DAWN AWAKENING

DAWN AWAKENING

THE DREAMWEAVER'S PACT™
BOOK THREE

RIVER TATUM

MICHAEL ANDERLE

DON'T MISS OUR NEW RELEASES

Join the Florid Romance email list to be notified of new releases and special promotions (which happen often) by following this link:

https://floridromance.lmbpn.com/about/sign-up-for-our-newsletter/

Published by Florid Romance
an imprint of LMBPN Publishing
2375 E. Tropicana Avenue, Suite 8-305
Las Vegas, Nevada 89119 USA

Version 1.00, May 2025
eBook ISBN: 979-8-88878-423-5
Print ISBN: 979-8-89354-742-9

PROLOGUE

The silence in the obsidian-walled chamber was profound, broken only by the faint, erratic pulse emanating from the tear in the Veil. It was a discordant thrum against the otherwise absolute stillness Malakar cultivated in this hidden sanctuary deep within the palace's forgotten passages. He stood before a scrying pool, its surface not water but a roiling canvas of corrupted dream-stuff, swirling eddies of shadow and sickly light, the chaotic bleed-through from a reality unraveling at the seams. His reflection stared back, composed as sculpted ice, silver hair immaculate, dark robes absorbing the chamber's gloom. But his eyes, usually calm pools of calculation, held a new, sharper intensity, like chips of volcanic glass reflecting a distant fire.

The recent confrontation had been... untidy. The unexpected resilience of the seamstress, Elara, fueled by nascent, potent empathy. The inconvenient return of Lord

Lucian, Caelum's ever-loyal shadow, armed with suspicion and righteousness. And, most unsettling, the surge of defiant power from the prince himself, fighting back from within his psychic prison. It was a setback, an irritation disrupting the delicate weave of his decade-long plan. But defeat? Malakar scoffed. Defeat was for lesser minds.

His long, elegant fingers traced the cool, smooth rim of the pool. Five years. Five meticulously planned years since that vibrant festival night, alive with the scent of roses and spiced wine, when he had first woven the tendrils of cursed slumber around the kingdom's darling heir. The court, blinded by sentimentality and grief, saw only tragedy. They mourned a promising young prince struck down by sudden, inexplicable illness. They never grasped the necessity, the grandeur, of the sacrifice. They could not perceive the true currents of destiny, or the encroaching darkness that he alone had foreseen and sought to master.

He allowed his mind to drift back, savoring the memory. Lanterns hung like captured stars, nobles swirled in silks, and Caelum stood at the center, radiating effortless charm. But Malakar, ever observant, saw beneath the gilded surface. He detected a faint, dangerous shimmer of innate power surrounding the boy: an untamed, intuitive connection to the kingdom's dreaming heart, the raw energy of the Veil itself. Caelum was not only an heir; he was a conduit, a living key to forces Malakar coveted but could never reach directly. Malakar's own power, built through decades of painstaking study and ruthless acquisition, was potent, yet it lacked that natural resonance. He could manipulate, twist, and control, but Caelum could channel.

Malakar had also read the future in the threads of fate, or rather, the future he chose to see. A looming storm approached, but it would be of his own subtle making. He foresaw a kingdom weakened by Caelum's untested leadership, the prince's sensitivity leaving him open to forces Malakar planned to unleash or deflect, as best served his aims. "Your destiny is not to lead this kingdom," he told the prince that night, the words wrapped in feigned sorrow, "but to protect it. Even at great cost." A perfect manipulation. Caelum's destiny, as Malakar defined it, was to become the vessel through which Malakar would guard the realm, shielding its magical core from misuse, or from any wielder but himself. The curse was not simple political murder; it was a harnessing, a repurposing of the kingdom's greatest asset into its greatest shield, governed by its most capable, if unrecognized, guardian. Caelum's sacrifice cleared the way for Malakar's quiet dominion, a reign secured not by birthright but by superior intellect and will.

For five years the plan unfolded with elegant precision. The kingdom stagnated under the so-called King's Sorrow, the court grew pliable, and Malakar consolidated his influence. The indispensable adviser tirelessly searched for a cure while subtly tightening the prince's psychic chains, siphoning whispers of dream power through his sleeping anchor.

Then she had appeared. Elara. An anomaly, a quiet guild seamstress whose thread inexplicably glowed with empathic light. He had dismissed the whispers at first, but closer observation revealed a resonance, a warmth that echoed Caelum's own dormant potential. Another dreamweaver, perhaps from a lineage thought extinguished? A dangerous wildcard. Once her potential was undeniable, bringing her under his wing, offering "guidance" while ensuring proximity for monitoring, had been the only prudent course. Keep potential threats close, cultivate them if useful, prune them if necessary.

Now Lucian. Back from the borders, fueled by misplaced guilt and unwavering loyalty. Lucian's suspicion was overt, his meddling in the archives irritating. A predictable, honorable fool, easily manipulated by his devotion, yet still capable of disrupting carefully laid plans. And Carmen, the ambitious guild rival, struggling against his subtle possession, was becoming unreliable. Loose threads, all of them.

Worse, Elara's connection to the prince was strengthening, developing an intimacy that threatened the foundation of the curse. He had felt it escalating: the shared power pushing back against his nightmare constructs, the emotional resonance that could awaken Caelum fully if left unchecked. That shared kiss in the dreamscape...a vulnerability, an anchor point he had not anticipated, dangerously pure. Severing their contact so forcefully last night had required a significant expenditure of his own energy, a sign her untrained power was becoming formidable when amplified by the prince.

His hand clenched. The shadow-stitch glamour held, masking the truth from the court for now. But Elara knew too much. Lucian suspected too much. And Caelum... Caelum was no longer a passive battery; he was becoming an active resistor, drawing strength from the seamstress's infuriating light.

Malakar turned from the scrying pool, the cold smile returning. Let them conspire. Let them seek scraps of truth in dusty scrolls. The tearing Veil, the spreading dream-bleed; they perceived only chaos. He perceived opportunity on a grand scale. Reality itself was becoming porous, thin. If controlling Caelum directly was becoming complicated, perhaps harnessing the encroaching dream-stuff, blurring the lines between worlds permanently, was the more elegant solution. Reshape the waking world with tangible nightmares, and solidify his power through fear made manifest. Elara and Lucian's interference had merely accelerated the transition to the final phase.

He glanced at the small vial resting on a nearby stand. The supposed headache remedy. The tracking charm woven within its glittering powder served him well, confirming Elara's meetings with the old crone Imelda, her furtive exchanges with Lucian. Let her believe she schemed undetected. Her power, her connection, would fuel his ascension, willingly or not. He needed to adjust the loom, tighten the warp threads of fear and control.

The pulse from the Veil quickened, a frantic, unstable rhythm in the chamber's oppressive silence. Soon. The final convergence was approaching. He needed only to guide the chaos, weave the encroaching nightmares into a tapestry of his own design, and ensure that when the Veil tore completely, it was his will that governed the merged reality. Caelum would be his eternal anchor, Elara his potent amplifier, and the kingdom...the kingdom would finally, irrevocably, dream his perfect dream. A dream of absolute order, shielded from all threats by his singular, enlightened vision. It was, after all, his destiny to impose it.

CHAPTER

ONE

Elara leaned her forehead against the closed oak door and inhaled. The corridor outside was quiet except for the faint hum of distant voices from the palace's main hall. Exhaustion clung to her like a shroud, heavier than the usual fatigue from late nights' stitching. The ordeal in the palace storeroom, during which she poured every ounce of her focus into the dreamshield while Lucian guarded her, had left her scraped raw, psychically frayed. They had pushed back the encroaching darkness and felt a flicker of hope ignite, but the victory was fragile, and the silence afterward echoed with the knowledge that Malakar remained unseen and undeterred. Their modest triumph might have confused his focus, yet she knew with chilling certainty that it had also alerted him. She sensed his watchful presence, felt his intricate schemes tighten like unseen threads, as though he anticipated their next move.

Behind her, Lucian crouched over the oak table, a

small silver ward-stone balanced in his hand. "I have finished carving the last lines of the ward," he said, his voice low with intent. "I hope it masks any magic we stir tonight," he added, his voice rough with fatigue that mirrored her own. He rubbed his shoulder, where Elara knew bandages lay hidden beneath his tunic, a souvenir from the storeroom defense. "Gods know I trust your skill, Elara, but after last night...this threshold feels different. More charged. More dangerous." He glanced toward the door, then back at her, his gaze unnerving. "After last night...I think Malakar's shifted his focus. He's still out there, but I think he's reinforced his influence within the dreamscape. It feels...watchful."

Elara pushed away from the door and forced strength into legs that felt like water. "The dreamshield bought us a reprieve, nothing more. It won't last." She drew a breath. "And." Her voice dropped, heavy with the weight of their limited success. "It didn't break the curse. He's still trapped, Lucian."

Caelum. The name was a silent ache in her chest. She pictured him lying pale and still in his distant chamber, unaware of the battle waged for his consciousness. "We need more than defenses," she continued, urgency sharpening her tone. "We need answers. We need to understand how Malakar anchored the curse so deeply, what those flickering runes in the courtyard truly signify, and what he's planning next."

Lucian looked at her, his eyes dark with grim understanding. "The archives yielded fragments, warnings...the notes we found hinted at Malakar using Caelum as a conduit but offered no clear way to sever it. We risk exposing ourselves to the King and Queen before we have proof they cannot ignore, not while Malakar's glamour clouds their judgment." He paced the small, cleared space, agitation radiating from him. "We need a clearer path, Elara, a weapon."

"Then we need to go to the source," Elara said, the decision solidifying even as the thought terrified her. The exhaustion and the risk were immense, but the memory of Caelum's fragmented whispers in her dreams, the feel of his consciousness brushing against hers, spurred her onward. She met Lucian's gaze. "We need to reach Caelum in the dream realm right now, both of us."

Lucian stopped pacing and stared at her as if she had suggested walking into fire. "Now? Elara, after last night? We barely have the strength to stand. And I... I'm no dreamweaver. My place is here, guarding you."

"I need you with me this time, Lucian," she insisted, stepping closer so he could grasp the shift in strategy and the heightened danger. "I know your role was to guard, to be my anchor in the waking world, but things have changed. After we pushed back with the dreamshield, the Veil feels thinner, more volatile, and I sense Malakar's influence is stronger within the dreamscape itself, more watchful, as if he anticipated this. Going alone feels dangerous." She shuddered, recalling the icy presence that had torn her from Caelum before. "I need your strength beside me, Lucian, your resolve as a guard there, not just here."

She saw the conflict in his eyes, ingrained duty

warring with deep distrust of this ethereal battlefield. She pressed on, appealing to the one thing she knew anchored him more firmly than any fear. "And... you're his friend, his oldest friend. Caelum trusts you implicitly. Your presence, your voice...it might help ground him within the dream, help me reach him more clearly and faster. We need to learn what he knows about the curse, about the runes, before Malakar senses our intrusion and seals him off." She held his gaze, pouring all her conviction into the plea. "The greatest threat feels internal now, Lucian. Please. Will you come?"

He searched her face, seeing the exhaustion that mirrored his own, the faint tremor in her hands, and the fierce, unwavering determination that burned in her dark eyes. He thought of Caelum, lost in shadow for five years. He thought of Malakar's suffocating control over the palace and the minds of the King and Queen. He looked back at Elara, at the impossible burden she carried, the fragile hope she represented. Apprehension warred with loyalty. Finally, drawing himself up, the soldier overriding the skeptic, he gave a single decisive nod.

"All right, Elara. If you believe my presence inside can help Caelum, if it gives us even a sliver of a chance..." He took a deep, steadying breath. "Then I'll face it. Guide me. Tell me what needs to be done."

"We need space, light, and focus," she said, her voice regaining some measure of calm now that the decision was made. Elara retrieved three precious waxed candles from her satchel, miraculously intact after their flight through the corridors, and set them in a triangle on the floorboards. Lucian knelt opposite her and pulled out the small silver ward-stone he had finished carving earlier.

"The runes are complete," he said, placing it carefully within the triangle of candles. His voice was low, tight with focus, though she saw his hand was not steady as he positioned the stone. "Hopefully, it masks any magic we stir tonight and gives us some protection from unwanted listeners." He glanced toward the door, then back at her. "I still cannot believe I'm doing this. Diving into dreams...I only ever watch you from the outside when you do illusions."

She moved closer, noting the tremor in his voice. He had ridden in battles and faced monstrous illusions that snarled in real corridors, yet this deliberate plunge into the dream realm unnerved him more than any blade. She reached across the table and touched his wrist. "I'll guide you. We'll be tethered by the incantation from the stolen texts, but you must keep focus. The illusions there can shift in an instant. If your concentration snaps, you'll drift away from me."

He inclined his head and exhaled through his nostrils as if steeling himself. "I trust you. Let's begin before our nerves talk us out of it."

Elara nodded and lit the candles. Their glow pushed back the gloom, casting long, dancing shadows among the discarded relics. The flames pulsed, reflecting the instability she sensed from the torn Veil. She placed her spool of glimmering thread on the floor beside the candles, its faint luminescence a beacon in the shadows. She retrieved the worn page copied from Mistress Imelda's restricted texts. This dangerous incantation, pieced together from Malakar's stolen notes, was their only key to the perilous realm. Without it, the shared journey would be impossible.

She settled beside Lucian at the edge of a pallet they had prepared, a flimsy substitute for a real bed. The three candles on the table flickered, casting a wavery light that made her spool of thread shimmer. She traced a glyph in the air above his forearm and pressed her finger to his wrist. "Reflect on your sense of duty," she whispered, letting her breath ghost over the ancient words. "Picture your protective instincts as a weapon. You'll shape it once we're inside."

Lucian's eyes half-closed in concentration. "Duty. The kingdom. Protecting Caelum...and you."

A spark of silver glided along Elara's fingertip and gathered at the glyph on his wrist. A warm prickle coursed through her arm as the incantation sank in. She lifted her finger, pulse hammering. "That should connect us in the dream state."

They stretched out on the makeshift bedding and lay side by side, their shoulders nearly touching. The glyph on his wrist glowed as a warm, vital point between them in the deepening darkness. Lucian kept his gaze steady on her, even as a muscle in his jaw twitched.

"All right," he said softly, then exhaled. "Let's do it."

She took his offered hand, and the brief contact sent a warmth through her, grounding her despite the circumstances. Lucian's hand was strong and callused, achingly real compared to the ephemeral world they were about to enter. She turned his wrist over. The skin was pale in the flickering candlelight. Her fingertip hovered above his pulse point. She drew another breath, channeled her focus past the fatigue tugging at her, then traced the complex, looping lines of the tethering glyph Imelda's texts had described.

As her finger moved, the air began to hum. The lines she drew glowed, leaving trails of silvery light on his skin like liquid moonlight. Lucian inhaled sharply at the sensation but remained still, his gaze fixed on the unfolding magic, his trust in her absolute. When she traced the final curve, the glyph flared with an internal glow that pulsed against his skin and hers. Elara felt the familiar drain, sharper this time, tugging at her reserves, a reminder of the dreamshield's cost only hours earlier. Keeping this connection tonight and guiding another soul across the frayed Veil would demand immense focus, pushing her depleted strength to its limit.

She placed the incantation page in the candlelight and began to chant. The archaic words lay thick and powerful on her tongue, echoing through the cramped space. The air grew heavy and charged. Candle flames stretched tall, licking at the shadows and casting grotesque shapes that writhed on the storeroom walls. Beside her, Lucian's breathing grew shallow, and his hand tightened into a fist.

Then came the shift, the lurch, the surrender. It felt less like falling asleep and more like slipping through a tear in thinning reality. The Veil, still wounded by Malakar's manipulations, filled the air with the unsettling potential of dreambleed. The transition felt unstable and precarious, like stepping onto rotten ice. The world tilted violently sideways. A drifting sensation wrapped them in dizzying weightlessness as the musty smell of the room vanished, replaced by the cool, sharp tang of raw magic, ozone, and something indefinably ancient. Colors swirled behind Elara's closed eyelids: silver, gold, and deep indigo, shot through with bruised purple and angry red. The vortex spun faster and faster, threatening to pull them apart before they even arrived, until everything merged into a blinding, silent white.

Then, stillness. An abrupt, unnerving quiet. They had arrived.

CHAPTER
TWO

Elara opened her eyes to the shifting, shimmering expanse of the dream realm's threshold. Before them stretched corridors woven from thought and memory, walls shimmering like living silk, constantly reforming, patterns shifting like water under wind. But tonight, the realm felt deeply agitated. The usual fluid grace was marred by jarring ripples, patches where the silver light seemed thin, almost transparent, revealing glimpses of raw, unsettling darkness beneath. The dream-bleed was palpable here, the fabric of this reality weakened, frayed.

"Anchor yourself, Lucian," Elara urged again, her voice calm and steady despite her own fatigue and the realm's unsettling energy pulsing around them. "Focus. Remember why we're here: for Caelum. This place responds to thought, to emotion. Fear makes the shadows deeper. Hold onto your duty, that loyalty. It will be your shield, your grounding here."

He closed his eyes for a moment, his breathing harsh, visibly fighting for control. Elara watched, sending a silent thread of encouragement toward him, feeling the subtle shift as he battled his disorientation. She saw the tension in his shoulders ease fractionally, his posture straightening as he drew on years of ingrained discipline, on his unwavering resolve. When he opened his eyes again, the raw panic had receded, replaced by the familiar, focused intensity of the soldier finding his footing, even on ground that refused to stay still.

"Alright," he said, his voice steadier now, clearer. "Duty. For Caelum." He focused inward, drawing a deep breath, and Elara felt a definite shift in the dreamstuff around him, a coalescing of purpose. Slowly, shimmering into existence in his hand, appeared a spectral sword. Not ornate silver like his physical blade, but forged from pure, unwavering resolve, its edges sharp with fierce loyalty. He tested its weight, flexing his grip, a look of grim satisfaction finally settling on his face as he felt its familiar balance, even here. He stared, incredulous. "This is from my sense of duty?"

"It's your resolve made manifest. It will protect you from illusions that attack here." She reached to rest her palm lightly against the gleaming sword's hilt, feeling its chill energy resonate like a heartbeat.

All around them, the dream realm breathed ominous shadows. The distant gloom rippled, revealing half-formed nightmares that watched them with glowing, hateful eyes. Elara coaxed luminous thread from her spool, letting it weave in the air around her. Each time she moved her hand, the thread floated in gentle arcs. "We must push deeper," she said quietly. "I think Caelum is here. I can sense him."

Lucian nodded, though worry tensed his features. "Then lead on."

They ventured forward, drifting through corridors that constantly shifted, walls swelling or receding. Strange shapes flickered at the edges of Elara's vision. She conjured a barrier of filaments whenever the shadows drew too close. Lucian raised his weapon to shatter illusions that lunged from the corners. The clang of his spectral sword rang out in the hush, and each strike left faint, rippling echoes along the corridor.

At length, they turned a curve and came upon a stretch of sudden darkness, its surface as smooth as liquid ink. A faint shimmer glowed in the distance. Elara squinted, realizing it was a glimpse of Caelum's familiar bearing: the tall, regal silhouette she recognized from countless dream encounters. He appeared caught in the gloom, as if illusions clung to him like tar. Her chest constricted at the sight.

"We need to hurry," she murmured, her voice hushed with worry.

Before Lucian could reply, a monstrous shape erupted from the blackness. It had no discernible face, only twisting limbs of shadow. It flung itself at them with a savage hiss. Elara flinched, threads swirling in chaotic arcs. Lucian stepped forward, spectral sword gleaming bright. He slashed boldly, cutting through the thing's midsection. Its shriek reverberated like shattered glass.

One half dissolved into mist while the other half leaked toward Caelum's silhouette.

Elara's heart thudded in anxiety. "They're trying to hold onto him," she whispered. "We have to clear a path."

A swarm of smaller nightmares coalesced. They danced right beneath the corridor's surface, slashing at the illusions Elara conjured for protection. Her spool of thread glowed hot in her grip. She advanced, weaving a protective swirl that shredded several of the approaching shadows. But for every nightmare destroyed, three more slithered forward.

Lucian pressed close to her side, sword raised defensively. "Elara, we can't hold all of them off at once."

She clenched her jaw. "We don't have to fight them forever, just enough to reach Caelum." She moved to charge, but the darkness swelled, forming a wall of sinewy illusions in front of them. The gloom churned with malevolence, and for a moment, Elara's courage faltered. Could they truly break through?

Lucian squeezed her free hand. Even in the dream realm, his grip felt solid. "We do this together. I'll cover you."

She nodded, inhaling shakily. Their joint determination seemed to spark a brighter glow in the sword and the threads. Lucian sliced forward, creating an opening. Elara followed, weaving shining patterns that tore holes through the illusions. Step by step, they carved a narrow path into the heart of the swirling blackness.

Ahead, Caelum's form grew clearer. She saw his pale face, eyes flickering with exhaustion. But there was a glint of recognition when he spotted her. He reached out weakly. "Elara..." The word echoed, muffled by the roiling illusions that clung to him.

Elara pulled in a deep breath and slashed her glowing threads through the final barrier of shadow. She was close enough to touch him now. She gathered the shimmering filaments around her hand and reached toward Caelum's wrist, trying to tug him free from the ink-like swirl that pinned him in place.

Yet at that instant, something lunged from behind, a stray nightmare, faster than she expected. She tensed, bracing for impact, but Lucian stepped between her and the attacker. His sword met the shadow with a deafening clash of dream energy-heartbeat. The blow knocked him off-balance, and the corridor surface buckled beneath his boots. Elara felt the wave of displacement ripple through the ground.

She spun around, snagging Lucian's sleeve to keep him from tumbling backward. He exhaled sharply, arms tangling with hers. Their gazes locked for a single, charged moment in the midst of chaos. She tasted panic in her throat. Panic and something else, a fierce gratitude that he had shielded her.

As the dreamscape shuddered under the weight of unseen forces, an impulse seized Elara. It wasn't her own desire; it felt cold, sharp, and utterly foreign—a marionette string suddenly pulled taut within her mind. She felt her body tense, an urge rising that wasn't born of longing but of cold command. Her gaze locked onto Lucian, who stood beside her, equally tense, his spectral sword flickering. A confused frown creased his brow as if he too felt a strange dissonance, a pull he couldn't explain. "Elara?" he started, his voice tight with sudden apprehension. But before he could say more, the compulsion intensified, a chilling pressure behind her eyes demanding action, forcing her forward against her will.

Against every instinct screaming defiance within her, Elara felt her body move stiffly, unnaturally, rising onto her toes. The dream ground seemed to recoil beneath her feet. Lucian's eyes widened in shock confusion as she reached for him, her hands feeling like clumsy wooden replicas of her own. His own hands rose defensively, but the same cold force seemed to grip him, freezing his resistance. The brush of their lips wasn't a spark of sunlight; it felt like ice scraping against stone. There was no warmth, no shared breath of longing, only a horrifying sense of violation, of being puppets maneuvered by unseen hands. This wasn't connection; it was defilement, a twisted demonstration of power that left her feeling hollowed out, trapped within her own skin as her body performed an act against her will. Lucian's face was a mask of confusion and dawning horror, his hands gripping her shoulders not in passion, but as if trying to push away an unwelcome phantom.

Her mind buzzed with conflicted emotions. She thought of Caelum, pinned only a few paces away in the swirling blackness. Then, out of the corner of her eye, she saw him. He stared at them with a solemn understanding that made her stomach clench.

She pulled back from Lucian, breath ragged. Lucian's

cheeks burned red, but he looked no less resolved than before. Caelum's gaze stayed on them for a moment, weariness and acceptance mingled in his expression. Without a word, he turned his face aside as if he respected what he had just witnessed but could not hold it in his sight.

Another wave of illusions attacked. Elara scrambled to shield herself, spinning her shimmering threads upward in a wide arc that ripped through the nightmares trying to close around them again. Lucian raised his sword, driving back the last few horrors that prowled behind them. Freed by this surge of magic, Caelum staggered forward, half-collapsing into Elara's outstretched arms. She felt the weight of him in this unreal domain, caught between relief and heartbreak.

A chorus of shrieks echoed from the walls as the illusions reeled under their combined force. Caelum's voice was faint. "We... must escape. You can't hold them forever."

Elara nodded, chest heaving. "We'll get you out."

She shot a desperate glance at Lucian, who angled his sword toward the swirling corridor behind them. The path they had taken was slowly dissolving into dark currents. There was no more time to linger. Gritting her teeth, Elara pressed a final wave of her magic into the spool, conjuring a luminous shield that surrounded the three of them. Lucian helped lift Caelum's unsteady form, and together, they backtracked through the drifting labyrinth, illusions clawing at them all the while.

Their combined might carved a channel back to

waking. Step by step, breath by breath, Elara felt the dream realm loosen its claws. Just before they escaped entirely, the corridor shook with one last wave of menacing energy from deeper layers of Malakar's illusions. Then, mercifully, the swirling silver pulled back. Everything turned to white noise. She let her eyes close—

She jerked upright on the workshop floor, candles sputtering to weak blue stubs. Lucian lurched beside her, bloodless and shaking as though the nightmare still clung to his skin. For a long moment they only stared.

Lucian finally spoke, voice raw. "That kiss was not mine to give."

"Nor mine to take," she whispered, cheeks stinging with remembered heat.

The violation wasn't about Lucian, not truly; it was Malakar's cruel puppetry, a defilement of any potential tenderness. Her heart ached with a different, purer pang for Caelum, whose image, trapped and vulnerable, was the true north of her compass. This forced intimacy with Lucian felt like a betrayal of that sacred connection, a stain she desperately wanted to cleanse, not a spark she wished to fan. The memory of Caelum's faint consciousness brushing hers in the dream was a beacon she clung to, and this felt like a muddying of those pure waters.

They had shared kisses of their own choosing before, but this one tasted of violation, a puppet-string pulled tight.

Her gaze fell on the spool. The glow flickered like a dying star. "Malakar can command us inside the Veil now. He wanted Caelum to watch, to bleed doubt."

Lucian's fists tightened around empty air. "Then he has found a new blade. And we handed him its edge."

Guilt coiled between them, sharp as any weapon. Elara drew a ragged breath. "We cannot let that moment be the thing Caelum wakes to."

Lucian nodded. "First, we shield his mind. Then we cut Malakar's strings. For good."

The candles guttered out. In the sudden dark their resolve gleamed brighter than any flame, but the aftertaste of forced desire lingered, a sober warning that the sorcerer's reach had grown.

And that tomorrow he would try again.

CHAPTER

THREE

Elara sank onto the narrow wooden bench, panting through a dull ache in her shoulders. Moonlight slanted through the workshop windows, illuminating the exhausted slope of Lucian's posture at her side. The two of them had just returned from doing battle in a domain that did not strictly obey the laws of flesh and bone, yet the bruises forming along her arms threatened to prove otherwise. Each breath she drew felt like a confession of frailty.

Lucian rubbed the back of his neck, then glanced over. "You alright?" His voice was hushed. A faint bruise marred the skin around his left temple, as if some creature in that twisted dream realm had struck him with claws of living shadow.

Elara flexed her fingers, testing the soreness. The ripple of pain confirmed what her eyes had already told her: dark illusions could leave tangible marks. "I will live," she said, though her voice trembled. "Still, I learned something tonight."

"Which part?" he asked warily.

"She swallowed, heat and shame tangling in her throat. "That kiss. Malakar wrenched it out of us. But it would be dishonest to claim I feel nothing for you. My heart is a snarl, Lucian, and Caelum is knotted at its centre."

She felt a flush of guilt even admitting that much to Lucian. The 'something' she felt for him was a confusing warmth, a camaraderie born of shared danger, perhaps even a fleeting physical attraction spurred by their intense proximity. But it was a flickering candle next to the steady, consuming flame of her devotion to Caelum. Every beat of her heart in these shadowed halls was for the prince, and any distraction, any misdirected affection, felt like a disservice to his desperate fight for survival. She owed Caelum her unwavering focus, not a divided heart.

Lucian's eyes darkened. "It felt as though iron hooks set into my ribs, dragging me forward. He can bend our wills now, not merely paint horrors."

Elara nodded once. "If he can puppet us, he can puppet anyone who crosses the Veil. Worse, he made certain Caelum saw."

Silence pooled between them, thick as pitch. They both knew jealousy would sap the prince's fragile resolve faster than any nightmare beast. Then, Lucian lifted his head and said, "about your feelings." Elara looked up. Lucian smiled sadly, as though he had suspected the truth for some time. "I understand. And I don't have any expectations" he answered softly. Exhaustion pulled at his eyes, but acceptance flickered behind them. "I still care about both of you. Whatever happens, I do not want either of you in danger."

Relief and sadness warred in her heart, leaving her feeling unsteady. "I only wish it were as simple as choosing." She traced the line of a purplish bruise crossing the back of her hand. "Yet Malakar's powers have grown stronger, and these bruises prove we are all at risk."

Lucian exhaled. "That mage once told the court illusions were harmless. Now we see they can injure and linger. If we do nothing, Malakar's nightmares, illusions, and now these... actions. They will devour everyone." His hazel gaze shifted toward the locked door, as if he expected to sense a creeping darkness under the gap.

The bench squeaked when Elara shifted her weight toward him. "Let's find Carmen," she suggested. "She needs to know how badly we fared. With the stolen texts she returned, maybe we will find a new lead."

Lucian nodded. "Agreed." Even in the gloom, his protective concern stirred warmth in her chest.

They rose, gingerly testing the stability of stiff limbs, and crossed the workshop to a smaller side room cordoned off by thick drapes. Candlelight glimmered from inside. They stepped through to find Carmen hunched over a table scattered with parchment. A steaming kettle sat on a small stove nearby. She glanced up, worry plain in her expression.

"You look like you crawled out of a bar fight," Carmen said, eyes firm but tinted with concern rather than mockery. "What happened to the both of you?" Her usually impeccable hair hung loose around her shoulders, testament to the tension ravaging them all.

Elara pressed her lips together and eased onto a battered stool. "They were vicious tonight. We barely escaped." She did not add that the illusions had once more singled them out, as though Malakar had begun studying their patterns.

Lucian managed a rueful half-smile. "Malakar happened. He can do more than conjure monsters: he seized our muscles, marched us like dolls."

Elara added, voice tight, "We felt the pull, Carmen. A compulsion in the marrow. If he can force us, he can force anyone who steps into the Veil."

Carmen's face drained of colour.

"So physical wounds are one thing, but if Malakar can steer our bodies too...then his magic is even more potent than we feared." Her knuckles whitened where she gripped the table's edge.

"A cut to the flesh we can salve, but a cut to Caelum's spirit could root the curse deeper. If Malakar floods him with envy, dread, even the smallest grief, the prince will have no footing to fight back."

Lucian nodded. "Hope and resolve are our armour. We keep his thoughts clear, or the sorcerer's illusions will feast on every crack."

Carmen's gaze flickered toward Lucian as he spoke, a complicated expression crossing her face: a hint of admiration for his unwavering resolve quickly masked by her usual guardedness. It was the kind of steadfastness she had once foolishly sought in Malakar, only to find deceit.

For a moment her focus on the scrolls wavered, a brief, almost imperceptible softening around her mouth before she straightened and snapped her attention back to the task at hand. She inhaled slowly and replied, "Which means Malakar doesn't need claws if he can tilt a heart the wrong way. Body, blade, nightmare beast; none of that matters once he owns the feeling that guides them."

Elara remembered Mistress Imelda's most urgent lesson: "Dreamweaving can mend hearts or shatter them. It can unravel curses or bind them tighter. The power is undeniably real, and it is intrinsically tied to your emotions. You must learn to master it, or risk being consumed by it."

"Exactly," Lucian said. "He yanked our muscles tonight, but the true strike was in the mind. If he floods Caelum with despair, he'll never claw free of the curse."

Carmen's frown deepened as she surveyed the parchment sprawl. "Then our first task is emotional armour. These notes"—she tapped a scroll with ink-stained fingernail— "speak of dream-spirits who answer sincerity. They are older than any mortal weave and can sever corrupt threads from the inside."

Lucian leaned slightly closer to the table, his gaze sharp as he scanned the scroll Carmen indicated. "A risky venture, relying on spirits," he murmured, more to himself than anyone, "but if Malakar is using these internal strikes, we need unconventional defenses." He glanced at Carmen, a brief, almost imperceptible nod acknowledging the potential value of her find, even if his tone remained guarded.

Elara leaned forward. "I used to sing children's verses about kindly watchers in sleep; I never guessed they might be real. What does it say about approaching them?"

"Empathy, vow, mutual defence," Carmen read. "And no duplicity. If they detect hidden motives they vanish, or worse, fight back."

Lucian traced the diagram: a circle within a circle, tiny runes for *truth* and *shared purpose* at each quarter. "It mirrors the ward we cast months ago, only turned inward. If we form that circle and keep our intentions clear, the spirits might help cut Malakar's strings."

"But the margin for doubt is razor-thin," Carmen warned. "The text claims they flee at the first scent of conflict in the summoners' hearts."

The words settled like frost. Elara thought of the tangled lattice of her own heart. Her abiding love for Caelum, the flicker of hunger for Lucian, and the guilt that threaded them together.

Lucian pushed upright. "I will fetch fresh compresses and see if the watch outside spotted any shadow-stirrings. Shout if you need me."

Elara offered a grateful tilt of her head while Carmen mouthed a quiet thanks. The door clicked shut, leaving the two women alone amid parchment and lamplight.

Carmen folded her arms. "You and Lucian looked as though a storm had rolled straight through you. Do I get the censored or the honest version?"

Elara rubbed her temples. "Honest, but... carefully so. Malakar forced a kiss between us. It was not the first time

Lucian and I have erred toward something more, yet this time it was a weapon."

Carmen's brows shot up. "If the sorcerer can twist affection, he'll use it where it hurts most: Caelum."

"That is what terrifies me," Elara whispered. "My feelings are no longer private terrain."

A soft creak sounded; Lucian slipped back through the door, a basin of water balanced on one hip and fresh cloths draped over his arm. His shoulders were tense, but his voice stayed low. "Hallway is clear. No shadow-stirrings." He set the supplies down, then caught the tail of their conversation with a rueful glance.

Carmen met his gaze directly, her usual haughtiness tempered by a shared gravity. "If Malakar can force actions like that, Lucian," she stated, her voice low and steady, "then no one is truly safe from his influence, especially those closest to the prince. We need to anticipate his next move, not just react to his horrors." Her practical assessment, devoid of her usual barbs, seemed to catch Lucian slightly off guard. He gave a curt nod, acknowledging the grim truth in her words.

"Before all this, I would have scowled," Carmen continued, turning back to Elara. "But I've watched how Malakar's compulsions gorge on even the smallest suspicion. If we let doubt or rivalry fester, we give Malakar an advantage." She upped the heat of the lamp's flame, sending flickers of gold across the table. "We can not let him exploit that."

Lucian inclined his head, speaking gently, "We focus on severing Malakar's new strings and shielding Caelum.

No matter the knots in our own hearts" His gaze slid to Elara for a moment, and she felt the ghost of that bond that had nearly tangled them into something more. "We will do it right this time."

An unexpected wave of gratitude filled Elara. For all their tension, the three of them had learned to stand together. She turned back to the text, scanning several cramped lines that looked like instructions. "It says that in order to summon dream-spirits, we must replicate a circle, yes, but also guarantee them a direct role in defending the dream realm from Malakar's compulsions and the nightmares he seeds. That might mean we have to vow to shield them from exploitation. They do not trust mortals after centuries of mages trying to enslave them."

Carmen poured the bitter tea into three wooden cups, its pungent aroma filling the cramped room. "We can handle that. I owe enough penance to these illusions," she said softly. "If it helps to promise them freedom, I will do it."

Elara's heart fluttered as she read further. "We will need to do it soon," she concluded. "Malakar has every reason to intensify his illusions after what we just thwarted. If we do not have reinforcements, we might lose ground again." She met Lucian's eyes. "You think you can anchor the circle with me? You helped me last time."

He nodded immediately. "I can. Let us plan the ritual for tonight, unless you are too battered."

She tried rotating her neck to gauge the stiffness. "I am exhausted... but if it gives Caelum an edge, I will push on."

She paused to sip the tea and grimaced at its bitterness. "That is wretched, Carmen."

Carmen smirked, though genuine worry still lined her face. "At least it will keep your eyes open."

Elara turned back to the swirl of notes. Her gaze flicked over one scrawled line describing a rumored meeting place: "the moonlit chambers." She recalled drifting through an ephemeral corridor in a prior dream, glimpsing strange lights flickering in the distance. Might that be the domain of these spirits? The text offered only partial clues: an arch shaped from woven illusions, a floor shimmering like pale water. The mention made her heart race.

Lucian touched the edge of the parchment. "I suggest we finalize the details. We replicate the circle ritual, but we expand it to invite these spirits in. If they trust us, they will bolster your illusions. If not... they might lash out." His eyes clouded with worry. "A risk we will have to take."

Carmen placed her barely touched cup on the table. "While you and Elara handle that part, I can arrange the last items for reinforcing Caelum's ward. The guild receives shipments of specialized crystal shards tomorrow morning. They will not look suspicious if I claim they are for a new tapestry design. I can slip them straight into the runic embroidery around Caelum's bed. That might protect him physically if illusions try to seize him again."

Elara nodded, gratitude warming her. "And that ensures if we fail in the dream realm, Caelum is still safe. If Malakar spawns fresh constructs the ward will keep their talons from his mind."

Silence settled for a moment, broken by the persistent drip of a leaky eave outside. Elara breathed in the pungent tea smell, thinking about everything that had come between them—jealousies, regrets, the sorrow of unspoken feelings. Yet here they were, forging a plan that might save the kingdom from illusions too potent to face alone.

Lucian set his cup down gently and ventured a slight smile. "Then it is decided. Elara and I will head to the dream realm again tonight and seek out these spirits in the moonlit chambers. Carmen, gather those crystals and any specialized thread you can. I want every precaution set before we return." He paused. "But first, we should rest, if only a little."

Carmen's gaze lingered on the fresh bruises along Elara's arms. "Yes, rest for a few hours, if you can manage it. I will talk to a few discreet guildmates so no one wonders why I need those crystals. Just promise me not to delve into the dream realm half-dead." She forced a shaky laugh.

Elara felt her lip tug upward in a weary smile. "I prom-ise. I am not keen on leaping into illusions half-blind, no matter how motivated I am."

Lucian let out a breath, relief tangling with determina-tion. "We have come too far to tumble now."

Carmen spun the battered kettle around on its base, swirling the last dregs of tea. Her expression softened, a far cry from the confident ridicule she once wore. "I am sorry," she said quietly. "For the ways I contributed to Malakar's rise... I want to make things right." The regret in her eyes seemed genuine, her once-honed vanity over-shadowed by fear for the kingdom and guilt for her part.

Elara reached out, resting a hand over Carmen's. "We will fix it," she said softly. "As best we can. You are here now. That is what matters."

Carmen's throat bobbed. "Then let us do this properly." Determination flared anew in her gaze. She set the kettle aside as if discarding old doubts.

They fell silent, absorbing the magnitude of what lay ahead. The battered workshop's wooden walls felt strangely comforting, a far cry from the lavish but treacherous castle corridors. Here, with only a handful of flickering lamps, a battered spool of shimmering thread, parchment scrawled in archaic runes, and three people clinging to the hope that their plan might redeem them all, they resolved to see this through.

Elara cleared her throat, letting that quiet moment root itself deep in her chest. "I will review the text a little longer," she murmured, tapping the lines describing the vow they would make to the spirits. "I need to be sure I do not offend them. I will do whatever it takes to convince them we are worthy."

Lucian touched her elbow. "I will help you practice the incantation. If we each memorize it, we can stand united in that dream corridor." His tone grew gentler. "But do not push yourself until dawn. Even dreamweavers must close their eyes now and then."

A soft laugh escaped Elara's lips, though it sounded more like a tired exhale. "True. And your own rest might help you stop reeling from those illusions."

Carmen snatched up a quill, scribbling an inventory list on a scrap of parchment. "Crystals, maybe a coil of silver wire. We can spin that into your ward threads. And I will hide them among standard shipments. No one will suspect anything."

Lucian nudged aside some wrinkled cloth to settle onto a stool, giving Elara room at the table. "We have a plan then: circle ritual for the dream-spirits tonight, wards around Caelum's bed reinforced by tomorrow. We keep our personal tensions locked down, or at least... balanced. No illusions feeding on our doubts."

Elara rubbed at the bruise on her shoulder, determined not to let the pain overshadow her. "That is right," she breathed. "We cannot fail Caelum. Or each other."

They spent the next stretch of minutes reviewing the archaic lines they would recite, Carmen's quill scratching across parchment every so often. The workshop's silence grew thick, though not unkind; for once, they accepted each other's presence without stinging barbs or hidden agendas. Every so often, Elara's eyes flicked toward Lucian's bruised face, and a pang of guilt bristled through her at the memory of how illusions had battered them both. But she also felt a gentle sense of comfort that, despite everything—her tangled feelings, the kingdom's nightmares—they faced it side by side.

Finally, as the first hint of dawn glimmered at the edge of the sky outside the workshop's small window, Carmen broke the hush. "Alright. I have enough for the next steps." Her tone sounded brisk, but a faint wobble betrayed her exhaustion.

Lucian pushed to his feet. "I will stand watch while Elara and you catch an hour or two of real sleep. Then we gather at dusk to attempt the summoning. Agreed?"

Carmen nodded, her eyes shining with a new purpose. "Yes. Tonight, we try. And we do not let illusions trick us into turning on each other."

Elara let out a slow breath. She rose, pushing the rumpled papers into neat piles. "Agreed. Let us rest while we can. Because once night falls, we enter the dream realm again."

They all seemed to hesitate, glancing around as if each carried a silent vow. The fragile calm among them felt as if it were made of porcelain. Needing no further words, Elara squeezed Carmen's hand, then let her go. She offered Lucian a small nod of gratitude, ignoring the ache in her arms. This alliance was imperfect, but if the dream-spirits demanded sincerity, she would give it.

With the plan settled, Elara retired to the corner of the workshop, where a rolled blanket and cushion served as her makeshift bed. Carmen busied herself finalizing her inventory, and Lucian quietly stepped outside to patrol. Though the city beyond remained cloaked in uneasy shadows, the three of them clung to a single hope: that tonight, they would reach the moonlit chambers and bring those elusive spirits to their cause. One chance to harness a power never before attempted, all for a kingdom they refused to watch crumble under Malakar's illusions.

Night pressed against the crooked windowpanes, rattling them with a wind that smelled of river-mist and distant fires. Lantern-glow etched long bars across the floor, catching motes of dust that drifted like tiny constellations. Somewhere a watch-bell tolled fourth glass; they were deep into the belly of the night, the hour when courage wavered. Elara let the sound settle inside her chest, counting each reverberation the way a tailor counts stitches. Four tolls: enough time to memorise the incantation, to bind thread to crystal, to gather whatever scraps of courage remained. When the fifth bell rang, she intended to be sleeping, if only so her spirit could stand straighter when dusk returned.

FOUR

Elara stepped carefully through the torchlit corridor that linked the workshop to the disused stables. At this late hour, the usual bustle of guild apprentices had quieted, leaving only the distant hum of wind outside and the low flicker of flames against cold stone walls. Weariness pressed her shoulders. She had spent countless hours at her workbench earlier, stitching wards onto delicate cloth. Every thread glowed faintly with the promise of dreamweaver magic. But the day's labor was done, and now she found only heavy fatigue in her limbs and a measured tension in the back of her mind. She inhaled deeply, reminding herself that nights grew more unpredictable with each passing day. Somewhere beyond stone and straw, Malakar schemed to yoke the entire kingdom through the dream realm; every ward she stitched tonight felt like a stitch in that wider battle.

She paused at the threshold leading to the stables. A battered wooden door stood ajar, revealing piles of dusty crates and half-rotted straw bales. Rusted lantern hooks, unused for ages, clung to the walls. Elara had rarely ventured here alone. She knew this corner of the castle grounds would be quiet enough to let her gather her thoughts without the prying eyes of courtiers or the well-meaning but overbearing concerns of the guild. Yet she had not expected to hear soft footsteps echo behind her.

She turned. Carmen stood at the corridor's turn, dark curls half shadowed by the wavering torchlight. Gone was the usual haughty tilt of her chin. Instead, she looked hesitant, her posture rigid with unspoken tension. Elara's pulse gave a small jump. She had not anticipated seeing Carmen here at this hour, especially not after the uneasy alliance they had forged in recent days. Though they had agreed to share information important to Prince Caelum's defenses, old habits of rivalry died hard. Elara forced herself to relax and offered a curt nod.

Carmen approached quietly, her heeled boots making light taps on the stone floor. A fleeting shimmer glazed Carmen's irises, the same silvery haze Imelda's severance ribbon had not yet fully chased away. She kept her arms folded across her chest. Her voice sounded subdued when she finally spoke. "I slipped out by claiming I had urgent guild inventory matters. That was the only excuse Malakar would accept without prying." She hesitated, eyes flitting to a half-open stable door as if checking for eavesdroppers. "He thinks I left in a hurry to assess new shipments."

Elara's mouth felt dry at the mention of Malakar. She knew the sorcerer had a habit of tracking Carmen's whereabouts. His illusions hovered in more corners of the kingdom than any of them dared count. A single misstep could destroy the brittle trust Carmen was trying to cultivate with him—and by extension, sabotage the hard-won progress she and Elara had pieced together for Caelum's sake. Elara placed a light hand on Carmen's elbow, guiding her deeper into the stables where the flickering torchlight could not easily reveal them to passersby. Dust rose at their feet, and the faint smell of old leather and rotting hay tickled Elara's nose.

"You managed to slip by him, then," Elara said softly. "I knew he would ask questions if you disappeared too abruptly."

Carmen gave a stiff nod. She released a trembling sigh, her gaze skittering away from Elara as if she could not bear to meet her eyes. "I had to pretend you were stuck in yet another magical rut, that I planned to gather your mistakes as evidence." A hollow laugh followed the words. "He seemed satisfied, or at least uninterested enough to dismiss it."

An uneasy silence fell. Elara observed the lines of exhaustion on Carmen's face. The other woman looked so different from the haughty guild star who once strutted through the workshop in gleaming attire. Gone were the elegant sneers and the easy condescension she always used to keep Elara in her place. Now her shoulders looked frail, tension coiling in her posture as though a single touch might shatter her composure. Elara could see the weight of too many secrets pressing behind Carmen's eyes.

"I... I need to tell you exactly what it cost me to remain

in Malakar's shadow." she began, voice cracking, betraying how frayed her confidence had become. "He showered me with attention first. Then, he promised coin, position, anything I wanted, *if* I reported on your weaving. I wish I could say that I he had possessed me by this point, but I can't. Because he hadn't. It was all me. My jealousy. My greed." Her eyes shone with tears.

Elara bit her inner lip. She had guessed portions of Carmen's struggle, but to see Carmen voluntarily speak it aloud sent a pang of sympathy through her. "You thought it was your chance," Elara said softly, "to surpass me. To have the recognition you believed you deserved."

Carmen nodded. Drifting forward, she rested a hand on a dusty saddle perched on a crate. Straw rustled under her palm. "It made sense at first. He had real influence at court. And I... I looked at your magic and felt so powerless." Her cheeks colored, and tears gathered in the corners of her eyes. "I told myself everything Malakar did was to root out forbidden illusions. I thought I was helping him keep the guild safe from overshadowing sorcery. But then it all twisted around. The requests grew darker. Each scrap I gave him helped him twist the kingdom's dreams." Her breath hitched. "Children, Elara. He terrorised children."

Unease churned in Elara's stomach. The corridor outside remained silent, but her mind buzzed with the memory of illusions that battered them in the dream realm, illusions that manifested in too many corners of the city at night. Through it all, Malakar's influence had only grown. She took a step closer, her voice gentle. "Why invest faith in him at all? You never seemed the type to be so—" She cut herself off, not wanting to insult Carmen further.

Carmen's mouth twisted into a bitter approximation of a smile. "So gullible, you mean? I believed I had control." She let out a shaky breath. "I saw him as this cunning ally who simply wanted a clever way to harness illusions for the monarchy's sake. I wanted to prove my worth by assisting him. Then I realized how far he would go—how far I had let him go. When I discovered the kind of illusions he unleashed on peasants... children. The nightmares that left them too shaken to speak." Her voice caught, and she gave a small, trembling shrug. "It hit me that I was not just a bystander. I had abetted him by handing him the knowledge about wards you invented. I gave him glimpses of your dreamweaver spool, your runes, everything."

Anger fluttered, but Elara shoved it down, even though it took effort. She recalled the nights she spent in a half-panic, warding Caelum's bedchamber with every ounce of dreamweaver skill she possessed. So many illusions had hammered at them from the dream realm. Each blow had grown stronger, more sophisticated, as if Malakar understood her strategies in real-time. Now she saw how Carmen had unwittingly funneled that information to him. She looked to be on the brink of breaking. Elara took Carmen's hand. "You have regrets."

Carmen let out a ragged breath. "More than regrets," she whispered. "I have nightmares. And shame. There was a time I wanted so badly to be at the top of the seamstress guild. I let envy blind me to the cost. I saw you weaving illusions so effortlessly, forging a path that drew the attention of the entire castle. I was terrified that if I did not do something dramatic, I would remain overshadowed forever." She drew herself back, eyes flicking to the stable entrance. "Now I see what I almost destroyed. You. Caelum. Maybe the entire kingdom."

Carmen glanced away, a bitter twist to her lips. "Even Lucian... his loyalty to the prince, his quiet strength... it's the sort of honor I once craved notice from, but always felt it directed elsewhere, usually towards you." The admission was soft, almost lost in the rustle of straw, a fleeting vulnerability before her defensiveness returned.

Elara heard the rawness behind the words. She remembered how Carmen once sneered and called her illusions cheap tricks. How Carmen had bragged about receiving better commissions from the nobility. Now all that posturing felt so distant. The woman standing before Elara was not just a rival anymore. She was an ally seeking atonement. Elara's chest squeezed with pity and an odd sense of kinship.

She glanced away, a bitter twist to her lips. "Even Lucian... his loyalty to the prince, his quiet strength... it's the sort of honor I once craved notice from, but always felt it directed elsewhere, usually towards you." The admission was soft, almost lost in the rustle of straw, a fleeting vulnerability before her defensiveness returned.

"We can make this right," Elara said gently. "Your knowledge of Malakar's methods will help us. If we strengthen the dreamshield for Caelum, we close off his mind to Malakar's illusions for good. Then the dream realm can be used for healing instead of terror."

Carmen's eyes lit with a faint flicker of hope. She turned for a moment, as if uncertain she deserved that kindness, but then she squared her shoulders. "I have already told Malakar that I grow skeptical of your so-called progress. I told him I believe you are faltering under the strain of advanced illusions. He believes I am still gathering evidence to show him how limited your powers are. That was enough to buy me time."

Elara exhaled, relief and tension tangling in her gut. "So, we maintain this ruse. You remain close to him, pretend you doubt my competence. Meanwhile you feed him only trivial illusions or half-truths. Enough for him to think he still has your loyalty."

"Yes," Carmen confirmed. "But if he suspects betrayal, he will lash out. I have seen what he does to those he thinks are no longer useful." She shuddered as if recalling a private horror. "I will not let him manipulate me further. And I will not let my envy endanger us again."

Watching Carmen struggle with that confession, Elara realized how different this encounter felt from all the times they had locked horns over petty guild politics. The stakes now reached far beyond personal renown. Carmen's remorse proved genuine, despite the many ways she had once harmed Elara. In that moment, Elara felt the last remnants of her anger dissolving, replaced by a fierce resolve.

She squeezed Carmen's hand. "This is not just about one dreamshield or one night's illusions. We have to weave something that repels Malakar at every opportunity. And you can help. Your illusions, even at a lesser strength than mine, can still bolster our wards. I saw the potential when we faced nightmares side by side before." She recalled the fleeting moment in a dream corridor when Carmen had mustered enough magic to keep illusions at bay. "We need every ally we can get."

Carmen swallowed, nodding. Her grip trembled around Elara's hand. "I was taught only minimal illusions. And what Malakar showed me was always tinted by his darkness. Yet, I will try. I confess I'm terrified that I will slip again."

"We are all frightened," Elara admitted, her own voice quavering. She thought of Prince Caelum, still haunted by the memories of the illusions that bound him for so long, and Lucian, who constantly guarded them in the waking world. Everyone carried fear. "But we do not have to face it alone. Malakar is strong, yet we have come far in unraveling his illusions. And we know he cannot cast them so widely if we block him from Caelum's mind."

Carmen closed her eyes. A tear trailed silently down her cheek, leaving a faint shimmer in the torchlight. Elara watched sadly, noticing how Carmen instinctively touched the thick, knotted ribbon on her wrist: the double-layered severance ward she'd stitched herself. Even now, weeks after breaking Malakar's primary hold, the fight wasn't entirely over; the sorcerer's influence lingered like a stain, ready to bleed through if her resolve faltered.

"I envy you, you know," she said in a hushed tone.

"Not just your dreamweaver gift. But how you hold onto hope. I wanted to be strong like that. I felt so overshadowed that I could not see how to stand on my own."

Elara's throat constricted with emotion. She recalled her own feelings of insignificance when she first joined the guild, how everyone overlooked her. She squeezed Carmen's hand again, gentler this time. "Strength does not mean never faltering. It means we keep going when we want to collapse. You are still here, trying to fix your mistakes. That counts."

They fell silent. Footsteps from somewhere beyond the stables made them both stiffen, but the sounds faded, likely just a passing guard. The flickering torchlight had burned lower, casting erratic shadows up the walls. Elara realized they had been speaking for longer than she expected. Dawn felt distant, yet she knew they had precious little time before Malakar might suspect Carmen's absence.

As if sensing Elara's concern, Carmen squared her shoulders. "I will pretend the conversation went poorly, that you cursed me out for demanding explanations of your illusions. I will gather bits of cloth and scribbled runes from the workshop to show him. He will think I am just searching for proof of your failings."

Elara allowed herself a thin smile. "And I will complain, loudly if needed, about how you invaded my space looking for something to flaunt in Malakar's face. The apprentices might overhear and spread that tale if we do it right."

Carmen nodded. Her tears had dried, replaced by

steely determination. "You will tell him next time that I put on an arrogant front, as if hoping he will reward me for humiliating you. He will not suspect I am funneling worthless scraps of illusion." She bit her lip. "But for that to work, you must continue your real progress with Lucian and the wards in secret. I promise to deflect Malakar, to buy you time to ready the shield for Caelum."

Elara placed a hand on her own spool of shimmering thread, which was tucked in a leather pouch against her hip. The spool felt warm, almost pulsing, as if it recognized the turning point in her heart. She inhaled. "Then we have a plan. As soon as I speak with Lucian, we will press forward with the final round of preparations. We need to anchor the shield with fresh runes and illusions. If you can bring me any leftover scraps of Malakar's notes or wards, we might learn how to disguise the shield's presence from him."

Carmen exhaled a sigh of relief. "I will do what I can. There are piles of half-distorted illusions I have glimpsed in his private trunk. Perhaps I can glean specific incantations that hide illusions from detection. If we invert them, we might cloak our dreamshield from him."

Warmth spread through Elara's chest despite the lingering shadows around them. In another life, Carmen might have remained the woman who ridiculed her daily. Now they stood together in the gloom, forging a fragile unity for Prince Caelum's sake, and possibly for the kingdom's. The bitterness that had once choked their relationship felt like a memory fading under the weight of greater truths.

She looked Carmen in the eye. "It is not too late for you to do right," she said softly. "Dreamweaver magic, illusions... they are only as good or evil as the intentions behind them. If your heart is set on protecting rather than destroying, then you have already chosen a better path."

Carmen blinked. The tears threatened to return before she lifted her chin in determination. "Thank you, Elara. I never imagined I would say that, but..." She trailed off, a half-smile ghosting across her lips. "Well, I suppose we are no longer just rivals."

They wrapped each other in a tentative embrace, the dusty stable air a silent witness to this shift. Wood creaked underfoot, and the single lantern's flame flickered in the corner, illuminating their tense but genuine moment. Elara could feel Carmen's tremors, her fear that Malakar might discover her duplicity, the remnants of shame for what had been done. But she also sensed Carmen's resolve.

After a few breaths, the two women stepped back, the hush stretching around them like a promise. Elara found her voice at last. "Let us seal this with a vow," she said. "We do what we must to protect Caelum from further harm. We dismantle Malakar's illusions piece by piece, no matter how deep they go."

Carmen pressed her lips together, then nodded solemnly. "Agreed. We will protect Caelum from that monster, whatever it takes. And if Malakar suspects, I will face him. I cannot run from this anymore."

Elara studied Carmen's eyes. She saw a flicker of the proud woman she had once envied, now tempered by regret and courage alike. Her own heart thumped loudly, but the moment of solidarity gave her strength. They had both made costly mistakes in the past. Yet, here in the dusty gloom, they were forging a vow that might reshape their destiny, and that of the kingdom.

She extended her hand, and Carmen clasped it firmly, sealing the promise in silence. In that gesture, Elara sensed the old bitterness melting at last, replaced by a fragile but determined unity.

They parted, each ghosting toward opposite exits. As Elara brushed straw from her cloak, a cold draft swept the lane. On an overhead beam a faint serpent-eye glyph flared, ember red, then vanished. Her heart lurched. Malakar was still watching. And the true test of their fragile pact had only begun.

FIVE

Elara shuddered from the faint chill that clung to Prince Caelum's bedchamber. It wasn't just the draft seeping under the heavy oak door; it was the lingering resonance of the dream realm, a place her spirit now visited as readily as her own workshop. Each visit strengthened her bond with Caelum, a connection pulsing through the spool inherited from her grandmother, but it also left her feeling perpetually drained, as if she straddled two worlds without fully belonging to either.

Despite the soft lamplight flickering against polished furniture, the space felt colder than midnight air. She stood at Caelum's bedside, only a few steps from where Lucian hovered, and fought to calm her racing pulse. The hour was late, and the corridors beyond lay in silence, giving them precious time to achieve what so many doubted: weave a ward strong enough to shield the prince from Malakar's darkest illusions.

She could feel the tension humming in the air. Carmen

waited at the edge of the room, a spool of ordinary gray thread slipping through her fingers. Lucian's hand remained poised near the hilt of his sword, as if expecting Malakar to burst through the doors at any moment. And there, in the bed's center, Caelum's tranquil face betrayed no hint of the danger creeping along the edges of his mind. His eyelids never so much as fluttered, but a faint pallor clung to his cheeks, reminding them of his fragile condition. Elara inhaled slowly, stirring dusty motes of light, and forced herself to believe they had a chance.

Carefully, she set down her spool of shimmering thread on the quilt beside Caelum. The spool glowed with the soft luminescence that had first caught her notice when she was only a lowly seamstress in the Tapestry Guild. Now, she knew it was the conduit of her dreamweaver magic, a link between illusions and reality. A link that had let her glimpse Caelum in the dream realm and guide him toward consciousness more than once. Tonight, she was determined to place one final safeguard: a layered ward to hide him from Malakar's grasp.

"This is the last piece," she murmured, letting her focus settle on the spool. "We have to do it quickly. Carmen, are you ready?"

Carmen stepped forward. Her lips pressed tight in a mix of worry and resolve. "Yes," she said under her breath. The ordinary thread in her hands looked unimpressive next to Elara's glowing spool, but that simple skein represented Carmen's choice to stand with them. She had explained it earlier with a slight tremor in her voice, describing how she once used the same thread to sabotage

Elara's illusions under Malakar's direction. Now, she intended to reverse that harm by lending moral support in the form of her own small dream-threads.

"We must be sure Malakar can't sense this," Lucian said. His voice was subdued but carried a note of command. "He has eyes and ears in more corners of the kingdom than we realized."

Elara nodded, and noticed Carmen give a short, almost imperceptible nod of agreement toward Lucian, a silent acknowledgment of the shared responsibility they now carried. The sharp edges of their old guild rivalry seemed to have softened, replaced by a grudging respect forged in the face of Malakar's pervasive threat. If they left so much as a ripple in the magic around Caelum, Malakar might strike while the prince was still too weak to defend himself. She carefully loosened the spool's end, letting the glowing thread slip across her palm. Then she glanced at the nearest table, where pages of stolen notes lay. She and Carmen had spent the last hour huddled over them, searching for a final phrase to conceal their work from prying illusions.

Her gaze fell on a margin note scrawled in uneven script, the same note that had caught her eye earlier in one of Malakar's purloined manuscripts. She repeated the words softly, a needling sense of urgency driving her:

"The illusions thrive on the echo of fear. Mask that echo in the hush of compassion. Let your thread be still as the quiet moon."

She recalled seeing that sentence scribbled in the corner of a page on advanced warding. Malakar must have overlooked it, likely too busy twisting the main incantation for his own ends. Elara prayed that this small hint would help them succeed. Looking once more at the sleeping prince, she whispered, "I will not fail you."

Steadying her breath, she inserted the needle into the intangible space above Caelum's chest, letting the shimmering thread gather. The motion looked like sewing the air itself, pulling a thin veil across his body. In truth, she was weaving illusions. Each pass of her hand shaped a protective mesh to keep out nightmares. Carmen scarved the edges of that mesh with faint pulses of her own illusions, forming a border that fused with Elara's dream-thread.

Lucian stepped closer, gaze sharp. Without speaking, he set his hand just above Elara's elbow, his presence grounding her. A faint pulse of warmth flickered where they touched, an unspoken reminder of what they had shared: fear and uncertainty, but also trust and comfort.

Her heart twisted with a familiar pang of guilt. Lucian's steadfast presence was an undeniable anchor in this waking world, a comfort she couldn't deny feeling drawn to, especially in moments of such intense pressure. Yet, the echo of Caelum's voice in the dream realm, the memory of their shared vulnerability, the profound connection woven into the very fabric of her magic and purpose – that was different, deeper, an irrefutable pull towards the prince's soul. She knew, with a certainty that ached, that Caelum was the core of this fight, the reason she risked everything. Any warmth she felt for Lucian, however genuine in its own right, was a gentle river current beside the powerful ocean tide pulling her towards Caelum. She had to be clearer, if not to Lucian, then at least to herself.

She angled her needle a final time, drawing loop after loop of glowing thread. Her arms ached from the strain, and the shimmering spool trembled in her grip. It felt as though all the magic she had left was pouring out into this ward, but there was no other choice. Caelum's life hung by that shimmering tether. If her illusions failed, Malakar might tighten his hold and destroy all their progress.

Lucian's brow furrowed as beads of sweat formed at his hairline. She sensed his energy feeding into her illusions, though he was no dreamweaver. The synergy between them was new, a bond that had taken shape when they crossed the threshold into the dream realm together. Elara, intent on her weaving, was only dimly aware of Carmen watching them. For a fleeting moment, she thought she saw a wistful flicker in Carmen's eyes when they rested on Lucian's intent profile, a longing Carmen quickly shuttered away as she returned to her part in the warding, her expression settling into studied neutrality.

Carmen muttered a short incantation, her voice wavering. With her free hand, she guided the ordinary thread around the edges of the bed. Lucian, standing sentinel, watched Carmen's precise movements as she wove her thread. He noted the focused frown on her face, the way her fingers, though trembling slightly, moved with a practiced skill he hadn't fully appreciated before. She wasn't Elara, her magic far less potent, but there was a meticulousness to her work, a determination to get the supplemental warding just right. He found himself giving a small, almost involuntary nod of approval when she successfully anchored a particularly tricky section of the thread.

To Elara's eyes, it glimmered faintly as Carmen's illusions danced along the drab fibers. Though Carmen lacked raw dreamweaver strength, her own brand of illusions was precise, able to fill in any small gaps Elara's more powerful but sometimes unwieldy magic left behind.

A swirl of light glowed, bridging Carmen's thread with Elara's shimmering spool. The effect surrounded Caelum's body in a halo that shimmered blue violet in the dim lamplight. He stirred, not awake, but his lashes twitched slightly. Elara clenched the spool more tightly, pressing the illusions forward, urging them to remain gentle yet firm. She felt no real change in the prince's shallow breathing, so she prayed that, at least, she was doing no harm.

Minutes bled into a hush of effort. The ward expanded around them, drifting outward until it resembled a faint shell curving over the bed. Lucian's closeness became almost palpable in her periphery. She heard him exhale softly, as if he worried that too sharp a sound might snap the fragile illusion. Carmen's lips moved at a silent pace, likely repeating a protective phrase gleaned from her stolen scraps of parchment. The air grew thick with the tang of magic, reminiscent of heated metal in a forge, layered with the faint spice of the herbal candles that still burned on the table beside them.

At last, Elara felt the ward reach its apex. The illusions steadied into place, humming with a power that seemed to stand as a barrier against every creeping shadow. Her entire body shook with fatigue. Her sleeves clung to damp skin beneath, and the needle trembled in her fingers. She drew one last loop of the shimmering thread, then tied it off with a quiet whisper: "Quiet as the moon, hidden from the echo of fear."

A trembling hush fell over the chamber. Murky lamp-light revealed the completed bubble of soft incandescence that encased Caelum in a protective aura. Small ripples of color swirled along its edges, reminiscent of moonlit water. Elara felt her heart stuttering under the strain of so much magic. She sagged forward, bracing her hands on the side of the bed for support.

Lucian's hand found the center of her back, his voice low. "Steady yourself. You did it."

She tried to lift her gaze, meeting his eyes for a fleeting second. She saw relief in them, and something deeper that made her pulse skip. Carmen stepped back, letting out a long exhale of her own. Her spool of ordinary thread dangled between her fingers, unwound and exhausted, no longer glimmering with illusions. It might have looked too humble to anyone else, but the flicker of satisfaction on Carmen's face spoke volumes.

"It looks stable," Carmen said quietly. She placed a hand on the ward, and faint rings of color expanded outward, then dissipated. "Elara, you're certain Malakar can't see it?"

Elara swallowed around a dry throat. "I used the

margin note from the stolen text. It should cloak our magic's signature. Malakar might sense Caelum is protected, but he shouldn't be able to pinpoint how we're doing it."

With a measured nod, Carmen turned her attention to Caelum's face. A shadow of regret flickered across her expression, perhaps a reminder that she once helped Malakar gather illusions that tormented him. She said nothing more, only folded her arms and let that remorseful quiet speak for her.

Elara tried to slow her breathing. The illusions glowed steadily, and Caelum's form, though still motionless, did not look in distress. She whispered a silent thank you in her head, not only to whatever power sustained her dreamweaver gifts but also to Lucian and Carmen for their part in weaving this fragile stand. Fragile, indeed. Malakar had been thwarted, yes, but not defeated. He was out there, his influence still poisoning the Veil. If he discovered this ward, she suspected his next move would be far less subtle, aimed directly at the bonds they had just risked everything to forge. But the alternative, leaving him unguarded, was far too dangerous. The quiet in the chamber felt less like peace and more like the held breath before a final, devastating storm.

In the quiet that followed, she peered at Lucian's still hand resting on the hilt of his sword. His knuckles were white, and faint tremors shook his forearm. "Are you alright?" she asked.

He managed a tight laugh. "I have never tried to infuse illusions this way. Feeling my own resolve braid into your dream-threads was… unsettling. Draining, though I have no talent for magic myself. Yet I felt it just now."

Elara's heart twisted. She knew exactly the odd pull he meant. As she watched him, a bitter image flashed—last night's dream, when she and Lucian had been yanked together by unseen strings, their mouths meeting while Caelum watched, powerless. She had felt the alien tug then, slick and cold, and knew now it had been Malakar puppeteering their bodies. Shame burned, but clarity followed: her heart had not chosen that moment; darkness had.

Carmen moved to the foot of the bed. She placed her spool on a small stand, as if she no longer wished to carry its symbolic weight. Then quietly, she said, "We have to stay alert. Malakar might try illusions in Caelum's vicinity, even if he cannot penetrate the ward. We should post a rotating watch."

Lucian nodded in agreement. "I will take the first shift. You both are exhausted."

Elara opened her mouth to protest, but her strength was ebbing. Faint arcs of colored light swam at the edges of her vision. Accepting his offer felt like a relief, but guilt hovered in the back of her mind. She hated leaving him to stand guard alone while she found rest. Still, her battered limbs offered no argument. She wiped sweat from her brow, letting her posture slump.

"Thank you," she whispered to Lucian. He dipped his head in acknowledgment. The simple act of his voice, his presence, eased the tension in her chest.

She sank onto a low wooden bench by the wall, letting

her eyes skate across the ward's shimmering glow. Caelum's face remained restful, the slight flutter of his pulse visible at his neck. Each gentle thump reassured her that he lived and that she had not overtaxed him with illusions. She wanted to believe it was enough. At least for tonight.

Carmen drew closer to Elara, touching her shoulder gently. "You did well. We needed this."

Elara nodded, biting back a surge of complicated emotion. She could not help remembering the flicker of longing she sensed whenever Caelum murmured her name. She recalled, too, the quiet comfort that bloomed each time Lucian steadied her hand in the dream realm. All of that now clashed inside her heart like two warring illusions on the brink of colliding.

Carmen stepped back, allowing Elara a moment to breathe. The heavy hush in the chamber was broken only by the muted crackle of the bedside lamp. Shadows danced against the walls, occasionally catching on the shimmering arcs of the ward. Outside, the corridor likely remained silent. The King and Queen had retreated into their own rooms hours ago, presumably drained by the day's endless wave of uncertainty. There would be no challenge to their methods tonight.

Elara found herself pressing fists into her skirt, trying to regain composure. The shield around Caelum had taken every ounce of her focus, and with it completed, she felt hollow, as if strangled by the swirl of emotion that accompanied her illusions. She could not let that emptiness linger or she risked unraveling the patchwork of illusions they had just painstakingly created.

Lucian's voice rose gently. "You should rest," he said to Elara, though his gaze flicked to Carmen in silent suggestion that she do the same.

Carmen nodded, her cheeks tinting. Elara noticed, but didn't think much of it. They were all exhausted. "We can switch watch at the next hour, Lucian. Wake me then."

Elara was grateful for the sense of determination in them both. They all knew Malakar would not simply slink away, not after exerting so much effort fueling the kingdom's nightmares. Yet, for now, they had done all they could to safeguard the prince. With Caelum slowly recovering from the illusions that once held him prisoner, this protective shell was their best weapon, a stand against Malakar's creeping power.

She rose to her feet, stepping back to the bedside. The ward glowed faintly, tracing gentle ripples across Caelum's cheeks. She placed a hand over his, feeling the lingering warmth of life, though he did not stir. "You are safe," she whispered. "We will keep you safe." The words rang with a quiet reverence, a promise she intended to keep.

An uncertain hush settled around them. Carmen cleared her throat softly. "If we notice any disturbance... illusions, or if Caelum's breath changes, we call each other. Immediately."

Lucian nodded, posture rigid. "Exactly. I will watch for the slightest sign."

Elara's chest felt both heavy and buoyant as she

turned away from the bed, letting Carmen guide her toward the far side of the chamber, where a cushioned chair had been set up. She recognized how easily exhaustion could unravel her illusions if she pushed herself to remain awake. Each step threatened to buckle her knees. Still, she spared one final glance toward the prince who lay beneath the shimmering tapestry of protective magic.

Doubt nagged at the corners of her mind. Was the concealment strong enough? Had she truly masked every trace of dreamweaver essence so Malakar's illusions would not find a single loose thread to pull? The tension made her teeth clench, but she forced her breathing to slow, summoning the last wisps of faith in herself.

When she sank into the chair, the weight of her exhaustion enveloped her. Lucian stood near the door, sword half-drawn, vigilant in the hush of the night. Carmen retreated to a corner seat with her spool of ordinary thread at the ready, eyes shuttered yet poised to spring up at a moment's notice. The flicker of the final layered ward danced across the walls, offering them all a fragile reassurance in the face of the kingdom's mounting fears.

Elara let her eyes slip closed. Beyond the swirl of fatigue, she felt raw hope flicker inside her chest. They had done something vital here. Though the threat loomed, Caelum was no longer defenseless against Malakar's illusions. Together, they had fashioned barriers beyond what any one of them could weave alone.

She opened her eyes once more, letting them roam the room. Lucian's gaze met hers, and unspoken understanding passed between them: a blend of triumph, longing, and a whisper of regret. Then, she glanced at Carmen, who cradled her spool in her lap, shoulders hunched in a posture of uneasy relief. Finally, Elara's gaze moved to Caelum, whose peaceful expression reminded her why this battle mattered so deeply.

Though none spoke, each of them felt the significance of that moment. The protective aura cast gentle patterns of light across the floorboards—signs of a fragile harmony woven from heartbreak and resolve. She knew their fight was far from over. Malakar would lash out when he sensed Caelum slipping further from his grasp. Yet the shield held. One obstacle had been overcome, if only for now.

Elara let a strained smile ghost across her lips. Despite the tangle of emotions, she sensed that the alliances they had forged, born in fear, tempered by love, and sealed with illusions. These bonds were stronger than any nightmares that might prowl the kingdom's sleepless nights.

By the time they completed the last thread, sweat dotted her brow, and Lucian's hand trembled near his sword. The field glimmered around Caelum, reflecting faint colors onto the walls, and Carmen exhaled in tandem with Elara. That final hush spoke everything they dared not say out loud: Malakar would not let this go easily, and Elara's heart still teetered between two affections. Yet for a brief, gleaming instant, all seemed whole. Hope had been stitched into the gloom.

In that shimmering quiet, they silently promised to stand together, braced for whatever illusions haunted the next hours. Malakar's hold might persist beyond these walls, but Caelum lay wrapped in protective light, beyond the immediate reach of nightmares. Elara pressed a hand to her chest, feeling her pulse race beneath her fingertips. This moment, at least, belonged to them. A small victory in a war that demanded all their strength.

Still, for a fragile, shining moment, they stood together, resolved that every bond they clung to, whether forged in dreams or in waking solidarity, must remain unbroken if they had any hope of dismantling Malakar's stranglehold on the kingdom.

Elara's spine felt stiff as she hurried down the long corridor leading to the palace library. Torchlit sconces cast shifting patterns on the floor, framing her rushed footsteps in fluttering shadows. Despite the evening hour, she still felt the tight coil of tension in her shoulders, a remnant of the day's grueling task of blocking illusions from infiltrating the king's private chambers. The memory of those illusions made her heart pound; more than once she had sensed cold tendrils of Malakar's magic slithering at the edges of the wards she had sewn.

Now she needed a moment of peace, somewhere no exhausted sentinel asked her for fresh wards and no trembling servant blocked her path with frantic pleas. The library alcove offered at least a semblance of solitude. She pushed through the heavy wooden doors and let them close behind her with a quiet thud. A faint hush enveloped the space. Most scribes left at dusk, and tonight even the occasional scuffle of parchment or scratch of quill was absent.

She wound her way between shelves crammed with histories, treatises, and yellowed scrolls. The scent of leather bindings and dust reminded her of simpler times before illusions and curses forced her into constant vigilance. Although her thoughts flickered to Prince Caelum's slow recovery and the swirl of politics around him, she tried to ignore the weight in her chest. She deserved a pause.

When she reached the end of the aisle, Elara found Carmen in a quiet alcove, not amidst scrolls as usual but staring blankly at a rain-streaked window. Tightness pinched Carmen's mouth, and her shoulders slumped with a vulnerability Elara had rarely seen. Unease prickled through Elara as she recalled Carmen's fleeting, complicated glances toward Lucian during the warding and the almost imperceptible softening that had vanished as quickly as it appeared.

"Carmen?" Elara began gently. "Is everything all right?"

Carmen turned, her eyes shadowed not with anger but with deep, weary sadness. "Elara," she started, her voice barely a whisper, "there's something...something I need to tell you. And it's the hardest thing I've ever had to say, especially to you."

Elara's breath caught. Sophia, one of her fellow seamstresses, had once warned her that Carmen's cunning extended to manipulating the air around her. Yet the flicker in Carmen's gaze spoke neither of triumph nor cruelty, but of desperation and, beneath that, quiet despair.

"Could we do this another night?" Elara asked softly, her voice strained with exhaustion and a thread of unease. "I don't think I can handle any more illusions today."

Carmen pressed her lips into a thin line, eyes flicking nervously toward the narrow walkway behind them. "No. It has to be tonight, or there might never be another chance. I need to say my piece."

Elara hesitated, anxiety evident in the tightening of her jaw. "All right," she whispered, barely audible. "I'm listening."

Carmen steadied herself, swallowing as if bracing against a surge of emotion. With a trembling sigh, she set the warding candle on a small side table. Its ghostly glow stretched their reflections across a row of dusty tomes. Her gaze dropped to her hands, twisting in her lap. "It's Lucian," she said, the words heavy with unshed tears. "I...I find myself feeling things for him, Elara. Things I never expected, never wanted, especially now." She looked up, her eyes pleading for understanding. "It's confusing, and it makes me feel...ashamed, after everything. He's been so steadfast for you, and I see the way he...cares for you. And I know your heart is with Caelum, as it should be." A tear escaped and traced a path down her cheek. "I don't want to cause trouble, Elara. Truly. But watching...sometimes it feels like he's holding onto a hope that might not be there for him. And it's tearing me apart, because I...I care for him."

Elara's breath caught. Carmen and Lucian? The pieces

clicked into place: the shared glances, the quiet respect she had occasionally noted. A wave of guilt, sharp and sudden, washed over Elara, but it wasn't for anything Carmen accused her of. It was for her own heart, for the confusing warmth she had allowed herself to feel for Lucian, the comfort of his presence, the memory of shared danger that sometimes blurred into something more. But it isn't love, a clear voice insisted within her. Not the love I feel for Caelum. That was a bedrock, a certainty that anchored her soul. Lucian was...a dear friend, a brave ally, even a fleeting, dangerous attraction born of trauma and proximity. But Caelum...Caelum was the missing piece of her own weave, the melody her magic sang for. Carmen's painful honesty was forcing Elara to confront the truth she had been avoiding: any ambiguity she projected was unfair to Lucian, and a disservice to the profound love she held for the prince.

Carmen continued, and her voice trembled despite her attempt at composure. "I've kept it to myself too long. At first it was a fascination, a silly way to feel close to him because you seemed to share something special. But lately I can't help noticing how he looks at you, how easily you two connect. I envy that closeness, how naturally you seem to understand each other."

The air in the alcove seemed to grow heavier, but Elara softened her posture, fatigue giving way to genuine concern. "Why tell me now?" she asked gently, unsure whether Carmen needed comfort or encouragement. "Have you talked to him about how you feel?"

Carmen bit her lip and glanced at the candle, which

flickered as though sensing their vulnerability. "Because I've seen the way you look at him, Elara. He watches you, and I know you see it too, even if you pretend not to. You try to focus on your stitching magic or your friendship with Caelum, but I can tell something more is there. I guess I'm just asking, could you maybe step back a little?"

Something stirred in Elara's chest, a complicated blend of guilt, worry, and understanding. Her day had been full of illusions hammering at the palace door, guards questioning her wards, and now her heart was laid bare before her friend. She took a gentle step closer, her expression sincere.

"You know I'd never want to hurt you," Elara said softly, choosing her words carefully. "Lucian will always make his own choices, and I will too. But that doesn't mean your feelings don't matter to me. Carmen, you're my friend."

Carmen's gaze softened, eyes bright with restrained tears. "You've always mattered to me too," she admitted quietly. "Ever since we were apprentices, I admired how easily magic came to you. I had to work so hard to keep up, but I never resented you for it. I wished I could find that kind of magic in myself."

Elara's heart swelled with empathy. She remembered their early days vividly, Carmen staying late to practice, always pushing herself. "You think it came easily? Carmen, when that spool of thread first glowed in my hands, I was terrified. Dreamweaver magic felt like a responsibility I wasn't ready for. I didn't ask for any of it. I always admired how dedicated you were, how determined. You inspired me."

"You still had something special," Carmen said softly, managing a small, self-aware laugh. "You got to stand beside Prince Caelum, to do something brave for the guild. And now Lucian sees you clearly and appreciates your strength. It makes me realize I want someone to see me that way too."

Elara reached out and placed her hand on Carmen's shoulder. "I'm also torn, Carmen," she whispered, guilt creeping up. "I care for Caelum. I risked everything to bring him back from that cursed realm. But Lucian... he's been there for me in ways no one else has, and it makes me feel like I'm betraying two men at once. Do you think that's easy for me?"

Carmen let out a shaky laugh. "At least you have options. I'm stuck in the middle, tangled in Malakar's games, misunderstood by half the guild, and always feeling a step behind you."

Hearing Malakar's name sent a quiet chill through Elara. She thought of the day's illusions pressing against the king's chamber doors and wondered if Malakar was behind them, wherever he remained hidden. The atmosphere grew heavier, and when she tried to speak, her throat tightened. She recalled Carmen once confessing she'd gotten caught up in Malakar's plans, though she'd sworn she regretted it.

"What about Malakar?" Elara asked softly. "Are you saying your feelings about Lucian and me are making it harder for you to resist him and fight the illusions threatening the kingdom?"

Carmen swallowed, tears brightening her eyes. "That's exactly why I'm talking to you now. I don't want to fall deeper into his web. This jealousy, this confusion, is hurting me. If I keep holding onto it, I'm afraid it will push me toward choices I will regret. But I need you to understand me, Elara. My feelings matter too."

Elara exhaled slowly, her shoulders relaxing slightly. She felt too weary to hold onto any anger. Her mind replayed the times Carmen had stood beside her, facing swirling illusions and risking herself to strengthen protective wards. Every action told Elara that Carmen genuinely wanted to break free of Malakar, not help him.

"Carmen," Elara said quietly, her voice gentle and sincere, "I wasn't sure I could ever fully trust you again after everything. But I see how hard you're fighting Malakar's influence. You've risked your standing in the guild to protect others. And about Lucian, I can't deny we have a connection, but I'm as confused about what to do."

A tear slipped down Carmen's cheek. She quickly brushed it away, embarrassed by the emotion. "I'm sorry for letting envy come between us. It drove me to mistakes I regret. I nearly damaged your work, and worse, I allowed Malakar to use me with empty promises. It doesn't fix the past, but you deserve to know I'm truly sorry.

In that moment, Elara saw not the rival she had once imagined Carmen to be, but a friend as tired and uncertain as herself. The warding candle flickered gently, casting soft shadows across the rows of texts behind them. Silence stretched between them, filled with quiet understanding.

Finally, Elara spoke softly, wanting to heal the wounds between them. "I should've been more open with you. If we had talked sooner, we could have spared each other a lot of pain."

Carmen gave a watery laugh, the sound edged with relief rather than bitterness. "We're both a bit responsible," she said gently. "And now we're here, liking the same man, sort of. We're both caught up in the kingdom's burdens, just from different angles."

Elara bit her lip, emotions swirling inside her. She pictured Lucian's steady gaze whenever illusions threatened to overwhelm her, his quiet, supportive presence. Then she thought of Caelum's gentle, thoughtful eyes, remembering the tenderness they'd shared in the dream realm. Confusion, guilt, and longing all tangled together in her heart.

She steadied herself with one hand against a bookshelf, barely noticing the dust settling on her palm. "I don't have easy answers," she whispered softly. "Lucian is kind, loyal, protective... and he cares for you too, Carmen. He's noticed the courage you've shown lately, especially how openly you've resisted Malakar. But his feelings aren't something I control."

Carmen drew a deep breath, voice wavering gently. "I know you don't control them. But it still hurts to see the way he looks for you when I'm standing right in front of him. It makes me feel invisible."

Elara felt her heart tighten sympathetically. "I'm not

sure what else I can say, except... I promise I'm not trying to make things harder for you. I need to be honest with myself, too. Caelum..."

Carmen hesitated, frustration flickering across her features. "Of course, there's Caelum. Sometimes it feels like you've always been a little out of reach, even when we were apprentices."

Warmth rose to Elara's cheeks, but her voice remained soft, free of accusation. "We both know I didn't ask for any of that attention. The bond with Caelum, the illusions: it all fell on me without warning. I've spent my life trying to catch up, never feeling truly ready."

Quiet filled the space between them. The warding candle's flame flickered low, bathing them in soft shadows. After a moment, Carmen's expression softened, her shoulders relaxing slightly. A wry smile tugged at her lips. "You know what's strange? I think we're after the same things: a sense of belonging, some control over our own stories, love, even if it's different for each of us. I'm tired of illusions, real or otherwise. And I certainly don't want to be anyone's villain anymore."

Elara felt a quiet ache in her chest. She remembered the feeling of being a girl unnoticed by most, a spool of thread glowing uncertainly in her hands. She'd never imagined ending up here, crafting wards, fighting alongside princes, and navigating complicated friendships. "I don't want us to be against each other either," she said quietly, sincerity warming her voice. "We've already lost so much time misunderstanding each other. Imagine what we could have accomplished together against Malakar if we'd talked sooner."

Carmen offered a tentative smile, eyes glistening with unshed tears. "I guess we have more in common than I realized," she said. "Look, Elara, it'll probably take years before I can redeem myself for all I've done, especially the jealousy and the mistakes it caused. And maybe part of me still envies you a little. But I promise to try harder, for both our sakes. I want to support Lucian properly too. If Malakar threatens any of us again…"

"We'll face it together," Elara finished, a wave of tension easing into cautious unity. She stepped closer and studied Carmen, hoping their newfound honesty could grow into something stronger.

Carmen drew a steadying breath. "I hate that I've spent so much time feeling second best," she confessed, sincerity clear in her gaze. "But Malakar's schemes are so much worse. The kingdom deserves better from both of us, and I'm determined never to fall back into that darkness."

Elara blinked back her own tears as emotions she'd long hidden surfaced at last. "I'm sorry I didn't recognize your struggles sooner," she said. "I was wrapped up in my fears, in feeling inadequate. The truth is, Carmen, I've spent all this time afraid: of letting down Caelum, Lucian, the royal family, even the villagers who rely on our magic. Sometimes it feels overwhelming."

Carmen reached for the warding candle, her expression softening. "We've both been struggling under impossible expectations," she said. "You, holding the kingdom together with a spool of glowing thread, and me chasing ambitions I wasn't even sure were mine. Maybe it's time we let go of those illusions."

Elara exhaled slowly as a quiet resolve took hold. She lifted her chin, eyes clear. "No more secrets, Carmen. If you truly care about Lucian, show him. If there's still something between us, let's talk openly. No more pretending, no more illusions of our own making."

A faint, genuine laugh slipped from Carmen. She nodded, tears shimmering in her eyes. "Honesty. I think I can handle that."

They stood silently for a moment, the earlier tension fading into a fragile yet comforting bond. Rivalries seemed insignificant beside the looming threat of Malakar. Carmen cleared her throat, brushed the moisture from her lashes, and blew out the warding candle. A thin trail of fragrant smoke drifted toward the ceiling.

Elara felt her heartbeat slow at last. "Tomorrow we'll need to strengthen the wards," she said, her voice steady despite lingering exhaustion. "If illusions are already reaching the king's chambers, it won't be long before Malakar tries something worse."

Carmen straightened, determination brightening her expression. "We'll stop him together. And Elara, if you ever need my help, ask. I promise not to second-guess you again. What matters most is freeing the kingdom, not competing with each other."

Elara managed a soft, grateful smile, her eyes growing warm. "Thank you, Carmen." Carefully, she extended her hand, unsure whether Carmen would accept. Carmen hesitated only briefly before clasping it. The sincerity of the gesture felt powerful, shielding them both from lingering shadows. Slowly, they stepped apart.

Together they walked toward the corridor in quiet companionship, their footsteps echoing against the library tiles. Their hearts still raced from the honesty exchanged and the understanding found. At the exit, Carmen paused and turned to Elara with gentle strength.

"Let's do better," she said. "We've fought through enough illusions already. It's time we took control of our own stories."

Elara nodded, her throat tight with emotion. "Agreed." Words lingered on her tongue, but she held them back, afraid they might unravel her fragile composure. They parted there, each turning down different hallways, yet neither felt alone.

As she walked away, Elara knew one thing clearly: she couldn't keep hiding from her feelings. It was time to choose—not only between Caelum and Lucian, but also the person she truly wanted to become. No more illusions, she thought with newfound resolve. She would step into her own truth and face whatever came next.

SEVEN

Rain slicked every cobblestone under Elara's boots, and wet twilight clung to the palace courtyard like a cloak of restless shadows. The downpour battered the torch sconces along the high stone walls, reducing their light to a weak, wavering glow. Still, Elara pressed forward. Her woolen cloak clung to her shoulders, heavy with rain. Her heart pounded with an uncertainty that felt at odds with the drowning hush of the evening.

She spotted Lucian leaning against a chipped marble column in the center of the courtyard. Lantern glow rippled across shallow puddles near his feet. He wore a short cloak whose hood had fallen back, allowing the rain to darken the close-cropped hair at his temples. He must have thought himself alone. His eyes stayed on a distant corner of the courtyard, as if he expected illusions to materialize at any moment. Even from across the rain-drenched space, Elara caught sight of tension in the set of his shoulders. Tension she guessed he carried since sunrise, possibly even longer.

She didn't speak right away. Instead, she lingered, noticing how the storm muffled every ambient sound and cast drifting droplets of water across Lucian's stance. His sword belt sat low around his hips, the hilt glinting each time lightning flared in the sky. She saw the subtle rise and fall of his chest, heard his shuddering breath. The sight worsened the knot of guilt sitting heavy in her stomach. He was exhausted, probably from the scattered patrols she knew he helped organize. The illusions prowling the city left few hours of true rest.

He finally sensed her presence and turned, hand twitching near the sword hilt. At once, recognition replaced alarm, and he released a taut breath. "Elara." His voice cut through the static hiss of the rain.

She stepped closer, drawing the hood of her cloak farther forward, though the damp fabric seemed unable to stave off the chill. "Lucian," she managed quietly. "I... I realized you didn't report back to the gallery. I grew worried."

He cast a fleeting glance upward, droplets glistening on the dark lashes framing his hazel eyes. "I needed a moment," he said. "One moment of quiet to think, though the storm saw fit to join me." A half-smile tugged at his lips, but it never reached his eyes. "You're the only other soul mad enough to be wandering around in this downpour."

Elara feared her own heart would betray her. She was bound, in some unspoken sense, to Prince Caelum. Bound by the dreams that drew them together, bound by that desperate, powerful magic she used to keep nightmares from consuming him. She was the seamstress turned dreamweaver, the one who had touched Caelum's consciousness in a realm few others could enter. Yet, here, under slanting sheets of rain, her pulse clamored for Lucian in a different way. Lucian's steadfastness was a comfort, a tangible warmth in the cold reality of the palace corridors. The memory of their impulsive kiss in the library still burned, a confusing mix of shared exhaustion and genuine affection born from the trials they faced together. Yet, it felt different from the pull she felt towards Caelum: that deeper, almost fated connection woven through the dream realm, echoing the half-remembered magic of the grandmother whose legacy lived in the shimmering spool she carried. Lucian anchored her here, in the waking world, but Caelum... Caelum felt like the anchor for her soul. The division left her heart aching, unsure how to honour both bonds without betraying one.

He cleared his throat softly. Lucian's eyes held a vulnerability Elara had rarely seen. "I know my timing is terrible," he said softly. "But after everything we've faced, I couldn't keep silent any longer. The nights we spent poring over texts, the battles against illusions: they changed something in me, Elara. You became more than just the seamstress I was tasked to protect."

Elara felt her chest tighten. She remembered those quiet moments in the library, the way Lucian's steady presence had anchored her when nightmares threatened to overwhelm. "Lucian," she began gently, "those moments meant something to me too. Your unwavering support gave me strength when I needed it most.

"I find it impossible to stop thinking about you," he admitted, voice descending into an almost ashamed hush. He pressed a palm over his eyes, as though the confession weighed more than he could bear. "Every time I see you stitch illusions out of that shimmering thread or talk about wards and dreamweaver magic, it reminds me of how different you are from anyone I've known. And... it reminds me of my own limits as nothing more than a man with a sword."

Lightning flashed, illuminating the courtyard's edges and turning the puddles into splashes of silver. Elara's heart thudded with conflicting emotions. She shook rainwater off her cloak. "Lucian," she said, trying to sound firm, though her voice trembled. "You're no lesser because you aren't... a dreamweaver. In truth, I rely on your sword more times than I can count, and on your strength, too." She forced a small, tired laugh. "Physically and otherwise."

He gave a faint huff of amusement. "It's not the same," he insisted. "When it comes to illusions or curses, a sword can only hack at shadows. Meanwhile, you're out here weaving threads into reality. You've saved more people than I ever could, just by your gift... by yourself."

She shook her head, stepping over a wide puddle that threatened to soak her boots. "Dreamweaver magic is terrifying, Lucian. If you saw half the illusions that swarm me in the dream realm, you'd understand how powerless I often feel. My needle might stitch protective wards, but I can't hold a formation or give courage to a patrol of frightened guards. That is something only you manage. Do you see? Your skill is just as essential." The words carried more intensity than she intended, each syllable throbbing with genuine admiration for his commitment.

He nodded, eyes flicking away as a soft rumble of thunder vibrated overhead. "I believe you, though I struggle with it." He angled his face to hers, gaze momentarily downcast. "I can't shake the images of you weaving illusions in the workshop, the quiet determination in your eyes. It draws me in like... like a tether I can't cut."

She swallowed at the swirl of heat in her chest, feeling her pulse intensify. His closeness made her hyperaware of the cold raindrops sliding over her cheeks. She pictured Caelum's half-lidded gaze from the prior evening, the hoarse whisper of her name on his lips as he drifted near wakefulness again. She recalled how her illusions had gently glowed around him, and how her heart had ached in joy at seeing him stir. Yet here she was with Lucian, drowning in an entirely different longing that curled through her senses.

"I care for you deeply, Lucian," Elara said, her voice thick with emotion. "In another life, perhaps... But my connection to Caelum goes beyond just affection. It's as if our souls recognize each other, forged in the crucible of shared dreams and nightmares. I can't explain it fully, but I know with absolute certainty that he is where my heart truly belongs."

Lucian's jaw tightened, but his eyes held no anger, only a resigned understanding. "I see it now," he said quietly. "The way you look at him, how your magic seems to resonate when you're together. I think, deep down, I always knew. I watch him sometimes when he sleeps," he continued softly, "I see his breathing steady or falter depending on your illusions. I know he's dear to you. I'd never want to jeopardize that." His throat moved in a tight swallow. "And yet, not a day passes without me thinking... perhaps there is room in your life for something else, some other comfort."

Her entire body felt taut, as though pinned between storms raging inside and out. She recognized the sincerity in Lucian's confession. He wasn't demanding she abandon the prince she had risked everything to save; he was only baring a raw piece of himself in the middle of a courtyard battered by unrelenting rain. Her chest tightened with guilt for even allowing herself to yearn for him. While Caelum lay in a precarious recovery, no less.

"You deserve far more clarity from me than I can give," she murmured, forcing herself not to linger on the shape of Lucian's lips. "I care about you, Lucian, more than I thought I would. But I can't betray one bond for another, especially when illusions run amok, and Caelum—" She trailed off, chest aching.

A gale swept across the stone, sending ripples through the puddles around them. Before Elara could finish her thought, Lucian gently reached out, half-closing the distance. His fingers grazed hers, as though testing whether her hand would recoil. But she found herself clutching his touch, an involuntary move that shot warmth up her chilled arm. She let out an uneven breath.

"Were the kingdom not tangled in nightmares," he whispered, "I'd ask you to walk with me under kinder skies. No illusions, no curses, just a night of calm. I hate these hidden confessions, these stolen moments in the rain. Still, I can't keep silent anymore."

She forced a shaky exhale. "I can't pretend this isn't real," she whispered, swallowing hard as the thunder rattled overhead. "But I also can't ignore all the people who rely on us, or the miseries that illusions still inflict on the kingdom. I can't stand the thought of betraying Caelum after all the nights we've shared in dreams. And Carmen—she... cares for you. I can't hurt her either."

At the mention of Carmen, Lucian's mouth hardened in a line. "She said something to me too, though not so directly," he admitted. "I don't want to wound her. She's come far, and she's trying to make amends for her part in Malakar's manipulations. But I won't lie to you and say my heart is free of feeling. You and I..." His teeth caught the corner of his lip, and he averted his gaze.

Lightning streaked the sky again, and in its after-flare, Elara noticed how close they were standing. She felt the heat radiating from his taut body, smelled the rain-soaked leather of his cloak, saw rivulets of water slip down the line of his jaw. A sharp longing rushed through her—unexpected and intense. It felt as though the entire court-yard shrank to just the two of them and the hush of the storm.

She was trembling, half from cold and half from that raw magnetism. Did she truly dare to close this gap, to risk what might happen if Lucian's lips met hers? She reminded herself of the tenderness in Caelum's voice when he whispered her name, the faint smile on his face mere hours ago. Her conscience twisted, urging her not to let the moment spiral out of control.

"You deserve someone who can give you their whole heart, Lucian. Someone who sees you as clearly as you've always seen me."

Even while she said the words, her heart hammered in a riot of confused desire, urging her to move just a step closer.

"Elara," Lucian breathed, "I—"

She never learned what he meant to say. They both felt the shift in the air the instant before Carmen burst into view at the courtyard's far end. The lamp in Carmen's hand flickered as she made for them, her cloak flaring behind her in the wind. Stark apprehension etched her features. Elara stiffened, quickly releasing Lucian's hand, although she suspected Carmen had already seen more than she should.

Carmen's eyes flicked from Elara to Lucian, then to the narrow inches that separated them. Rain trickled from the curls plastered to Carmen's face. For a tense heartbeat, she seemed at a loss for words, hurt flickering across her expression. Then, she drew a breath and pasted on a mask of urgency. "Elara, Lucian," she said, voice betrayed by a slight tremor. "Something is happening on the southern edge of the city. Another surge of nightmares. People are panicking, running indoors." The wind whipped her words almost into shards, but her meaning was unmistakable.

Elara stepped away from Lucian, the cold air instantly filling the space he had occupied. The heat of him evaporated, and she felt a lurch of regret so strong it took her a moment to speak. "How bad is it?" she asked, wiping moisture from her eyes.

Carmen steadied the flickering lantern in her grip. "Bad enough that the local watch tower signaled for urgent backup. They claim illusions formed twisted shapes that the usual wards can't contain. We have to intervene."

Lucian exhaled, a muscle tight in his jaw. "Then we'll gather the knights immediately. I'll handle a patrol. Elara, can you—"

"I can try weaving any illusions or wards the people might need," she finished for him. She stole a look at Carmen. Guilt flared in her chest again when she recalled Carmen's heartfelt confession the day before. But Carmen gave a curt nod in acknowledgment, letting no further emotion slip. "We'll do everything we can," Elara said softly.

A sheet of rain swept past them, and thunder rumbled low, echoing the tension in all their hearts. Lucian glanced at Elara, then at Carmen, and squared his shoulders. "Right," he said briskly. "I'll coordinate with the inner watch. We can meet near the city gates to share what we learn."

Carmen's gaze lingered on Elara a moment longer, a swirl of pain and resignation shadowing her dark eyes. "I only came to fetch you," she said, addressing Elara in a tone that balanced politeness with unspoken betrayal.

Then she turned on her heel, lantern bobbing as she disappeared into the storm to sound another round of warnings.

Sudden silence claimed the courtyard. The yearning that had crackled between Elara and Lucian felt distant now, replaced by the sobering reminder that illusions still ravaged the kingdom. She became acutely aware of her own torn heart, battered by too many emotions to name. If Carmen's abrupt arrival had not shattered the moment, Elara wondered what she might have done—what both of them might have surrendered to in the hush of the storm.

She inhaled, tasting the raw tang of rain in the back of her throat. Lucian dipped his head in a resigned gesture, some unspoken grief tucked behind his eyes. "Let's focus on what's important," he said at last. "Saving people from these nightmares."

Elara nodded, ignoring the trembling in her legs. She forced her attention away from the ache in her chest. This was bigger than her, bigger than any confusion flaring in her heart. "Yes," she agreed softly. "That comes first."

They started toward the castle archway, footsteps splashing through puddles and echoing against towering walls. Elara hugged her cloak closer, refusing to meet Lucian's gaze again. The memory of that almost-kiss made her heart pound viciously. Duty, she reminded herself. She had to protect the kingdom, defend Caelum, and help contain the illusions. No matter how torn she felt, the cause demanded everything she had, or more.

Another gust of wind dulled the last of the torches outright, plunging the courtyard into near darkness.

Neither Elara nor Lucian paused to relight them. A deeper fear kindled in her mind: fear of fueling more jealousy or dividing the fragile alliance that had grown between them and Carmen. She swallowed hard. Each step through the rain took her away from the heated confessions under that flickering torchlight—and shoved her back into the relentless struggle that waited in the city beyond.

At the main threshold, Carmen reappeared, cloak dripping, her posture braced for the next onslaught of illusions. Heated tension still flickered in her gaze, but she covered it with an air of purposeful resolve. Elara could only manage a polite nod in return, steeling her spine and reminding herself why they all fought. The unspoken conflict in the courtyard would have to wait. Malakar's conjurations threatened their people more urgently than any single tangle of hearts.

"Onward then," Elara said, forcing an even tone. "We have work to do."

Lucian and Carmen both inclined their heads. The three departed into the gloom, hurrying through winding corridors that led away from the courtyard. The rain hammered on every window they passed, lightning continuing to flicker. Elara's heart still thudded with leftover longing, but she pushed it aside. This night demanded her illusions, not her affections. Maybe one day she would untangle the threads binding her to Lucian and to Caelum, but for now, the kingdom needed her more than ever.

Her armor was neither steel nor leather—it was the spool of shimmering thread at her side and the unwavering promise she had made. She vowed silently that she would see another dawn free of illusions. She clung to that thought as they crossed into the corridor that led toward the city gates, resolute in the face of whatever nightmares lurked beyond. Even if her heart fractured with guilt and forbidden desire, she would stand firm.

At the end of the passage, they paused to check the outer doors, and Carmen turned with a half-compelling glare. "We can't let people be devoured by illusions," she reminded them. "Are you ready?"

Elara straightened. "As ready as we can be." She let her own gaze wander from Carmen to Lucian. She saw the swirl of unspoken emotion in both sets of eyes but knew that in this moment, they had no choice but to set it aside. "First priority," she murmured, voice shaking a little. "We save the kingdom."

Lucian's expression darkened with quiet determination; Carmen gave a curt nod. Together, they pushed through the palace doors and vanished into the stormy night, bracing themselves for the illusions that threatened to twist reality into chaos. Elara did not look back at the courtyard's lonely torches or the echo of that interrupted moment. She pressed forward, bearing the ache in her chest. There would be time for the turmoil of longing later, if they were fortunate. For now, duty guided every step.

EIGHT

Elara could not remember the last time she had slept more than a handful of hours. Every morning arrived in a swirl of shrieks and rumors—terrifying illusions rampaging through the city, conjured beasts that vanished in seconds but left scattered debris and frightened citizens in their wake. The palace gates stood half-barricaded, and the King and Queen found themselves relying more and more on Malakar's supposed remedies. Under his direction, riders patrolled the streets, stifling dissent as swiftly as the illusions sprang up. Only a select few realized that Malakar's cures were often as frightening as the conjurations he claimed to banish.

She stood in the dim corridor leading to the war council chamber, waiting for news about the latest outbreak. Guards brushed past with grim expressions, barely acknowledging the young seamstress who once went unnoticed everywhere. Now, hushed whispers trailed her steps: some called her a secret witch, others the kingdom's sole hope. Either way, the eyes that followed her glimmered with dread.

A door at the far end opened, and Carmen hurried out, her features drawn in tight worry. Elara moved to meet her, but Carmen seized her by the wrist and tugged her into a corner, fearful of eavesdroppers in the corridor.

"They are rounding people up," Carmen whispered, breath ragged. She smelled faintly of smoke. Her richly curled hair clung to her cheeks, damp with sweat. "All it takes is one rumor that someone has spoken against Malakar, and the soldiers come knocking. The jails are overcrowded. I heard a blacksmith's apprentice got dragged away just for complaining that illusions distorted his home."

Elara's stomach twisted. She had tried to keep up with the city's turmoil but had hardly left Prince Caelum's side these last days. "Does the King know? The Queen?"

Carmen's grimace deepened. "They know something is wrong, but they are desperate for Malakar's help. They see illusions tearing through the city, then watch as he waves his hand and banishes them, for a moment, at least. They are half-blind, Elara. Fear has them signing anything he puts in front of them."

A knot of helpless anger tightened in Elara's throat. Each new decree granted Malakar more authority, and with that authority, his agents carried out arrests at will. "We have to do something," she said, voice unsteady. "Citizens are fleeing, barricading themselves indoors. The illusions feed on terror, and Malakar knows it."

Carmen nodded. "I keep thinking if I can just slip into

his records or find some damning note, I could sway the King and Queen. But Malakar is careful. He presents only polished lies."

They parted when Lucian strode up with a messenger in tow, his boots echoing sharply on the stone floor. At the sight of him, Elara's thoughts tangled with guilt. She had not forgotten Carmen's confession about wanting him. She had also not forgotten her own tumultuous feelings that surfaced whenever Lucian offered her a steadying hand during her illusions. Their conflicting emotions lingered in the air, unstoppable as the illusions outside.

"Elara," Lucian said, ignoring the tension that coiled between the three of them, and pointing at the messenger standing beside him, "He arrived saying that phantom creatures manifested in the west side of the city last night. They ravaged two storage warehouses and terrified the watch. Malakar's men subdued the illusions, but half the workers have been arrested on suspicion of conspiring against the crown."

Elara saw the messenger's eyes, usually alert, flicker with a profound, almost unnatural depth of despair for a moment. He swallowed, his Adam's apple bobbing. "They... they say there's no hope left, mistress," he mumbled, his voice hollow, before shaking his head as if to clear a sudden fog. He then straightened, trying to regain his composure, though the shadow of that bleakness lingered in his gaze.

Elara pressed her lips tightly together. "Then Malakar will spin this as if he himself quelled another crisis. More arrests, more fear... more illusions strengthening him."

She exhaled slowly. "We cannot let Caelum remain vulnerable in this chaos. Our dream-shield must be reinforced before Malakar tries again to twist Caelum's mind."

Lucian hesitated, hazel eyes flicking to Carmen, then settling on Elara. "We only started weaving tonight's protective layers. Are you sure you have the strength to continue?"

She forced the closest thing to a smile she could muster. "I have to. Otherwise, Malakar might find a way to break through again." She swallowed, remembering how Caelum's eyelashes had fluttered two nights ago, how softly he had whispered her name in a moment of half-lucidity. Each time he stirred in his bed, relief warred with apprehension. She did not want him to see how broken the kingdom had become in his absence.

They hurried down the corridor toward the next flight of stairs that led to Caelum's chamber. Soldiers stationed outside gave them sour looks but stepped aside, albeit reluctantly—perhaps uncertain whether Malakar would want them to block Elara's path or allow it. When they reached the door, Elara lifted a hand to knock softly, then entered.

The chamber smelled of jasmine incense, lit to cover the medicinal tang of potions that physicians had poured down Caelum's throat earlier. He lay in a large bed, sunlight from the narrow window spilling across his pale features. Though he appeared calm for the moment, Elara knew illusions often prodded at him. His last moments of awareness had been laced with an edge of fear she had never seen him display before.

Carmen whispered, "He stirred again an hour ago. He kept calling your name. I tried to calm him, but he only eased when he heard your voice in the corridor."

Elara brushed the back of her hand against Caelum's cheek. A faint warmth answered, but his lids remained closed. She drew in a steadying breath, then began unwinding the spool of shimmering thread that rarely left her side. Settling onto a small stool, she placed her palm over his sternum, letting her intuition guide the glowing strands to form protective loops around his chest and forehead.

Her power flared bright for a moment, but exhaustion gnawed at her concentration. The illusions outside seemed louder than ever, as if they howled at the palace walls, threatening to break in. When she tried to weave a fresh ward, her stitching faltered, and the glow flickered unevenly. A monstrous shape, half-formed, started to slip into the corner of her vision—a writhing presence. She bit down on her lip and forced her magic into a coherent pattern, finally beating the shape back into the shadows.

Lucian caught her elbow as she swayed on the stool. "Elara, rest. You cannot keep going like this."

Her eyes burned with unshed tears, but she straightened her shoulders. "I do not have the luxury of rest. Malakar is making arrests by the hour. People are terrified. If we lose Caelum to another surge of illusions, there will be no hope left at all."

Carmen knelt at Elara's side, a spool of ordinary thread in her hand. Though Carmen's illusions were less potent, she had learned enough about dream-craft to boost

Elara's efforts. "Let me help. Show me how to layer the base pattern again."

Elara nodded, grateful for Carmen's sincerity, even if the tension over Lucian was a constant ache. She guided Carmen's hands, placing them over the softly shimmering design. Carmen inhaled deeply, then released a slender wisp of magic, weaving it into Elara's light. Elara tried to focus on the synergy of their combined illusions, but at times, her gaze moved to Lucian, who stood behind them like an ever-watchful guardian. The memory of how he had once held her in the corridor made her heart pound with shame. Carmen had seen that closeness. Carmen had asked her outright to keep away from him. Elara's own desire collided with the knowledge that she might be hurting both Carmen and Caelum.

She forced her attention back to the threads. "Steady," she murmured, fusing her voice with the pattern. "We need the shield unbroken."

Carmen clenched her jaw in concentration. For several moments, their illusions wound together, spinning a protective barrier around Caelum's slumbering body. Sheer, pale light enveloped him, flickering like silk in a breeze. Lucian helped by pacing the perimeter, occasionally pressing the small, warded amulet at his belt whenever the magic wavered.

Elara could sense Caelum's heartbeat flutter against her magic, like a moth seeking warmth. She tried to will calmness into him, reminding him in dream-space that he was not alone. A surge of appreciation pulsed back, and she caught the faint movement of his lips forming her name.

Gradually, the light coalesced into a firm shield. Elara exhaled, her limbs shaking. Carmen let out a ragged breath, brushing sweat from her brow. Lucian stepped closer, wiping a damp strand of hair from Elara's face.

"It is done for now?" he asked gently.

"It will hold him safe," Elara answered, though her voice tremored. Her entire body felt hollow. "At least until the next wave of illusions or Malakar's next order."

She rose unsteadily, and Lucian's hand found her elbow again, stabilizing her. His concern was obvious, but she noticed the way Carmen's gaze flicked down, caught somewhere between frustration and sympathy. Despite everything, Carmen had cast aside her resentments to stand by Elara's side. Yet that strength came at a cost: the lingering knowledge that Carmen's heart was not so easily healed from envy or from her own growing feelings for Lucian.

They relocated to a small alcove just outside Caelum's chamber to talk more freely. The air felt stale, weighed by unspoken truths. Lucian folded his arms, his expression grave. "We cannot keep this pace forever. Malakar is strengthening his grip on the throne's decrees while we are trapped here, weaving wards around Caelum."

Elara nodded, pressing her palm to her forehead to ward off a wave of dizziness. "Every day we struggle to keep Caelum shielded. Every day Malakar expands his illusions farther into the city."

Carmen's voice cracked. "And each arrest feeds the

fear. People blame the monarchy, or blame you, or blame anyone who stands in Malakar's way. There are rumors of entire families vanishing overnight." She swallowed. "I heard one courtier call you a deceptress for conjuring illusions in the palace. Another insisted you are the only spark of hope. The city is so divided, I can hardly see how we mend it."

Elara's shoulders sank beneath the weight of it all. She remembered the hesitant gratitude in the King and Queen's eyes whenever Malakar displayed his swift illusions to chase out phantom beasts. They had grown too desperate to question his sincerity. Even if they felt a flicker of doubt, their fear kept them silent. After all, Malakar was the only one who claimed to contain illusions that seemed unstoppable to others.

An urgent knock on the adjacent door cut through the hush. A startled servant burst into the alcove, breathless. "Phantom serpents in the orchard courtyard," he announced. "They slithered through solid stone walls, terrifying courtiers. The Captain of the Guard is requesting additional wards."

Lucian glanced at Elara. "I can handle the orchard courtyard. You should rest."

"I will help," Carmen said, pinching the bridge of her nose. "I can manage basic illusions to hold the serpents at bay. Malakar's men are sure to show up, but perhaps I can buy the city more time."

Elara wanted to join, wanted to bury her anxiety in action, but she could barely stand. Her legs trembled, and she sensed that if she tried to conjure illusions directly against the phantom serpents, she might collapse and lose hold of the dream-shield around Caelum.

Lucian placed a firm hand on her shoulder. "Stay. Protect Caelum from here. If the illusions assault him directly, you are the only one who can reinforce the shield." His gaze flicked to Carmen. "I will meet you at the orchard courtyard. We must hurry."

Carmen cast Elara a lingering glance—an odd mixture of compassion and defeat. Then she followed Lucian out, steps echoing in the corridor. Elara sighed and slumped against the wall. She was too tired to chase after them, too tired to untangle the swirl of guilt that clenched her heart every time she caught Lucian's anxious stare or felt Caelum's shallow breaths under her palm.

Lucian stood near the edge of the courtyard, his face grim as he watched another group of frightened citizens being escorted away. Carmen approached, her usual confidence tempered by the gravity of the situation.

"Any word on when this madness might end?" she asked, her voice low.

Lucian shook his head. "Every hour brings new reports of illusions. It's as if Malakar's influence is spreading faster than we can contain it."

Carmen's gaze lingered on him, noting the tension in his shoulders. "You look exhausted," she said softly. "When was the last time you rested?"

He gave a wry smile. "Rest feels like a luxury we can't

afford right now." His eyes met hers, and for a moment, the shared weight of their responsibility passed between them.

AT LEAST HALF an hour passed before she forced herself back into Caelum's chamber. She perched on the edge of his bed, letting the hush wrap around them. A mild gray gloom pressed through the window, muted by the heavy rain clouds that had rolled in. An occasional flash of torch-light from the courtyard below played across Caelum's cheek, highlighting the faint tension in his brows. Even asleep, he sensed the illusions prowling through the corridors.

Elara blinked blearily, feeling the prick of tears she refused to shed. She spread her hand over the shimmering barrier protecting Caelum's chest, watching the faint ripple of magic as it reacted to her presence. How many more nights could she keep this up? She felt stretched to the breaking point, torn between the dream-bond she shared with Caelum and the undeniable tenderness she felt blossoming in moments with Lucian. Carmen's longing for Lucian only deepened the guilt. The air felt stifling, no matter how she breathed.

A faint cough made her jolt. Caelum's eyes fluttered and opened. Though his gaze remained distant, he turned his head slightly in her direction. His lips parted, breath rattling. "Elara..."

She leaned closer, throat tightening. "I am here," she

whispered, brushing a light hand across his damp brow. "You are safe."

He exhaled slowly, tension easing from his posture. Her illusions must have seeped into his dream, offering him a reprieve from the encroaching darkness. For a moment, she felt renewed hope surge through her exhaustion. Nothing mattered more than preserving his fragile claim on consciousness and ensuring that when he woke, the kingdom would not lie in shambles.

But just as quickly, the hope curdled with dread. Another wave of illusions could strike at any moment. Every precious minute she spent weaving wards was a minute Malakar used to tighten his grip outside these walls. Every breath Caelum took was threatened by rampaging horrors that roared through the streets. And in the space between illusions, Elara's own heart warred with a tangle of conflicting needs, dividing her soul.

She gazed at Caelum's placid face, remembering how fiercely he had once advocated for unity in the guilds—how he had shown interest in Elara's stitching talent the night before his curse took hold. Now, he hovered on the brink of wakefulness in a kingdom spiraling into nightmare. She choked back a sob, gently smoothing the hair away from his forehead, anchoring him in the protective barrier's glow.

Every ounce of her magic was bound up in preserving him, yet her emotional balance could unravel at any moment. She thought of Lucian's soft-spoken devotion, Carmen's confession, the city's terror, the King and Queen's half-blinded trust in Malakar. Despite it all, she would not abandon Caelum. She would not surrender to Malakar's illusions. But weariness had eroded her determination.

Elara leaned down, pressing her ear to Caelum's chest. The drum of his heartbeat offered the barest promise that this kingdom might not succumb to fear. If she failed to keep her illusions stable, if the shield fell, every pact of love would be swept away by Malakar's manipulations. The thought made her pulse pound with a sickening sense of inadequacy.

She rose carefully, trembling from the strain, and sealed another strand of shimmering thread onto the ward. It was the best she could do. Outside, distant shouts and the clang of weapons drifted in the hush—Carmen and Lucian no doubt battling more phantom apparitions. Elara closed her eyes and inhaled slowly. She had to hold on.

By week's end, her efforts showed in the bundle of fine, glowing lines that now cocooned Caelum. Yet her body and mind paid the price, each day a repeated struggle not to faint. Even Carmen's renewed loyalty, even Lucian's gentle hand at her back, failed to ease the dread in her soul. She stood at Caelum's bedside late one evening, the final threads of her magic trembling around him. The city's screams still resonated in her head, and Malakar's triumphs echoed through every corridor.

Her vision swam with fatigue, but she did not abandon her post. She touched Caelum's chilled fingers, feeling him respond with a tiny flex of his hand. A single question swirled in her thoughts, pounding louder than her heart: If she failed to save him and curb Malakar's illusions, did any vow of love matter at all?

That came last in her mind, a quiet statement that crystallized into a haunting truth. As she stood there, trembling from exhaustion, a single, agonizing thought echoed in her mind:

If she failed to save him and curb Malakar's illusions, no vow of love—whether dream-forged or born in harsh reality—would ever matter again.

CHAPTER

NINE

E lara exhaled slowly as she positioned the third candle on the small stand near the head of Caelum's bed. The flame sputtered for an instant, then steadied under her quiet, watchful gaze. Moonlight crept through the parted drapes, imbuing the chamber with a soft silver sheen that made the warded lines glimmer across the floor. Those lines were the fruit of sleepless nights and near-desperate determination. She pressed her fingers against the spool of shimmering thread tucked at her waist, reminding herself that tonight was no time for doubt.

Carmen stood opposite her, meticulously adjusting the boundary of glowing thread that circled the bed. Fatigue lingered in the slight tremble of Carmen's hands, but Elara sensed the resolve pooling beneath that carefully controlled posture. The other seamstress had labored tirelessly for the past few days, eyeing illusions with a mix of guilt and anger that pushed her to master wards Elara once feared Carmen would never learn. Now, in the hush of Prince Caelum's bedchamber, they would put all that training to the test.

Quiet footfalls approached from behind. Elara glanced over her shoulder to see Lucian step forward, sword balanced lightly in his hand. Shadows carved sharp lines across his face, accentuating his worry. She tried to offer him a reassuring smile, but the gravitational pull of the moment weighed too heavily on her heart.

"Are you certain you can both manage the spell?" he asked, voice low to avoid waking any attendants outside. His eyes flicked from Elara to Carmen, the hazel depths revealing how much he worried about them.

Elara drew a steadying breath. "We have to do it," she replied. "If we hesitate much longer, Malakar's influence in Caelum's dream will tighten its grip again." She saw no point in adding that her own exhaustion began to fray the edges of her concentration. Carmen's presence told the same story, but there was no alternative.

Carmen, arms folded against her chest, lifted her chin. "We have studied the runes every spare minute. Elara has guided me," she said, giving Elara a determined look. "I might not be as adept as she is, but I will not let Caelum down." The words slipped out in a hushed rush, as though she wanted to outrun her own fears. She inhaled. "I owe it to all of you."

A fleeting silence fell. Elara understood why Carmen spoke those words. Guilt had haunted her every step recently, a weight she struggled to turn into something useful. Tonight, success would free the prince who had spent years imprisoned in illusions. Each swirl of candlelit shadow reminded Elara they faced more than one person's redemption. If they failed, Caelum's mind might collapse entirely, taking what remained of the kingdom's hope with it.

"All right," Lucian said, shifting his grip on the sword. "Remember, I will be right here. If anything threatens you on this side, I will see to it that it does not succeed." His gaze settled on Elara. "You have my word."

The unwavering support in Lucian's eyes eased a fraction of her nerves. Over the past few weeks he had proved a steadfast guardian, working day and night to bolster their enchanted defenses, rally the palace guards, and watch over the prince. She tore her gaze from him and focused again on the ward circles flickering around Caelum's bed. On the mattress the prince lay still, his breathing shallow under layers of protective illusions meant to keep Malakar's nightmares at bay.

"Give us a moment," Elara said. She moved around the bed and lit a final sliver of incense. The pungent scent curled upward in pale ribbons. Then she turned to Carmen, lifting the spool of enchanted thread from her belt. "Carmen, show me your wrist."

Carmen held out her arm. Her dark curls shifted across her shoulders as she stooped, and Elara traced the ephemeral sigil with the tip of her sewing needle. In earlier lessons Mistress Imelda had explained how a dreamweaver could create a shared conduit, allowing two souls to descend into another's dreamscape together. Elara's heart fluttered as she recalled how rebellious this magic had once seemed to her, yet now it felt like their only chance to save Caelum.

She spoke softly, loud enough for Carmen to hear. "The incantation is the same one we practiced, but draw your focus from your compassion, not your guilt. Lean on that need to protect him." She lifted Carmen's palm and pressed it gently until the tracery of light shone like a faint silver tattoo where the needle had touched.

"I understand," Carmen said, her gaze flicking between Elara's face and the swirl of luminous thread. "I do."

Elara gave a short nod, then closed her eyes to steady herself. She laid a hand on Caelum's forearm, feeling the faint pulse beneath his skin. Wordlessly, she began spinning the spool of thread between her fingers and recited the incantation under her breath, mindful to keep her voice measured. Carmen joined in, quieter at first, stumbling on a syllable before finding a steadier rhythm. Elara sensed the tremor beneath Carmen's forced calm, the raw edge of someone terrified of failing yet desperate to atone. The severance ribbon beneath Carmen's glove must be straining, holding back the silvered echo of Malakar's will. This joint venture was as much a test of Carmen's fractured spirit as it was a mission to save the prince.

Pressure grew in the air, as though the temperature in the room dropped. The candle flames shivered, casting elongated shadows across the bed. Elara heard a sharp gasp from Carmen but kept her own senses disciplined. Their voices wove together in chanting hums. She felt the spool's subtle tension pulling her deeper into dreamweaving.

Lucian stayed silent near the bed, sword angled across his body in a protective stance. His watchfulness was a tangible shield behind them. Elara reminded herself that if any illusions spilled into the physical realm, Lucian would hold them off, and she could not afford to squander energy worrying about that.

Time stretched. Each breath conjured new shapes in Elara's mind, images of swirling corridors and shifting tapestries rising from the dark corners of her thoughts. The spool in her hand glowed softly. Then she felt the sensation of sinking. Her stomach lurched as though she had stepped off a ledge, and pebbles of cold energy skittered along her spine. Carmen's voice trembled once, but she maintained the chant. Together, they dropped into a single stream of power and snapped the link to Caelum's subconscious wide open.

Elara's body tensed. She had not moved from the chamber, yet her mind soared into a different plane. Beside her, Carmen's presence flickered like a wan torch, uncertain but determined. With a final wave of psychic force, the bedchamber fell away.

Elara blinked into her new surroundings. A corridor of living silk stretched before her, undulating as though caught in a perpetual wind. Some sections tore and reformed at the edges, as though resisting her intrusion. She sensed Carmen's spirit-form flicker at her left. Despite the ethereal surroundings, Carmen's expression looked as real as it had under candlelight: guarded, anxious, but resolved.

The corridor's walls pulsed with deep violet light, each beat suggesting Caelum's precarious life force. The dream realm had grown labyrinthine. Some illusions manifested as tall shapes etched with shifting designs, while others turned corners into dark hallways that taunted with half-heard whispers.

Elara curled her hand as though still gripping a needle and released a thread of her own shimmering energy, which illuminated a twisting path ahead. "We move carefully," she said, not daring to speak too loudly. Even in a dream, sound might echo into illusions best left dormant. "Stay behind me. Your shield illusions will keep the worst from breaking through." She shot Carmen a sideways look. "Keep steady."

Carmen nodded, her lips pressed into a firm line. Elara caught a flicker of uncertainty in her eyes. "Are you sure you're ready for this?" Elara asked gently.

Carmen squared her shoulders. "I have to be. After everything I've done, I owe it to Caelum...and to you." Vulnerability colored her voice in a way Elara had only recently begun to hear.

She took a stiff step forward and conjured a translucent bubble around them both, soft pink and gold gleaming in the haze. The bubble rippled whenever a wave of blue or purple flickered across the corridor. "I will try to expand it if anything attacks," Carmen muttered.

Elara kept her gaze forward. The corridor curved gently, revealing twisted silhouettes ahead. They looked like giant calico banners flapping in a phantom wind. Only on closer approach did she realize these banners were illusions cleverly woven into the dream's tapestry. They were watchers. Their faceless folds trembled as though alerted to intruders.

Be brave, she told herself. She stepped toward the watchers, bracing for sudden hostility. At first, they did not move, only fluttered in place. Then, with a faint rustle, one spun inward, forming a funnel of cloth that aimed directly at them. The funnel hissed with an echo of Malakar's presence. Elara felt it scrape across her mind like a chilling breeze. A memory of Malakar's unctuous voice slithered through her thoughts, mocking her illusions as trivial parlor tricks. Her heartbeat hammered.

Carmen stepped beside her, illusions shimmering at her fingertips. "Go," she whispered. "I will distract them." She hurled a half-finished incantation at the funnel-like watcher, and it briefly became a swirl of golden sparks. One of the watchers twitched violently, rearing until it loomed overhead in the shape of a serpent.

Elara seized the moment, brandishing her spool's radiant thread. She guided it in a graceful, tightening loop and severed the watcher's connection to the corridor. The gloom parted at the seam, unraveling the funnel with a silent scream that vibrated in the dream's fabric. The mothlike watchers trembled and melted into the walls.

Carmen lowered her hands, breathing hard. "It worked," she said, relief mingling with wonder on her face. Her eyes darted around them, searching for new threats.

Elara nodded, trying to slow her racing pulse. "We keep going. Caelum is somewhere deeper, and Malakar's illusions will only get more cunning. Do not drop your guard." A gentle swirl of light drifted down the hall, beckoning them onward like a lantern in the distance. Elara felt a pang in her chest, recognizing it as a faint echo of Caelum's presence. He was near, perhaps struggling beyond these illusions. She forced her feet to move.

The corridor narrowed until Elara had to edge sideways along a wall of soft, shifting cloth. Under her palm, the fabric felt slimy, pulsing with faint malice. She clenched her jaw and prayed Lucian was safe outside, that no illusions had slipped from this realm to snag him unaware. The musty taste of dream-ether weighed on her tongue, thick as stale incense.

Carmen, pinned by the corridor's narrowness, let her illusions flicker, preserving enough of the shield to repel sudden attacks. "I do not like how quiet it is," she whispered. "A moment ago, watchers ambushed us, and now nothing."

Elara glanced over her shoulder. "It may be a lull, or it may be Malakar's way of steering us where he wants." In the distance, the faint glow she associated with Caelum's consciousness pulsed again. Her heart jumped. She reached out mentally and let her dreamweaver power attempt the smallest thread of contact. Caelum's presence responded with a flicker of light, but a cloying darkness coiled around that brightness. She felt it clamp down, as if fangs sank into his energy.

She sucked in a breath, alarm prickling at her core. "He

is in trouble," she muttered. "Hurry." She slid sideways along the corridor, ignoring how the walls constricted.

Carmen bit back a soft cry when the silken surface snaked around her ankle. A flick of her shield illusions shattered the snare, and they hurried forward into a new chamber that opened with violent abruptness.

A swirling mosaic greeted them, formed of thousands of glittering shapes. No watchers patrolled here, but the mosaic expanded across the floor in overlapping hexagons, each one swirling with color that threatened to mesmerize. Elara shuttered her gaze, trying not to stare too deeply. She recognized a trap: illusions that enthralled unsuspecting intruders and drained them until their defenses collapsed.

Carmen's voice trembled with awe. "I did not realize illusions could be so...intricate."

Elara tightened her grip on the spool, unraveling a slender strand of her dreamweaver magic. "Stay close," she warned, her voice taut. She stepped forward and let the shimmering thread anchor a fragile path across the treacherous mosaic. Each step sent prickles of unease skittering along her skin, as though the mosaic itself scrutinized her every intention. She fixed her thoughts on vivid memories of Caelum, his half-lidded gaze in the waking world and the gentle call of her name whenever the illusions receded. That unwavering devotion blended with her magic, forming a fierce clarity that repelled the mosaic's sinister pull.

Behind her, Carmen advanced, her illusions weaving a protective shield across her torso. When the tiles trembled beneath their feet, Carmen fired a burst of blinding magic at them, scattering sparks and dampening the mesmerizing colors. Together they crossed half the chamber in wary silence. At the edges of their vision, shadows writhed hungrily, restless and waiting.

The swirling mosaic finally gave way to a curtain of thin fabric suspended in midair. Elara sensed something heavier beyond it, an oppressive presence thick with malevolence. She steadied herself, heart pounding. "This must be Malakar's final barrier. Are you ready?"

Carmen swallowed hard and squared her shoulders. In unison they pulled the curtain aside. A biting gust of air slammed into Elara's chest, stealing her breath. Beyond lay a chamber cloaked in a darkness deeper than any corridor they had passed. Flickers of violet lightning danced across the ceiling, illuminating for an instant a sprawling nest of tangled, nightmarish illusions. At its heart she saw Caelum's faintly glowing aura, shackled by dense coils of living shadow.

Carmen seized Elara's forearm, her voice trembling with alarm. "Elara, look!" Her words were nearly swallowed by a roaring wind. Above them the illusions twisted and writhed, quickly fusing into monstrous hybrid shapes, part human, part beast. From deep within the vortex a low, sinister laugh echoed, unmistakably Malakar's. His presence surged, powerful and wrathful, reverberating from every crevice in the nightmare chamber.

"What's happening?" Carmen gasped, panic edging into her voice as her illusions began to flicker dangerously.

Elara's pulse hammered in her ears. "Malakar knows

we're here. He's collapsing the dream realm to trap us inside!"

The chamber walls began to drip and distort, horrific shapes emerging from the liquefying surfaces. Elara and Carmen found themselves battling not merely illusions, but the dreamscape itself as it tore apart around them.

Chaos erupted instantly. Piercing shrieks rose from attacking illusions, tendrils of savage darkness snapped violently from every shadow, and Carmen let out a sharp cry of fear. Elara swiftly cast a swirling net of dream-thread overhead, deflecting the brutal initial assault. Her arms quaked from the impact. Malakar's influence was undeniable, his dark power intent on keeping Caelum's mind eternally imprisoned.

"Focus on breaking whatever chains hold him!" Elara shouted over the deafening cacophony. "I'll keep these nightmares at bay!"

Carmen cast a quick glance at Caelum's motionless form, then steeled herself, jaw clenched with determination. Her illusions flared in brilliant, golden intensity, forming razor-sharp needles of light that pierced the tangled bindings. Elara planted her feet, hurling her own powerful conjurations upward into the swirling darkness above. The monstrous illusions howled in fury, battered by the combined strength of two seamstresses turned fierce warriors within the dream.

Outside, in the dim, candlelit bedchamber, Lucian stood tense and vigilant. Unable to glimpse the battle raging in the dream realm, he nevertheless saw the strain etched across Elara's and Carmen's pale faces. Their rigid postures and the tightness around their mouths revealed an unseen peril. Lucian tightened his grip on the hilt of his sword, scanning the room's shadowy corners with fierce suspicion, alert for any physical intrusion Malakar might attempt.

The candle flames dipped low, nearly snuffed by a sinister, unnatural draft. The trio teetered on the brink of darkness. Lucian murmured a fervent prayer, his gaze on Caelum's ghostly features. In his heart he begged for the prince's liberation from the relentless nightmare, praying it would end that night.

CHAPTER

TEN

Elara's breaths came in sharp, uneven bursts as she crossed through the ragged veil of pulsing darkness. The battle behind them faded into a churning haze, part of the endless labyrinth they had navigated for what seemed like an eternity. Even with her physical eyes sealed shut, she perceived every detail of the dream realm vividly: walls formed from writhing fabric and hallways saturated with Malakar's lingering menace. Every step felt simultaneously numbing and electric, as if lacking a physical body intensified each sensation to the brink of pain. She risked a glance at Carmen, who stood beside her, eyes wide, threads of glowing illusion twisting delicately around her fingers.

In fleeting moments, Elara glimpsed the physical world beyond the dream: Lucian at Caelum's bedside, standing guard with unwavering vigilance, refusing to leave the prince unattended even for a heartbeat. That steady image bolstered her dwindling strength. She reminded herself that Caelum's life, in the waking world, now hung precariously by the slenderest thread. If she and Carmen failed to breach this final pocket of Malakar's nightmares, that fragile tether might snap forever.

They pressed forward into the gloom. The air in the dream corridors felt acidic in her lungs, thick with the taste of cold ash and decaying silk. Malakar's laughter rippled through the silence at unpredictable intervals, each echo leaving her uncertain whether it was real or merely a memory intended to disorient her. Carmen's voice broke through the oppressive quiet.

"Are you certain this is the right way?" Carmen asked, her illusions trembling along the corridor walls. "The passage behind us felt like it was collapsing."

Elara nodded, pushing aside her doubt. "It was collapsing. The illusions imprisoning Caelum despise any intrusion. If they're trying to seal us out, we're drawing close to his core consciousness." She reached ahead with a slender thread of her dreamweaver magic and felt the comforting yet faint warmth of Caelum's essence flicker somewhere ahead. "He needs us, no matter how terrible this path becomes."

They moved forward, united in cautious silence. The corridor narrowed dangerously in places, forcing them to reshape their illusions into sharp-edged strands that sliced at clawing shadows erupting from the walls. Carmen crafted her magic into thin, needle-like missiles that flashed forward, dissolving shadowy figures before they could fully materialize. Meanwhile, Elara twisted her illusions into a delicate yet resilient shield around them, repelling surges of dark, nightmarish energy. Together, they were an unlikely pair, given Carmen's former taunts in the seamstress guild, but past rivalries now seemed trivial. The city, the royal family, and Caelum himself were at stake, and all their fates hung in the balance.

The air grew colder and sharper. The swirling illusions peeled back, revealing a hallway strewn with shredded, half-torn tapestries. Frayed threads gaped open, exposing the walls beyond. Elara glimpsed fragmented memories. She saw Caelum, younger and carefree, exploring the city streets alongside Lucian. She saw Carmen, hunched in a shadowed corner, stitching while she longed for recognition that never came swiftly enough. Finally, she saw herself, thin and desperate, bent over her earliest commissions. Malakar's magic had plundered their pasts, shaping the memories into phantoms meant to torment and weaken. Her throat tightened.

"These illusions are exploiting our past," she murmured. "They want to undermine us through guilt and regret."

Carmen flinched as her gaze fell on a vision of her younger self mocking Elara near a sewing table. The memory flickered, then shattered. "I wasn't kind to you," she whispered, her voice thick with shame.

"We can face that when we're all safe again," Elara replied. She fixed her gaze forward and conjured a thin thread of luminous magic to light their path. Caelum's presence lay beyond these twisted memories, and she would not let specters break their resolve.

Their hallway curved abruptly and opened into an

immense, shadow-filled antechamber. At first glance, Elara thought the space was empty, but then she sensed an unnatural stillness. It was too quiet, as though even the illusions held their breath, waiting in sinister anticipation. In the span of a heartbeat, a grotesque form erupted from the ceiling and assembled into a skeletal beast with impossibly long jaws. Carmen's illusions flared in alarm and lit the chamber with a flash of golden brilliance.

Instead of retreating, Elara steadied herself. She drew a sharp breath and flung her spool of shimmering dream thread upward. She wove a net of glistening strands around the creature and bound it as it thrashed and shrieked. Carmen leapt forward and unleashed a volley of magical needles that impaled each spectral limb. The beast broke apart into swirling particles of black dust.

Elara lowered her spool, a tremor running through her hands. "They're growing stronger," she murmured. "Heavier. Malakar's illusions have never felt this...tangible before."

Carmen wiped the sheen of sweat from her brow, her voice taut with strain. "It's because Malakar senses we're close. He's unleashing everything he has left against us."

Elara opened her mouth to reply, but a strangled sob rose in her throat. She fought against the fear threatening to unravel into despair. It wasn't only the unrelenting horror lurking around every bend. The crushing knowledge of Caelum's frail body lying helpless in the waking world, and the anxiety radiating from Lucian's unyielding vigil, weighed on her. She knew that if they faltered now,

Malakar's illusions would tear at Caelum's spirit, leaving no trace of consciousness behind.

With renewed determination, they moved onward, winding carefully through passages that pulsed ominously beneath their feet. Eventually, they reached a pair of battered stone arches leading to a corridor bathed in a sickly violet glow. The eerie light seeped from jagged cracks in the floor, accompanied by a nauseating scent of corrupted, decaying magic. Each cautious step twisted Elara's stomach, yet she pressed forward, Carmen walking resolutely beside her. They braced themselves for another assault.

Instead, the passage ended in a swirling vortex of thick, impenetrable darkness. Elara exchanged a worried glance with Carmen, then extended a slender thread of her magic toward the border of the vortex. It sparked, crackling with ominous intent.

"What do we do?" Carmen whispered. "If it lashes out again, we're out of illusions strong enough to counter it."

"We push through," Elara said with quiet resolve. She reached for Carmen's hand, intertwining their fingers. "Whatever lies on the other side, we'll face it together."

Carmen nodded, unable to hide her apprehension. "Then let's face it."

As one, they stepped forward. The vortex trembled around them, frigid and suffocating as tar, threatening to extinguish their magic. Panic surged within Elara, but she resisted it and looped a strand of glowing energy around Carmen's wrist so they could not be separated. Her pulse pounded as the dark swirl sought to invade her memories, bombarding her with flashes from her past: her first confrontation with Malakar in the guild hall, her heartache and confusion over Lucian's unwavering loyalty, the blend of anguish and love each time Caelum stirred weakly in his bed. Clenching her teeth, she poured every ounce of strength into resisting the darkness, guarding those precious moments from being twisted against her.

In a rush, the vortex dispersed. Elara dropped to her knees, coughing as the dream world slowly stabilized around them. She felt Carmen's reassuring presence at her side, solid and grounding. When she lifted her gaze, she realized with an icy chill that they had emerged into an immense, cryptlike chamber.

Her breath caught. Torn royal banners hung in charred tatters from the ceiling, their edges scorched black. Jagged shards of stained glass littered the floor, catching and distorting faint glimmers of wavering, sinister light. The entire hall radiated forbidding emptiness, the oppressive silence heavy with dread, as though no living being should ever set foot inside. Even in the gloom, Elara's gaze fixed on the figure suspended at the chamber's heart, and her chest tightened at the sight.

It was Caelum.

He hovered limply just above the fractured stone floor, his body half swallowed by writhing shadows that coiled around him like serpentine chains. Dark strands tightened around his wrists, ankles, and torso, forming bindings that pulsed with maleficent purpose. Flickers from distant illusions made his features appear both chillingly inert and achingly vulnerable. Each shallow breath only underlined the toll Malakar's magic had taken on him.

Elara swallowed. "Caelum," she whispered, her voice thick with emotion. Fear pounded through her veins. She stepped forward, glass shards crunching under her boots.

Carmen sensed her intent and tried to follow, but the dark chains binding Caelum surged to life. They snapped through the air like living whips, lashing toward the women. Elara reacted on instinct. She flung out a shimmering, translucent shield, and her threads of dreamweaver magic collided with the restraints. Sparks burst across the chamber in blistering showers.

"Look!" Carmen gasped. The shadows peeled away from Caelum's body and coalesced into spectral forms. They advanced like ghosts, each twisted into a mockery of the ancient royals who had once ruled the kingdom. Malevolence radiated from their contorted features, a sick parody of Caelum's lineage.

Elara's heart hammered against her ribs. She recognized some of the faces from faded palace portraits, now corrupted and weaponized by Malakar. She pictured his triumphant sneer and felt rage and sorrow churn within her.

"We must reach Caelum," she said, her voice tight. "These are only illusions wearing his ancestors' faces. We cannot let them hold him."

Carmen gave a resolute nod, her brow knit in concentration. She raised her hands and summoned illusions shaped like glittering, needle-thin missiles. "Cover me," she murmured. "I will hold them off."

The specters hissed, their lifeless eyes blazing green. Before they could engulf Elara, Carmen loosed her barrage. Needles of pure illusion rained on the specters, striking hard and bursting in brilliant flashes. Several recoiled, their forms wavering and dissolving under the assault.

Elara seized the opening. Her pulse thundered as she sprinted toward Caelum. She collapsed to her knees beside his suspended, fragile form. The dark chains remained tight, alive like serpents poised to crush. Her fingertips hovered above one restraint, and she braced herself. Expecting coldness, she recoiled instead as searing energy sliced into her astral form. She hissed in agony and pulled back. As her skin grazed the restraint, a shriek of bending metal filled her ears, and the power of the illusions felt terrifyingly tangible. She sensed their potential for permanent harm if she lingered. Elara glanced at Caelum's face. He seemed partially awake, features contorted in silent torment. She felt his consciousness stirring, fighting beneath the cruel bindings.

"Stay with me," she pleaded, tears burning her eyes. "We're here to take you home."

Behind her, Carmen cried out, battling the advancing specters. More illusions flooded the chamber, merging into monstrous forms. Carmen lacked extensive dreamweaving experience and struggled under the strain. Gritting her teeth, Elara pressed her palm against the first chain, enduring the agonizing needles of pain stabbing through her.

"Hold tight!" Lucian called in the bedchamber,

squeezing Caelum's clammy hand. He felt every tremor racing through Elara's body, her features drawn in silent anguish. "Do not let him go, Elara," he whispered, fear clawing at his chest. Outside, footsteps hurried, muted voices questioning the tremors rattling through the corridor.

Inside the dream, Elara channeled her energy, layering luminous threads atop the dark chain. At first it sparked uselessly, dread twisting inside her. Then a hairline fracture appeared, splitting the chain like overheated glass. Encouraged, she poured herself into the conjuration, recalling Mistress Imelda's teachings and Caelum's gentle, determined smiles. Empathy and determination flowed from her into the bonds.

A shattering scream echoed through the chamber as the chain at Caelum's wrist exploded into black fragments that scattered into oblivion. Relief surged through Elara, but she quickly steeled herself, noting that the bonds around his ankles and chest still pulsed malevolently.

She spun at Carmen's cry. The specters closed in, twisted arms extended menacingly. Carmen pierced one with a luminous needle, but three others surged forward, overwhelming her defenses. Carmen's illusions faltered, blinking in and out erratically.

"Carmen!" Elara shouted, guilt and panic gripping her heart. Carmen's bravery had carried them this far. Elara searched for a way to help without abandoning Caelum. The chamber shuddered, dark tendrils creeping from its corners and feeding on their fear.

She steadied herself. "Stay focused," she muttered,

expanding her illusions into a protective barrier around Carmen. Even from a distance she sensed Carmen's exhaustion, her desperate fight to remain standing. They had fought nightmares before, and Elara clung to the hope they could do so again.

Outside, the corridor echoed with commotion. Guards shouted, torches flared brighter, and their light trembled as though in fear. Lucian turned, heart pounding, while shadows stretched across the floor. "Malakar," he breathed, dread filling his chest as cold, malicious laughter drifted down the hall.

At that instant, the chain binding Caelum's chest ignited, sending sparks flying. Elara gritted her teeth and pressed on. She brushed her hand across Caelum's face, ignoring the searing pain. She felt his rapid heartbeat beneath the chains and saw his eyelids flutter. For a moment, his lips moved as though whispering her name. That fragile recognition renewed her determination and drove her illusions deeper into the hateful chains.

Another piercing shriek scraped through her consciousness. Dizziness washed over her and nearly dropped her to the floor, but she gripped the spool tighter, her lifeline. Behind her, Carmen rallied, illusions flaring with renewed hope. A specter dissolved in silent howl, yet others surged forward.

Metal groaned and splintered, shaking the chamber. The next chain fractured, dark shards dripping like viscous tar. Caelum inhaled sharply, chest heaving as though drawing his first breath in ages. Elara's vision blurred with tears. They were agonizingly close to freeing him.

The oppressive gloom above coiled for a final assault. Elara met Carmen's exhausted but determined gaze. Both women nodded, silently affirming their pact.

Elara summoned the last of her strength, pouring radiant threads onto the final link at Caelum's chest. She thought of Caelum's reassuring smile, Lucian's courage, and Mistress Imelda's steadfast belief, refusing to yield to fear.

Back in the bedchamber, Lucian clutched Caelum's trembling hand. He refused to let go, eyes fixed on Caelum's tortured features.

In the dream, Elara met Carmen's gaze again. "We do this together," she called.

Carmen nodded.

Elara unleashed a final surge, determined to shatter the vile chains and bring Caelum back from the nightmare.

ELEVEN

Elara's lungs burned, each breath thin and desperate as she fought to draw air within the dream's suffocating confines. Her fragile inhalations entwined with delicate strands of magic spiraling from her outstretched fingers, embedding themselves deep into the malicious illusions that imprisoned Caelum. Every second stretched painfully between hope and raw terror. She pressed her trembling fingertips against the dark, coiling restraints at his wrists, feeling their sharp resistance scrape against her senses like rusted wire.

Beside her, Carmen gasped in urgent breaths, seizing every fleeting opportunity to cast blazing illusions toward the encroaching specters. Those shadowy entities gathered ominously around Caelum, their contorted faces radiating silent, seething menace, Malakar's lingering fury made manifest. Distantly, crackles of blue lightning flickered, casting eerie reflections upon the chamber's walls of drifting, silken gloom. Elara anchored herself in desperate conviction, certain Caelum's spirit still lingered beneath these insidious chains, chains that sought relentlessly to consume his consciousness entirely. Guilt sharpened her determination. Failure now meant the illusions would reassert their strength and annihilate him from within.

"Focus!" Carmen's voice sliced through the oppressive stillness. Both her hands flung outward, conjuring thin rays of brilliant gold-white illumination that hissed upon contact with the surging specters. "Elara, hurry! They're closing in!"

Elara's eyes darted across the chamber strewn with fractured banners and shattered mosaics. Carmen's illusions flared, each radiant beam piercing the creeping, faceless entities that inched ever closer. Beneath the writhing illusions, Caelum lay wrapped in shadowy tendrils, motionless except for the faint tremors of his chest, his breath shallow but present. The battered spool of luminous thread at Elara's waist vibrated, as if imploring her forward. Her throat raw, she swallowed, seized the spool, and channeled its potent energy through herself.

"Carmen," she rasped, desperation thickening her voice, "keep them back. I need a few more seconds."

Carmen nodded, sweat beading along her forehead. She spun, unleashing a searing arc of golden illusions that sliced through multiple specters. Shadowy fragments exploded silently, dissolving into nothingness. The circle of nightmares shrank, though Elara felt the final bindings around Caelum's ankles surge violently, drawing renewed strength from the darkness. Black threads slithered across the ethereal ground like serpents, ravenous to consume her resolve. She refused to yield.

Steeling herself against fatigue, Elara pressed her knees into the intangible floor. She placed her palm on Caelum's forearm and grasped the cursed restraint still anchoring him. The spool glowed, pulsing brighter and filling the dream realm with flashes that echoed a heartbeat. Caelum stirred beneath half-lidded eyes, his breathing irregular. Elara's heart clenched with protectiveness. He hovered close to freedom, yet each dark coil strained to pull him back into Malakar's grasp.

A flash of gold drew her attention toward Carmen, who fought the illusions in a dazzling display of conjurations. Razor-sharp shadows cascaded around her, each vicious slash met with radiant defiance. The chamber trembled, the quake rippling through every fiber of the dreamscape. Elara gritted her teeth. She looped the spool's glowing thread around Caelum's wrists and wove a spell of release. The illusions shrieked on contact, shattering into luminous motes that scattered across his skin, each fragment dissolving into the darkness from which it came.

Outside the dream, Elara caught an echo of Lucian's shout. Even without seeing him, she sensed his presence as a bulwark in the waking world. The knowledge reminded her they were not alone. She pictured him bracing Caelum's physical body, making sure no stray illusion tore through the wards. Though the dream realm had become its own battleground, the trust they shared across the thresholds of reality gave Elara strength.

A shriek tore through the chamber. With a lurch, the

floor cracked, revealing an endless abyss swirling beneath her feet. Elara's heart pounded. She kept her hold firm. A metallic taste spread across her tongue, a sign that the illusions were trying to undermine her resolve.

"Hold on!" Carmen shouted as she rushed forward. She flung a barrage of luminous needles at the largest cluster of specters on their flank. "Elara, do you see the chain at his ankles?"

She did. A roiling cord of pure black magic wound around Caelum's left leg, wreathed in twisting runes that reeked of Malakar's handiwork. Fueled by terror, it pulsed with each ragged breath Caelum took. Elara drew a slow, purposeful breath and sank deeper. She let every scrap of love she felt for Caelum guide her illusions. She remembered the curve of his smile during the fleeting nights he stirred in dreams and the quiet determination in his voice whenever he tried to reassure her that her calling was more than mere convenience.

Gathering that tenderness like starlight in her hands, Elara pressed her palms against the black coil locked around his ankle. Heat blistered her fingers, the illusion's dark energy sparking violently in response. At first her magic sputtered, nearly overwhelmed by the potency of Malakar's curse. For an instant, white sparks burned across her wrists, threatening to wrench a cry from her lips, yet she swallowed the pain. No. She would not falter now. Clenching her jaw, she poured her spool's luminous dream thread over the coil and channeled relentless radiance.

Her illusions sliced through the coil's surface. She

pictured herself unraveling a corrupted tapestry from within, each dark thread peeled from Caelum's spirit. The coil thrashed, possessed by a will of its own, but Elara refused to relent. The spool's glow intensified into a fierce blaze, igniting sparks that devoured the tether strand by strand. The darkness hissed, then retreated, and Caelum's ankle fell free.

A deafening crack shattered the chamber and nearly knocked Elara off balance. She pressed a palm against the shaking floor to steady herself. The illusions saturating the ground splintered. Carmen barely managed to leap clear as a jagged fissure cut toward them. Specters stumbled, some vanishing into the void beneath. As the dream realm fractured under the strain of their magic, dread surged through Elara. If the dream collapsed, Caelum's mind might shatter in the chaos. She had to finish this at once, before the realm tore itself apart.

"Elara!" Carmen's cry pierced the cacophony. The final coil around Caelum's torso tightened, a living vice intent on squeezing the last breath from him. His lips parted in silent agony, chest trembling against the confines. Fury blazed inside Elara and propelled her forward. She lunged, the spool flaring in her left hand, her right arm sweeping protectively across Caelum's heart.

Something immense burst through the far side of the chamber, a shape writhing in shadow and blotting out what little light remained. Its tendrils lashed, the form a grotesque hybrid of serpent and demon, saturated by Malakar's malevolent will. Dozens of blood-red eyes glowed with hate, each fixed on them. Malakar's voice vibrated through the oppressive air, echoing his twisted ambition as the tendrils bristled with razor-sharp illusions.

"We are out of time," Carmen whispered, raising her chin as her illusions crackled at her fingertips. "We end this."

Elara tightened her grip on Caelum. She felt the spool's final reserves of energy swirl up her arms, an inferno of shimmering light. The monstrous shape struck, slamming a barbed limb at them. Carmen dove to intercept, flinging illusions in jagged arcs that battered the creature's advance. Sparks erupted as illusions clashed in midair. The creature reared, letting out a thunderous roar that rattled every shred of dream fabric surrounding them.

Elara pressed closer to Caelum, her breath ragged. Her heart thundered in her ears, but she clutched the spool with new resolve. She remembered every dream-kiss they shared, every ephemeral embrace that kept his spirit tethered to life. She recalled the first time he whispered her name in that moonlit corridor, how those quiet syllables had lit her up with a hope she never knew she possessed. Now that hope roared through her, forging a glimmering shield around Caelum. White fire raced along the boundary of his body, defying the monstrous illusions.

She splayed her fingers over his chest, letting the spool's blazing threads anchor him to her. Tendrils of black illusions sizzled at every contact, then evaporated in bursts of radiant motes. The final coil loosened. A savage roar tore from the abomination as if it felt each severed link inside its own vile core.

Carmen pivoted, illusions swirling like a hurricane of gold needles around her. She hurled them in rapid succession, tearing through each of the nightmare's thrashing limbs. It retaliated with wild slashes, but each blow weakened as the illusions anchoring Caelum fell away. Cracks spiderwebbed across the creature's torso, and threads of Malakar's hate-laced magic began to fray.

A violent shockwave slammed the chamber, toppling Elara over Caelum's body. She clutched him tight, ignoring the bruising impact to her elbow. The spool glowed hot under her grip, pulsing as it siphoned the last vestiges of dreamweaver might from her heart. She knew what needed to be done.

Summoning every shred of devotion and defiance, Elara raised her gaze, locked it on the towering nightmare, and channeled all her illusions into one final surge. Light exploded in a fierce corona around her, staining the chamber with gold radiance. The beast shrieked. Carmen's illusions rushed in tandem, scores of needle-thin arcs driving into the creature's center. They cleaved the monstrosity's form from within, scattering lumps of black shadow into shards that dissipated into the swirling air.

Outside, Elara felt Caelum's body jerk against Lucian's supporting arms in the physical realm. She could almost hear Lucian's triumphant shout as the wards flickered bright. The protective circle glowed anew, standing firm against any last-ditch illusions. She thought she caught the faint echo of a woman's voice, possibly a nurse or attendant, sobbing in relief. Yet here in the dream, she and Carmen fought to seal the final break. The monstrous figure was not quite finished. Rivulets of darkness reassembled at the edges, seething in a scramble to re-form. It reached for Caelum with one hideous tendril, determined to steal him back into endless sleep.

"No," Elara rasped. Her spool vibrated in her hand, weaving a net of shimmering threads around the last horrifying limb. In a decisive motion, she snapped her wrist and unleashed a swirl of illusions so pure and bright they blinded even her. She poured into every thread the vow she had spoken so many times, that she would save him.

The tendril recoiled as light tore it apart. Dead illusions fell away in droves, leaving only swirling dust. A hush stretched across the battered chamber, broken only by the trembling echo of Elara's breaths and Carmen's ragged gasps. The gilded illusions faded with slow pulses, revealing Caelum sprawled on the fractured floor, chest rising and falling in shallow but free respiration.

"Elara..." Carmen's voice wavered as she stepped over the crumbling remnants of the nightmare, illusions flickering at her fingertips. "Is he...?"

Elara pressed her ear to Caelum's chest. The heartbeat, faint but steady, resonated beneath her palm. Relief blurred her vision. With a trembling sigh, she sat back and brushed damp strands of hair from his forehead. "He's alive. We did it, Carmen."

She half expected the illusions to surge again, some new horror conjured by Malakar's unholy flair for cruelty, but the dream was eerily still. The chamber's edges quivered as if deciding whether to collapse entirely or remain stable for another moment. A swirl of silver dust drifted across the remains of the monstrous shape, dissolving among the battered, dream-built banners overhead. A hum of quiet energy grazed Elara's wrist, reminding her that the spool, though nearly spent, still responded to her emotions.

Caelum's eyes fluttered open. Though his gaze remained distant, he turned his head slightly in her direction. His lips parted, breath rattling. "Elara..."

Time seemed to stand still. Elara's breath caught in her throat as she met Caelum's gaze, no longer clouded by dreams but clear and present. A rush of emotion washed over her: joy, relief, and a deep, aching tenderness.

"I'm here," she whispered, voice trembling. "You're safe now. You're really awake."

Carmen nodded, sweat glistening at her temples. "We need to hurry," she murmured, her voice hushed with worry.

Elara sensed the fragility of the moment. Caelum was awake but still vulnerable. She turned to Carmen, gratitude welling inside her. "Thank you," she said softly. "I couldn't have done this without you."

Carmen's eyes widened slightly, surprise and warmth flickering across her face. "We did this together," she replied, a hint of her old confidence returning. "We need to go. If the dream collapses while we're still here, it could tear Caelum's mind." Her illusions shimmered out of existence, leaving her hands trembling at her sides.

"Yes," Elara whispered, clinging to Caelum's shoulder. Except... if they woke him too abruptly, might the shock undo all they had done? Her heart twisted. She closed her eyes, letting the spool's faint glow soothe her. The bond she shared with Caelum pulsed, vibrant and hopeful, reminding her that they had faced this darkness together many times before.

Behind them, the fractured floor gave an ominous shudder. Pieces of the chamber walls peeled away in sheets of dissolving fabric, unveiling a haunting emptiness beyond. Elara sucked in a breath. "We can't linger." She slipped one arm around Caelum, gently supporting his unconscious form in the dream. Carmen nodded, and together they hoisted him to an upright position. In reality, they were not lifting physical weight, but the strain felt crushing, nonetheless.

A roar of wind shot through the chamber. Leftover illusions vanished as the corridor behind them ruptured. The dream at last recognized that the final tether was broken. The illusions that had imprisoned Caelum no longer held sway, and the swirling hush devoured everything. Elara's spool flared once, as if guiding them toward the exit. She squeezed Caelum's arm, unable to contain the wild burst of gratitude in her chest. They had conquered Malakar's final gambit. She could almost taste freedom in the air.

Yet a pulse of lingering blackness caught her eye. The shattered remains of the monstrous shape quivered in a far corner. Its edges flickered, congealing into a final coil like a dying snake lashing out. Elara's nerves blazed with fresh alarm. She saw the remains slither along the ragged floor, creeping toward Caelum's unguarded left side.

Carmen gasped, but exhaustion hissed in her muscles, her illusions slow to respond.

Elara lunged and hooked her spool's last thread around the final coil. Her body shook under the strain, but she funneled every ounce of will into a swirl of magic that glowed as bright as a star. The coil sizzled, struggled for an instant, then disintegrated with a final, ear-splitting shriek. The echo reverberated through the chamber, knocking both women to their knees.

For a beat, Elara heard nothing but her own pulse roaring in her ears. Darkness threatened the edges of her vision, her illusions drained to the point of near collapse. She felt Carmen slump against her shoulder, panting. Caelum stirred, a shudder wracking his body, but his face looked peaceful beneath the swirling afterglow of freed illusions.

As Elara clung to him, she could not stop her tears. They burned at the corners of her eyes, a blazing mixture of relief and exhaustion. Her entire body ached, from the tips of her calloused fingers to the soles of her feet. She forced a breath, tasting the crisp, otherworldly air. A faint glow pulsed at Caelum's heart, reassuring her that he lived, that this rescue was no dream conjured by desperation.

In the far reaches, the monstrous presence had gone, scattered to the void. Malakar's fury had left behind an empty hush. Elara met Carmen's gaze and found the same astonishment in her tired eyes. Together, they had shattered the final illusions tethering Caelum to Malakar's darkness.

A jagged tremor tore across the chamber, walls peeling like torn fabric. The dream rumbled, threatening to pull them under if they did not return to the waking world. "Now," Carmen murmured. "We have to go. Pull back."

Elara nodded and pressed her forehead to Caelum's. She whispered a soft, tremulous promise, telling him everything would be all right. Then she squeezed the spool in her hand and willed them upward, straining to break the barrier that separated mind from body. Visions blurred by swirling lights flooded her senses. Carmen's illusions carefully cradled Caelum. Elara shut her eyes, imagining Lucian's shout of encouragement, the wards around the bedchamber in the real world holding strong.

Her heart thundered as she channeled one final wave of power. She felt the dream's floor drop away beneath her. The spool's energy escalated in a hot rush, then surged outward in a burst of brilliance. All at once, the illusions tethering Caelum collapsed. The final coil dissolved around his torso, reducing Malakar's last barrier to a swirl of harmless dust. Elara pressed both palms firmly over his chest, letting that radiant bond invigorate him.

They were so close. She felt the dream realm buckle beneath them, an avalanche of swirling fragments pulling them toward consciousness. Carmen's silhouette flickered, still upright but shaking with the effort of holding her illusions poised for quick defense if needed. At the edge of Elara's vision, Caelum's eyelids quivered, as if he were edging toward true wakefulness. She drew in a stuttering gasp. The spool's last shimmer flared in unison with the fierce love she held for him.

Around them, the dream chamber fractured, threatening to collapse. The monstrous remnants surged in a last attempt, but Elara's resolve was unbreakable. With a final surge of strength, she unleashed her illusions, dissolving the darkness. Silence descended, punctuated only by the tremulous breaths of victory. Elara pressed her forehead tenderly against Caelum's, a promise whispered softly: everything would finally be all right.

Her eyes burned with tears as she poured all she was into that moment, letting Malakar's vile imprint dissolve forever beneath her unstoppable wave of blazing truth. She refused to yield an inch. She tore through every shred of darkness anchoring him to the curse. For Caelum, for the kingdom, for the fragile hope beating in her own chest, she would not fail.

She threw her head back, inhaling the echo of victory. Their illusions flared in concert, harnessing every dream-kiss and spark of shared courage. Faintly, from somewhere beyond the unraveling chamber, she heard Carmen's voice shaking with equal parts terror and triumph. The spool heated in Elara's clutch, its magic leading her toward dawn.

Now, as the final coil disintegrated and Caelum's breath steadied, Elara felt certainty like a sunrise in her heart. She had leaned on her deepest feelings: loyalty, devotion, and a fierce need to protect him. The illusions tried to cling to his spirit, but her dreamweaver power cleaved them away. One by one, those black threads shrieked and vanished.

When there was nothing left but the raw hush of triumph, Elara felt the dream swirl around them, eager to eject them back into reality. Tension throbbed through her limbs, but she welcomed it. She had done what she came here to do.

Then, gripping the spool tightly, she gathered Carmen and Caelum close, feeling reality beckon them homeward as the last shreds of Malakar's darkness dissipated forever into nothingness.

TWELVE

Elara tasted lightning on her tongue as the final tether began to splinter. The entire dream chamber vibrated with tension, each corner choked by serrated shadows that refused to release Prince Caelum. She knelt beside his unconscious figure, her trembling fingers pressed against the last coil of Malakar's dark illusion. There was no time to think of her own panic. This was the final step in shattering a curse that had held him prisoner for years. Her spool of shimmering thread glowed with intensity, each filament charged by everything she felt for him: loyalty, determination, and an aching love so fierce it made her chest hurt.

A brutal roar tore through the stale air. High above, the monstrous illusion Malakar had birthed, a shapeless beast of nightmares, howled around the chamber's periphery. Carmen stood a few paces away, breathing hard and drenched in sweat. She had conjured a ragged, translucent shield of woven illusions to hold the worst of the monster's wrath at bay. It trembled with every impact, bright sparks fizzling and vanishing in the gloom. Yet Carmen never lowered her arms, even as fatigue shook her frame. Elara caught her gaze for a moment, noted the flicker of determination behind the fear, and felt bolstered. For far too long they had fought as rivals, but now they fought side by side.

Elara turned back to Caelum's chained form. Victory or failure would hinge on this moment. She inhaled and let her illusions funnel into the last thread of blackness binding him, picturing the spool's power as a cleansing wave. With each breath, bright filaments flared along the tether, sizzling like molten steel against the dark coil. The illusions hissed in protest, and a jolt of agony speared through her astral form. She gritted her teeth. Yielding to pain was not an option.

A thunderous crack reverberated through the chamber. The monstrous illusions overhead howled in unison, as if they understood something precious had broken. Elara felt the shock wave course through her body. It was as though she had loosed an arrow into the final knot of Malakar's deceit. The thick coil disintegrated in her palms, leaving a swirl of glowing motes that fluttered away like burned scraps of parchment.

For an impossibly still instant, the dreamscape froze. Her heart thudded loud in her ears. Was it truly done?

Then, in a noisome shriek, the monstrous beast roared its fury from across the chamber. Crimson arcs of illusion spat from its half-formed jaws, bombarding Carmen's shield. Elara's gaze darted up, alarmed to see her friend's illusions wobble precariously. "We're close," Elara shouted, voice shaking, "just one more push!"

Carmen spared a breathless nod, sweat gleaming on her cheeks. She shaped her own illusions into needle-like missiles that sliced through the swirling darkness. Each needle impacted with a flash of gold, forcing the writhing beast backward. Elara sensed Carmen's raw determination, fueled by regret and an unspoken desire to make things right. Not long ago, Carmen would have cursed Elara for outshining her. Now the two of them were a single front of defiance.

Elara pressed a quivering hand over Caelum's chest. He lay unmoving except for a faint tremor in his pale wrists. For years, illusions had invaded his body and bound his mind, all orchestrated by Malakar's twisted ambition. A pang of sorrow coursed through her. She bent close, letting the spool's final threads swirl around her arm and stream into him. She spoke no words. Her illusions spoke for her, weaving a lit path back to consciousness. In the flickering dream-light, his lashes fluttered.

And then, all around them, the dream-chamber shattered like glass struck by a hammer.

A violent crack distended the air, driving Elara to her knees. Loose debris made of nightmares rained around them, black shards dissolving in midfall. The monstrous beast shrieked a final time, its roar so guttural that Elara's ribcage vibrated with it. Carmen stumbled backward, hissing in pain as she summoned every illusion left in her to deflect the final barrage. Elara braced her arms around

Caelum and refused to let any fragment of illusion tear him away now that she had freed him.

An echo of thunder resounded, and lightning-like flashes streaked across the dream's horizon. Through the chaos, Elara watched dark illusions peel away from Caelum's limbs in long, ragged ribbons. They drifted upward and vanished in midair, dissipating like steam under a blazing sun. Each fallen chain revealed an inch more of Caelum's true form. His chest rose in a shaky attempt at a breath, and his eyelids flickered. Elara pressed her palm to his cheek, a sob building in her throat.

When his eyes opened, they locked on hers. He blinked rapidly, his eyes struggling to adjust to the light. A soft groan escaped his lips as he tried to move. His muscles were stiff and uncooperative after years of disuse. The simple act of breathing required immense effort, each inhale accompanied by a slight wince. As he stared at her, dazed confusion rippled across his face, then recognition chased it away.

Elara had rehearsed this moment countless times, picturing how she would reassure him, how she would stand tall and greet him without tears. Now the reality stole her voice. She stared down, tears shining while she fought for breath.

Caelum opened his mouth, but no sound came. At last, a faint groan slipped out, balanced between pain and disbelief.

She leaned in, and he anchored himself by curling his fingers around her wrist. He made the smallest move-ment, an attempt to rise, and instantly trembled so violently that Elara feared he would crumble. He had been deprived of movement for so long, and the dream realm's gravity still quaked beneath them. She wrapped an arm around his shoulders and gave him the support his frail body demanded. She felt the thump of his heart pulsing, hope echoing through her entire body.

"Caelum," she managed. It was all she could say, his name full of relief, gratitude, and unspoken devotion.

He gave a faint nod, lips parting. "Elara…" His voice was barely audible, like a reed flute struggling for wind, yet it sent a jolt of warmth through her. It was the first time she had heard him speak in the physical realm, or at least close enough to it. "Thank…you," he whispered, tears lining his lashes. His shoulders tensed, head bowing against hers. Every word cost him enormous effort, but he still tried.

A cry cut the air behind them. Elara whipped her gaze around to see the beast lash out a final time, but Carmen had not faltered. She hurled one last wave of illusions in a sweeping crescent, scything through the monstrous shape. The beast roared in agony, shriveling into a tangled silhouette. Even in its death throes it flailed and spat. Raw magic sizzled across the chamber floor, rattling the dream's foundations. A flash of bright gold exploded outward. Elara shielded her eyes and clutched Caelum tight.

Shafts of golden light fractured the dream horizon. Cracks spiderwebbed the walls, letting pure illumination pour in until the entire chamber looked like broken stained glass. The monstrous shape thrashed once more, roaring so loudly that Elara's teeth rattled. Then it collapsed into watery blackness. Moments later, the blackness itself vanished. Gone. The monster Malakar had conjured no longer held Caelum captive.

A wave of searing brightness overtook them. For a heartbeat, Elara thought she was lost in that light forever, a swirl of half-formed illusions and dream residue clinging to her ankles. Then Caelum's weight shifted against her, real and solid, and she heard Carmen's uneven breathing. The dream was giving way, preparing to spit them back into waking reality.

Outside this battered dream, Lucian had stayed beside Caelum's physical body, monitoring the wards that flickered each time illusions raked the boundary. Elara heard faint echoes of his muffled voice calling to them. Even in the suffocating hush of the disintegrating chamber, she imagined him bracing himself with sword in hand, ready to fend off any threat that might cross the threshold. She could feel his tension, sense his fierce protective stance.

She steeled herself. "Hold on," she whispered to Caelum. He clung to her arm as though no other anchor existed. Carmen, bruised and panting, staggered over, illusions flickering around her hands like dying embers. Triumph shone in her eyes, and a shaky grin curved her mouth. Elara and Carmen shared a brief, exhausted look, an unspoken acknowledgment of how far they had come from sniping at each other in the Tapestry Guild. She squeezed Carmen's wrist in gratitude, and Carmen nodded.

A final quake rattled the dream, and the floor dropped

from under them. Elara tightened her hold on Caelum, heart stuttering in alarm. They fell through a swirl of searing brilliance. She had no sense of up or down, only the swirl of dream threads unraveling around them as they plummeted toward consciousness. It felt like being inside a star, everything luminous and infinite yet heartbreakingly fragile. She heard Carmen gasp and tried to steady Caelum against her shoulder.

With a burst of dizziness, Elara opened her eyes to the real world. The bedchamber's lamplight replaced the dream's glare. She felt softness beneath her knees, where plush rugs spread across the stone floor. The spool of shimmering thread dangled from her belt, still tingling but dimmer than before. She blinked, disoriented for a moment, until a strangled sound of joy drew her attention. Lucian knelt opposite them. His eyes shone with raw relief, though his posture was stiff from the tension that had held him.

Caelum lay propped against Elara's chest, eyes half-lidded but open and glimmering. Wakeful light gleamed on his lashes. He drew a shuddering breath and forced himself upright an inch. The wards Elara had stitched around the walls blazed with new vigor, as if recharged by the dream's victory.

"Elara?" Caelum croaked, voice weak but resonant. He coughed, blinking at his limbs and moving them gingerly in disbelief.

She braced him and felt his heartbeat under her hand. Carmen dropped to a crouch on Caelum's other side, trembling from exertion. The chamber's torches illuminated the sheen of sweat on her brow and the dirt smudges across her cheek. She exhaled a wavering breath. "You're awake," she whispered to Caelum, though it sounded more as if she reassured herself.

From the bed's far side, Lucian pressed a hand to Caelum's shoulder. His voice came out hoarse. "He's truly awake," he murmured, as though uncertain it could be real. Relief, pride, and something akin to longing flickered across his face, but the moment held no room for jealousy or regret.

Caelum swallowed another painful gasp. His eyes darted around as though trying to place each figure in the room. Then he rasped, "Carmen... Elara... you saved me." He tried to speak again, but emotion barreled through him. Tears slipped down his cheeks, each track shining in the lamplight. "I can't..." He abandoned words and let a trembling laugh break free instead. It was the laugh of someone tasting life again.

"Don't strain yourself," Elara murmured. Her hand hovered at his hairline, smoothing back damp locks. The memory of holding him in dream corridors flashed through her mind, moments when he was intangible, only half real. Now she felt the weight of his body, the warmth of his breath. The reality threatened to undo her.

With an unguarded exhale, Carmen sank onto her heels beside them. She, too, had tears brimming in her eyes. Her illusions flickered one last time, then went dark, no longer needed to parry nightmares. She pressed both palms to the floor for balance, trying and failing to hide the quiver in her shoulders. "I thought for sure we were going to lose him," she whispered. "But we did it."

Lucian eased Caelum's arm around Elara's shoulders, stepping aside so they could gather more comfortably. The prince still looked dazed, but the relief in his gaze was unmistakable. Lucian swallowed hard, emotions swirling behind his guarded expression. He let go of Caelum's elbow, giving the newly awakened prince a measure of dignity, though the subtle ache he wore revealed that some quiet part of him needed time to process the miracle.

The wards that banded the walls continued to shimmer, but the presence of Malakar's illusions had vanished, leaving behind only the muffled hush of a chamber set free. The air felt lighter, purer, as if every candle flame now burned with renewed brilliance. Elara felt her pulse steady. Her entire body still buzzed with leftover adrenaline, but a growing sense of peace settled over her. The spool of thread at her hip hummed softly, a silent echo of triumph.

"Caelum," Elara said again, tears threatening. "You're safe." She could think of no other phrase. Those two words carried the weight of everything they had fought for. His half-lidded eyes glimmered with gratitude so palpable it made her heart hiccup.

He drew a faint breath and managed, "Thank you... both." He tried to shift his gaze to Carmen, but his head swam. His body had spent too long in enforced slumber. The attempt alone spoke volumes. Carmen nodded back, lips curved in a trembling smile.

In the corner of her vision, Elara spotted a faint swirl

of ephemeral dust in the air, residual illusions dissolving like footprints in the sand. She realized that Malakar's stronghold in Caelum's mind was truly broken. Her chest constricted with a complicated swirl of elation and weariness. She looked at Carmen, who returned the glance with a watery grin. Whatever bitterness once existed between them had been replaced by hard-won camaraderie.

Carmen gently brushed a stray lock of hair from Caelum's forehead. "We should get you comfortable," she said softly. "Illusions may still claw at your mind if you stay upright after such a shock."

He managed to nod, but before they could help lay him down, a pulse of awareness ran through the bedchamber. It felt like a ripple in the wards, signifying that the last threads of dream magic had collapsed. Lucian's eyes flicked to a corner of the room, as though expecting a lurking shadow, but found nothing. After weeks of dread, it was surreal to face a chamber free of nightmares. With nothing left to fight, the tension in Lucian's shoulders ebbed.

Caelum lifted a trembling hand as if to wipe his own tears. His voice, hushed and scratchy, carried a hard edge of vulnerability. "I never thought...never thought I would see you like this. Awake.," he added, blinking in disbelief. "You're... more vibrant than in my dreams," he murmured, awe coloring his weak voice. "I never imagined... colors could be so bright." Fresh tears spilled again, and he let out a shaky laugh.

Elara's heart caught in her throat. She remembered all the nights she had glimpsed him in the dream realm, valiantly clinging to life while illusions battered him from every side. Gently, she turned to him so that their eyes aligned. "You fought too," she reminded him, her voice thick with emotion. "We all did."

He opened his mouth to speak, perhaps to protest that she and Carmen had done everything, but the words faltered. Instead, he pressed his forehead to Elara's shoulder and breathed in shallow, uneven spurts. Subdued lamplight flickered against his hair, and for a moment time hung suspended in the hush of that reunion.

Carmen rubbed her bruised arms and shifted her weight. She closed her eyes as if centering herself, then glanced at Elara. "We need to be sure," Carmen said gently, "that nothing remains of Malakar's illusions." Her voice still shook from exhaustion. "Do you feel anything else clinging to him?"

Elara paused, summoned the faintest glimmer from her spool, and sent a careful ripple of dreamweaver intuition over Caelum's form. The spool's threads revealed no remaining chains, no malignant shadows lurking. Instead, she felt the steady hum of Caelum's actual life force, bright and unwavering. "He's free," she said, relief trembling in her tone. "The illusions are gone."

A strangled laugh of joy escaped Carmen's throat. She slumped with exhaustion and pressed her palms against the mattress for support. Then, with that same shaky smile, she found Elara's arm, her fingers locking around it. They had never been close. Their entire relationship had been built on petty barbs, resentments, and sabotage. Yet in that instant they clung to one another, deliriously relieved.

Outside the bedchamber's tall windows, the city was dark except for scattered torches. Elara guessed it was past midnight, the hour when illusions often crept through unguarded corners. But the wards here shone strong, and in Caelum's eyes, she saw sunrise. A new dawn for him, for them all.

She turned to check Lucian, who stood a pace away, regarding them with unreadable eyes. He exhaled slowly, then offered Caelum a small, proud nod. Whatever complexities had haunted his heart, whether lingering guilt, conflicting affections, or fear that his friend might never wake, slipped aside now. When he finally spoke, his voice was hushed. "Welcome back, Your Highness."

Caelum swallowed and fought the urge to reply with something formal. He managed only an earnest, "Lucian... thank you." The rest came out in a breathless rasp. When Lucian stepped forward to clasp Caelum's shoulder, a fragile peace settled among them, a promise that old grudges and uncertain affections would not overshadow this hard-won victory.

Elara blinked through tears. For the first time in her life, she sensed that she truly belonged here. Prince Caelum's half-reclined figure, Carmen's panting frame, and Lucian's quiet watchfulness formed a circle of battered loyalty that no illusion could tear apart. A faint hum of residual magic skimmed the air, almost like a sigh of relief from the spool of thread that had guided her all along.

Still, her heart hammered with the knowledge that Malakar had not been confronted beyond the dream. The illusions in Caelum's mind were gone, but the threat to the kingdom might remain. She forced herself to stay anchored in this reprieve. They would deal with Malakar's continuing menace soon enough.

Caelum's breath hitched, and he pulled back to meet Elara's gaze once more, tears gathering. "I never thought I'd speak your names outside those nightmares." His eyes flicked between hers and Carmen's, wonder in his expression. "I'm free."

Carmen, cheeks damp, exhaled and lifted her chin. "And we're not letting him or his illusions take you back." She brushed tangled hair from her face, fresh determination sparking in her tone. "We can't rest forever, but just for tonight, can we allow ourselves this moment?"

"Yes," Elara whispered, cradling Caelum's hand against her heart. "Yes, we can." She felt him squeeze her palm in unspoken gratitude.

Lucian, still standing nearby, stepped back to give them space. The wards overhead shimmered again, as if celebrating the end of a long journey. Elara's weary limbs threatened to collapse, yet her spirit soared with a unity she had thought impossible.

A flicker of leftover dream light traced along the bedchamber walls, as ephemeral as memory. Carmen saw it too, her eyes shifting to the vanishing glow, the last echo of the monstrous illusions dissolving for good. In that fading luminescence, Caelum's voice cracked with gratitude when he spoke the women's names, tears brimming at a freedom he had never expected to taste again.

Lucian released Caelum's arm and stepped back a half pace, unsure where he belonged in this raw moment. Pride and a quiet ache crossed his gaze, reflecting everything they had faced, while relief outweighed all else, for now. Even Carmen, once the face of rivalry and sabotage, felt life surge in her chest, a battered sense of redemption.

Together they shared a fragile moment of joy, hearts pounding at the knowledge that Malakar's illusions might still lurk in the kingdom but could no longer cage the rightful prince.

THIRTEEN

A shaft of sunlight pierced the thick drapes in Prince Caelum's bedchamber, casting a pale beam across his bed. Elara hovered near the foot of his mattress, her heart pounding so hard it smothered every other thought. For five years she had carried his face in her mind, first as rumors, then as a fragile form trapped in illusions, and finally as a figure she had touched through dreamweaver magic. Yet every glimpse before now had been in half-light, never quite real. This morning she could no longer deny the reality.

Caelum's eyes fluttered, struggling to stay open in the faint sunlight. His lips parted, releasing a ragged breath that sounded as though it scoured his raw throat. Elara's pulse jumped at that simple sound of life. She swallowed, fighting to keep composure. She had expected his awakening. Last night's dream battle with Carmen confirmed it, but seeing him shift and stir on his own felt perilously close to a miracle. She stepped closer and quietly rested a hand against the edge of the bed for grounding.

Lucian stood by Caelum's side, brow furrowed, bracing the prince's shoulders. He offered an encouraging nod, a silent acknowledgment of all that had led them here. When Caelum tried to push himself upright, a violent tremor seized his arms. His body remembered only years of stillness, and muscle and bone had forgotten movement. Wavering, Caelum let out a faint, rasping sound, and Lucian quickly gripped him around the chest.

"Easy," Lucian murmured, voice tight with concern. "Your body needs time to remember how to move." Caelum nodded, his breathing labored. "Everything feels... heavy. And yet, somehow insubstantial. As if I might float away if I'm not careful."

Lucian kept his hold firm so Caelum wouldn't collapse. A wave of empathy rippled through Elara. She had seen Lucian fight illusions with no hint of hesitation, but the tenderness in his eyes now was different, raw and protective in a way that stole her breath.

Footsteps and raised voices echoed down the hall, and a moment later the King and Queen rushed into the room. King John's face was pale beneath his neat beard, while Queen Meredith's hair had slipped from its pins in her haste. At first neither of them spoke. They lunged for their son, once unmoving and now trembling closer to wakefulness.

The queen pressed shaking fingers to Caelum's cheek as King John sank to a knee beside the bed, tears glinting in his eyes. "My boy," the king choked out. "You... you're truly..." He could not finish. Instead, he grasped Caelum's hand, then brushed sweaty curls from the prince's forehead with trembling fingers. The queen covered her mouth, half in disbelief and half in relief.

Elara shifted back, wanting to give them room for this long-awaited reunion. Warmth flickered in her chest as she watched mother and father cradle their son, tears mingling with faint laughter of disbelief. The tender sight threatened to unravel her composure. She pressed her palm to the spool of shimmering thread at her belt as if to assure herself the dreamweaver power was real and that they had broken a portion of the illusions binding him.

Behind them Malakar stepped through the threshold, each measured footstep echoing on the stone. His smooth voice slid into the chamber like oil, seeming to take control of the moment. "It is a relief to see him stir at last," he pronounced. He clasped his hands in front of him, a polished veneer of calm, yet something in his posture felt charged, ready to deflect blame or seize credit.

Elara's stomach twisted. She had spent too many hours studying illusions and too many midnights weaving wards not to sense the tension radiating from Malakar. Lucian's eyes flicked toward him with open distrust. When Malakar leaned closer, Lucian placed himself between the sorcerer and Caelum, forming a human barrier. Lucian offered no words, only a sharp glare that seemed to say, "Stay away."

Queen Meredith noticed. She tore her gaze from Caelum and locked it on Malakar. Her tears glistened even as her voice hardened. "What exactly have you done to him?" she demanded in hushed alarm. "Five years of searching, and only now does he truly open his eyes. Yet my son claims..." She inhaled, darting a desperate look at Caelum, then back at Malakar. "He claims he saw your shape prowling in his dreams."

At first, Caelum tried to speak, but his voice was barely a rasp. "I...remember...illusions." He swallowed with a painful shudder. Elara wanted to run to his side, to soothe that dryness, but the tension crackling between the royals and Malakar kept her toes planted where she stood.

King John gathered himself more quickly than the queen. He rose, drawing himself to full height, anguish flashing across his features. "Explain yourself." He directed his words at Malakar, who stood calmly at the edge of the chamber. The king's voice trembled with unleashed fury. "Our son speaks of your silhouette haunting his mind. That is not a trifling matter, Malakar. If you had a hand in whatever cursed him..."

Malakar gave a shallow bow, dark hair shifting back from his brow. "Your Majesties, I understand your alarm. My presence in his dreamscape was not from malice but from necessity. We pursued advanced healing interventions that may appear...unorthodox." His tone settled into practiced calm. "I told you that illusions can heal as well as harm if guided correctly. Would you not say this morning's outcome proves my methods were worthwhile?"

Lucian hissed under his breath, clearly not believing a word. He kept one bracing palm on Caelum's back, supporting the prince as he tried to remain upright. The king's lips pressed into a thin line, while Queen Meredith crept closer to Caelum, cupping his face as though to anchor him to reality. Caelum's eyes darted from Malakar to Elara, confusion etched in the lines of his brow.

Elara's heart ached at his overwhelmed expression. He was caught between waking nightmares and disjointed memories of illusions. She yearned to soothe him, to speak plainly about Malakar's deceptions, but the storm of suspicion swirling around the bedchamber silenced her.

Malakar continued, unspooling his explanation in even, measured rhythms. "We should focus on Prince Caelum's victory over this torment, not rehash every step of the past," he said. "He is free, is he not? Let him recover. We will speak about details...later."

The queen's eyes narrowed. "And how exactly can we trust you after such claims? Our son is too weak to speak fully in his defense, but we know illusions ravaged his mind." She glanced at Elara, voice gentling. "My dear, step forward."

Elara stiffened at being singled out. Even so, she obeyed, crossing the floor with cautious steps. Caelum turned his head slowly, seeking her face. When their eyes locked, blue to hazel, a tremor of recognition coursed through Elara's chest. She had only known him in the dream realm or in fleeting glimpses of half-consciousness. Now he was alert, truly seeing her. That intensity made her spine tingle.

The queen's hand found Elara's shoulder. "You were the seamstress who stitched illusions to rouse him, correct?" She exhaled, struggling to keep her composure. "Tell me, child, did you witness Malakar's presence in those illusions you wove? Did you sense any wrongdoing in his methods?"

Elara's throat tightened. Malakar's gaze bored into her, daring her to speak out too boldly. She recalled the times he had lurked at her side, praising her illusions, gleaning knowledge from her spool of thread. Countless nights of dream battles she had waged with Carmen felt frayed and hazy, but she remembered the creeping presence that always pulled at Caelum from the darkness, scenes of black magic swirling with Malakar's chill.

She inhaled, voice trembling. "I..." She caught a flicker of terror in the queen's gaze, and that sight hardened her resolve. Carefully, she forced calm. "I can confirm that illusions shaped his slumber. Malakar...guided my training to an extent, yes. But the illusions were not only to heal." She shivered at the memory of black serpentine shapes. "There were...darker threads at work."

The King's posture stiffened. "Darker threads? Malakar, is that not precisely what you said you had under control?" he demanded. "You assured us months ago that your illusions would purge malignant curses, not compound them."

Malakar chuckled, low and controlled, as if he found the confrontation cumbersome.

"Your Majesties, I said illusions have two edges. Some illusions require a measure of darkness to fight darkness. My silhouette may have appeared menacing in the dream, but it was all in service of jarring the prince awake. Stress awakens dormant instincts."

Elara's nails pressed into her palms. Stress awakens

dormant instincts. The words churned her stomach. She had witnessed enough illusions to know how Malakar's magic thrived on chaos.

"Speak plainly," Lucian shot back, voice vibrating with tension. "You expect us to glean that your part in his nightmares was beneficial? Or are you spinning another lie?"

Malakar's gaze flicked to Lucian. "You stand at the prince's bedside, but do you truly understand healing illusions? I suspect not. With all due respect, your sword cannot slice through a dream."

Lucian's jaw tightened, but before he could retort, Caelum mustered a whisper. "That...shape, in my mind," he began, throat raw. His breath rasped in soft gasps. The queen stroked his arm. "I remember...so many shapes, so many illusions. I...saw an outline, always in the corner of my vision, urging me deeper into suffocating darkness." Wincing, he slid another unsteady look at Malakar. "Was that you?"

The question fell into the hush that gripped the chamber. Every attendant, every guard posted at the threshold, and even Carmen, who hovered in the hallway, eyes wide, seemed to hold their breath.

Malakar's carefully constructed façade rippled with a flash of annoyance. "Prince Caelum," he said, adopting a gentler tone, "your memories may still be clouded. Let us not jump to conclusions."

King John reaffirmed his stance, shoulders squared. "We are not ignoring this." His tone brimmed with a father's protectiveness. "We want the entire truth,

Malakar. Now." His gaze flicked between the sorcerer and his son. "If your so-called healing illusions brought him here, then explain how he has vivid recollections of nightmares bearing your likeness."

"Yes, explain that," Lucian growled. He steadied Caelum's shoulder, ensuring the prince's precarious balance remained. "Because Elara has done far more for his healing than you ever did. She's the one who truly reached him, not your illusions of terror."

A tremor of rage flashed in Malakar's eyes, but he masked it with a careful smile. "Need we overshadow the boy's wonderful first conscious morning with these petty accusations?" He sighed. "We can delve into every nuance later. For now, Caelum is awake at last. This is cause to celebrate, not bicker."

The queen stood, the sadness in her tear-stained face giving way to indignation. "How dare you call these accusations petty? My son has suffered for years." She drew a shaky breath, trying to keep her voice steady. "He claims he saw you. So, if you indeed followed him into dreams, we have a right to know why."

Malakar opened his mouth, no doubt prepared to recite another polished excuse, but Caelum's hand shot up, palm shaking as he silently asked them to pause. His breathing remained labored, but his eyes sparked with the same quiet determination Elara had encountered in the dream realm.

"Mother... Father," Caelum croaked, his voice hoarse. "I understand your fears. But let me speak with Elara... alone. Please."

Elara's heart kicked. She felt Malakar's gaze drill into her again. The king and queen both turned, startled by Caelum's request, but they showed no reluctance. The queen answered softly, "As you wish, my son." A hush spread through the chamber.

Lucian hesitated, glancing from Caelum to Elara. Then his hand slipped from the prince's shoulder. "If that is your choice," he said quietly, clearing enough space for Elara to approach. The tension in his eyes showed he disliked leaving Caelum unguarded while Malakar still hovered, but the prince's request was clear.

King John kissed Caelum's brow. "We will wait outside. But we must continue this discussion. We must get to the bottom of these illusions." He clenched a trembling fist, struggling for composure. "I do not plan to let suspicious talk be brushed aside any longer."

Malakar dipped his head in courteous acceptance, though a ripple of disdain marred his features. The queen lingered a moment longer to touch Elara's arm, whispering, "Give him any comfort you can." Her voice dropped. "He must recover from this curse, no matter the cost. We need him."

Elara nodded, her pulse roaring in her ears. She watched the King and Queen withdraw and usher the few attendants along, among them a flustered Carmen who cast a conflicted look toward Elara. Lucian stayed near the door, offering one final protective glare at Malakar before stepping into the corridor. Malakar followed, pausing only to bow smoothly to Caelum with an air of false reverence.

The door closed, and an unsettling hush settled over the room.

Elara moved forward, her chest tight. She knelt by Caelum's pillow, still hardly believing this was real. He was upright, conscious, and gazing at her. A faint glimmer of pain flashed in his brilliant eyes. He licked his cracked lips. "I will not ask for the entire story now, but...you have stood in my nightmares, haven't you?"

Tears threatened to break her voice. She managed a shaky nod. "I did," she whispered. "We tried so hard to reach you, Lucian, the guild, even..." She swallowed. "Carmen. We wanted you back."

The corner of his mouth quirked in a semblance of a smile, though fatigue carved lines in his face. "I felt you," he said softly. "Felt that spool of light, that tether. It saved me when the illusions, and Malakar himself, clawed for every breath."

Elara closed her eyes, relief flooding her veins. She brushed a stray lock of hair from his damp forehead. "We freed you because you fought too," she said. "This was not just me."

He let out a ragged sigh and pressed his hand gently over hers. His grip lacked strength, yet it held a warmth that made her heart ache with gratitude. "Thank you for believing I could come back," he said, each word sounding as if it cost him physical pain. "That alone gave me hope."

She shifted her weight, afraid to rest all her emotions on the cusp of this moment. Even as her heart soared with joy, the echoes of Malakar's illusions lingered. Outside, a muffled swirl of voices showed that the King and Queen still demanded answers. Malakar was no fool. He would keep spinning truths until no one remembered which way was up, and they all knew illusions did not vanish overnight.

Caelum followed her worried glance at the door, a determined glint sparking behind his exhaustion. "Elara," he said, his voice dropping to a rasping hush, "I need to speak with you alone. No watchers, no illusions. The others mean well, but I cannot rest until I know exactly what happened. I must understand how Malakar twisted my dreams, and I will not let him hide behind half-truths."

Elara's chest tightened. "We can talk as long as you want," she whispered, though emotion threatened to close her throat. "But your strength..."

He inhaled in a shaky attempt at composure. "I know," he murmured. "I am weak... but not helpless. Not anymore."

His eyes locked on hers, revealing a flicker of the regal determination she had glimpsed in the dream realm. "I will speak with you privately, and then I will face him. I swear I will not let the shadows that once caged me linger unchallenged."

Though exhausted and far from fully recovered, Caelum insisted on speaking with Elara privately, promising he would not let the shadows that once caged him linger unchallenged.

FOURTEEN

Elara stood in one of the castle's lesser corridors, heart pounding at the flurry of excitement echoing through the walls. A constant shuffle of finely dressed courtiers passed by, each determined to slip into the gilded antechamber ahead, eager to lay eyes on Prince Caelum. A day ago, most of them had seemed resigned to the notion that his mysterious coma would never lift. Now they pressed against the ornate doors with breathless anticipation.

Elara shifted her weight from one foot to the other, trying to quell her nerves. She had never been the sort of person to crave attention, yet she sensed eyes flicking her way. Those curious gazes, once dismissive of her plain clothing and humble background, now carried questions: Who was this unknown seamstress rumored to have done the impossible?

A jolt of self-consciousness swept over her. She smoothed her skirts beneath trembling fingers, still wearing the same modest gown she had donned before dawn. Sleepless nights had stolen what little patience she had for polite frivolities. She wanted to ensure Caelum's well-being, not parade through a sea of prying stares. But so much had changed in mere hours, and duty weighed too heavily on her to hide.

A guard in gold-trimmed livery gestured for her to move into the antechamber. She swallowed a tight breath and stepped forward, overwhelmed at first by the swirl of perfume and chatter. Glittering chandeliers illuminated every polished column, and the floor gleamed with reflections of the crowd's jewel-toned finery. Ahead she spotted Lucian. He stood at Prince Caelum's side, supporting the newly awakened heir with a steady arm around his shoulders.

At that sight, Elara's chest twisted with mingled relief and worry. Though Caelum stood on his own two feet, an unimaginable triumph after his long slumber, he looked pale beneath the flush of excitement. Perspiration beaded on his forehead, and his shoulders sagged with exertion. His gaze, once distant and dream-bound, now scanned the crowd with a flicker of both determination and unease. He had insisted on appearing today, though the healers warned he might not possess the strength to endure so many voices at once.

"Elara," he murmured upon seeing her, words softened by a weary smile. He tried to lift a hand to beckon her closer, but the movement wavered.

She approached, heart thumping. "Highness," she said gently, though the formality felt strange after all their private moments in the dream realm. "You should sit if it becomes too much."

Before Caelum could answer, Lucian guided him toward a carved wooden bench near the antechamber's side. Elara followed, but a group of courtiers swept in around them, brandishing questions for the newly roused prince. She clasped her hands against the chaos, alarmed at how these wealthy lords and ladies leaned in, voices overlapping as they clamored for details.

"Forgive us, Your Highness," one plump noble said, his voice quavering with excitement. "All the kingdom rejoices at your recovery. Might you spare a word about how you were saved?"

A tall, angular woman wearing emerald silks fanned herself and spoke before Caelum could reply. "We have prayed for this day. Lord Malakar often assured us healing illusions would bring you back. Clearly, he held part of the key, did he not?"

Elara's chest tightened. The mention of Malakar's name stirred a flash of anger she barely contained. She wove through the bodies to stand beside Caelum, hoping her presence might calm him, but their circle of questioners only widened. She could not help noticing how some glances fell upon her spool of shimmering thread. Rumors abounded that her illusions, not Malakar's, had broken the darkness gripping Caelum.

"Please," Lucian interjected, his voice firm, "give the prince a moment to breathe."

The crowd subsided a fraction, but the hush crackled

with anticipation. Caelum inhaled slowly. Elara watched him steel himself.

"I appreciate your concern," he said softly, "and I thank every soul who offered prayers. Restoring my health took more than one spell."

He was about to continue when two chamberlains in matching royal livery strode in and called for all to gather in the Great Hall. The King and Queen had convened a council to discuss Caelum's return, and every courtier was expected. At once, the jubilant throng swelled like a wave, carrying Caelum, Lucian, and Elara along. She tried to keep her composure, reminding herself to walk with calm rather than cling to Caelum's arm, yet the swirl of movement made her stomach flip, and she yearned for an inconspicuous corner to hide in.

They entered the council room under marble arches that rose high above them. Tapestries depicting heroic battles lined the walls, but the hush that settled over the assembly drowned any sense of grand ceremony. Advisors, nobles, and officials parted to let the newly awakened prince pass. Elara edged behind Caelum and Lucian, keenly aware of each stare drilling into her.

At the far end of the room, the king and queen stood flanked by several high nobles. Queen Meredith's eyes gleamed with the same joyous tears Elara had glimpsed the night before. King John wore an expression that bordered on disbelief, though gratitude softened the lines of worry etched across his brow. When Caelum reached them, both monarchs stepped forward to embrace their son. Elara's heart swelled at the tender sight.

Silence followed the royal greeting until the king cleared his throat. "Good people, we are gathered to discuss the path forward now that Prince Caelum is awake. Our hearts brim with relief. We owe thanks to all who aided him." He paused, his gaze flicking to Malakar, who stood behind the gathered lords. "We must also clarify how illusions were employed, and whether any danger remains."

Malakar bowed with practiced poise, dark hair catching the light. "Your Majesty, no further threat lingers from my illusions. As I have long stated, they were used only to support the prince's mind against darker forces. It is a blessing he has resurfaced."

Elara's fist clenched at the sorcerer's confident tone. He glided into a place of prominence as though he were the champion behind Caelum's recovery. She swallowed a rebuttal, uncertain whether she dared to break the council's order. Next to her, Lucian stood rigid as a statue, jaw tight in barely concealed disgust.

King John nodded gravely. "Then how do you explain the continuing illusions that plague some of our outlying districts? Reports arrived this morning of strange sightings and night terrors. Are they truly random, or did something else disrupt your illusions, unleashing chaos?"

Malakar dipped his chin in apparent regret. "Rogue magic pockets, Your Majesty. Traces of older curses that occasionally flare without warning. I have done my utmost to contain them, yet some resentful folk in the guilds or scattered villages may be experimenting on their own. We cannot rule out misguided novices fueling these phenomena." His voice never rose above careful politeness.

Elara felt her pulse hammer. Anger pressed against her ribs. She wanted to shout that this man had woven illusions powerful enough to steal Caelum's mind for five years. She tasted the memory of countless nights fighting swirling shapes in the dream realm, each one bearing Malakar's vile signatures. Yet a single glance at the King's uncertain expression held her back. Perhaps she feared that naming Malakar's guilt too openly would cause a backlash, especially when so many in the court had admired the sorcerer.

An older counselor, nervous in posture, slipped forward. "Malakar, court records show at least four contradictory edicts. Each bore the King's signature, yet included odd instructions regarding illusions. Are you honestly claiming they were oversights by minor assistants? This appears far too consistent for mere mistakes."

A flutter of agreement rippled through the room, and a few bold heads nodded. Elara noticed two advisors exchanging pointed glances, as if they had long harbored suspicions but lacked the nerve to speak. Across from them, a cluster of courtiers hoisted up ledgers bound in ribbon, their pages rustling with collected evidence of illusions gone awry.

Malakar shrugged, a controlled flick of his shoulders. "Assistants can be...overzealous, especially when pressed for results. I never approved any illusions that compromised official decrees, I assure you."

Elara could hardly believe the brazenness. Did he truly

expect them to accept such a feeble excuse? She shifted her attention to Caelum. Though he remained upright as best he could, she saw the tremble in his knees. Exhaustion weighed on him, and the swirl of half-truths only intensified the frustration etched on his features.

Slowly, Caelum lifted his chin. "I remember illusions in my mind," he said, voice unsteady. "They were not supportive. They dragged me deeper, made me doubt reality. I..." He paused, swallowing, and Elara realized the burden it took for him to speak at all.

The Queen stepped forward, pressing a gentle hand on his arm. She looked at Malakar, eyes shining with a mix of gratitude and concern. "Malakar, our son believes your silhouette appeared time and again in his dreams. Can you explain that?"

For a frozen moment, no one spoke. Hatred pricked at the back of Elara's throat. She could taste the lies on Malakar's lips. He offered a slight, regretful tilt of his head to the Queen. "Your Majesty, illusions can be misunderstood. I never took a harmful step into Prince Caelum's mind. Perhaps he saw my reflection from our healing sessions. Dreams distort reality in unpredictable ways."

A hush settled over the council. Elara felt everyone's gaze shift from Malakar to Caelum, as though waiting for a clearer accusation. Her breath caught; she was unsure if the moment had come to speak. Yet Caelum stumbled forward a step and nearly toppled from dizziness. Lucian stepped in to brace him, the scrape of his boot slicing the silence. The king lifted a hand to quell the rising murmurs.

"Peace," said King John, voice tight with suppressed

dread. "We will not let rumors overshadow the prince's joyous return. We recognize that illusions might still linger, and we need swift measures to stop them. Malakar, we order you to…"

But the king's words halted when a handful of advisors grated in protest. "If he has caused these anomalies," one snapped, "then the palace must investigate him further. We cannot trust the same illusions that nearly destroyed the prince."

Others, particularly those who had profited from Malakar's supposed healing magic, spoke in hushed, protective tones and insisted no wrongdoing existed. Their voices clashed across the table, tangling in a knot of speculation and dread. Elara's cheeks flamed with the intensity of it all. She wanted to defend Caelum openly, yet the wave of conflicting opinions crashed over her and urged her to stay silent, or risk further chaos.

She clenched her fists and swallowed every word of accusation. Now that Caelum stood in the room, trembling from fatigue, she did not wish to spark an uproar that could damage him politically. The tension threatened to fracture the unity needed to keep illusions at bay. She glanced at Lucian, who seemed equally torn, his eyes locked on Malakar with a glare that could cut stone.

Malakar, taking advantage of the disarray, wove new declarations of innocence. He offered half apologies about administrative confusion and invoked vague cautionary tales of how illusions, once started, might spring up in new forms without the original caster's knowledge. At times the king and queen appeared half convinced by his soothing tone, though their son's distress weighed on them heavily.

At last, the king rapped his knuckles on the table for silence. "We will hold a formal inquiry," he announced, exchanging a glance with Queen Meredith. The mix of relief and anxiety in her eyes spoke volumes. "Until then, Prince Caelum shall recover in peace. This council will reconvene to decide how we address illusions beyond the palace. Our people need answers. They need hope."

Caelum leaned on Lucian and nodded faintly, though Elara saw disappointment carved into his face. The conversation had twisted in circles, achieving little beyond stoking more suspicion. Whispers flitted from noble to noble, spurred by Malakar's ambiguous remarks.

Queen Meredith cast Elara a look that bordered on a plea, as if silently asking for a statement that might cut through the swirling accusations. Yet Elara hesitated, weighed down by caution. One misstep could fracture the fragile support Prince Caelum had only recently regained. She swallowed the burn in her throat. Better to wait than watch Malakar spin her words.

Moments later, the King declared the council adjourned, instructing everyone to depart in an orderly manner. The lords and ladies murmured among themselves, stepping away from the table with measured bows. Elara released a long, shaky breath. The palace staff began funneling from the hall, latching onto the next wave of rumors to dissect. Adjusting her spool of thread at her hip, Elara tried to quell the racing of her heart.

She lingered near Caelum, desperation churning in her

gut. Malakar, surrounded by his admirers, exuded an air of confidence that made her want to scream. He did not scurry away like a guilty man, nor fling accusations. He existed as if he had won. If she could have, she would have ripped the truth from his smirk, but she remained frozen.

As the last of the courtiers drifted into the corridors, the King turned to speak quietly with Caelum. Queen Meredith reached out to place a comforting hand on Elara's arm. "We will find clarity," the queen said softly. "Do not lose heart."

"Yes, Your Majesty," Elara managed to reply. She thought of how Malakar's illusions still lurked in distant towns, weaving nightmares. She wanted to help rid the kingdom of them, but suspicion and rumor closed in from all sides. It felt like standing inside a tightening snare.

Lucian caught her eye, brow furrowed. He must have read the frustration on her face. He did not speak, yet his silent nod offered reassurance he, too, would keep pushing for the truth. Caelum, straining to remain upright, shared Elara's concern with the slightest tilt of his head. She realized it would take more than a single council session to strip away Malakar's veneer.

By the time the council dissolved, rumors of treason and illusions swirled in every corridor, building an invisible pressure that threatened to tear the court apart.

FIFTEEN

Elara eased her way down the winding corridor, clutching a small bundle of notes in one hand as a guard led her toward the sitting room Prince Caelum had requested. She had hardly slept the night before, consumed by roiling thoughts. Despite everything she had endured, including sabotage in the guild, Malakar's manipulations, and her own doubts, it felt surreal to walk these palace halls for a private audience with a prince who, days ago, had lain unresponsive. Yet she could not deny the flutter in her stomach, equal parts relief and anxiety.

She reached the sitting room at last. A gentle glow filtered through tall windows, gilding the plush chairs and polished table. Morning light fell in wide bands across the floor and illuminated the dust motes that danced in the stillness. By the window, Caelum stood with one hand braced on a carved mantel. His posture was straighter than the day before, though a faint quiver ran through his limbs when he shifted his weight. A physician hovered at his side, urging him to remain seated, but he earned only a polite shake of the head from the prince.

"Elara." Caelum's voice was soft as he tilted his chin, beckoning her closer. The rasp in his words made her chest tighten, yet the warmth in his eyes was undeniable. She caught herself staring at how different he appeared while awake, no longer a distant figure bound by nightmares, but a man determined to stand on his own.

"Your Highness," she said, dipping into an awkward curtsy.

The physician glanced from Caelum to Elara, concern etched on his features, then withdrew. She guessed the poor man had spent sleepless hours trying to convince the prince to rest. Caelum clearly had other ideas.

"Please." He gestured to a cushioned stool near the window. "Sit with me."

She obeyed, perching on the edge of the seat. Sunlight spilled over her lap, highlighting the spool of thread she had pinned at her belt. Even after all this time, she preferred to keep her spool close. It was both comfort and shield.

Caelum inhaled slowly. She noticed the subtle tension in his jaw, as though every breath still carried echoes of old pain. Then he offered a delicate smile, warm but tired. "I have been told," he began, his voice low, "that you risked everything to keep me from slipping further into those illusions. You have my eternal thanks for... for pulling me back into the light."

A flush crept over Elara's cheeks. She was not used to

such direct praise from someone of his status, though she had glimpsed his gentle nature in the dream realm. Even so, hearing it in open daylight struck a tender chord in her heart. "I... you are welcome, Highness," she replied softly. "I only did what needed doing. I could not bear to see you lost."

He leaned against the arm of the chair placed beside hers, his shoulders tense, as though propping himself upright demanded all his strength. "You owe me no formality," he said. "Not when I have caused so much pain. It seems I slept for five years, letting illusions crawl through this kingdom unchecked."

"That was not your fault," Elara insisted. She remembered how he had flinched in the dream corridors, confused by the illusions. He had no control over what happened in his cursed sleep. "None of us realised the full extent of Malakar's magic," she added.

He exhaled a shaky breath, his lips curving in a faint, wry smile. "Yet I am the prince. The burden belongs on my shoulders, along with the guilt that I was not awake to protect my people. You, on the other hand... you have borne that responsibility in my absence." His gaze caught hers, unwavering. "You fought illusions, overcame rivalries, and faced so many accusations to keep me alive in the dream realm. I have heard murmurs of what you have endured, though I suspect I have not learned half of it."

Her heart pounded. It was strange to think of him taking note of her troubles. She could barely reconcile the difference between the inert figure she had visited day after day in that cold bedchamber and this earnest young man determined to stand tall. She swallowed, pushing back the tangle of emotions swirling inside her. "I did face obstacles," she said quietly, "but only because Malakar twisted every advantage he had. Most guild members were not sure if my illusions were real or dangerous. And Carmen... she..." Elara's voice trailed off, uncertain how many details she should share about Carmen's sabotage and eventual remorse.

"I have gathered that your guild faced its own tensions," Caelum said, fatigue lacing his tone. "I want to know everything, but first, I must ask for your patience. My physician tells me I must not press myself too hard, though I find it impossible to remain idle."

Elara nodded. "You should rest. We can speak more later." She suspected he had insisted on this meeting out of sheer willpower. Even now, his voice trembled slightly.

He lifted a hand as though to dismiss that notion. "I will rest when I must, but first...I must learn how you overcame the illusions that trapped me. I remember some pieces of the dream realm. I recall shadows shaping themselves into attackers. I recall hearing your voice...your spool of thread, glowing in the darkness." A faint wonder lit his eyes, as though the very mention of her spool conjured long-lost comfort. "Tell me, please, how you broke through those illusions."

She paused, considering where to begin. The entire path had been riddled with doubt. She finally decided to speak plainly. "I found half-burned texts that described something known as dreamweaving. Mistress Imelda encouraged me to explore those arts, though at first, I did not even realize I possessed them. My illusions started small, a bit of glow here, a flicker there, never anything strong enough to heal a curse."

Caelum listened intently, though a shadow of dizziness crossed his features. He closed his eyes for a moment, and she rose halfway, ready to steady him if he swayed. But he opened them again and exhaled. "I am fine," he managed, his voice hoarse. "Continue, please."

She sank back onto the stool, resting a hand on the arm of his seat to be sure he would not topple forward. "Over time, I learned the illusions could be woven to protect rather than deceive. We discovered your mind was not entirely lost in sleep. You...you fought from within, even if you did not always realize it. Lucian helped me gather more texts and push deeper into the dream realm. He was at my side many nights, standing guard so I could concentrate without fear of physical threats."

At Lucian's name, Caelum's jaw tightened. She noticed the flicker of hurt in his eyes, and her stomach did an uneasy flip. She had feared this moment ever since he awakened, the complicated truth that she had grown close to Lucian while trying to save the prince she only fully knew in dreams. She would never deny the bond that had formed with Caelum, but she also could not pretend that Lucian was a mere bystander.

"I see," he said warily. "He spoke of you often, even when I lay half-entombed in illusions. I suppose I observed glimpses of his presence, though at the time, the boundaries of dream and reality blurred." The corners of his lips twitched in a faint, rueful smile. "I remember once...I thought I saw him standing at the edge of my bed. And another time, I saw you and him... never mind. I was not sure if that was real or yet another trick."

Elara swallowed. "It was real. He watched over me to keep Malakar from stepping in. And the other time...was real too. It was Malakar. Lucian never...meant to come between you and me. But I leaned on him. I was so exhausted from the illusions, and at times, I feared it was hopeless."

Caelum took a slow breath. She saw the tension in his throat as if the words were difficult to swallow. "You do not need to defend him. Lucian is my friend, and I owe him more than I can say. He has always been loyal. If you grew close, it must have been through shared trials."

She nodded. The guilt she felt was less about wrong-doing and more a swirl of emotions left tangled from the weeks of desperation. "I cared for him," she admitted quietly. "Yet you were in my dreams, day after day. My heart was never simple."

A brief silence settled, broken only by the rustle of the garden breeze through the open window. Warm sunlight caressed Caelum's cheek, throwing gold highlights into his eyes. When he spoke again, his voice had softened. "There is no shame in that. All of us have carried more burdens than we expected. You had no choice but to stand with whomever offered help, especially in the face of Malakar's illusions." His hand twitched against his knee, betraying a flicker of tension. "It still stings a little," he confessed, voice dipping lower. "I fought so long in my dreams, clinging to the thread of your presence. At times, that was all I had."

His honesty took her breath away. She reached for his hand without thinking, curling her fingers gently over his. There were faint lines across his knuckles, a reminder of battles fought in both real and unreal planes. "I always came for you," she whispered. "No matter how many illusions Malakar cast."

"And for that, you have my undying gratitude." He squeezed her hand, eyes clouded with something deeper than simple thanks. "But Malakar is not finished, is he? Even I can sense the unrest in the kingdom. Word trickles in about nightmares prowling the city after dark, illusions that confuse travelers and stir panic in the countryside. I fear this is the same twisted magic that trapped me. He wields illusions like a puppet master, seeding terror to maintain a semblance of control. Only, he is no longer at the palace." Caelum's tone dropped, weighted with dread. "He has scattered illusions like shards of glass. They must be linked to the same foul power that once bound my mind."

Elara felt her chest tighten. So many had suffered sleepless nights and turned to the guilds for wards or illusions of calm. She remembered the gatherings in the corridor, where even noblemen trembled with fear. "Yes," she said softly. "He is far from done, even though you are free of his direct curse. His illusions remain out there, haunting both the streets and people's dreams."

They fell silent. The hush made her shoulders tense until Caelum gently uncurled her fingers from where they still lay across his. His gaze searched her face as though seeking the corners of her heart. Perhaps he looked for reassurance the same way she did. She held his hand more firmly, letting warmth pass between them.

"Yet it does not mean we have surrendered." His voice trembled slightly, but determination shone through. "I have awakened, and you remain at my side. Lucian stands guard, the guilds are rallying, and despite every ounce of heartbreak we have shared, we stand with a common purpose." He paused, swallowing. "None of you have given up on me, so I will not give up on the kingdom."

She blinked back an upwelling of emotion, biting her lower lip. "You should not blame yourself for the illusions that run rampant now. We will stop them, just as we freed you."

He exhaled an unsteady breath that settled in a half smile of gratitude. "Sometimes, in the nights...while my mind wandered, I half believed you were just a dream spun from my desperation. I would cling to that fleeting vision, trying to glean strength from the possibility that there was someone out there who believed I still lived. I thought of you as my...light in the darkness." He cleared his throat, and that raw rasp returned. "I owe that light more than I can ever repay."

Heat flooded her cheeks, and she wished she had something more eloquent to say, but the words caught in her throat. She squeezed his hand in silent acceptance.

Struggling against a wave of dizziness, Caelum closed his eyes briefly and leaned forward in the seat. With her free hand, she pressed gently against his upper arm to steady him. Up close, she caught the faint scent of floral salve, a remedy the physicians had used on his bruises. He looked at her and whispered an apology for his weakness. She shook her head.

"There is nothing to forgive," she murmured, her voice thick. "Your strength has always been there, even if your body needs time."

A grateful look crossed his face, but she also glimpsed guilt flickering in his eyes. "I stole so many years from the kingdom, so much time from you," he said, his voice hauntingly fragile. "You have carried burdens that should never have been yours."

She forced a shaky smile to show him that the blame lay elsewhere, with the man who orchestrated this entire mess. Malakar alone deserved that ire. "We both survived," she said softly. "That is what matters."

He gazed at her, and for a stretched moment the morning light sparkled around them, a hush settling that felt too intimate for any palace corridor. He brushed an unsteady hand along the side of her face and let his thumb linger at her jaw. Her pulse kicked at the warmth of his touch, and her heart hammered in her chest.

"Surviving is only half," he said, his voice dipping to something that made her blood rush. "I want more than survival. I want life. I want a future unchained by illusions, a kingdom that breathes freely...and I want so much more with you."

Elara's pulse stuttered. She saw the flicker of devotion in his eyes, a sentiment that reminded her of how he had stared in those dream corridors, reaching out despite the illusions. She recalled the weightless hope she had felt each time she glimpsed him fighting the nightmares, pressing forward just to rest his palm against hers.

He reached for Elara's hand, intertwining their fingers. The warmth of his touch sent a shiver through her. "I've dreamed of this," he said softly, "being able to hold your hand without fear of illusions tearing us apart."

He tilted her chin up so she could not shift her gaze away. The tension between them felt electric, fueled by heartbreak, gratitude, and something achingly close to longing. Then his lips touched hers, soft and uncertain, as though he too marveled at the privilege of kissing her in the living world. Elara's breath caught. She might have gasped if not for the sweetness of that moment, the hush sweeping through her.

Her eyes fluttered closed. It was a fleeting press of warmth, gentle as sunlight. Behind her lids, the last remnants of fear and guilt seemed to shimmer and dissolve, leaving the prince who had once been lost and the seamstress who had pulled him back. She let her free hand slide over his shoulder, felt the flex of his muscles and realized how real this was. When he broke the kiss, she tasted salt on her lips, uncertain whether it came from him or herself. His breath fell shallow, his cheeks tinged with color. Then he whispered, as if confessing a secret, "Thoughts of this kept me going in the darkest corners of my dreams. When everything else felt like it slipped away, I held on to the vision of your face. I wanted to return so I could...kiss you in real life." His eyes swept her features.

"And to touch all of you, not merely a phantom in the shadows."

His words tugged at a yearning in her chest. She leaned closer, heart thrumming. For a second, she let that want wash over her and forgot the illusions creeping beyond these walls. He exhaled, as though some weight crashed back into his mind. "I suppose I must save the kingdom first," he said, a faint, self-mocking smile curving his lips. "Do not let me get lost again in any illusions. Not when I want so much more time...with you."

Elara pressed her forehead to his, warmth expanding behind her ribs. "Yes, you do," she said, her voice trembling with equal parts laughter and tears.

Caelum pulled her closer, resting his forehead against hers. "In all my dreams, I never imagined a moment as perfect as this," he murmured. Elara closed her eyes, savoring the closeness, the reality of her prince's presence.

CHAPTER

SIXTEEN

Elara wandered along the edge of the palace courtyard, the late-afternoon sunlight slanting across her shoulders. She should have felt relief at the recent swirl of council meetings and wards set along the palace walls, but her chest remained tight with a complicated mix of triumph and unease. Caelum had awakened. The news spread hope everywhere. Yet nightmares and illusions still prowled beyond each corridor, and together they all fought a war that never quite slowed. Elara could hardly recall the last time she had sat still without her mind sprinting to the next threat.

She stopped near a carved stone bench beside low hedges. The courtyard path extended to her left, where a series of old practice dummies had been erected for guards to hone their fighting forms. An occasional guard passed by, acknowledging her with a quick bow or a respectful nod. She offered small smiles in return, but her thoughts drifted to Caelum, who had quietly asked her for a brief respite that afternoon. The prince had insisted she find a moment of her own to clear her head, promising he would rest properly in his chambers. Warmth stirred in her at the memory of his gentle concern. Despite all the chaos that had shattered his life, he still worried about hers.

The subtle glimmer of wards caught her eye. Pale lines flickered at intervals along the courtyard's perimeter, placed to deter illusions that might creep in through the heavy iron gates. In the lively glow of day, the wards were barely noticeable, like faint ripples in the air, yet Elara's awakened senses could feel their hum of power. She inhaled slowly, trying to steady herself. Her spool of shimmering thread, tucked at her hip, gave a tiny pulse, as if urging her to remain vigilant.

A dull thud caught her attention. On the other side of thick hedges, she heard a series of forceful blows landing on something solid. Concerned that illusions might be manifesting again, she made her way down a winding path. Stepping around a tall rosebush, she found a training circle paved with smooth cobblestones. At its center stood Lucian, sword in hand, hammering at an old practice dummy. Sweat darkened the collar of his tunic, and each strike echoed with the fierce ring of metal against burlap and straw.

Elara's pulse hitched at the sight of his rigid posture. His shoulders were taut, his expression grim. She had grown used to Lucian's calm discipline, his unwavering presence whenever Caelum needed a loyal defender, or she needed a partner in dreamweaver research. Now the anger in his eyes seemed unrestrained. She recognized the tension in his stance, the unspoken frustration that had simmered since Caelum emerged from the cursed slumber. Guilt panged in her stomach. She knew Lucian had never begrudged Caelum's awakening, but something gnawed at him.

Her feet carried her closer, though she stayed behind a chipped column rather than announcing herself. She did not want to disrupt him if he needed the release. She wondered if any words she offered would bring comfort. The question of what she represented, friend, potential lover, or simply the seamstress who had once turned to him for nights on end in the dream realm, had lurked since Caelum's heartfelt gaze first settled on her.

Lucian paused mid swing, chest heaving. The dummy sagged with fresh gouges, straw poking from beneath the ripped cloth. The wards along the courtyard boundary shimmered, sending tiny sparkles along his blade. Elara turned her gaze aside to give him a moment of privacy. She sensed something raw and vulnerable in him, and she felt a prickle of sympathy for how the palace demanded so much from him. Since Caelum's return, questions of loyalty and old jealousies had complicated every step.

A glimpse of movement drew her focus to the left. Carmen entered quietly, weaving around a line of stacked crates near the courtyard's boundary. Her hair, coiled in a sleek bun, gleamed in the angled sunlight. She wore a fitted cloak that emphasized her poised silhouette. Elara's heart caught. She still remembered the rancor Carmen once directed at her, spurred by ambition and jealousy. Yet the woman had changed. Carmen had helped in the final push to break illusions around Caelum's sleeping mind and had apologized for her earlier sabotage. Even so, Elara sensed Carmen still wrestled with guilt. In the reflection of the wards, her figure flickered slightly, as though she stepped between two uncertain paths.

Lucian, unaware of Carmen's approach, resumed a punishing rhythm against the dummy. He muttered something under his breath, curses about illusions and half-truths if Elara guessed right. When Carmen halted within a few paces, Lucian pivoted, blade raised as though expecting an enemy. Recognition flashed in his eyes, and he blew out a sharp breath.

"Looking for pity?" he asked, voice edged with bitterness. "Sorry if I disappoint you."

Carmen's posture stiffened. She twisted one hand around the small ring of warding keys that jangled at her hip. "I'm checking the wards. I meant no intrusion."

Elara winced at the tension crackling between them. She almost stepped forward to mediate, but instinct told her this was not her moment to speak. She slid back a little, half hidden by the column's shadow, torn between giving them privacy and wanting to know how two complicated hearts would converse.

Lucian tightened his grip on the sword's hilt. "If you're here to see me thrash a stuffed dummy, fine." His gaze flicked to the wards at the courtyard's edge. "But I doubt that helps you measure the wards."

The ring of keys in Carmen's hand rattled again. She swallowed. "I suspected you might be here," she admitted softly. "I know you're angry. More than angry."

He snorted. "That obvious?"

"Yes," she said, taking a careful step forward. "I understand if you resent me too. I resented Elara for so long, and I caused both of you more harm than I can repay." Her upper lip twitched as though anticipating his barbed reply. "I told you once I was... drawn to you." Her voice lowered, laced with quiet vulnerability. "But I assumed you saw that as another scheme to get ahead."

Lucian remained silent for a moment. His lowered sword glinted in the last golden rays of sunlight. Finally, he jammed it into the ground with a dull thud. "It's still confusing. Everything about this is." He shrugged, tension thick in his shoulders. "I devoted myself to protecting Caelum, especially after the illusions overtook him. Then Elara came along with her dreamweaver magic, changing everything. I..."

He trailed off, his gaze flicking into the distance. Elara's heart clenched. She feared he might name her directly, describing how their nights of shared research and tentative closeness had morphed into muddled feelings. She could almost feel the weight of guilt pressing on him. Even from several yards away, she recognized that swirl of contradictory longing in his eyes.

Carmen drew a shaky breath. "I can't claim to know half of what you've endured, but I see the strain eating at you." She bowed her head, the usual bright confidence in her posture dimmed. "And I'm not sure how to help. I only know I'd prefer real honesty to false alliances right now."

Lucian ran a hand through his dark hair, leaving it disheveled. "I don't want pity," he repeated, his voice softer but no less troubled. "I definitely don't need more illusions. The entire kingdom is drowning in them."

Carmen's eyes narrowed with shared frustration. "Malakar used me, used all of us, planting illusions everywhere. I was so blinded by envy that I..." She paused, swallowing the words. "I betrayed people I never meant to harm."

A bird fluttered along the courtyard ledge, then took flight, the sound of its wings punctuating the heavy silence. Lucian exhaled. He looked as though he might argue, but something in Carmen's expression, maybe a flicker of remorse, softened his stance. "The damage is done," he said quietly. "The best we can do is keep standing against the chaos Malakar left behind."

Carmen nodded, relief mingling with sorrow on her face. "Then do we... start fresh? As allies?"

A wry smirk curved the edge of Lucian's mouth. "That depends on whether you keep calling me a fool behind my back." His tone held a teasing edge that hinted at a shred of acceptance. "But perhaps we can try."

She flushed, letting out a small breath. "No harsh words, not anymore." She gestured to the battered dummy. "You have enough storms to fight without me throwing more insults."

They let the moment settle. Lucian glanced at the wards again, their faint glow dancing across his face. "We do have bigger battles," he conceded, voice low. "If illusions rebound or if Malakar tries something else, we need to be ready. I hate how intangible it all feels. I grew up believing swords could fix everything, but illusions slip through the blade." His gaze dropped. "And then there's... my own regret."

Carmen approached him slowly. "You're allowed regret," she said, her voice surprisingly gentle. "Everything changed the moment Caelum woke. We all have to find a new normal."

From her vantage behind the column, Elara pressed a hand to her racing heart. She knew she should return to Caelum, or at least slip away and give them space, yet she could not tear herself from their conversation. She sensed Lucian grappling with his jealousy, not only over Caelum's place in the monarchy, but also over Elara's affections. Guilt tangled inside her as she remembered the times she relied on Lucian during her darkest hours, the same hours that bound them in an odd closeness.

She felt a pang of regret that neither love nor loyalty could be this simple.

Lucian tried to speak but paused, uncertain how to frame his feelings. At last he lifted his gaze. "I look back at how you used to torment Elara. Part of me wants to remain furious with you." He inhaled. "But your honesty in the last few weeks, your willingness to stand beside us against illusions...it means more than you might guess."

Carmen looked momentarily struck by the sentiment. "I never expected forgiveness for everything I did," she admitted. "But I'll do whatever it takes to keep this kingdom from collapsing and to prove...maybe I'm not the same woman who schemed in the shadows."

Lucian's expression flickered with something like empathy. He studied her in silence long enough that

Elara's heart pounded in anticipation. The hush felt charged with possibility. Slowly, Lucian allowed a small, rumpled grin. "Maybe we both need to move past old resentments," he said. "We spend enough energy fighting illusions. We don't need to fight each other too." He glanced at Carmen, and for a moment the hardened suspicion in his eyes softened into something closer to understanding. He saw not only the rival who had once tormented Elara, but a woman fighting her own battles against Malakar's influence, wrestling with guilt and a desperate desire to atone. Perhaps, he mused, redemption deserved a chance, even for someone who had caused so much pain.

Carmen's posture relaxed as if an invisible weight slid off her shoulders. She offered him a nod, then gestured to the wards behind them. "I should reconfirm their strength. They're flickering in the western corner. Will you help me check?"

He glanced down at the sword still embedded in the dirt. He pulled it free and carefully placed it against the courtyard wall, letting the battered dummy remain as it was. "I'll come."

They turned together toward the perimeter, stepping beyond Elara's direct line of sight. The wards shimmered there, throwing faint glints across the stone walkway. Elara, breath caught in her throat, followed from a distance, her quiet footsteps masked by the rustle of leaves. She wanted to ensure no illusions lurked behind the hedges, and she could not ignore her curiosity about the growing tension between Lucian and Carmen.

Trailing carefully, she watched them walk side by side, soft conversation drifting through the air. She saw Carmen point at a small bronze amulet hanging from a bracket, and Lucian studied it as if checking for cracks. Sunlight now tinted gold by the late hour, lit Carmen's face. Her eyes shone with a dedication Elara rarely saw in her. Elara saw Lucian notice that detail too, his expression gentler than usual.

He removed his gloves and tipped the amulet into his palm, the wards swirling in response to his touch. Carmen watched, her lips curving into something close to a real smile. She murmured a question. He replied with an earnest nod. From the angle of his body and the turn of his face, Elara sensed his guarded walls had lowered. The dryness in his eyes had been replaced by genuine warmth.

Elara's heart ached with a blend of relief and bitter-sweet acceptance. Carmen no longer looked like the woman who once sneered across the guild workshop, and Lucian, long locked in guilt over Caelum's fate, seemed to find an unexpected kinship here. Elara saw the tension dissolve as they spoke.

Slowly, mindful not to interrupt, she stepped back. It was time to let them have this flicker of calm. If Lucian was beginning to notice Carmen's softer edges, that might help both of them heal. She swept her gaze across the courtyard, then turned toward the palace doors, a swirl of quiet emotion in her chest. By day's end, she realized, Lucian might discover a newfound admiration for the woman who had once been his enemy.

Elara felt a faint smile touch her lips. For all the illusions that plagued this kingdom, some truths ran deeper: people could change if they allowed themselves to see one another clearly. She let the hum of the wards guide her steps back toward the main corridor, leaving Lucian and Carmen to their shared duty and to something more meaningful than either had expected.

SEVENTEEN

Elara felt the cold weight of dread settle in her stomach the instant she heard the guards' frantic whispers. Word had arrived that Malakar, once lauded as the kingdom's resident miracle worker, had deserted his rooms without warning. He left behind not so much as a single personal chest, only a handful of scrolls decorated with twisting symbols that flickered under torchlight like trapped embers. His abrupt disappearance rattled every corner of the palace, and servants scuttled through corridors loaded with speculation. Some declared he had fled when he realized Prince Caelum was stronger than he had hoped, while others whispered, he pursued a new scheme to restore illusions now that Caelum's curse had weakened. The fractured rumors drummed against Elara's thoughts, each more unnerving than the last.

She barely had time to catch her breath before a messenger relayed the king's proclamation: there would be widespread searches for Malakar. Soldiers galloped off at daybreak to comb the city's main avenues and outlying farmland, and additional knights departed on horseback to check trade roads. Despite the flurry of activity, each search team returned that evening dazed and unsettled, reporting strange illusions that warped their paths. They spoke of roads twisting into thick forests that vanished when approached and of farmland where ghosts of cows flickered in and out of sight. As Elara made her way through the palace corridor, the frantic hush of voices and clanking armor kept her nerves on edge.

A part of her wanted to pretend she had never learned the name Malakar, never glimpsed the cunning behind his cultivated smile, yet she could not deny how deeply his illusions had tainted every layer of court and city life. She recalled the nights when illusions had crawled around Prince Caelum's slumber, and Malakar had feigned innocence. Now he was gone, leaving behind a swirl of suspicion that spread like an ink blot on parchment.

She passed a small group of guards exchanging dire updates near the fountain in the courtyard. They looked up at her approach, relief flickering in their eyes. They probably recognized her as the one who had helped awaken Caelum. Their expressions carried a tinge of hope but also desperation, for if Malakar had conjured illusions that sent men in circles, how long would it be before entire districts became prisons of fear?

As she stepped into the library's main hall, Lucian and Caelum waited off to one side. A basin of oil lamps lit the shelves, sending wavering shadows across centuries of records. Their faces confirmed all she had heard. Prince

Caelum leaned heavily against a table, his posture tense, yet he forced a faint smile when Elara joined them. Lucian stood close by, arms crossed, scanning the door as if expecting an enemy to burst in at any second.

"You heard the news?" Caelum asked, his voice warm but laced with concern.

Elara nodded and wiped her damp palms on her skirt. "The entire palace is whispering that nobody has a clue where Malakar has gone."

Lucian exhaled. "Searchers scoured half the roads leading out of the capital. They found illusions that tricked them into backtracking. A captain even reported glimpsing Malakar on a hillside, but when his archers approached, the figure dissolved like mist." He shook his head, face grim. "They suspect illusions can be cast over stores of supplies too. Some caravans vanished along farmland routes."

The mention of lost caravans sent a chill through Elara. "So, Malakar is free to sabotage the kingdom from the shadows. That's what we feared."

Any retort from Lucian died when Carmen slipped into the library, her footsteps halting inside the threshold. She wore a fitted tunic and a cloak drawn tight, as if warding off scrutiny. Though she had earned a measure of respect after helping break Caelum's curse, Elara sensed lingering tension in Carmen's movements. Yet Carmen came anyway, choosing to stand beside them at a narrow reading table stacked with a mountain of scrolls. Those were Malakar's remnants, salvaged from his deserted apartments.

"I gathered everything I could before the guards locked down his rooms," Carmen explained, her voice subdued. "It's not much. Most of his private papers have vanished, probably carried off with him. But a handful of coded writings remain."

Elara examined one scroll's edges, charred in places as though Malakar had tried to destroy it but left abruptly. Its surface teemed with odd shapes that coiled into each other in a pattern that made her eyes ache if she stared too long. Scribbled notes in the margin showed partial translations that Malakar must have attempted. She unrolled another parchment and winced as those same swirling sigils seemed to pulse with leftover magic. It felt unsettlingly alive.

Caelum cleared his throat. "We suspect these may detail illusions powerful enough to trap entire towns," he said, sliding a dusty sheet toward her. "Look at the corners. They mention dreamweaver nodes." His cheeks paled. "This matches some of the lore we uncovered before. Malakar wanted to expand illusions on a massive scale."

Her heart pounded as she scanned the lines. Many fragments described a weaving technique that harnessed communal fear to feed illusions. If Malakar had mastered it, he could strand entire provinces in endless nightmares, all without ever setting foot near them. As she rubbed the back of her neck, Elara felt how fragile the kingdom's morale was. She could taste the tension in the air.

"How do we stop illusions from a phantom we can't locate?" Lucian muttered, his gaze flicking up at Caelum.

"We can't even be sure whether these illusions are local or if Malakar has found new allies elsewhere."

"That's what we need to figure out," Caelum replied, setting a trembling hand over a tattered scroll. His brows drew into a worried line. "I only just woke, and the kingdom is already on the brink of a new crisis. I refuse to let him strike unchallenged. Not again."

The door creaked open, and a weary steward bowed and announced the king's latest edict: new patrol rotations at the outer gates, bigger escort units for merchant caravans, and a strict curfew after sundown. Elara's pulse tightened at the thought. Curfews would keep citizens locked away in their homes, fueling even more paranoia. She pictured an entire city cowering behind shuttered doors, illusions thrashing outside.

"Could Malakar be working with a faction beyond the city?" Carmen asked, once the steward departed. She smoothed her cloak over her arms, as though the library's lamplit warmth could barely touch her. "I recall him meeting travelers from the north, scribes from smaller courts...he might have been forging alliances in secret."

Elara's stomach twisted. "The question is, how do we outmaneuver illusions that can fold entire roads?" She stared at the scrawled glyph on the page before her. The lines looked jagged, as though capturing something vile. "If Malakar planned this, he must have left a clue in his notes. Perhaps it indicates an anchor or a focus for remote illusions."

Lucian reached over her shoulder to point at a recurring symbol: three spirals coiled inward. "I've seen that in earlier references to dreamweaver runes," he said quietly. "Mistress Imelda once said twisted coils sometimes appear in curses meant to bend entire landscapes. She told me illusions can tie themselves to emotional energy, like fear or suspicion. The bigger the fear, the more illusions can manifest from a distance."

Elara closed her eyes and inhaled slowly. Malakar had manipulated fear from the start, turning the city's discomfort into nightmares. She remembered how Caelum's coma had nearly consumed any hope for the monarchy. Now that the prince was awake, Malakar aimed to warp other corners of the kingdom instead. The notion that he might employ illusions to devour entire villages churned her gut. She opened her eyes again and mustered her resolve. "We'll need every guild and every ally we have," she said firmly. "If illusions can't be traced to a single location, we can still anchor wards in each district or at least warn people how illusions behave."

Caelum's lips curved into a grateful half smile, though tension remained in his eyes. "We can't sit idle. It doesn't matter if Malakar is physically here or lurking in some hidden fortress. The illusions are real, and people are vanishing. We must act."

A faint rustle of parchment drew their attention to Carmen, who had begun carefully sifting through the scattered notes. She pulled forth a page with smaller writing. "This line mentions corruption entwined with the monarchy's lineage," she said, her voice catching at the end. "I'm not sure what it means, but Malakar's margin notes indicate something about Caelum's bloodline powering illusions, possibly a leftover effect from the coma."

As Carmen spoke, Lucian felt a sudden, cold spike of irrational anger flare toward her: a vicious, unbidden thought that she might be withholding more, perhaps even still subtly aligned with Malakar. The intensity of it shocked him, so alien to his usual assessment of her recent efforts. He clenched his jaw and forced the ugly suspicion down, a muscle twitching in his cheek as he fought the unnatural wave of distrust. It receded as quickly as it came, leaving him inwardly shaken and frowning at the disturbing intrusion.

Caelum gripped the edge of the table. "So, he discovered more about my family than we realized." His voice wavered, but determination flickered in his eyes. "He is delusional if he thinks I'll stand aside while he exploits old secrets tied to my bloodline."

Lucian, recovered from his earlier bout of unexplained ire, stepped closer. "We'll disprove his illusions by exposing him. The question is, how do we gather enough evidence when half the kingdom still believes him a savior?"

Carmen's gaze dropped. "Some courtiers remain convinced he cured the prince. They keep calling him a hero. Now, with him gone, they sound certain he ventured off on a mission to rescue the kingdom again." She rubbed her brow with stiff fingers. "They do not see the illusions, or they think illusions serve some hidden purpose for the greater good."

Elara laid a hand on Carmen's wrist, offering silent

empathy. "The illusions feed on fear and ignorance. If Malakar's missing, he can let them run rampant while the courtiers bicker over whether he is a villain or a hero."

They fell silent. The library's lamps hissed, throwing flickers on the high shelves. Outside, the wind howled, and Elara could imagine illusions creeping through the gardens, twisting flowerbeds into shadow labyrinths, then dissolving before frightened eyes could confirm them.

"We must inform the king at once about these advanced illusions," Caelum said at last. "Father already sent out patrols, but they don't know how to handle illusions that vanish on contact. We need a strategy beyond swords and watchtowers."

Lucian gathered the scattered scrolls into a neat stack. "I'll coordinate with the knights, see if we can station them at key crossroads. We can lay down wards or chalk signs to help travelers recognize safe routes. If illusions try to alter the roads, people might notice mismatched markings."

Elara recalled how wards had once protected smaller corners of the palace from stray illusions. Though those wards required constant upkeep, they had saved lives. "We have to warn the guilds, too...not just blacksmiths. We might need every artisan to replicate wards citywide." She paused, remembering how Carmen had used illusions to help when she abandoned Malakar's side. "And we'll need illusions of our own to counter his, coordinated illusions anchored in honesty, not fear."

Carmen bowed her head, swallowing. "I can help." A hint of her old fire touched her tone. "I regret the times I aided him, but at least I know how illusions can be stitched across large areas. It's not enough. I realize I might face suspicion, but I refuse to stand aside after what he has done."

A reluctant smile tugged at Elara's lips. She was grateful for Carmen's shift in loyalty. "The city has room for every skilled mind it can hold, as far as I'm concerned. Malakar won't know where we'll strike if we unite. But we must spread word that illusions can no longer be dismissed as mere rumors."

Caelum pushed away from the table, though the tremor in his hand did not go unnoticed. "I'll speak with my father. He must give me leave to address the citizens directly. If we show them that illusions can be fought, fewer will succumb to panic." His gaze lingered on Elara, pride mingling with worry. "We managed to break illusions around my coma. We can do it again, for everyone."

She wished she felt as confident as she tried to appear. Her spool of thread at her hip buzzed softly, an echo of magic that reminded her how illusions had once consumed many. "We have to try. Malakar is counting on our fear to splinter us."

Outside, a rumble of thunder echoed, or it might have been the stamp of boots in the courtyard. Elara set her jaw. "Let us find these clues and share them with the King. We can approach Mistress Imelda, too. She might decipher a few runes that slip past us. We're missing pieces, but we will piece them together. Malakar may be out of sight, but his illusions still plague us."

Lucian pressed a hand to the hilt of his sword, as

though reassuring himself it remained at his side. "Agreed. We should start now. Soldiers are panicking. The commoners are confused. We need them calm and prepared, not frantic and trapped by illusions."

The four of them walked from the table to a smaller corner of the library where a battered chest waited. Inside lay more items left behind in Malakar's apartments: broken quills, half-finished maps, and a single leather-bound ledger missing entire pages. Elara swallowed her nerves and leafed through them, dread swelling in her chest. Each missing page teased that Malakar had secrets that extended far beyond empty pathways and farmland illusions. If he was forging alliances, they had to uncover them quickly. If illusions could devour farmland, caravans, and entire roads, they might soon swallow the entire kingdom's sense of what was real.

A muffled crash echoed from the corridor, making Elara jump. Carmen set a steady hand on her shoulder and offered a faint nod, signaling that it was only a passing guard tipping a stray box of old manuscripts. Even so, tension coiled around them, an unspoken certainty that illusions prowled beyond the palace walls. If caravans were missing and farm workers refused to tend fields haunted by ghostly duplicates, Malakar's reach was truly staggering.

They managed to glean a few more lines from Malakar's scribbled translations. Some mentioned "shackling dream realms" across great distances, and others implied that illusions could leech power from any lingering scraps of sorrow or resentment tied to Caelum's cursed years. The prince's hands trembled as he paused over those lines, letting the parchment curl inward.

"We should find a way to disprove these illusions," he said quietly. "If he means to blame my lineage for something, we must show the people that we stand with them."

Elara watched him square his shoulders and force steadiness into each breath. Waking him from that coma had been a triumph, but this new crisis threatened to test them all again. She touched his forearm, and he offered a faint, grateful nod.

They stood together, the four of them, listening to rain tap against the windows. The king, reeling from Malakar's flight, had ordered every messenger on alert, yet not a hint of the man's location had surfaced. Instead, illusions trailed every rumor, meant to disguise him or frighten away prying eyes. In the city below, suspicions festered, half the populace cursing Malakar's name, and the others hailing him as a misunderstood savior.

Caelum reached for the last scrawled glyph on the corner of a parchment, the lines wavering in the lamplight. He turned to Elara and Lucian, quiet resolve filling his gaze. "His illusions may be unstoppable unless we confront him directly. We all know the cost if we fail."

A hush settled. Elara nodded, her heart pounding with responsibility and determination. She remembered every phantom she had battled in Caelum's dreams, every frantic night she had spent keeping illusions from swallowing the light that remained in him. The king's best knights and the city's guilds might rally, but if Malakar was forging illusions from afar, the kingdom's nightmares were only beginning.

Lucian scanned the cryptic symbols, his knuckles white against the table's edge. "We exposed his treachery once, but that was only pulling back the curtain. He will strike harder now that he knows we stand united."

"And he is counting on our fear to let him roam freely," Carmen added, bitterness lacing her tone. "I will not let him keep twisting hearts as he twisted mine." At that, Caelum's mouth tightened. "Then we have no choice but to prepare for whatever final confrontation he engineers." He inhaled and braced himself. "No more illusions in the dark. No more hidden curses. We stand together this time, and the entire kingdom stands with us."

Elara turned from the page, the swirling glyph dancing in her mind's eye. "Yes," she managed softly, pressing a hand to her spool of shimmering thread. The time for half measures had passed. Every step from now on would lead them closer to the biggest battle illusions could conjure. Yet she refused to yield to panic. They had come this far, awakened a prince once lost to nightmares. They could face Malakar's illusions again.

She felt the swirl of anxiety and hope ripple through her. If Malakar attempted to bury entire cities in shifting illusions, they would push back with wards, dreamweaver defenses, and the unflagging resolve of a prince who refused to sleep even one more moment while his people suffered. The risk loomed vast and terrifying, an entire kingdom on the brink, but Elara did not shrink away. None of them did.

They parted from the library with urgent tasks. Lucian would organize new guard rotations, Carmen would assemble illusions designed to counter Malakar's trickery, and Caelum planned to inform his father of the newest revelations. Elara lingered a moment longer, picking up the last scrawled glyph Malakar had abandoned. She traced the lines with her fingertip and felt an odd pulse of magic spark against her skin. A storm of illusions threatened to consume the land, and Malakar might be out there weaving nightmares for them all.

Her pulse pumped faster, but she steadied it. Whether she was a seamstress or the kingdom's only dreamweaver, her role was clear. She would stand by Caelum's side and help shield people from the illusions that threatened reality.

When she joined the others in the corridor, each face told the same story: this crisis was growing, fueled by fear, illusions, and Malakar's manipulations. They knew exposing Malakar's treason was only the first step, and a final confrontation loomed on the horizon, a storm they must brave together if they dared to save the kingdom from illusions that threatened to devour reality itself.

EIGHTEEN

Elara folded her arms as she stepped into the palace's main corridor. The tapestries hung motionless, but the silence felt ominous. News of Malakar's misdeeds had spread swiftly through the city. Day by day, more frightened citizens came to the palace gates, pleading for guidance or relief. Illusions haunted the poorest alleys and the richest mansions, leaving no corner safe. Stories circulated of peasants seeing hungry apparitions in their barns, and of nobles waking at night to find ghostly shapes creeping along their bedchambers.

She could almost taste the fear as she walked toward a small antechamber near the throne room. Two young maids huddled near a side table, sharing rumors that Malakar had learned to slip nightmares directly into people's minds. At her approach, they fell silent. Elara heard them whisper her name as they hurried away. She wished she had comforting words, but all she could offer was a weary nod. She, too, felt the suffocating tension that thickened the castle air.

When she entered the antechamber, she found Prince Caelum at one of the windows. He spoke in low tones to a steward and leaned against the stone sill. Every step he took these days was deliberate, as if he had to measure his energy. Still, he insisted on seeing the guild leaders and sending messengers. His daily reemergence, although exhausting for him, brought hope to those who had once believed him lost forever. In the pale morning light, his hair looked almost bronze, and the dark circles beneath his eyes contrasted with the regal lines of his face.

The steward bowed when he saw Elara, then slipped away. Caelum turned to greet her, posture calm but drained of the easy vitality that once defined him. Determination shone in his eyes, a look she had come to know well. He offered his hand, inviting her to stand beside him at the window.

"How are you?" he asked, his voice subdued. He searched her face for signs of strain.

Elara forced a small smile. "Not half as tired as you must be," she murmured. "But I am keeping busy. The guild leaders have started giving me quiet invitations to speak in private. They trust you, but Malakar's illusions have driven them to desperation, and they want reassurance from anyone who seems to understand dream-borne threats."

She had been at the center of a flurry of secret talks during the last few days. As Malakar's illusions adopted bolder shapes and sharper edges, fear gnawed at every corner of the realm. Merchants refused to transport goods at night. Farmers abandoned fields after sunset, and city watchmen could do little when intangible nightmares threw entire streets into chaos. Elara's dreamweaver abilities offered the hope people needed, yet the weight of their expectations pressed at her temples whenever she closed her eyes.

"Any success in holding everyone together?" Caelum asked softly.

"If chatter alone can hold them, yes," Elara replied. "But they are terrified. Each time a rumor of wraiths in a barn circles back, someone claims it as proof that illusions have gained physical form. They are uncertain where to pin their frustration, and some blame the monarchy for not crushing Malakar's schemes sooner."

Caelum's jaw tightened. She knew he blamed himself more than anyone else. Although he had only recently awakened, he still carried the burden of having been the cursed heir who slept haunted for years. His eyes flickered with regret, then he drew a measured breath. "We will address them all soon," he said, his voice resolute. "Together."

She nodded. "Lucian has been pacing the castle halls for hours, too. He says illusions could lurk behind every column from here to the outer wings. Carmen was with him earlier, checking wards in the corridors, and I believe they are trying to reassure the guards by telling them that illusions feed on fear more than anything else." A wry smile curved Elara's lips. "This entire place feels ready to combust."

Caelum straightened. "We need to keep each faction from splintering. When the blacksmiths and scholars stand behind us, others will follow."

Elara touched his forearm in a gentle gesture of agreement. "You should rest more, though. You look pale."

"I can spare my strength for a few more days," he replied. "Once illusions grip a city, half the harm lies in the panic that follows."

They spent another moment in silence until the clang of a distant bell signaled the start of a meeting. Elara helped Caelum navigate the passage toward a set of broad double doors. Servants waited with thick torches, making sure every corner was lit, as if to repel any illusions. The smell of melted wax hung in the air and mingled with the tang of old stone.

Inside the meeting chamber, tension hit at once. Several guild representatives had gathered around a long table strewn with worn ledgers and torn scrolls. The blacksmith Roderick stood near the head, arms crossed, a scowl etched into his features. Carmen leaned against a side pillar, her expression guarded. Lucian hovered beside her, arms folded, scanning the room as if he expected a spectral form to appear at any moment.

Caelum entered with Elara at his side. The attendees bowed in cautious reverence, yet energy crackled in the air. No one was calm. They were tired, on edge, and hungry for reassurances no one could fully give.

Roderick wasted no time. He planted his hands on the tabletop. "Malakar roams freely, or so it seems," he said, his voice gravelly. "You have heard the stories. Farmers in my district speak of illusions that drive their animals into stampedes. It might not be a physical blade, but folks have been trampled all the same."

A murmur of agreement rippled through the group. A young scholar raised a shaky hand. "We have tried to overlay anti-illusion sigils in some alleyways," she said, adjusting her small spectacles. "In the morning, residents report that illusions detour around the wards. It is as if Malakar's illusions can shift with ease."

Lucian exchanged a look with Carmen and said, "We have been marking safe zones within the palace, but we cannot replicate that in every district without more ward crafters. Skilled blacksmiths are forging protective amulets, but we lack resources for the entire populace. Each day the illusions grow. They flicker in broad daylight." His voice held quiet fury.

A blacksmith's apprentice slammed a hand on the table. "Tell us, Your Highness," he demanded, looking at Caelum. "How can illusions create injuries that feel real? Are we not told illusions are intangible, nothing more than shadows?"

From the back, a usually quiet weaver, a woman known for her placid nature, cried out, "It's a trick! He's still cursed! Malakar was right to keep him contained!" Her voice was shrill, laced with venom that startled every-one. A moment later, her face crumpled in confusion, her hands flying to her mouth as if horrified by her own outburst. She sank back, trembling, as whispers of shock rippled through the attendees. Elara felt a cold dread. That sudden, uncharacteristic fury felt chillingly familiar, like the strings Malakar had pulled before.

Lucian watched the weaver collapse back into her seat, her face pale with shock at her own words. A jolt went through him. Cold recognition. He remembered the library, analyzing Malakar's notes, and the sudden, inexplicable flare of rage he'd felt toward Carmen. It had been sharp, ugly, and wrong. He had dismissed it as stress, but seeing the same unnatural discord sown here, twisting a peaceful woman into spewing hatred...he understood now. It was Malakar's touch, a subtle poison dripped into the cracks of fear and suspicion. He met Carmen's gaze across the tense room, a flicker of apology in his eyes for the doubt the sorcerer had tried to plant within him.

All eyes shifted to Caelum, whose face seemed whiter in the lamplight. He gripped the back of a chair for support and inhaled carefully before speaking. "Illusions themselves might not be solid," he said, "but fear leads people to react as if they are. A horse spooked by a stirring shadow might bolt into a crowd. Someone running from a wraith in their home might trip in panic. Chaos itself becomes lethal, even if the illusions never physically lay a hand on you."

A hush fell. Caelum's words were calm, and a flash of sympathy passed over Roderick's rugged features. The blacksmith might have been rough in manner, but seeing the prince standing before them, still weak from the years stolen by Malakar, softened his anger.

"Sir Roderick, I understand your frustration," Caelum continued. "I have watched illusions nearly consume my own mind. I will not let them devour this kingdom. But we cannot rely on a single measure to hold Malakar at bay. We need everyone's craft, every guild's strength." His eyes traveled the room. "Blacksmith forging, scholar sigils, seamstress wards, the watchmen's vigilance, all together."

The blacksmith apprentice glared a moment longer, then unclenched his fists. "We can craft a protective lattice," he muttered, sounding a bit more mollified. "Metal frames hammered with runic lines that might interfere with illusions crossing thresholds. It will take time and labor."

The scholar who had spoken earlier gave a decisive nod. "Scholars can draft new anti-illusion sigils if we combine references from older texts. We simply need time to refine them, and supplies for the inks that can hold enchantments."

At that, Carmen tilted her head, her dark curls shimmering in the torchlight. "The seamstresses still have stockpiles of resistant thread. We can embroider wards directly into the edges of cloaks, banners, and possibly even gloves for commoners. Once our spinners and weavers join the cause, we can help. People need to trust us again."

A low hum of agreement swelled among the guild leaders. Despite the tension, Elara felt a simmer of unity forming, as if each craft recognized it could not fight illusions alone. In the shadows near the door, Lucian quietly exhaled in relief, while Roderick pressed his hand firmly on the table again.

"All right," Roderick said, his tone gruff yet calmer. "If

we combine efforts, perhaps Malakar will find less space to exploit our fears. It is time we show him we are not cowering in the dark."

An echo of cheers and murmured approval spread through the chamber, though worry lingered in many eyes. Elara breathed easier. This was the alliance she and Caelum had hoped to forge. Looking at the prince, she saw the faintest trace of color return to his cheeks, as if the room's renewed energy fed his spirit.

Someone closed the meeting with final notes on forging the protective lattice and distributing ward materials. The blacksmiths would coordinate with the seamstresses for the right threads, and the scholars would share new sigil designs with the palace scribes. The quiet vow spilling from each corner was that they would all do their part to stifle these nightmares.

Elara helped Caelum dismiss everyone. Many bowed in respect before filing into the corridors. Outside, the wind seemed to pick up, rattling the old windows. She caught glimpses of anxious faces but also saw a few stewards exchanging grateful nods that the monarchy was taking control.

At her elbow, Carmen cleared her throat. "You realize," she said, voice low, "Malakar will strike back at the first hint of defiance. He feeds on fear. People are banding together, yes, but if illusions spike again, that unity might crumble overnight."

Elara nodded. "I know. But this time, we are not alone."

Lucian approached them, arms still folded. He gave a

hesitant smile in Carmen's direction, then rested a hand on the hilt of his sword. "I will patrol the corridors again this evening and ensure no illusions slip inside. The more we prepare, the less Malakar can do on short notice."

"Thank you, Lucian," Caelum said quietly, stepping close enough to squeeze Lucian's shoulder in gratitude. Elara felt a pang of warmth at the renewed understanding between them. Though tensions had once run high, they seemed more aligned now than ever before, each man determined to safeguard the kingdom no matter the cost.

A distant rumble echoed above the castle. Thunder. Outside, the sky had darkened with thick clouds threatening rain. Elara thought of the many city streets under those clouds, the flickering lanterns that might not hold back illusions creeping along the walls. She caught Caelum's gaze once more and saw a trace of exhaustion etched there.

"Let us go back to the main hall," she suggested gently. "We cannot solve everything in a single night, and you need to sit for a while."

He gave a small nod. "Only for a moment," he said. "Then I must send word to the blacksmith forges, ensuring they stay supplied."

She guided him out of the chamber, Carmen and Lucian following at a measured pace. The corridor's torchlight flickered with each breath of wind outside, and every step under those shifting shadows reminded Elara how Malakar's illusions could sneak past the fortress of hope they had begun to construct.

Trudging through the winding hallway, they reached

the main hall, where a few courtiers still lingered, exchanging rumors and updates with frantic intensity. Caelum's arrival silenced them at once. He walked with careful dignity, refusing to let fatigue show any more than it already did. Elara walked at his side, hands clasped behind her back in an effort to channel a sense of composure.

One of the courtiers, an older woman with braided hair, approached with urgent eyes. "Highness," she pleaded, "we hear that illusions are already lurking near the southwestern gate, scaring off the merchant wagons. Will you address it?"

Caelum offered her a reassuring dip of his head. "My guards will investigate. Remain calm. We are forging new wards and illusions to counter these nightmares. I promise we will do everything possible to protect you."

The woman bowed, tears shining in her eyes, then darted away. Elara felt a tightening in her chest: these people were placing their hope entirely in Caelum, in her, and in all the guilds. Even Carmen's posture stiffened, as though she, too, felt the weight of that responsibility. A guard beckoned from the far side of the hall, holding a stack of new dispatches. Caelum drifted to speak with him while Carmen and Lucian stepped aside, murmuring quiet strategies about patrolling the southwestern gate.

Elara stood briefly and still, letting the swirl of voices fade to a dull buzz in her ears. She could almost sense Malakar's presence like a coiled snake in the rafters, even though he was nowhere near the palace, or so they presumed. He might be hidden somewhere far beyond the city walls, conjuring illusions in secret. The thought sent a chill up her spine. From the start, illusions had specialized in exploiting weakness, and fear was the kingdom's greatest weakness right now.

She swallowed hard and glanced at Caelum. He braced himself against a column while a guard hurried him through another round of messages. Even from across the hall, she saw the feverish gleam in his gaze, a fierce resolve to face whatever came next. She remembered how he had once been so close to losing everything in that cursed sleep. Now he stood here, battered but defiant.

Outside, the sky thundered again. A flash of lightning lit the stained-glass windows in bright fragments of color, momentarily painting the floor in vibrant hues. Elara's pulse kicked faster. The city was on edge, illusions had grown monstrous, guild members were frantic, and any sign of fracturing could let Malakar's nightmarish intrusions unravel them all.

When Caelum finished with the guard, he paused to steady his breath. He spotted Elara and made his way over, each footstep measured. His lips curved into the faintest smile, warm yet determined. "It will be all right," he said, almost as if he were telling himself as much as he was telling her.

Elara inhaled and clasped her trembling hands to hide the nervous quiver. "I believe you," she whispered, and in that moment, she realized how tightly a fragile alliance of guilds, dreams, and a newly awakened prince held their fractured kingdom together.

Somewhere above, thunder echoed more fiercely, a

herald of storm clouds gathering over the palace. Carnage might have lurked beyond the horizon, but they had no choice except to prepare and hope. Elara turned her gaze to the tall windows, feeling the rumble pass through the floors, and she thought of how illusions could twist a simple storm into citywide dread if people let fear guide them.

Carmen and Lucian moved closer. Carmen offered a timid grin, a silent reminder that even a former rival could stand side by side with them when darkness gathered. Lucian placed a protective hand on the hilt of his sword, jaw tight with guarded determination. A faint thread of solidarity bound them all together, and Elara clung to that thread like a lifeline.

The meeting had ended, the plan was set, and the guilds were resolved to act. Yet it felt like the calm before a deeper battle, one in which illusions could tip the entire realm into pandemonium. Crashes of thunder reverberated outside, matching the tension that gripped the halls.

Standing close to Caelum, Elara breathed in the faint scent of ink and parchment that clung to his doublet. He was exhausted, but she sensed strength in him. He had faced nightmares that devoured his mind for years, and now he was determined to save everyone else from a similar fate. She exhaled slowly, longing for a gentler world where illusions did not run rampant.

As thunder rumbled over the battlements, Elara glanced at Caelum's pale face, her heart clenching with equal parts admiration and dread. She knew that any slip in their newly formed unity would be exploited by Malakar's monstrous deceptions.

CHAPTER

NINETEEN

Elara pressed the back of her hand to her forehead, blinking away flickers of fatigue that threatened to cloud her vision. The warehouse still smelled faintly of smoldering tallow and old burlap, relics of another busy evening in the workshop district. Long bolts of cloth lay piled in towering stacks, half embroidered with protective sigils that looked strange under the glow of a few guttering lanterns. Every corner bustled with motion. Seamstresses huddled in small knots around low tables, swiftly stitching ward designs into cloaks and banners. Though the night was deep, energy crackled through the space like a pulse of nervous excitement.

She pivoted on her heel and gestured for one of the junior seamstresses to pass her the spool of shimmering thread. The spool felt too warm in her hand. Weeks earlier she might have taken comfort in the gentle glow of her dreamweaver spool, but tonight the constant call to craft illusions felt like a burden. Everyone wanted reassurance.

Every guildhouse demanded more cloth wards and more illusions to chase away the nightmares haunting the city's corners. Elara felt the strain digging into her bones.

Carmen's voice rose above the clamor, clear and authoritative. "Spread out. Pair off if you can. Each set of hands should share a single pattern, so nobody loses pace." She stood near a makeshift dais at the center of the warehouse, her dark curls shining in the lamplight. She wore a determined expression that lent her features a new sense of purpose. Gone was the familiar sneer or flicker of jealousy. These days Carmen's ambition had found a more honorable outlet, rallying the seamstresses to stand against Malakar's illusions.

Elara had to admit it: Carmen directed the operation with impressive skill. She knew exactly which seamstress specialized in borders, who excelled at runic motifs, and who could track commissions from the blacksmiths or scholars. Every time a newly recruited seamstress faltered at the thought of illusions, Carmen was there with a firm word of encouragement or a reminder that Prince Caelum himself had awakened and was counting on them. The mention of his name often sparked fresh determination in the exhausted workers.

At one long table, three seamstresses were meticulously testing rows of stitches loaded with faint glimmers of warding sigils. Elara paused beside them and checked that the lines of thread aligned with the runic shapes Mistress Imelda had taught her. The patterns were correct, slightly crooked with fatigue. The younger woman's eyes were sunken from endless hours of stitching. Elara pulled a wooden stool closer, then leaned down and pointed at their embroidery. "Good work so far. Be sure to keep your tension even. The wards become stronger when every stitch is consistent."

One of them, a girl named Roselle, managed a thin-lipped smile. "We will. Does it...help if we keep the lines straight?" her voice trembled. "I overheard some folks saying illusions can twist wards no matter how neatly we sew."

Elara rested a reassuring hand on Roselle's shoulder. "Illusions feed on panic. A well-formed ward forces them to spend more energy fighting the pattern. It won't stop everything, but it weakens the illusions enough for the city's watchers or the blacksmith wards to finish the job."

Roselle nodded, her hand tightening around her threaded needle, and she returned to her task. Another seamstress, eyes rimmed red, carefully repositioned her spool.

At the back of the warehouse, Roderick towered over a trio of blacksmith apprentices. A loud clang reverberated through the space when he tested a newly forged locket by pressing it against a small illusion draped across a crate. The illusion flickered like a half-snuffed flame, then dissolved on contact. The apprentices whooped in triumph, and Roderick gave a brusque nod of approval.

"That's a third success," he announced in his gravelly voice, running a thick hand across his beard. A hint of relief softened his features. He turned to Elara and Carmen. "We might have a workable design. This metal holds the runic lines well enough that illusions can't stand up to direct contact."

Carmen stepped down from her makeshift dais and approached him. "Master Roderick, if we can replicate enough of these lockets, we can start distributing them outside the city center." She glanced at Elara. "We'll need to coordinate with the seamstresses and make sure each new piece is embroidered with the insignia that matches your spool's resonance." She fixed Elara with a pointed look. "That final touch is supposed to help them ward off illusions more effectively."

Elara nodded. Her spool glowed faintly in her hands, and she felt a weary ache spread from her fingertips to her shoulders. "If we want the lockets fully charged, I can weave a minor dream-thread across the wards, but I'll need help from one or two others. My strength is...not endless." She smiled shyly at Roderick. He had always intimidated her, but now she sensed no judgment from him, only a practical acceptance that her magic helped keep illusions at bay.

He eyed the faint circles under her eyes. "Understood," he said curtly. "We'll handle the forging, you handle that fancy thread. Let me know if you need more breaks or if the illusions get too strong."

She offered a grateful nod, then turned as her name was called from across the warehouse.

Lucian stood at the entrance, his broad frame outlined by a single torch set in a bracket on the wall. He scanned the bustle, looking for her. He wore a well-fitting guard's tunic embroidered with a few runic sigils, small wards that might have come from the same spool in Elara's hand. The sight of him brought a warm flicker to her chest, but it also reminded her of the confusion stirred by his unwavering presence these past nights. Whenever she looked at him, she recalled the hours they had spent in hushed corners of the castle library, rummaging through forbidden texts. She remembered how often he chased away illusions at the palace perimeter, never once yielding to fear. She also replayed moments when his quiet gaze lingered on her too long, telling her how he felt, though the words never left his mouth.

"Are you all right?" he asked gently as he approached. His voice held more worry than reproach. "You've been at this for hours. I thought you were going to pace yourself."

Elara tried to summon a confident smile, but it wavered. "I wanted to check on everyone's progress. The wards won't stitch themselves, and if we can't keep illusions away from the supply caravans, we'll run out of basic materials next week."

Lucian exhaled, glancing around at the frantic pace. "And what about you? If you burn out, it won't help any of them."

Before she could respond, Carmen hailed them both, gesturing for them to join her near the dais. Elara gave Lucian a small shrug and moved to where Carmen stood, addressing a group of seamstresses who had paused their embroidery. The women exchanged exhausted looks, so Carmen spoke in a tone she rarely used before these troubles began: gentle empathy.

"You have all worked tirelessly," she told the seamstresses. "And I know how tempting it is to push through, ignoring aches and hunger. But if we keep pushing on empty, we will end up collapsed. We are meeting with Caelum soon, and we need to show him we are strong enough to keep going, not that we are on the verge of keeling over." She glanced at Elara, then back at the gathered seamstresses. "Thirty minutes. Find a corner, eat, drink something. After that, if you are still feeling faint, speak up. We have to pace ourselves because the illusions will not stop if we do."

Some flicker of admiration stirred in Elara's heart. Carmen's transformation from bitter rival to a commanding, organized leader felt almost as miraculous as Caelum's awakening. That reminder made Elara's thoughts drift toward him. Though he had told her he would rest at the castle, he insisted on visiting each guild in person to express his gratitude. She could see how it boosted everyone's morale, but it also worried her. Last night, he nearly collapsed while trying to speak to a district gathering. The memory twisted her chest.

A clamoring of voices echoed toward them, and a group of dyed fabri merchants bustled in, carrying fresh bolts of linen. They looked wary, as if illusions might leap out at them from behind the crates. One of the older men approached Elara, doffing a worn cap. "Beg pardon, Mistress Elara," he said. "We've brought supplies as requested. Are...are these wards enough to keep us safe going back to the docks? There's talk that illusions spin up extra strong after midnight."

Elara steadied her shoulders. "You will need one of the

new lockets from Roderick's forge. And if you can keep calm, illusions are less likely to hold you hostage. I'll have a seamstress anchor a quick ward into your cloak. It's not foolproof, but it helps."

The merchant bowed his head gratefully before hurrying off to ask for Carmen's directions. Elara sighed and rubbed her eyes. Each new wave of anxious visitors required reassurance. Anxiety had become a suffocating presence throughout the city. Some nights, illusions of swirling shapes or phantom cries rattled entire neighborhoods, leaving people trembling at dawn.

She felt a nudge at her elbow. Lucian handed her a small tin cup. Steam rose from the surface, carrying the pungent aroma of herbs. "Mistress Imelda's blend," he said softly. "Tastes bitter, but it should help keep you upright. Drink."

She caught a faint quiver in his voice. Perhaps it was only the warehouse clamor, but she thought she heard genuine concern. "Thank you," she murmured, wrapping her hands around the warm cup. She sipped, wincing at the sharp tang. The brew made her eyes water, but she already felt the edges of her fatigue lift. She wondered if it was truly the herbs or the comforting presence at her side.

A few steps away, Carmen directed new arrivals to vacant seats, showing them how to replicate the simplest ward lines. Under Carmen's guidance, the seamstresses who once cared only for coin or prestige now bent over cloth with resolute focus. Elara found a brief satisfaction in seeing them unify. Malakar had once exploited vanity and fear, preying on them to strengthen illusions. Now that they had discovered their own power to push back, they worked with a fervor that rivaled the illusions themselves.

A distant clatter at the warehouse entrance made everyone pause. The door swung open, revealing Prince Caelum, taller than Elara remembered from the day before, though that might have been her wishful thinking. He wore a subdued cloak embroidered with a handful of wards. A watchful guard hovered behind him. Caelum's breathing looked shallow as he stepped over the threshold, scanning the scene. Even from across the room, Elara noticed a slight tremor in his hand, but a glow in his eyes countered it. Around them, hushed whispers rippled: the prince was here in person.

He raised a hand, beckoning people to resume their work. "I do not wish to interrupt," he called, "but I had to see the progress myself. Regardless of how exhausted you all must be, you stand firm, and I...I thank you." The last words came out breathy but sincere. He attempted another step forward. His legs shook. The guard hurried to his side.

Elara gave Lucian a quick nod and set her cup aside. He positioned himself to help if the prince faltered. Caelum reached the central aisle, and murmurs of respect followed him. Seamstresses who once might have avoided royal eyes stood in direct awe of him now.

He turned slowly, acknowledging each cluster of workers with a regal nod. "Your wards, illusions, and forging efforts are saving lives. I cannot express how much that means for the future of this kingdom."

Elara's heart squeezed as she watched him try to maintain composure. If she had not known him so well, from the dream realm and the nights of wrestling illusions, she might have been fooled. But she saw a faint grayness along his cheekbones and heard the suppressed hitch in his breathing. Everyone else seemed uplifted by his presence. She felt compelled to step closer, ready to catch him if he faltered. Her spool of thread hummed in sympathy at her hip as if echoing her concern.

Carmen approached him first, offering a respectful dip of her head. "Your Highness, we didn't expect you tonight. We could have brought any updates to you tomorrow."

He gave her a faint smile. "I trust your abilities, Carmen, but the people deserve to see more than reports. They deserve to know that we stand with them, no matter how dire the illusions become." He breathed in, and his shoulders trembled. Then he added softly, "Your leadership here has been admirable."

Carmen's eyes shone for an instant, perhaps with gratitude or a deeper, more complicated emotion. Elara suspected Carmen rarely heard praise for anything except her beauty or cunning. Yet now Carmen had a chance to use both for good, and the monarchy recognized it. The tension among them all seemed replaced by something more hopeful.

Still, Caelum's cheek twitched with the effort to keep standing. Elara moved to his side and slipped her hand beneath his elbow. She felt momentary stiffness in his arm, then his muscles relaxed. He turned his gaze to her, relief flashing in his eyes.

"You see, Elara," he said in a hushed tone only she could hear, "I told you I would visit. But perhaps I should have paced myself better, yes?"

She let out a small, worried laugh. "Yes, my prince." He blushed. She added, softer this time, "You're pushing too hard. The illusions might not come for your dream again, but your body is still healing."

He gave a rueful nod, glancing at the seamstresses, blacksmiths, and scholars working in frantic unison around them. "Maybe so. But they push themselves just as hard. I want them to know I share that burden."

Before she could protest further, he turned to address the newly arrived blacksmith apprentices, praising their lockets. Roderick hovered in the background, arms crossed over his broad chest. His normally impassive face glowed with satisfaction at the acknowledgment. Meanwhile, groups of seamstresses grinned at one another, whispers swirling about the prince's unexpected appearance and how it bolstered their determination to keep illusions at bay.

Only a short while later, Elara felt Caelum's weight shift more heavily onto her arm, and she realized he was moments from collapsing. He caught her concerned look and exhaled slowly. "All right," he admitted, forcing a thin smile. "Perhaps we can be done for tonight."

A wave of murmured disappointment spread. Nobody wanted to see him go, but no one voiced it. Lucian signaled that he would help escort Caelum back to the palace. As they walked him to the door, Carmen gave Elara a subtle nod and stepped forward to reassure the still workers. She launched into calm instructions about finishing the current batch of wards before morning. The synergy between them and the blacksmiths continued within the warehouse even after Caelum slipped outside with Lucian and Elara.

Outside, the evening breeze felt cool against Elara's flushed cheeks. Lucian supported Caelum on the other side, letting him catch a steadier breath. The prince tried to straighten, and a flicker of pride lit his face. "Thank you, truly," he said, voice raspy. "I'm thankful you're both here."

"Of course," Elara replied softly. She meant it. Every day she found new resolve in him, even as her exhaustion grew.

They walked a few steps away from the warehouse door, where a small carriage waited. The two men conferred about the best route back to the palace. Elara lingered for a beat on the threshold, the faint hum of voices drifting from inside like an undercurrent of hope. She knew she would return soon to the workshop. The city's illusions would not relent, and neither could she.

After ensuring Caelum was settled on the carriage bench, Elara called a quick farewell. She would remain at the warehouse for another hour or two to finalize the wards that needed her spool's magic. Even if her bones ached, she had little choice. She refused to let down all those who looked at her illusions for protection.

She reentered the warehouse to find the seamstresses forming new circles, sipping water, or nibbling on scraps of bread Carmen had procured. Roderick kept watch near the forging station, and a few blacksmith apprentices hammered softly in the background. The scholars hunched over cramped desks, frowning at runic scripts by lanternlight. Through every corridor, people looked anxious, yet inspired by Caelum's brief visit.

Elara retraced her steps to the low stool she had abandoned earlier. She lowered herself onto it. The spool dug into her hip, and she stifled a groan. Her entire body throbbed with fatigue. The pungent brew she had sipped earlier lingered on her tongue, promising temporary relief if not lasting comfort. She closed her eyes for a moment and let the swirl of activity fade from her senses. Her spool of shimmering thread rested in her palm like a small, persistent heartbeat.

CHAPTER

TWENTY

Carmen urged her horse over the final crest of the muddy road, scanning the distant sprawl of farmland with wary eyes. The early morning light had given way to a dreary, overcast afternoon, and the thick clouds overhead threatened another downpour. She could almost taste the tension in the air. It was as though the land itself braced for the illusions lurking just beyond sight.

Lucian rode beside her, sword sheathed at his hip. He was a silent presence for most of the journey, keeping an attentive watch on the periphery of the fields. Whenever they passed a cluster of tilled earth or half-toppled fences, he slowed, scanning the horizon for any flicker betraying a phantom's outline.

They had come at Prince Caelum's request. The outskirts of the kingdom's farmland, vital to the people's survival, had been besieged for days by terrifying illusions that prowled through barns and across fields at night. The illusions did not strike in a physical sense, but they unraveled the nerves of anyone who glimpsed them. More troubling, the illusions spooked livestock, often driving the beasts into crazed stampedes. The farmhands, desperate to intervene, grew prone to accidents, trampled underfoot as they tried to halt the chaos.

Carmen nudged her horse closer to Lucian's. "I see a barn up ahead," she said. She pointed toward a structure that leaned slightly, its walls pocked with old planks. Though the sun hovered low, long shadows crept around them, lengthening across mashed patches of mud. "We should start there."

He nodded and steered his mount toward the barn. When they reached it, a handful of farm workers scurried out, eyes wild. A middle-aged woman with a frayed shawl grabbed Carmen's stirrup in frantic appeal. "Please," the woman begged, her voice strained. "Inside the barn...it quakes. We heard howls that turned the horses mad. Two stable boys were nearly crushed when the animals bolted."

Lucian dismounted first, extending an arm to help Carmen down. He murmured to the woman, "We will handle it. See if you can gather the others at a safe distance, and keep them calm."

While Lucian soothed the farm workers, Carmen advanced toward the barn entrance. Her heart sped at the faint, pulsing hush in the air. She knew illusions were intangible constructs spun from fear and twisted magic, yet crossing that threshold still sent a wave of cold prickles across her skin. She gripped a spool of ordinary thread she carried for basic illusions, leftover scraps from

Elara's dreamweaver craft. Although Elara's conjurations glowed with deeper resonance, Carmen had practiced enough under the young seamstress's tutelage to weave simple illusion-dampening spells, and she prayed they would suffice.

She slipped inside. Straw littered the ground, and in the gloom shapes seemed to twist just beyond her peripheral vision. The rafters overhead were thick with cobwebs. She inhaled and calmed her racing pulse. "It's just fear," she told herself under her breath. "No illusion can harm you unless you let it feed on panic."

A glide of shadow flicked across one rafter. She stiffened. The shape resolved into a dark swirl, like a serpent coiled in midair, trailing along the wood. It had no physical body, yet its presence throbbed like a living thing. The nearest horse, stomping in a stall, jerked with violent force, white showing at the corners of its eyes. Dread swelled, but she set her jaw and raised her spool. She traced a small pattern in the air and whispered a short incantation gleaned from nights of study with Elara. A faint shimmer rippled from the thread and drifted upward.

The swirl above huddled in on itself, flickering and growing less distinct. Then it popped out of sight in a quick burst, leaving only drifting motes of gloom. Carmen exhaled in relief. It was not a perfect fix. She lacked the sharper edge of dreamweaver magic, but it was enough to banish lesser illusions or at least weaken them. Nose wrinkling at the smell of manure and musty straw, she turned to check the rest of the barn.

A squeal erupted from the far side. One of the smaller farmhands, no older than fourteen, ran toward her, wide-eyed. "The illusions got into the next stall," he cried, pointing with shaking hands. "I th-thought I saw a giant dog or something."

Lucian stepped in, placing himself between the boy and any lurking phantom. The gloom parted slightly, revealing a flicker of a trembling shadow dancing near the stall door. Carmen narrowed her eyes, advanced, and repeated her basic ward. Each swirl threatened to coalesce into a monstrous snout or claws, but they dissipated once she poured more concentration into the illusions she controlled. Another horse let out a terrified whinny, kicking the side of the stall so hard a plank gave way, splintering near the floor.

"Easy," Lucian muttered, planting himself by the riled animal. He kept an even tone, though tension cut across his shoulders. "We must get these farmhands out of here."

Carmen signaled to the nearest worker, guiding them to lead any spooked horse outside. She walked the length of the barn, weaving small illusions at intervals. She curbed the stronger pockets of phantom shapes, though sweat gathered at her brow. She had not yet fully mastered the technique, and the more illusions she dispelled, the heavier the weight behind her eyes felt. By the time she and Lucian coaxed the final stable boys to safety, the barn had quieted. Some phantom traces still lingered in corners, flickers that might reappear by night-fall, yet their immediate threat was quelled.

They spent the rest of the day traversing nearby farmland, riding through drifts of cold drizzle. Word spread that two travelers bearing wards had arrived, so frightened families emerged from half-barn shelters, begging for help. Carmen did her best to calm illusions creeping into sheds or drifting along fences. Lucian offered a steady presence, standing guard at doorways, sword half-drawn whenever he sensed a swirl of fear taking shape. The illusions, relentless, did not cause direct physical harm, but each time a horse or cow started thrashing, Carmen's heart seized at the idea of more injuries.

The hours slogged by in a relentless cycle of illusions and weary farmhands. By late afternoon, the drizzle turned into steady rain, drenching them both. The roads devolved into watery mud, slowing their mounts. Carmen's cloak, once elegantly embroidered, hung limp and spattered with muck. She was shivering by the time she and Lucian found a ramshackle shed on a rise of land at dusk. It was only half finished inside, likely a store for grain sacks, but its roof remained intact enough to shield them from the pounding storm.

Lucian dismounted and led his horse beneath an overhang. Carmen followed suit, pushing back strands of wet hair clinging to her cheeks. The gloom deepened quickly under the leaden sky, and within the shed, it was pitch black except for fitful flashes of lightning in the distance.

He rummaged through his saddlebag and produced a small warding talisman, a simple bronze medallion etched with runes from the Blacksmith Guild. He propped it against the door frame, pressing it firmly until it latched onto a nail. Meanwhile, Carmen lit a tiny lantern with trembling fingers, savoring its meager glow.

She measured the walls of the shed with her gaze. "I should weave an illusion-dampening seal around us," she said quietly. Her voice rasped from the chill. "We have no idea if these illusions roam after dark, or if the wards around that barn have fully banished them."

Lucian nodded. "Do what you can." His expression softened as he watched her stoop to the ground, spool in hand. She etched a circular pattern along the perimeter of the shed's interior and chanted in a low voice. Threads of faint, silvery light rose from her spool and coated the walls with a whisper of protection. After a few minutes, the seal took shape, glimmered, and then faded to near trans-parency.

Exhaustion wrapped around her like a heavy cloak. She stumbled to the center of the shed, then sank onto a stray wooden crate, shoulders hunched. Lucian set the lantern on a crate beside her and gently offered a blanket he had pulled from his saddlebag. The night air felt merci-less, and though her illusions could hold off phantom beasts, she had no immediate remedy for the cold.

"You should rest," he said softly, shrugging off his cloak. He draped it beside them, hoping it might dry before morning. "Today was hard on you. I can keep an eye on the door."

She managed a weary grin. "We can both keep watch..." A thunderclap rattled the roof as though to mock her suggestion. She braced her hands on the crate and wiped rain-soaked hair from her eyes. "Sitting for a moment might be smart."

Outside, rain drummed incessantly on the thatched roof, loud enough that they would have to raise their voices to be heard if not for their closeness. In the cramped shed they sat shoulder to shoulder, both of them spent. Her pulse steadied in the hush that wrapped them. Carmen tucked her soaked hair behind her ear, aware of Lucian's gaze flicking over her. Normally she would have teased him or made some half-taunting remark about how unkempt they both looked, but tonight there was nothing left to muster except gratitude that they had survived the illusions for another day.

She felt the clammy chill seep into her bones, making her shiver. He shifted closer and placed a warm hand on her shoulder. "You're freezing," he said, his tone gentle. "We can share the blanket if it helps."

She swallowed and nodded. When he wrapped the blanket around them both, she exhaled in relief. The small lamp flickered, lighting the planes of his face in golden shapes. His brow, usually furrowed with worry, revealed tenderness now that they had a quiet space to breathe.

She could not ignore the warmth radiating from his body. She leaned in and let the tension unravel from her spine. They had spent days in the workshop district forging wards, studying illusions, always on the move. Rarely had they paused to contemplate the ripples of tension that stretched between them. Night after night, she had felt how steady his presence was. She could no longer resist that attraction now that they were alone.

He glanced down, concern shading his eyes. "Carmen," he murmured, "you look exhausted." His hand lingered on her arm. "You did good work today."

His voice steadied something deep in her, though it also stirred an ache. She had spent weeks wrestling with jealousy, regrets, and unspoken yearnings. She was tired of denying that what blossomed between them was more than a passing alliance. Her breath caught as his hand slid along her shoulder, calming and inviting at once. She turned her face toward him, and their gazes locked.

The air felt charged. The day's mud and sweat, the relentless illusions—none of it dampened the sudden clarity that she wanted him near. One kiss, she thought, and everything might tumble from the fragile walls she had built around her heart. She saw a flicker of uncertainty in his eyes, as though he too recognized the line they were about to cross.

She tilted her chin up. He leaned forward, lips parting in a slow breath. Thunder rumbled again, and the hiss of rain enveloped them. Their mouths met in a tentative brush—a single, trembling moment. It was enough to unleash the longing she had buried. One desperate kiss became two, then three, each more urgent. She shifted closer, sliding her arms around his waist. Her heart pounded so loudly it echoed in her ears.

Carmen pulled back, uncertainty flickering in her eyes. "Lucian, I... I don't want to be a consolation prize," she said softly. "I've spent so long feeling second best."

Lucian cupped her face. "You're not second to anyone, Carmen," he replied, his voice low and sincere. "What I feel for you is real, and I want to explore this, if you'll let me." He waited, breathing heavily.

Carmen studied him for a moment and nodded. Lucian resumed grazing her cheek, then slid his hand behind her neck and pulled her deeper into the kiss. Neither spoke. They needed to feel something real after so many illusions, so many nights of fear. The taste of raindrops lingered on their lips, mingling with the frantic cadence of unspoken desires finally set loose.

They melted into each other. Breath caught, hands parted cloaks and garments in subtle, urgent motions. The crackle in the air was not lightning now but the pulse of two people desperate for closeness. She gasped at the feel of his touch along her waist, and he murmured her name softly, as if unsure that this moment was truly allowed.

Wave after wave of tension poured away, replaced by a slow, molten heat. She closed her eyes, letting his warmth chase away the chill in her limbs. They sank onto the straw-strewn floor, blanket splayed beneath them. Amid the thunder and torrential rain, Carmen lost herself in Lucian's heartbeat, in the quiet sounds they made as they navigated each other's bodies with hungry reverence.

They gave in. Their world shrank to the press of lips and the clutch of hands, the warmth of skin on skin. Carmen felt tears prick her eyes, equal parts relief and release. Never had she allowed herself to be this unguarded with anyone. As thunder pounded in the sky, they wove a fragile cocoon of solace in the battered shed. Their kisses turned frantic, then slowed, savoring each gasp of pleasure until everything else faded. In that expanse of longing, they forgot illusions, curses, and the kingdom's troubles.

Some time later the storm's fury eased to a steady, quieter patter. Carmen lay beside Lucian, her body still tingling. His arm circled her shoulders, and she rested against his chest, the blanket draped over them. Lantern light flickered low, but it still lit the contented curve of his mouth.

He brushed damp curls from her forehead and offered a lazy grin. "I never thought," he began, then paused, exhaling. His voice held soft wonder. "I guess I never allowed myself to think about this, about you... in this way." He shook his head, amusement glinting in his eyes. "Tell me I'm not imagining it?"

Carmen traced a fingertip along his collarbone, a shy smile inching across her lips. "If you are, then I'm imagining it too," she teased. Her own voice had lost its usual edge, replaced by a tenderness that surprised her. She had not felt so unashamedly alive in a long time. She once believed closeness could only make her weak, but she recognized now how untrue that was.

They exchanged gentle touches, half laughing when Lucian brushed a stray piece of hay from her hair. He told her a story about racing through the palace corridors as a child, chasing a younger Prince Caelum with a toy sword, both of them convinced they were unstoppable knights. She pictured it, and, for once, envy did not cock its ugly head inside her. Instead, she felt an affectionate pang at the notion that even the bravest men had once been carefree boys.

They passed the rest of the night in warm, tired conversation, their voices hushed against the lullaby of rain. Outside, illusions might still have prowled the edges of the farmland, but inside the tiny shed, a sense of calm anchored them. The warding talisman glimmered faintly at the door, and the illusions Carmen had set along the walls kept any flickers of nightmare from pressing in.

Come morning, the overcast sky glowed with muted silver. The rain persisted, though it was gentler. She stirred against Lucian's shoulder and noticed the cramped ache in her legs and the cling of dried mud on her arms. Yet the discomfort felt trivial compared with the warmth that spread through her chest. She propped herself on one elbow to watch him, taking in the quiet satisfaction on his face. She had never seen him look so unburdened.

TWENTY-ONE

Elara tightened her grip on the reins as she and Prince Caelum passed under the palace's grand archway. The cobblestones were slick from a recent drizzle, and the clamor of frightened voices greeted them before they reached the inner courtyard. Her mind reeled with snippets of farmhands' terror, half-substantiated rumors about entire blocks vanishing behind illusions, and dire warnings of missing shipments. She dreaded what the city must look like now.

They slid from their mounts, and Elara sensed tension crackling in the air. Guards standing in uneven lines tried to direct confused civilians to "safe routes" that led deeper into the palace grounds. Most of these paths were marked by hand-drawn chalk symbols or scraps of faded cloth tied to railings. She saw families huddled in clusters, staring at any corner that seemed suspiciously still. A mother held her weeping daughter, muttering about a phantom herald who had called out contradictory news, then dissolved into swirling shapes.

Elara's heart pounded as she glanced at Caelum. He stood straighter than he had a few days earlier, yet she saw a slight tremor in his posture. His slumber had ended weeks before, but full strength would not return overnight. She thought back to the frantic ride she and Carmen had shared with Lucian. They had spent days on the outskirts, chasing illusions that spooked livestock and threatened scattered villages, only to find a new onslaught ravaging the city itself.

Caelum's eyes flickered uneasily over the courtyard. Though his expression looked calm to anyone who did not know him, Elara noticed the taut line of his jaw. As they stepped onto the slick stones, a breathless steward rushed forward. It was George, the man who often organized gatherings and juggled the court's precarious schedules. Ink smudged his left cuff, and Elara saw the trembling of his fingers as he tried to compose himself.

"My prince," George gasped. "If we cannot quell these illusions soon, citizens will storm the palace gates. Families are barricading themselves indoors, refusing to trust any voice but yours. I, along with the King and Queen, hope you have a plan."

Caelum nodded, though he looked paler than usual. "Gather as many guild leaders as you can," he said quietly. "We must show them unity. In the meantime..." He paused, swallowing hard. "Help the guards keep people to the marked routes."

George bowed, looking nowhere near reassured. He

hurried off, probably to wrangle a handful of local black-smiths or seamstresses into an impromptu council. Elara exhaled, the tension in her temples flaring.

"Have you slept at all?" she asked softly, stepping close enough to keep her voice private. She hoped he would not push himself until he collapsed, but the strain in his eyes already answered her.

"Barely," he admitted. "But these illusions are growing bolder every day. If I hide in bed, the city will think I've lapsed again, that I am unfit." A flicker of frustration crossed his face. "At least, that's what some courtiers suggest."

Elara felt a stab of sympathy. Word had spread among the fearful masses that the illusions were feeding off lingering unease, and many believed only the presence of the newly awakened prince could bolster morale. Others whispered that illusions had become so overwhelming that not even a rightful heir could banish them. The city teetered on the edge of panic.

Before she could speak, the courtyard erupted in shouts. A fresh cluster of travelers stumbled in, some rumpled from running. A gaunt older man lifted his hands at the guards, his voice cracking as he told them how he had nearly walked into a street that seemed perfectly normal until the cobblestones warped beneath him. He would have plummeted into a murky void if not for a quick-witted neighbor dragging him back. Hearing this, a huddle of watchers scowled, murmuring that the illusions grew more cunning, masquerading as ordinary roads one moment, then shifting into labyrinths the next.

Elara felt a chill ripple through her. In the past, illusions had manifested as fleeting shapes or nightmarish apparitions, but these accounts made them sound dangerously elaborate. She recalled how Malakar had once boasted of illusions that could disguise entire corridors. She had hoped, after the anchor runes were destroyed, such illusions would weaken. Instead, they multiplied here in the capital, twisting fear into something stronger with every passing night.

She spotted Lucian crossing the courtyard to speak with a group of guards. His stance radiated urgency as he demonstrated the flick of a torch to check a zone for illusions. A small wave of relief washed over her at the sight of him, for he knew the city's layout well and had begun stationing watchers on vantage points to keep a lookout for suspicious glimmers. He was speaking in quick, clear instructions, urging them to watch the rooftops at dusk and to rely on chalk or flagged symbols for safe passage.

She drifted closer to him and caught a sliver of his instructions: "If a route changes or flickers under your torchlight, do not proceed alone. Signal by whistling three times. We need watchers in pairs."

"Understood, sir," one guard said, saluting. The group dispersed to strategize with others. Lucian glanced at Elara and gave a small, distracted nod. She noticed the strain in his face and offered a swift, encouraging smile before letting him return to duty. They had no time for more.

Moments later, Carmen emerged from another section of the courtyard, arms crossed. She wore an air of grim focus Elara had seen only in the past few days. Carmen had scoured the warehouse district earlier, searching for shipments that might have vanished into illusions. Judging by her pinched expression, the news was poor.

Elara hurried to her side. "Did you find anything?"

Carmen pressed her lips into a thin line. "Not much. Two caravans meant to supply the palace never arrived. No wreckage, no sign of the wagons themselves. The dock officials swear they saw them set out, but the drivers vanished along the route. I suspect illusions devoured entire loads."

Elara's stomach tightened. Although illusions usually tore at minds rather than consuming objects, victims sometimes suffered real harm in panicked flight. If that danger now extended to caravans, the situation was dire. She remembered the scalding frustration each time illusions had led travelers astray in the outskirts, and now no corner of the kingdom seemed safe.

A frantic guard directed them to a platform near the courtyard's far side. The King and Queen had arranged a short address for Caelum, hoping to calm swelling fear. Elara overheard the guard say a crowd was gathering beyond the palace gates, begging for reassurance. She wondered whether that was even possible.

She leaned toward Caelum, who stood with his hand braced on a low wall. His complexion had grown paler. She spoke quietly. "You don't have to do this alone. Let the guild leaders speak, or your father."

He shook his head, and surprising firmness colored his

voice. "They need to see me moving about, not cloistered behind the throne. Even if it's only for a brief time."

Thick clouds pressed down on the city, sealing in the sense of claustrophobia. As Caelum climbed the short flight of steps to the hastily assembled platform, Elara and several watchers stationed themselves along the edges, scanning for suspicious ripples of illusion. The King and Queen hovered a little behind, unwilling to overshadow their son. Carmen stood rigid, arms still crossed, while she peered into the near-empty streets lacing the city. Lucian remained at the foot of the platform, his gaze fixed on the high vantage points along the ramparts.

The group of citizens who had mustered to listen looked worn. A few clutched children, others carried crude torch stumps they likely kept lit for self-defense. The hush that fell when Caelum raised his hand was eerie. Elara's heartbeat thudded in her ears as she waited, praying illusions would not erupt in the middle of his address.

He cleared his throat. Although his eyes flickered with exhaustion, his voice rang with quiet conviction. "You have heard tales...that illusions now prowl entire districts. I won't lie to you. These threats are real. But know this: I am awake. I stand with every last one of you who has felt terror clamp your heart."

A few murmurs rippled through the sparse crowd. One woman gave a muffled sob, another scowled as though unconvinced. Caelum pressed on, knuckles white against the wooden railing.

"Malakar will not win," he said, raising his voice until it carried above the restless stirring of the watchers. "His illusions feed on our fear, and we have watchers marking safe routes, we have guilds forging wards, and we have each other. Stand with us, and illusions be damned."

A few scattered cheers rose, uncertain but earnest. Elara felt tears prick at the corners of her eyes. His words rang with the faint echo of the prince she had glimpsed in the dream realm, the one who refused to let curses define him. Though the applause was halting, it bridged a moment of unity in the gloom.

Caelum's shoulders trembled almost imperceptibly once he finished speaking. The strain of his forced composure was taking its toll. He stepped back from the railing and blinked hard as though dizzy. Elara rushed closer, worried he might faint in front of the city. Lucian moved from the crowd's edge, but a guard had already supported Caelum's arm and helped him step down from the makeshift platform.

The hush that followed was laced with pity, though no one voiced it aloud. Even the minimal cheering had cost Caelum a great effort. Elara rested a hand on the guard's shoulder and nodded her thanks. She saw how Caelum tried to draw a full breath, but the cool air made him wince. A swirl of gulls cried overhead, lost in the haze that hung above the palace roofs.

Though the platform was only a couple of feet above ground level, Caelum leaned heavily against the guard's arm after he descended. Elara planted herself at his side, one hand hovering near his back should he falter. She looked around for some sign of hope that the crowd had remained steadier, but they were already dispersing in anxious clumps, stepping carefully along the chalk-marked roads. A few watchers followed, calling out instructions about the routes that might still be illusions. Only the occasional spark of torchlight broke the gloom.

As Elara guided Caelum away, her gaze shifted to where Lucian had gone. She spotted him near the courtyard's perimeter, standing partly hidden by a stone column. Carmen was there too, her face lit with a relieved smile Elara scarcely recognized. Elara watched Carmen rest her hands on Lucian's shoulders. The tension Carmen had once worn faded entirely from her posture. In its place bloomed something genuine, a softness that flickered across her features as Lucian drew her into a playful kiss. They seemed unaware of who might be watching, or perhaps they no longer cared.

Elara felt a small catch in her throat, half surprise and half a distant sort of joy on their behalf. She remembered how Carmen's jealousy had once sparked bitterness, yet now, in their shared trials, something deeper had grown. Elara's heart twisted, not in sadness, but in gratitude that the friction among them had transmuted into unexpected bonds. It was one less worry to weigh on Caelum's shoulders, one less wedge to fracture their precarious alliance.

As Caelum straightened with obvious difficulty, Elara gently touched his elbow. "If you want, we can find you a quieter spot inside. Let the guards handle the rest outside for now."

His breathing was shallow, but a spark of relief flickered in his eyes. "I think that might be wise," he managed. Then, against all odds, he let out a soft laugh. He angled his head to glance at Lucian and Carmen's private moment of affection, the corner of his mouth curving in faint astonishment. The sight lent him a subtle, genuine sense of comfort. For the first time that day, his shoulders loosened.

"They look... happy," he murmured, his voice ragged but no longer entirely forlorn.

Elara watched him, noticing the faint shift in his expression. Something like reassurance lit his features, as if he realized Lucian would not be his rival in matters of the heart. A breeze rustled the courtyard's tattered flags, stirring the last anxious citizens into scattered lines. Caelum let out a breath that eased a hidden burden inside him.

He took one last look at Carmen and Lucian, then braced himself once more on the guard's arm, a fleeting hint of renewed strength glowing in his gaze.

CHAPTER

TWENTY-TWO

Twilight settled over the castle spires, staining the sky deep purple and crimson.

In the great throne room, flames sputtered in tall iron sconces and sent wavering shadows dancing across rich tapestries. Elara stood near the center of the gathering, her heart pounding as she surveyed the crowd. The dusk wind rattled the high windows and made the torches flicker, but no one risked looking away. Every guild leader felt the urgency that had drawn them here tonight.

At Prince Caelum's request, palace guards had admitted blacksmiths, seamstresses, scholars, and other allies, each escorted by a royal steward. The hush in the chamber was startling. Even in past meetings filled with tension, an uneasy murmur or the rustle of parchment lingered, but now a chilling silence held them. Caelum remained upright before the empty throne. His breathing was labored, and his normally bright eyes looked heavy with fatigue, yet he refused to sit. His posture betrayed an unyielding determination, and Elara silently willed him to conserve his strength.

She noticed a faint tremor in his hands. His time in cursed slumber had weakened him, but his spirit burned with a resolve that seemed to radiate through the room.

She looked to her right and spotted Lucian leaning against a tall pillar. He kept his arms folded in guarded attentiveness, one ankle crossed over the other, his gaze sweeping the gathered guild members. The torchlight revealed faint lines of worry etched in his brow.

Roderick, the blacksmith master, stepped forward. His muscular arms showed beneath rolled sleeves, and he struck an imposing figure. He spoke in a gravelly baritone, grim and direct. "My wards are failing," he declared. "We hammered each piece to exact standards, but Malakar's illusions twist them at the edges. The designs corrode, as though something is eating away at the runes from inside. We have used every forging technique we know."

A troubled murmur rose in the assemblage. The statement alone would have alarmed any castle advisor, but the sight of Roderick's usually fearless stance was even more sobering. He gripped his thick belt, his eyes flicking between Caelum and Elara, silently apologizing for bringing ill news. Elara's pulse thrummed in her temples. She felt an aching fatigue in her arms, a reminder of how many protective illusions she had woven lately. If even Roderick's metalwork faltered, the threat had almost certainly escalated beyond the scope of their earlier efforts.

Next, a trio of scholars stepped to the center, carefully

carrying tattered scrolls and grimacing at the runic characters that shifted impossibly on the parchment. A wiry older scholar bowed curtly to Caelum. "Your Highness, entire sets of runic defenses have turned indecipherable," he explained, voice trembling. "We compiled these scrolls only last week after collaborating with the seamstresses' wards, but now they make no sense. The letters twist the instant our scribes set quill to paper. It is as if Malakar is inside the ink itself."

A rumble of dissent spread among the guild leaders. Nerves frayed from sleepless nights and demoralizing illusions turned these men and women into an anxious mass. Some blacksmiths exchanged uneasy glances. A few seamstresses lowered their eyes, worried about the possibility that the illusions might infiltrate their embroidered wards next. Elara swallowed her dread before it climbed into her throat. She could sense the malicious web Malakar had spun, pressing in on every corner of the kingdom.

Carmen cleared her throat from a different corner of the throne room. Her voice trembled, but she stepped forward with her chin lifted, curly hair pinned in a neat bun that accentuated her intense expression. Lucian's mouth curved slightly in approval as he watched her. "I have found...references," Carmen began, her usual poise faltering for a moment. "I pieced them together from Malakar's stolen notes. A handful of half-coded scraps kept pointing to the same location. Then I cross-referenced gossip I heard from a minor official who once carried Malakar's messages to the western corridors, and it all pointed to a hidden stronghold in the catacombs."

At her words, a fresh ripple of alarm swept through the hall. The palace catacombs had a notorious reputation even before illusions began ravaging the realm. Elara recalled glimpses of those underground passages in older books, always described as labyrinthine and damp with ancient secrets. If Malakar had claimed such a place for his illusions, it might explain why their wards broke so easily above ground.

Carmen continued, her voice raw but resolute. "These catacombs contain a rumored chamber that amplifies illusions. Some palace staff call it 'the hollow cradle.' That might be how Malakar feeds illusions across half the kingdom. If we disable whatever he established there, the illusions may begin to lose power."

A moment of stunned silence followed. One of the blacksmiths barked an incredulous question, but Roderick's low grunt of affirmation cut him short. "Hear her out," Roderick said, dipping his head toward Carmen. "I have heard rumors of old stones in those catacombs with runic channels carved into the walls. That is exactly the type of place Malakar would nest."

Caelum's jaw tightened. He pressed his left hand against the back of the throne for balance, and Elara stepped closer, ready to support him if he wavered. The prince closed his eyes for a moment, as if mustering the strength to speak. When he finally did, his tone was quiet but commanding. "At first light, we mount a strike," he said. "We will coordinate wards across the city to keep illusions at bay, then concentrate our best defenders in those catacombs. We must uproot Malakar's anchor once and for all."

At the mention of a dawn attack, several voices rose in concern. They worried about resources, the illusions that strengthened at night, and whether they stood any chance in cramped stone tunnels where phantoms might coil unseen. Elara's heart hammered. She knew how much Malakar hated the prospect of losing control, and a direct assault might provoke him to unleash even more desperate tricks.

Lucian pushed away from the pillar and spoke with steady calm. "We have begun training squads to detect illusions. Our watchers are no longer easily fooled by flickers or shifting shapes. And with Roderick's wards, plus Elara's illusions," he said, glancing at her, "we can carve a path through. We need everyone's efforts combined."

He nodded at Carmen, pride clear in his eyes. Her cheeks reddened, though she lifted her chin in satisfaction. When a seamstress at the back of the hall applauded, the gesture proved contagious, and a ripple of applause rolled through the throng. Even the scholars joined, though they looked more relieved than celebratory. Carmen's plan offered the first clarity they had seen in days.

Elara's mind whirled. She imagined a labyrinth of shadows waiting below, illusions that might appear as monstrous silhouettes or intangible nightmares. She pictured Malakar gloating in darkness, twisting runic energy to his own ends. The spool of shimmering thread in her pocket felt heavier than ever. She had used so much magic lately that her illusions sometimes faltered midcasting. Determined not to show that weakness before so many onlookers, she drew a careful breath and lifted her head.

Caelum turned toward her, his gaze softening despite the tension that charged the air. For an instant he studied her face, as if searching for reassurance. She exhaled slowly, letting him see she was ready to stand by him, no matter how frightened she felt inside.

"Seamstresses," Caelum said, raising his voice to address their cluster, "I ask that you sew protective cloaks and hoods with embroidered wards. The blacksmiths can supply the necessary metals to reinforce them, and scholars will handle the runic designs, so we combine illusions, forging, and scholarship. We are strongest when we work together, and tomorrow's mission requires every skill we have."

He cleared his throat, pushing back a hint of breathlessness that threatened to derail his speech. "And we are all grateful to Carmen for tracing these leads," he added, inclining his head to the woman who had once been so quick to sabotage Elara. Carmen pressed her trembling lips together and managed a small bow of acknowledgment toward Caelum, eyes shining with unexpected relief.

Gradually the council erupted into urgent discussions: blacksmiths huddled to confirm forging schedules, seamstresses argued over designs for the new cloaks, and scholars debated the best way to preserve runic symbols that tended to warp under illusions. The throne room bustled with an undercurrent of hope. Despite the exhaustion weighing every step, Elara felt a surge of unity in the air.

She swallowed a pang of anxiety and allowed herself to believe that this time they stood a real chance. Malakar's illusions had battered them all, but each fresh blow had taught them how to fight back. With the anchor in the catacombs destroyed, the illusions aboveground might erode like dust on the wind.

Amid the clamor, Caelum raised a weary hand, signaling the meeting to an end. Torches flickered, as if echoing his silent call for calm. The hush returned, and everyone in the throne room turned toward the prince once more.

"Dawn," he reminded them gently. "Return to your guild halls tonight. Prepare for the morning. We cannot afford fear or hesitation."

A chorus of determined voices answered. Roderick nodded curtly, Carmen squared her shoulders, and the scholars held their scrolls tight. Elara offered Lucian a brief smile. He dipped his head in her direction, as if silently saying, We will manage.

When the council finally adjourned, a subtle wave of optimism flowed through the departing crowd. The city might still quake under illusions by sunrise, but they had a plan to strike at the source. Elara lingered by Caelum's side as the throng receded. Heat flooded her cheeks once the final guild member exited, leaving only a handful of guards near the door, with Lucian and Carmen quietly discussing details under one of the tall windows.

Caelum's exhaustion showed in his slumped shoulders, yet his eyes gleamed with tender intensity. He gestured for Elara to step closer, and she did so willingly. He reached for her hand, brushing his thumb across her knuckles. The softness in his touch sent a rush of warmth through her body, and for a moment the worrisome swirl of illusions and catacombs faded to the background.

He dipped his head to meet her gaze. "You are trembling," he said softly. She tried to protest with a shaky laugh, but he hushed her with a gentle squeeze of her hand. "I know you have pushed yourself. I have asked so much of you, and tomorrow we will ask even more."

Elara's eyes pricked with tears she fought to contain. All her frustrations and fatigue threatened to spill over: the nights spent weaving illusions to calm frightened villagers, the constant fear that Malakar would discover a new way to manipulate her magic, the guilt that she could not always reassure the people counting on them. Yet Caelum's presence steadied her in ways she could not explain. Even after his long curse, even with the trembling in his own hands, he moved her heart with his quiet resolve. She parted her lips, but no words emerged.

He inhaled, his expression turning raw with emotion. He slid a hand across her waist and tugged her gently closer. Elara set her palm on his chest, feeling the uneven rise and fall of his breath beneath. Despite the eyes that might still linger, despite the two watchful guards at the far door, she leaned in without shame or hesitation.

His kiss was tender but full of longing that swept away the tension of the council. She slid her fingers to his shoulder, returning that gentle pressure. The throne room, draped in flickering torchlight, receded into a quiet ring around them. She could feel his pulse hammer against her fingertips, matching the rapid beat in her own veins.

When he finally pulled back, he kept one arm around her, as if unwilling to surrender that closeness. "Let us take an hour or two," he murmured in a voice for her ears alone, "have a good hearty meal, rest our bones, and just let me look at you. Would that be alright, my love?"

The words sank into Elara's heart, dissolving the last of her self-consciousness. She felt the slightest laugh bubble in her throat. How she had yearned for a moment of calm in the midst of chaos. Even a single meal together sounded like a life-saving balm after all they had endured.

She smiled and leaned in to return his kiss, cradling his cheek with her free hand. "Yes, my love."

TWENTY-THREE

The lingering scent of ozone and the faint, acrid smell of extinguished illusions still clung to the air in the upper rampart walkway where Caelum had led Elara. Below them, the palace courtyards were slowly returning to a semblance of order, the urgent shouts fading, replaced by the weary murmurs of guards and the distant clang of blacksmiths already at work strengthening the city's defenses. The storm that had mirrored Malakar's fury had passed, and a tender sky, mottled like a bruise, carried the first stars of evening.

Elara leaned against the cool stone parapet, the rough texture a stark contrast to the turmoil churning within her. The weight of the day, the council, the decision to descend into the catacombs, and the raw terror of Malakar's splinter illusions pressed down on her, an almost physical ache. She closed her eyes and tried to draw a breath that didn't taste of fear or exhaustion.

"You're trembling." Caelum's voice was soft beside her, a balm to her raw nerves.

She opened her eyes and found him watching her, his expression a blend of concern and tenderness that made her heart ache in another way. The borrowed finery he had worn for the council was gone, replaced by a simple linen tunic that did little to hide his weariness, yet his gaze was steady, clear, and fixed on her.

"Tired," she managed, an understatement. "And a little overwhelmed by what comes next."

Caelum nodded, his shoulders slumping. "The catacombs, Malakar's final stronghold, or so Carmen's notes suggest." He let out a slow breath, starlight catching the silver threads in his hair. "It feels as though we've traded one prison for another. I escaped the curse, and now the kingdom faces these splintered nightmares."

"But you are free, Caelum," Elara said, her voice firm. She reached out and brushed his arm, and a spark of warmth, her dreamweaver magic reacting to his presence, pulsed between them. "That makes the difference. You're awake, you're here. Malakar can't anchor his darkest spells through you anymore, and that gives us a fighting chance."

His hand covered hers, his grip still weak but undeniably real. "Because of you, Elara. You never stopped weaving hope into the darkness." He turned fully toward her, the rampart's low wall forming an alcove of intimacy against the vast night sky. "My father...my mother...they see you as a savior. The guilds look at your courage. Lucian and Carmen trust your judgment. Do you see yourself as they do?"

Color crept up her neck. "I see a seamstress who stumbled into a power she barely understood and is trying not to let everyone down," she whispered, "and who is still afraid."

"We are all afraid," Caelum murmured, his thumb tracing circles on the back of her hand. "But you, Elara, weave that fear into strength. I felt it even in the deepest shadows of the dream. Your light was the only thing that felt true."

The sincerity in his voice, the weight of his gaze, chipped away at the exhaustion around her heart. For so long, she had been Elara the dreamweaver, Elara the solution, Elara the conduit. Rarely had she simply been Elara, the woman.

"I asked you to the council today," Caelum continued, his voice dropping lower and drawing her into the hush between their breaths, "not only for your counsel on illusions, but because I needed... I needed you there. Your presence steadies me in a way I can't explain. Even when every instinct screamed that Malakar's influence was still too strong, seeing you across that table reminded me of what we're fighting for."

Elara's breath hitched. The raw vulnerability in his admission mirrored the unspoken emotions swirling within her own chest. The memory of their kiss in the garden after his awakening, so full of tentative hope and overwhelming relief, rushed back, vivid and potent.

"Caelum..."

He lifted her hand, turned it over, then pressed a soft kiss to her palm. The gesture was so tender and filled with unspoken reverence that tears pricked her eyes. "I've spent five years lost in a world of phantoms, Elara. Five years when touch was a memory and warmth a forgotten dream. When I finally woke, truly woke, it was your face I saw, your hand I felt. It was your magic that pulled me back."

He looked up, his blue eyes luminous in the starlight, reflecting the myriad stars that now blanketed the heavens. "I know the kingdom needs its prince. I know there are battles still to fight, a sorcerer still to bring to justice. But tonight, Elara... tonight, can the kingdom spare its prince for a few hours? Can the dreamweaver set down her spool?"

Her heart ached at the plea in his voice and at the profound weariness that clung to him despite his resolve. He was asking for respite, not only for himself but for her too, a moment stolen from the relentless march of duty and fear.

"Yes," she breathed, the word a release. "Yes, I think they can."

A slow smile spread across Caelum's face, a genuine, unburdened smile that lit him from within and reminded her of the vibrant prince he had been before the curse, the prince he was slowly becoming again. He tugged her hand gently. "Come with me. There's a place, a place I used to go when the burdens of being an heir felt too heavy. Before..." His voice faltered, the shadow of the past flickering in his eyes.

Elara squeezed his hand. "Show me."

He led her away from the main ramparts and down a little-used stone staircase that spiraled into the quieter, older sections of the palace. The air grew cooler, scented with damp stone and the faint, sweet fragrance of night-blooming jasmine clinging to unseen crevices. Their footsteps echoed softly in the narrow passage, a counterpoint to the distant, muted sounds of the city settling into an uneasy night.

Finally, he stopped before a heavy, iron-banded wooden door tucked away in an alcove almost swallowed by shadows. He produced a tarnished silver key, one she suspected he had not touched in years, and, with a grating click, turned the lock.

The room beyond was small, circular, and surprisingly warm. A single, narrow window, high above, revealed a sliver of the star-dusted sky. The only furnishings were a wide, cushioned window seat, a small, low table bearing a decanter of what looked like wine and two goblets, and a thick, plush rug spread across the stone floor. A brazier in one corner glowed with embers, chasing away the night's chill. It was a hidden sanctuary, a forgotten haven.

"My mother had this room prepared for me when I was a boy," Caelum said, his voice softened by nostalgia. "A place to escape tutors and council meetings. I haven't been here since..." He did not need to finish the sentence. Since before the curse.

Elara stepped inside, feeling the oppressive weight of the palace's expectations begin to lift from her shoulders. The quiet here was profound, a stark contrast to the fear-laced hum of the throne room or the frantic energy of the guild warehouse.

Caelum closed the door, the sound a definitive sigh, and turned to her. The ember light from the brazier cast flickering shadows across his face, softening the lines of exhaustion and highlighting the gentle curve of his lips.

"No guards, no courtiers, no splintered illusions," he murmured, stepping closer. "Just us."

He reached for her cloak, his fingers brushing her neck as he unfastened the clasp. The rough wool slipped from her shoulders, and she stood in her simple gown, feeling more vulnerable, more herself, than she had in weeks. He laid the cloak carefully over the window seat.

"You're still cold," he observed, taking her hands in his. Her skin was chilled from the rainy ramparts, but his touch was warm, sending a shiver through her that had nothing to do with the temperature.

He led her to the brazier, its gentle heat a welcome comfort. They stood there for a long moment, side by side, not speaking, simply absorbing the peace of the hidden room and the shared solace of being away from the world's demands. The only sound was the soft crackle of the embers and the distant, muted sigh of the wind.

Elara leaned into his warmth, her earlier exhaustion giving way to a different kind of weariness, the weariness of a heart that had carried too much for too long.

Caelum turned, his body angling toward her. He lifted a hand, his knuckles gently grazing her cheek. "You are so beautiful, Elara," he whispered, his voice thick with an emotion that made her breath catch. "Even when you are weary, even when you carry the weight of the world...your light shines through."

She looked up at him, her own gaze tracing the noble lines of his face, the sincerity in his eyes, the way the firelight caught the gold in his hair. He was the prince she had fought for in dreams, the man whose spirit had called to hers across the abyss of a curse. And he was here, real and warm and looking at her as if she were the most precious thing in his world.

"Caelum," she began, her voice trembling, "I..."

He silenced her with a finger to her lips. "No words. Not now." He drew her closer, his other arm circling her waist, pulling her gently against him. The scent of him, a mix of sandalwood, old parchment, and the clean fragrance of rain, enveloped her.

Her own arms found their way around his neck, her fingers tangling in the soft hair at his nape. The world outside, with its lingering nightmares and looming battles, seemed to fade away, leaving only the two of them in the warm, amber glow of the hidden room.

His head dipped, and his lips found hers. This kiss was different from the one in the garden, less about triumphant relief and more about a slow, deliberate rekindling. It was a kiss of shared exhaustion and burgeoning hope, of fears acknowledged and comforts found. It spoke of sleepless nights and silent vows, of a bond forged in the crucible of dreams and tempered by the harsh realities of their world.

Elara melted into his embrace, her body molding against his, her senses alight. The taste of him was intoxicating, a blend of the spiced wine he must have had earlier and a deeper, more intrinsic sweetness that was purely Caelum. The brush of his lips was hesitant at first, then grew firmer, more confident, as if he were relearning the language of touch, of desire, after years of forced silence.

Her fingers tightened in his hair, pulling him closer still, deepening the kiss. A soft sound, half sigh, half moan, escaped her lips as the last of her carefully constructed defenses crumbled. There was no room for guilt here, no space for the confusing warmth she felt for Lucian. In this moment, in Caelum's arms, there was only this undeniable, soul-deep connection, this overwhelming sense of coming home.

He broke the kiss, his forehead resting against hers, their breaths mingling. "I've dreamt of this," he rasped, his voice husky with emotion. "Not just being awake but being with you. Truly with you."

He led her toward the plush rug before the brazier, then sank down and pulled her with him. They settled there, nestled in the warmth, his arms still around her. Elara rested her head on his shoulder, feeling the steady beat of his heart against her ear. It was the most reassuring sound she had ever heard.

"Tell me about your grandmother," he murmured after a long, comfortable silence, his fingers gently stroking her hair. "The one who left you the spool. Was she a dreamweaver too?"

Elara felt a pang of sorrow mixed with quiet pride. "I... I don't know for sure. I barely remember her, just faint images, the scent of lavender and old books. But the spool...it always felt different, alive. Mistress Imelda believes the magic is in my bloodline, passed down." She paused. "Perhaps that's why I could reach you when no one else could. Our magic...it recognized each other."

Caelum pressed a kiss to her temple. "Your magic saved me, Elara. Your courage, your empathy...you saved me."

They lay there for a long time, sharing quiet words, whispered confessions, and gentle touches. He spoke of the formless terror of the curse, the disorienting fog of the dream realm before she arrived, the agonizing frustration of being trapped within his own mind. She, in turn, spoke of the guild, the initial fear of her powers, the small, desperate acts of weaving hope for him, and the unwavering support of Lucian, and the surprising, late found allyship of Carmen.

With every shared memory, every acknowledged fear, the bond between them deepened and strengthened. The embers in the brazier burned low, casting a soft, intimate glow over them. Elara felt a profound sense of peace settle over her, a quiet joy that was all the more precious for its rarity.

Slowly, tentatively, their kisses resumed, no longer only tender but tinged with a rising passion that had been held in check for far too long. His hands explored the curve of her back and the slope of her shoulders, kindling a fire within her that matched the hunger in his eyes. She met his touch with her own, her fingers tracing the strong line of his jaw and the pulse that beat in his throat.

The simple linen of her gown felt like a barrier, and she

shifted, a soft gasp escaping as his lips trailed down her neck and sent shivers across her skin. He unlaced the ribbons at her bodice with trembling fingers, his gaze never leaving hers, his silent question answered by her fervent nod.

They shed their clothes, leaving them forgotten on the rug beside them, and then there was only skin against skin, warmth against warmth, breath against breath. The last vestiges of fear and exhaustion melted in the rising tide of their shared passion. He explored her body with a reverence that made her tremble, his touch both gentle and exacting, awakening senses she had not known she possessed. She, in turn, discovered the strength that still lay within his recovering frame, the lean muscles and the surprising heat of his skin.

Their lovemaking became a dance of discovery, a tender exploration of shared vulnerabilities and deep desires. It was a celebration of life reclaimed, of a bond that had defied curses and nightmares. Every touch, every kiss, every whispered endearment was a stitch in the new tapestry they wove together, a tapestry of love, hope, and a future finally free from shadows.

In the quiet intimacy of that hidden chamber, shielded from the still-troubled world outside, Elara and Caelum found not only respite but a rekindling of souls. They found solace in each other's arms, a love that was both a sanctuary and a promise, a promise of a new dawn not just for the kingdom but for the prince and the dreamweaver who had at last found their way back to the light together. As they lay entwined, peaceful sleep for the first time in what felt like a lifetime claimed them. Their mingled breaths formed a soft rhythm against the dying embers of the fire, a quiet prelude to the battles yet to come.

For this night, though, they were simply Caelum and Elara, home at last.

TWENTY-FOUR

Elara stood beneath pregnant storm clouds, her heart pounding as raindrops spattered against the breastplates of assembled knights. Dawn's light was a pale glow beyond the roiling thunderheads, and the courtyard bristled with whispers as people steeled themselves for a battle that might decide their future. The air tasted of ozone and dread.

She tightened her fingers around the spool of shimmering thread at her belt. Beside her, Prince Caelum drew a quivering breath. His recently regained strength still came in pieces, yet he stood resolute in the gray half-light, chin lifted despite the pallor on his brow. Beyond him, Lucian and Carmen exchanged a brief nod, muttered final instructions to the rows of knights, and turned to join Elara and Caelum at the courtyard's center.

Standing one pace behind Caelum, a steward called the roll of those assigned to the upcoming mission. Each name was answered by a sharp, determined "Present."

The blacksmith Roderick answered first in his gravelly timbre, patting the warded lockets fastened to his belt. Carmen's voice, though subdued, held a steely edge as she confirmed her place. Finally, Lucian responded, voice clipped with focus, confirming his readiness to lead an advance party. Elara felt her own pulse throb. She was included in this mission by necessity. Hers was the only dreamweaver magic that could truly unravel the illusions fueling Malakar's final stronghold.

The courtyard lay quiet but for the drumming of rain and the clank of steel greaves on wet cobblestone. The king and queen watched from the top of the palace steps, their anxious expressions revealing they knew how real the danger was. Elara offered them a small reassuring nod, uncertain whether it brought them any comfort. She remembered, with a pang, how the king and queen had once pressed her for answers, lost in illusions they barely understood. Now they placed full trust in her and this ragtag group, hoping to salvage whatever peace might remain for their kingdom.

A distant rumble of thunder cut through the hush. Caelum raised a hand, drawing every gaze to him. Though lines of exhaustion framed his eyes, his voice rang clear enough to carry across the courtyard. "We march into the tunnels beneath the western ramparts," he said. "Be strong, be united. What we face underground might threaten our minds as much as our bodies."

For a moment, no one dared break the silence. Then Roderick grunted and stepped forward with the blacksmiths to heft satchels filled with forging tools and small lumps of metal. "We're with you, Highness," he said, patting the warded locket around his neck. "Let's see these illusions conquer good steel and stouter hearts, if they can."

Lucian cast a quick glance at Elara to gauge her reassurance. She managed a small smile, adrenaline thrumming in her veins. Beside him, Carmen rolled her shoulders with a grace that belied the tension in her body. The two had spent days patrolling the outskirts and training watchers, and now their skill and Elara's illusions would be tested in a place said to amplify nightmares.

With final orders murmured among the knights, the advance party moved as one into the mouth of an old stone stairwell that led underground. Torchlight flickered, carving shifting shadows on the walls. Elara felt Caelum's hand graze hers, and for a single trembling moment he inhaled her presence. Then he set his jaw and led them down the spiraling stairs.

The temperature dropped sharply. Damp air clung to Elara's face, and the reek of stale water and rotting stone made her stomach lurch. She recalled rumors of these neglected passages, labyrinthine corridors said to hold half-formed illusions left behind by Malakar's spells. Her steps slowed as the group passed a shattered archway where wisps of blackish shimmer crawled along the ceiling. Two knights swung their torches overhead, revealing twisting shapes that looked like worms made of living darkness undulating across the mortar.

"These illusions appear incomplete," Carmen murmured. The faint luminescence of her own thread, less potent than Elara's but still present, glowed at her finger-tips. "They're remnants, maybe. Not fully shaped, but dangerous all the same."

Lucian steered two knights toward the wall. "Careful," he warned. "They might lash out if disturbed."

At the sound of his voice, one writhing mass peeled itself from the rock and dropped onto the dusty floor. A hiss like escaping steam slithered through the corridor. Instinct took over. Elara gripped her spool and drew a thin strand of glowing thread. Carmen spoke a short incantation that sharpened the torchlight, and a rippling barrier of faint illumination spread between the illusions and the knights. The wormlike shape sputtered, flailed, and finally crumbled into ash, leaving a foul smell in the air.

Caelum pressed a hand to his forehead, steadying his breath. "We go on," he said. His voice shook, but he stayed resolute, ignoring the alarmed glances from a few watchers. They all knew his curse might flare anew at the slightest conjuring. Even so, he refused to stay behind.

They pressed deeper. The corridor opened into a broader, vaulted passage, dripping with condensation. Lanterns revealed columns worn smooth by centuries of damp, each carved with runic patterns that flickered when light played over them. A hush folded around the group, broken only by the shuffle of boots. Elara tried to maintain calm, focusing on the spool at her waist. She could almost feel the threads humming in reaction to the illusions swirling in these walls.

After several minutes of careful progress, they reached an iron gate, half rusted, that barred the way forward. Two knights forced it open with a groan of protesting metal. Beyond, the air felt heavier, as if each step pushed them farther from the world above. Elara's heart clenched when she inhaled a slight tang of sulfur. Each breath seemed thick with tension, stirring old memories of the dream corridors where she first sensed Malakar's dark presence.

Carmen exhaled a shaky breath. "We must be close. Feels like there's something... coiling beyond that hall." She pointed ahead at a corridor branching right, where a faint luminescence pulsed along the walls.

Lucian nodded, signaled for two knights to stay behind and guard their rear, and motioned the rest forward. The passage curved in a slow arc, leading them toward an area the stolen scrolls had called the "breach point." Elara recalled scribbling the runic instructions late last night, fighting her own fatigue. If they could disrupt the illusions' anchor here, the widespread nightmares might collapse under their own weight.

Ahead, the corridor opened into a cavernous chamber. The knights fanned out along the threshold, torchlight flaring across a massive floor engraved with arcane symbols that seemed to pulse like a diseased heartbeat. Elara's gut churned at the sight. Streaks of blackish flame flowed beneath the stone, forming patterns reminiscent of Malakar's brand. Half-formed illusions flitted along the edges, curling shapes that bled into the walls, too hazy to identify. At the chamber's far end stood a dais of cracked granite. It glowed with an unnatural gleam, like burning coals hidden behind thin paper.

Caelum held his breath, blinking against a fresh wave

of dizziness. Lucian stepped to his side and placed a steadying hand on the prince's shoulder. For once, Caelum did not refuse the help. He turned to Elara with eyes that looked older than his years.

"We must do this," he said quietly. "If Malakar wanted a failsafe, I imagine it is linked to these runes. He may not even need to be here physically for them to wreak havoc. I refuse to let illusions choke my people again."

Elara nodded, searching his face. The scars at his wrists, barely visible but still reminders of the dream bondage he had endured, remained a chilling testament to Malakar's cruelty. Caelum closed his eyes for a moment, as though summoning nerve. Then he stepped forward and ignored Carmen's hushed protests that he stay farther back.

The knights formed a protective ring around them, and Elara, Carmen, Lucian, and Caelum approached the dais. Each footstep echoed hollowly as if the stone was not entirely solid. A spike of chill air brushed Elara's cheek, raising goose bumps. She swallowed hard and withdrew her battered parchment of dreamweaver notes. The edges were torn, smudged from her frantic scribbling over the last few days, but the incantation was still legible.

"This is it," she whispered to Carmen. "Remember, we have to chant in unison. I will anchor the illusions so you can disrupt them from within."

Carmen licked her lips, her eyes flickering with apprehension. "Right. Let's do it quickly."

They smoothed the parchment on a flat section of stone at the base of the dais. The first lines were words in an archaic script gleaned from the dreamweaver texts. Elara's mind returned to the nights she spent hunched in the library, racing against time to decipher them. Now each syllable carried a weight that made her chest tighten. If they failed, illusions might intensify and devour the city above, leaving them helpless in these dank halls.

She glanced at Caelum. He offered a tremulous nod. Even in his weakened state, he was determined to stand at her side. Lucian hovered nearby, blade half drawn, scanning the shifting recesses of the chamber for any threat. The tension of an imminent fight crackled through the air.

Together, Elara and Carmen began chanting. Their combined voices echoed against the runic symbols that glowed beneath the dais. The lines of black fire seemed to recoil at first, as though uncertain whether to shrink away or lash out. Motes of swirling energy drifted around Carmen's feet. Elara felt her needle tremble at her hip, the spool's glow brightening in her peripheral vision.

"You can do this," Lucian murmured from behind Elara. She barely heard him over the pounding in her ears.

As they reached the Qethri phrase of the incantation, a sinister rumble pulsed through the floor. The dais flickered. Then, all at once, the runes on the walls blazed with malignant light, intensifying into pulsating arcs that spread across the floor in a web of black. Elara reeled. The toxic surge scorched the air, filling her mouth with a bitter tang.

A tremor rattled the chamber. Caelum stiffened with a ragged gasp, eyes going wide. Elara's incantation faltered as she whirled to see him clutching his chest, the faint scars across his arms blazing with the same black fire. The runes must have recognized him as the original victim, a direct link to Malakar's twisted illusions. Panic flashed across his face as he sank to his knees, breath rasping.

"No," Carmen hissed, fear making her voice jump. "They're pulling at him!"

Lucian lunged with quick reflexes, locking an arm around Caelum's shoulders before he could collapse entirely. In the same heartbeat illusions spun outward in savage arcs, forging monstrous silhouettes that took shape around the dais. Knightly instincts took over among the guards: a half-dozen men rushed forward, warded lockets clanging, while others formed a defensive circle.

Elara's pulse hammered. She had to protect Caelum, had to keep chanting. But the illusions multiplied too fast. A nightmarish figure loomed where the stone met the darkness, a towering shape with glinting eyes that seemed to swirl with starless black. Its limbs stretched and contorted like living smoke, the tips glowing with violet sparks. It gave a high, keening sound that made the hair on Elara's arms prickle.

Lucian's jaw clenched. He seized his sword with one hand while keeping Caelum upright with the other. "Those anchor runes give these nightmares enough solidity to wound us," he growled, voice echoing across the roaring illusions. "This is no mere trick of the mind!"

One of the illusions lunged at a knight, clawed hand slicing a wicked arc through the air. The knight stumbled, a ragged tear appearing on the side of his armor as if an actual blade had struck him. He cried out and regained his footing only with help from a comrade who held up a locket that glowed faintly, pushing the illusion back.

In the flickering torchlight, Carmen scrambled for an opening to finish the incantation. She caught Elara's eye, lips pressed into a thin line of desperation. They both knew time was short. If they could not weaken the anchor, the illusions might bloom unchecked. Above them, in the city, thousands of people cowered behind chalk markings and wards that would mean nothing if Malakar's final hold remained intact.

"Elara, chant!" Carmen hissed. "We must disrupt it. I'll help with the illusions."

Elara forced a shuddering breath, stepped closer to the dais, and recited the passages they had prepared, rhythmic lines meant to unravel Malakar's tether. Haze bled from her spool of thread and wrapped around her arms as she coaxed dreamweaver energy into the swirling darkness.

Meanwhile, Carmen braced a foot on the dais's lowest step and chanted a separate line that wove illusions of her own. She cast shimmering shapes that clashed with the monstrous silhouettes, each one bursting in a crackle of eerie light. One lesser illusion shrank back, hissing, while another snapped at the barrier Carmen formed. Above the din came Caelum's ragged breathing.

Elara's voice quavered. "Prince Caelum, hold on," she whispered fiercely. "We're not losing you again." She slammed a hand against the carved runes and let her spool's glow seep into the stone. The reaction was immediate: black flames sparked, swirling in violent eddies that battered her senses. Her heartbeat thundered, but she refused to break.

Lucian barked an order at the knights and locked them into a wedge formation. They rushed the illusions, warded amulets gleaming in defiance. Sparks lit the dim air as steel parted half-solid nightmares. The illusions spasmed, shifting shape like ink scattering in water. Each step the knights took bought Elara and Carmen precious seconds. Carmen flung a hand outward, illusions spinning from her fingertips, tangling with the nightmarish forms.

"We need a little longer," she gasped.

Sweat dotted her temples, but she clung to her illusions, shaping them into ephemeral nets that pinned two wraithlike shapes against the cracked walls.

Elara's chanting rose in pitch. She visualized every rebellious flicker of dream energy and harnessed the love and desperation that had fueled her powers since the day she first glimpsed Caelum in that dream corridor. Another line of archaic text hissed from her lips, the spool blazing with a brightness that hurt her eyes.

Caelum's tremors surged. He gave a choked moan as though Malakar's claws raked at his mind. For a heartbeat, Elara feared he might slip back into that cursed sleep or worse. Lucian's bellow snapped her focus.

"Fight it, Caelum!"

Caelum's eyes fluttered. A raw determination sparked there, despite the illusions' onslaught.

"I... I'm not giving in," he croaked, clutching Lucian's forearm to stay upright.

Dark shapes seized the far edges of the dais, thrashing

in unearthly silence. Each time one lurched forward, Carmen's illusions harried it and forced it back. Knights advanced in disciplined arcs, shouting as they pushed the nightmares toward the corners of the chamber. Still, new shapes formed along the walls in an endless cycle, fed by the anchor's power.

Elara pressed a hand against the dais. Her incantation reached its third and most crucial verse. Energy surged in her spool like water behind a cracking dam, ready to flood the illusions.

The runic markings across the chamber flared with violent intensity, as though Malakar himself roared from beyond. The stone vibrated underfoot, forcing the knights to brace themselves. Caelum groaned, arcs of dark power dancing across his clothes. The swirling illusions around them grew frantic, lashing with renewed fury.

Heart hammering, Elara locked eyes with Carmen. Each woman was nearly paralyzed by the knowledge that if they failed to disrupt this anchor, thousands of citizens above could drown in nightmares. They summoned whatever dreamweaver strength they could muster as a deadly force gripped the subterranean air.

TWENTY-FIVE

Elara's breath caught in her throat the instant she felt the double pull of magic: one set of threads kept her grounded in the catacombs, and another yanked her spirit into the shifting corridors of the dream realm. Around her, blades and torchlight clashed with ever-shifting shadows. The air howled with a malignant hum that threatened to choke any human sound. Yet she knew she could not falter. Too many lives depended on her. She shot Carmen a look of determination, noting the faint tremor in Carmen's fingers as she looped silver thread around her own wrist. They would face Malakar's illusions on both planes.

To Elara's left, Prince Caelum and Lucian pressed back-to-back. Their swords glinted with each flare of torchlight, bouncing off the grim stone walls. She saw Caelum's lips pull into a tight line as he strained against the weakness that still haunted him. Each parry rattled his arms, yet his resolve burned bright. A newly carved ward mark glowed on his vambrace, courtesy of the black-smiths' last-minute forging. The hum of illusions battered them, shrieking across the corridor with half-formed voices. Through the haze of flickering shapes, Elara caught only glimpses of the prince's face. Each time their eyes met, it felt like a promise that he would not let illusions devour any more of the kingdom.

"Form a circle around them, protect their bodies at all costs!" Caelum's voice echoed, raw with command.

In response, half a dozen knights scrambled into formation. They braced shields fitted with hammered sigils, each symbol shining faintly under the catacomb's sickly torchlight. The catacombs themselves felt alive, dank stone seeming to breathe with an unnatural pulse. Grooves in the floor were carved into twisting runes that glowed black and violet, as if feeding on the dread saturating the air.

Elara closed her eyes for half a heartbeat and let the swirl of her own fear settle. She let her fingertips graze the spool of enchanted thread that now hung against her hip, then exhaled. "Ready?" she called softly to Carmen, who blinked away the sweat stinging her eyes. A curt nod was Carmen's only reply.

Elara drew out a single strand of shimmering thread and tied one end around her wrist. Her voice dropped into a low chant, a stabilizing ward meant to anchor her consciousness here in the physical realm. She felt a sudden tug, a dizzying wave that made her heart thud, and the corridor's torchlight dimmed. The dream realm was calling. She had to balance bodily awareness so her limbs would not slump helplessly if illusions struck. For that, she relied on the anchor. The spool's glow pulsed, growing brighter for an instant as though in acknowledgment.

Carmen mirrored Elara's action, coiling a slender piece of glowing thread around her left wrist. Illusory sparks flickered around Carmen's fingertips, forming ephemeral veils that hovered protectively around them both. The knights standing guard gawked at how the shimmering illusions took shape in the stale air, swirling like subdued ribbons of moonlight. A lesser illusion from Malakar's runes snarled in the corner, rattling chains against the wall. The knights moved quickly to corral it, jabbing with warded spears until it broke apart in a ripple of smoke.

Elara let out a shaky breath. "Now," she murmured.

Together, she and Carmen stepped forward, crossing the boundary between the physical catacombs and the intangible realm of dreams. Her vision blurred. For an instant, her body felt painfully heavy, yet a rush of heady magic enveloped her senses. When her mind cleared, she and Carmen stood on a landscape both horrifying and ethereal: a dream corridor choked by winding paths of cosmic threads, each strand shimmering with malevolence.

In this mental battlefield, everything looked tinted violet. Waves of sickly luminescence rolled across the sky like thunderheads. Malakar's illusions reared up in monstrous shapes: a serpentine cluster of eyes rotating in midair. Flickers of black flame rimmed the corridor, coalescing into jagged silhouettes that snarled and bared dripping fangs. Elara's pulse pounded so hard she thought it might burst, but she kept going.

Behind them, Carmen's form flickered, though Elara sensed her friend's presence as a warm glow. Carmen raised her hands, illusions twisting from her fingertips in a bright spiral, and muttered incantations Elara recognized from their training sessions. The illusions formed ephemeral barriers that absorbed the first lunging wave of shadow creatures. Each time an abomination collided with Carmen's net, shrieking echoes rattled the dream corridor.

Elara steeled her resolve and trudged deeper. She spotted the anchor's cords, a tangled knot of shining black threads embedded in the distorted corridor floor. They pulsed like veins, each one feeding illusions into the waking world. She directed a sliver of dreamweaver magic at them and tried to pry one away. Raw force slammed back at her, knocking her a step to the side.

A tortured cry echoed faintly from the physical plane, and she nearly slipped back into awareness. No. She forced herself to remain calm. She had heard Lucian's voice cursing as a monstrous shape lunged. Illusions pressed them from every angle. She balled her fists against the guilt twisting in her gut. If she and Carmen did not unravel these illusions, the knights could fight all night without winning. "Focus," she whispered, swallowing her panic. "We can do this."

Carmen shot her a nervous glance. "One strand at a time?" Elara nodded and crouched near the black cords. Her spool glowed, and she reached out with trembling fingertips. The cord nearest her hissed like a living serpent, twisting away when her thread touched it. She pivoted and sent a wave of her own illusions onto the anchor, bright swirling motes that crackled with violet-gold light. If illusions were thoughts made real, she would counter them with determined faith in her cause. She had grown from that timid seamstress starved for coin. She had stood by a prince ravaged by curses. She had found hope in a bond that transcended nightmares. She clung to that hope and let it fuel her magic.

Hissing arcs of shadow shot up and hammered into Elara's illusions with enough force to buckle her knees. She clenched her teeth and funneled more dream thread into the cords. Finally, with a wrenching sound, one cord snapped free of the anchor and dissolved into glimmering dust. She heard a distant cheer in the physical realm, no doubt Caelum or Lucian noticing a horde of illusions vanish. Encouraged, she attacked another cord.

Meanwhile, Carmen struggled overhead, illusions swirling around her. A cluster of savage shapes battered Carmen's shimmering nets, each blow draining her energy. The sweat rolling down Carmen's face told Elara how hard she fought to stand her ground. Still, Carmen kept chanting, forging fresh illusions to keep the worst monstrosities at bay. At one point, a clawed phantom struck Carmen's shield so hard that she stumbled backward. Elara hissed through her teeth, wanting to help, but she knew the anchor took priority.

Carmen caught her footing, eyes ablaze with fierce

determination. "Don't stop!" she shouted. "Rip them all out!"

Elara forced a taut nod, ignoring the ache in her chest. She pressed her spool of shimmering thread against the second black cord. Dark magic seared her illusions, crackling with electric bursts that tremored in the dream corridor's floor. For a terrifying moment, her mind reeled with images of her lonely attic room, Carmen's scornful sneers from months ago, and the battered spool in her hands. Her insecurities threatened to drown her. Was she truly strong enough to challenge the illusions of a master sorcerer? She closed her eyes, inhaled slowly, and recalled Prince Caelum's blue gaze, splendorous even after five years spent in cursed sleep. She remembered his voice trembling with resolve not an hour ago, urging them all forward. She pictured Lucian's unwavering loyalty and Carmen's redemption. She was no longer alone.

That fresh surge of confidence ignited her illusions, lending a soft golden shimmer to her thread. She willed that power through her fingertips and shook off the malicious grip that tried to drag her under. The second cord snapped. Manipulative illusions sparked in protest, then fizzed out. Two down. Still more to go.

Simultaneously, the world jerked, and a wave of cold laughter echoed from behind them. Elara felt her blood run cold. She recognized that voice, so calm and elegant on the outside, but riddled with malice: Malakar. His presence manifested in the dream corridor as a tall, cloaked figure whose face flickered between grim smiles and an empty black mask. Wisps of darkness coiled around his silhouette. Carmen gasped, her illusions faltering. Even from a distance, Malakar radiated a potent destructive force that crackled against their illusions.

"And here I thought," Malakar purred, eyes glinting, "I had more time before you meddlesome dreamweavers arrived. How convenient that you delivered yourselves to my doorstep."

Elara's throat tightened. She remembered every moment he had manipulated her in the palace, the honeyed words that concealed his treacherous designs. She took an involuntary step back but forced herself to stand firm. This time, she would not be outplayed. She flicked a hand toward Carmen in silent support. Carmen squared her shoulders beside her, illusions thrumming around both of them. Even if fear clutched at their hearts, they could not yield.

Malakar swept his arm in a graceful arc and released a swirl of illusions that bled outward like living ink. They formed spined shapes that slithered over the dream corridor's walls, each hissing with savage hunger. "Step aside," he said, a quiet, lethal command. "You cannot hope to break runes I have embedded with my own blood and ambition."

Elara's jaw clenched. She forced a calm she did not feel. "Watch us."

Carmen hissed a short incantation, and a volley of shimmering needles rained down, piercing the illusions creeping along the walls. Malakar barely spared them a glance, his gaze shifting to the anchor cords Elara had broken. He snarled, real fury darkening his features.

Another wave of illusions poured forward in response, larger and more lethal. They looked like reptilian phantoms with barbed tails and snapping jaws that glowed with sickly purple flame. Carmen leaped to intercept them, illusions forming a thick barrier. Sparks flew, and the corridor vibrated with the collision.

Elara seized the moment to edge past Malakar's manifestation, aiming for the anchor's key wards. She spotted a cluster of filaments that shimmered with deeper black fire, marking them as crucial. If severed, the illusions in the catacombs above would weaken. But Malakar sensed her intent. He shouted a trio of words she did not recognize, and the ground beneath her feet exploded into writhing tendrils. She staggered, biting back a cry as they coiled around her ankles.

"Not so fast," Malakar growled.

She battered the tendrils with a swirl of her illusions. They recoiled, but Malakar twisted his wrist again, sending more illusions lashing. She blocked them with her spool's shimmering thread, though each clash drained her strength.

An echo from the physical plane reached her, a distant shout from Lucian. She caught the tail end of his furious words: "One more fucking trick from Malakar, and I'm dragging him from his damned hidey-hole myself!" Elara's heart twisted. The illusions in the catacombs must be intensifying. She pictured Caelum's trembling sword hand, the knights forming a protective ring around their slumped bodies. They had come so far. She refused to let Malakar's illusions devour them now.

She channeled her dreamweaver magic again. This time she shaped illusions drawn from memories of warmth and unity: a circle of seamstresses sewing wards side by side, blacksmiths forging protective amulets, scholars leaning over dusty tomes with scrawled runes, and Prince Caelum's unwavering eyes. The dream corridor brightened in response. Tiny motes of light flurried around her ankles, driving back Malakar's conjured tendrils. When Carmen noticed the shift, she poured more energy into her protective illusions. The monstrous shapes recoiled, battered by the sudden wave of luminous threads.

Elara took a precious second to breathe. Her arms felt weak, and her head throbbed from the sensory overload. She saw Malakar's expression waver, frustration etched in the tense line of his jaw. He advanced, illusions swirling from his outstretched hand in a violent torrent. Carmen braced herself, conjuring a mirrored shield that deflected some of the illusions. They shattered in an eruption of shrieks.

"We have to destroy the rest of those anchor wards," Carmen shouted, her voice breaking. "Quickly!"

Elara exhaled sharply and crouched again near the tangled cords. She placed her spool gently over them, ignoring the daggerlike illusions that sprang up to block her path. Carmen stood guard at her side, illusions tossing and colliding with Malakar's monstrous apparitions. Slowly, Elara coaxed her thread to fuse with the anchor cords, feeling every malicious twinge that sparked beneath her palms. She pressed her illusions forward, letting each surge of empathy unravel the curses Malakar had spent so long weaving. A third cord fractured with a flicker of swirling embers.

Malakar's presence slammed into them. A wave of black flame roared, jarring Elara's illusions away and making her spool vibrate so violently that she nearly dropped it. She gasped, fighting the swirl of dizziness that followed. Carmen screamed as her illusions collapsed under the blast, the force flinging her across the dream corridor. Elara's stomach clenched, certain that on the physical plane Carmen's body must have fallen limp for an instant. She pushed back a rush of panic. If they were ripped from the dream realm now, all their progress would be undone.

"Fools," Malakar hissed. "I shaped these illusions over years. You cannot unravel them in a night."

"Maybe not alone," Elara managed, her voice shaking. "But I'm not alone."

She heard Carmen's ragged breath behind her. Despite the pain, Carmen rose unsteadily. "We will undo you," Carmen spat, illusions sparking to life again around her trembling hands. The words were clumsy, but the defiance was clear. She mustered another wave of illusions that took the shape of silvery spears. Attention split, Malakar snarled in frustration and pivoted to shield himself from Carmen's assault.

Elara seized the opening and refocused on the anchor wards. Symbols etched into the threads glowed blood red, and a thick cord of black flame threatened to coil around her hands. She hissed in pain and grappled with the surge of dark magic. Forcing calm, she visualized each thread of the curse as an enemy to be severed. She guided her spool's shimmering strands between the cracks, searching for the runic pattern that would unravel them. Her entire body shook from the strain. Flickers of pale gold spun from her spool, merging with the cords and burning away knots of toxic illusions.

Finally, she tore through another ward. A pulse of brightness rippled outward, weaving through the corridor like a shockwave. She sensed illusions weakening in places. On the far edge of her hearing, she could taste relief in Lucian's triumphant shout and Caelum's fierce rally. The anchor was failing them, but Malakar had arrived to defend it personally, determined to snuff them out before the unraveling could finish.

He loomed closer, his voice echoing in the dream corridor like rolling thunder. Carmen braced herself, illusions crackling around her, yet exhaustion carved harsh lines across her face. Elara's heart thundered as she saw Malakar raise an arm, channeling an enormous swirl of illusions that churned overhead like a conjured tornado. He would strike them both down in one massive blow if they could not defend against it.

Adrenaline thrummed through Elara's veins, and she steadied her stance. She could not give in to terror, not when they teetered so close to victory. Fear flashed in Carmen's eyes, but she nodded, prepared to counter. Elara clenched her spool of thread, the spool that had first glowed in her lonely workshop what felt like ages ago. She fixed her gaze on Malakar, quiet hatred and unyielding hope fueling each breath. Defending her kingdom, saving Caelum, forging a new path with her allies, she would let all those convictions merge. It was the only way forward. Malakar's illusions triggered a hush, as though time itself had paused in horror.

His cold laughter rolled across them again, thick with contempt. Through the nauseating swirl of illusions, Elara found Carmen's gaze. Together, they waited for the onslaught. Elara's heartbeat roared like a drum. She steeled herself. Their unraveling was not finished.

Adrenaline thrummed through Elara's veins and she steeled herself. There could be no more hesitation. They had to keep unraveling, no matter how lethal Malakar's illusions grew.

TWENTY-SIX

Elara's heart pounded like a war drum as the darkness in the catacombs came alive around her. She felt the duality of reality pressing upon her: the cold, damp floor beneath her cheek and the roiling, half-formed dream corridor tugging at her mind. She forced her eyes shut and reminded herself to breathe. Each inhale tasted of stale earth and the lingering bitterness of Malakar's illusions. Somewhere nearby, water dripped against stone with a faint plink-plink, the only calm sound in the frantic chamber. Torches sputtered in the narrow passages, but their flickers offered little solace when colossal illusions loomed in both realms.

She could hear Caelum's voice echoing across the catacombs in the waking world, urging the knights to form up, to keep her physical body safe. Her pulse spiked at the protective strength behind his tone. She clung to it like a lifeline as she let her consciousness plunge deeper into the dream realm. The shift felt like pitching headlong into a raging tide. One moment, she lay on the cold stone, struggling to sit upright; the next, her vision clouded with flickering strands of dream-stuff.

Within that mental landscape, Carmen stood just ahead of her, illusions wreathing the rival seamstress's silhouette in a glimmering shield. Carmen's face shone with equal parts guilt and resolve. She tightened her jaw, her eyes narrowing. "Elara," she said, her voice thin but unyielding, "we hold him off together, yes?" Her illusions flared in a halo of silver, and Elara nodded, swallowing a wave of exhaustion. She felt a momentary pang of shared admiration for Carmen. They had come so far, from petty rivalries in the Tapestry Guild to standing shoulder to shoulder, fighting nightmares that threatened everyone.

Neither woman spoke further as Malakar's dream-spirit manifested before them like a vile storm cloud condensed into a figure. He was an amalgamation of twisted limbs and mocking faces, each feature flickering with raw malice. Static-laced blackness rippled across his torso, as if his body were riddled with tattered illusions ready to shred anything in sight. His voice lashed through the dream corridors in a low hiss that clung to every wall. "You meddling fools think a prince's heartbeat and a seamstress's thread can unmake me?"

The contempt coiling around his words made Elara's stomach twist. Instinctively, she flexed her fingers, conjuring a swirl of violet light that danced around her spool of shimmering thread. Her dreamweaver magic crackled along her arms, fueling her illusions. "I won't let you trap another soul," she said, forcing her voice to remain steady. "And I'm done letting you twist mine."

Carmen extended her hand, illusions radiating from her fingertips. "I regret everything I ever gave you," she spat, with no trace of her usual haughty sarcasm. "You used me to expand your power. I'm taking it back." She flung strands of shimmering illusions forward, forming a wavering net of brightness designed to isolate Malakar's form. Malakar only laughed, a guttural echo that disoriented Elara in the dream realm.

His shape pulsed with a terrifying energy, and the arena around them trembled. Massive, integral illusions surged upward, forming monstrous shapes that circled like predators. Their outlines dripped in smoky darkness, limbs bending at impossible angles. Teeth glinted in the gloom, too numerous to be anything but nightmares. Elara's mouth went dry. The hiss of these beasts mingled with Malakar's laughter, intensifying the dreadful pounding in her chest.

Back in the physical world, Caelum's command rang out in the catacomb's echoing passage: "Form the wedge! Push them aside!" Metal clanged as knights advanced, steel tips glinting in the unsteady torchlight. Elara felt the reverberation of real swords piercing illusions that had grown tangible enough to wound. She prayed the wards etched into the knights' lockets would hold. She could almost see Lucian's stance in her mind: blade leveled, ready to stab through living shadows. Caelum would be near him, sword raised, despite the unsteady bend of his knees. They had each come too far to surrender now.

In the dream realm, Elara braced her feet on a shifting plane of swirling color. She felt every drop of adrenaline fuel her illusions. Her spool of thread glowed bright, pulses of vivid gold-capped violet swirling around her wrists. She focused on every emotion that had driven her here: her love for Caelum, her fear for the kingdom, her gratitude for Lucian's unwavering support, and even her surprising camaraderie with Carmen. Blended together, these feelings became her greatest source of magic.

Her illusions flared in a halo of light, illuminating the dream corridor as though a midday sun had broken through. The monstrous shapes surrounding her and Carmen roared in protest, thrusting spined tendrils that cracked the surface of the dreamscape. Carmen gritted her teeth, holding her net of illusions in place. A shimmering barrier that blocked the worst of the onslaught.

"Do it!" Carmen shouted over the chaotic din. "I can't keep them all back forever!"

Elara lifted her spool as if brandishing a weapon. The thread coiled between her fingers, shining so brightly it stung her eyes. She directed that radiant energy straight at Malakar's shapeless form. He recoiled, his expression twisting from smug taunting to fury.

"Whelp!" he snarled, his face contorting through the illusions swirling around him. "You have no idea what you toy with. I command the nightmares of this realm!"

"Not anymore," Elara whispered, thrusting the last ounce of her dreamweaver resolve forward. Her illusions erupted in a burst of color, arcs of violet and gold surging through every ragged tear in Malakar's shape. She pictured the knights in the catacombs, Caelum's determined face, Carmen's outstretched hands—everyone she refused to lose. This was her final stand, an exorcism of fear.

Threads of molten silver wove through Malakar's spirit, fracturing his illusions at their very root. For an instant, the dream corridor blazed with blinding light, almost pure white, as Elara funneled her entire soul into the strike. She heard Malakar's anguished roar, a sound so sharp it made her ears ring. Then the realm cracked around them like lakeshore ice in winter, shattering into a thousand shimmering fragments that scattered into darkness.

In the physical corridor, that simultaneous break caused every monstrous shape to collapse. The illusions—grotesque creatures that had threatened to crush the knights against the stone walls—crumbled into dust, leaving behind the faint smell of ozone and something acrid. Elara's eyes snapped open just in time to see Lucian and Caelum, swords raised, crossing their blades in one decisive swing that scattered the final wisp of nightmare prowling in the torchlight. A resounding silence rolled through the catacombs. The anchor runes, once glowing like black coals beneath the arches, flickered and died.

A chaotic blend of panting and gasping filled the chamber. Elara's body trembled, both from the strain of battling Malakar's spirit and the cold, unyielding reality of the stone beneath her. Carmen, kneeling a short distance away, exhaled shakily and let her illusions dissolve. Sweat streaked into her eyes as she sagged back into Lucian's arms. He had rushed forward to steady her, and she clung to him as though the room might still tilt beneath them.

In the center of the corridor, Caelum lowered his blade. The raw relief on his face tugged at Elara's heart. His breathing was uneven, his cheeks flushed, but triumph shone brightly in his eyes. He lifted his gaze from the runes—now dimmed to mere etchings in the stone— and turned to Elara, relief radiating from every battered line of his posture. A flicker of the mesmerizing strength she had first glimpsed in their dream encounters lit his features. Carefully, he stepped through the scattered rubble, his boots scraping against broken shards of illusions that still fizzled into the air. At last, he reached for her with trembling hands.

"Elara," Caelum said, his voice hoarse from relentless effort. "Are you—" He broke off, words faltering in that moment. Instead, he crouched on unsteady legs and touched her cheek as she forced herself upright. A wave of exhaustion crashed over her. Her spool of thread hung limply from her fingertips, its glow reduced to faint embers of magic. She realized she was shivering, partly from the cold, partly from the emotional intensity of the final strike.

Lucian steadied Carmen before moving to Elara's side. He rested a supportive hand on her shoulder, his expression grim yet relieved. "Well done," he murmured. "I couldn't see exactly what you two did in there, but it worked."

Carmen let out a shaky chuckle, though tears glistened at the corners of her eyes. "I never... I never want to see illusions like that again," she whispered, her voice trembling, stripped of its usual pride. For all her mistakes, she had stood by Elara in that final moment. Her illusions had shielded them, buying the precious time Elara needed to deliver the strike that dismantled Malakar's presence.

Lucian nodded, his gaze sweeping cautiously across the corridor. "Where is he?" he asked, his voice hushed as though Malakar might still be hiding in the shadows. "Only that twisted spirit showed up here. We have no idea where his physical body is."

Elara's mind churned. She remembered the monstrous apparition in the dream realm, the savage laughter, and the sense of a mind controlling illusions from somewhere else. All of it had vanished, leaving behind only absence. Caelum took a torch from a knight and raised it toward the far corners of the catacombs, but nothing stirred beyond the circle of light. The damp stone walls reflected only the shine of the flickering flame.

Carmen closed her eyes and leaned against Lucian's chest. "Without the anchor," she said softly, "he can't sustain illusions on a grand scale anymore. But pockets of nightmares may remain like embers waiting to be fanned back to life unless we find him. We have to purge them."

The oppressive tension that had filled the underground chamber snapped. The knights who had formed the wedge breathed in unison, relief mingling with the raw shock of survival. One knight rolled his shoulders as if testing whether the illusions had wounded him for real. Another coughed into his fist and lowered his shield. The terror had felt so tangible, but now only faint wisps of gloom lingered at the edges.

Caelum exhaled a trembling breath. He sheathed his sword and surveyed the battered state of his companions. Carmen wavered, still half collapsed, and Lucian tightened his arms around her shoulders, trying to mask his own shakiness. Elara pressed a hand to her chest, her heart threatening to smash through her ribcage. She glanced at Caelum. "We did it," she rasped.

He nodded, pushing damp hair from his brow. "We did, but we still need to track him down. We'll send scouts at once. He will not blindside us again." His voice rippled with quiet, exhausted strength. "He can't hide forever now that the anchor is gone."

Elara rose from the cold floor. Her legs shook, but she managed to stand. Lucian helped Carmen to her feet, supporting her at the waist. Several knights lit additional torches, revealing the stone columns that had glowed with vile energy. Empty arcs now snaked across the walls, blackened lines showing where illusions once pulsed. It felt like stepping onto a battlefield after a catapult storm had ended. No one dared to rejoice too loudly, but victory glimmered in the exhausted eyes of everyone present.

He raised his head and rubbed the scar on his wrist, a mark that once pulsed with the same dark magic they had banished. The relief on his face made Elara's heart ache with fierce affection. She closed her eyes, recalling the tension of the dream realm moments earlier, and let the memory guide her breathing. They had severed Malakar's illusions from their strongest source. She could hear the hush of the catacombs acknowledging the triumph.

TWENTY-SEVEN

Elara stood at the threshold of the great hall, blood still rushing in her ears as she surveyed the figures gathered beneath the high-arched ceiling. Torchlight and a scattering of narrow windows gave the chamber a dim glow, lending everyone's expressions a tense cast. She could feel the palpable dread in the air: the kingdom had been plagued by illusions for too long, and tonight's gathering would determine whether any hope of peace remained.

Lucian stood near the heavy oak doors, boots planted as if preparing for a siege rather than a council. His hand hovered near the hilt of his sword, and his sharp eyes scanned each corner of the hall as though expecting Malakar to lunge from the shadows. Elara caught a glimpse of a fresh scratch on his forearm, battle scars from illusions they had recently faced in the catacombs, no doubt. He offered her a quick nod, a silent assurance that he was ready if any threat emerged.

Carmen lingered at Elara's side, her posture uncharacteristically subdued. She still wore a stylish cloak meant to frame her elegant silhouette, but no sign of her usual boasting or proud smiles appeared. Instead, she kept her arms folded over her midsection, gaze darting whenever a door creaked or someone shuffled too close. Despite her cool face, Elara sensed Carmen's underlying determination. They had come to rely on each other's illusions more than once, and that uneasy alliance now felt like a lifeline.

Farther into the hall, Caelum stood at the council table. His hair, still growing thicker since his awakening, brushed the collar of his regal tunic. A recent wave of dizziness had forced him to place one hand on the table's smooth surface. Elara saw him grit his teeth, refusing the help of an attendant, even though a tremor still ran through his legs. The king and queen stood just behind him, wearing matching expressions of concern.

"My son," Queen Meredith murmured, "you should sit." Her auburn hair and tear-bright eyes underscored how deeply she had worried for years.

Caelum exhaled through parted lips. "I will be fine, Mother," he answered, voice gentle yet firm. "We cannot waste time, not when the illusions grow bolder. I'm not collapsing tonight."

Elara felt a pang of sympathy. She knew how determined Caelum was to prove himself, both to the kingdom and to himself. The illusions had once held him prisoner in a cursed sleep, and much of the realm's chaos had festered under Malakar's manipulations. Although Elara had partially undone that curse, Malakar still lurked somewhere, weaving fresh nightmares for unsuspecting citizens. New rumors of coded splinter illusions weighed heavily on them all.

King John cleared his throat, a father's protectiveness evident in the way he hovered. "We trust you," the king said, shifting his gaze to the cluster of guild representatives waiting for the official start of the meeting. "Let us begin."

Caelum dipped his head in gratitude, then pushed himself upright. A hush fell over the gathered onlookers: blacksmiths, a few palace scholars, and two seamstresses from Elara's guild. Roderick the blacksmith had positioned himself near a pillar, thick arms crossed, a scowl etched into his face. Mistress Imelda was absent, as she seldom attended large gatherings, but her notes had guided many of Elara's dreamweaver discoveries.

Elara moved closer to the table, ignoring the flutter in her stomach. She sensed Carmen stepping forward too, as though they drew courage from each other's presence. Across the table, Caelum inclined his head, silently encouraging Elara to speak. Her pulse quickened. Two months ago, she had been just another overlooked seamstress. Now she was crucial to the kingdom's survival, and any slip of her words could rattle already frayed nerves.

She breathed in, projecting her voice across the hush. "When we destroyed the primary curse-anchor in the catacombs, we weakened Malakar's illusions. But we've discovered remnants of illusions seeded throughout the realm. We call them splinter illusions, each designed to feed off fear. If people struggle with nightmares or panic, these illusions manifest more strongly."

A ripple of alarm stirred among the council. A few guildspeople shifted uncomfortably, and one of the palace scholars whispered to his neighbor. King John's mouth formed a grim line, while Queen Meredith pressed her lips together, nodding in solemn acknowledgment. Caelum absorbed Elara's words, brows drawing close as she continued.

"If we do nothing," Elara said, "Malakar can still manipulate these splinters from afar. His presence may not be physically among us, but the illusions strip away reason, inciting chaos. We risk letting fear cripple the kingdom."

A flicker of movement at the hall's doors jerked Lucian into motion, his sword half drawn. A guard burst through, eyes wide with fright. He nearly tripped over himself before regaining balance. "My Prince," the guard gasped. "Another outbreak of illusions erupted near the eastern district. Shadows are gliding in the alleys, and people call them plague apparitions. They vanish like smoke, but we have injuries from panic. Some soldiers are losing their composure."

Murmurs of dread rippled through the assembled group. Caelum's knuckles whitened against the table, and Elara felt a surge of empathy for him. Though pale, he lifted his chin.

"Spread the word," Caelum instructed the guard. "Reinforce the wards in the eastern district. Direct the soldiers to use the newly forged amulets." His breathing was labored. "No one abandons their post."

"Yes, my Prince," the guard said, bowing hastily before retreating.

In the ensuing commotion, the King slammed a hand on the table. "We cannot allow these illusions to keep us cornered inside our own walls. Malakar put our son in a coma for five years. I refuse to let the rest of the kingdom sink under illusions."

A wave of agreement swept through the men and women in the hall. Roderick spoke next, his voice gruff. "We can distribute more warded lockets by nightfall, but it'll only slow the illusions, not stop them. We need a decisive end."

Elara glanced at Carmen, who nodded. Taking that as her cue, Elara said, "We do have a plan. Carmen and I can push deeper into the dream realm to uproot the illusions at their source. My needlework alone is strong, but if she helps me anchor a wide-scale dream shield, we might dismantle the splinters."

Some muttered warily. A stout, older seamstress from Elara's guild frowned. "But illusions in the dream realm are lethal if you lose focus, aren't they? I've heard stories of people not waking up." Her eyes flicked to Elara with concern rather than derision.

Carmen lifted her chin. "That is precisely why we plan carefully. The illusions feed on terror, so we must remain grounded. We have new incantations gleaned from the texts Mistress Imelda translated, and we have each other's support."

The King and Queen exchanged a look. At last, Queen Meredith spoke softly. "Elara, Carmen—if you venture into the dream realm, what do you need from us here in the hall? How do we protect your physical bodies from illusions while you fight?"

Lucian's voice cut in, crisp and steady. "My knights and I will guard them. Any illusions that attempt to manifest physically will be cut down before they reach the dreamweavers. We lost too many to illusions in the catacombs, so we stand ready now."

He made it sound so simple that Elara felt a surge of gratitude. Her cheeks warmed at the memory of his unwavering presence in earlier battles. Yet she caught Caelum's gaze across the table—he, too, had been her anchor, not just in the dream realm but in the fragile steps of daily life since his awakening. A brittle tension burned behind her lungs; she forced a careful swallow, reminding herself that unity mattered more than whatever tangled feelings still haunted her heart.

The King exhaled. He glanced at Caelum, who was leaning on the table once more. "Son," the King said gently, "your mother and I know you mean to fight. But your health is not fully recovered. These illusions: do you truly want to stand at the front of them?"

Every eye turned to Caelum, who breathed unsteadily. Yet a certainty brightened his expression. "I have let illusions rule me for five years," he said. "I cannot stand in the background while my people tremble. I will fight, in whatever capacity I can. They need to see I am with them."

A hush followed. Then the Queen nodded, reluctance

warring with pride in her eyes. "We trust you, Caelum," she said softly.

Elara inhaled, her chest prickling with a swirl of admiration and worry. She wanted to urge him to rest but knew better. If he stepped aside, the kingdom might suspect he was too frail to lead. And Malakar fed on doubts like that.

Gathering her courage, she cleared her throat. "We have identified the splinter illusions in multiple districts. They appear at random, but one thing is consistent: fear. If we can reach the root of Malakar's magic, his final stronghold, and if we demonstrate no fear, the illusions lose their potency." Her voice shook. "Easier said than done," she amended, "but that is the core principle."

Caelum's voice carried a quiet intensity. "Then let us unify the guilds, the knights, our volunteers. We hold the city while Elara and Carmen strike at the illusions directly through the dream realm. Meanwhile, Lucian will command a rebel force in case Malakar's illusions spawn again physically."

Lucian frowned. "I only fear Malakar might appear in person. We still have no proof that he is gone or cowering. Our scouts scoured half the outskirts and found no trace, but he might be hidden under wards. If that's the case, we must be ready to engage him physically while you two do your work."

The King and Queen each offered firm nods. Then the monarch turned to the assembled hall. "You hear the plan. Blacksmiths, prepare every protective amulet. Seamstresses, craft wards onto standard-issue cloaks if you can.

Scholars, finish any incantations that might unravel illusions in the city's busiest squares."

A charged excitement began to build. The anxiety remained, but now it mingled with a spark of collective purpose. Caelum gave Elara the faintest smile of encouragement. She clenched her fists, letting that sense of solidarity fortify her.

Then Carmen touched Elara's shoulder lightly. "I have informants," she said in a low voice, audible only to their nearby circle, "some of whom once reported directly to Malakar. They are frightened but willing to help. If Malakar resurfaces, we could know before illusions overtake us."

"This could be our best chance," Lucian said, raising a brow at Carmen. "I might dispatch a few scouting parties, armed with wards, to those contact points you mentioned. We don't want to be blindsided if Malakar tries to strike again."

Elara saw the King overhearing that final exchange. He drew in a breath, then addressed the entire hall. "We must trust each other now. Enough clandestine alliances have damaged this kingdom already. If Carmen's network can alert us, we will adjust swiftly."

Queen Meredith's gaze swept across the hall, noting the wide range of expressions—hopeful, afraid, resolute. "The sun will set soon," she said. "Before it does, make sure each district leader understands their role. We meet again at sunrise if there is no immediate threat during the night, or sooner, if illusions strike."

In that moment, Caelum straightened as if his body no

longer weighed him down. He nodded, then inclined his head to Elara, Lucian, and Carmen. The softness in his eyes told her he appreciated them more than words could express. For a heartbeat, she remembered the night she first glimpsed him in the dream realm, how intangible he had seemed. Now he stood among them, a living testament to what courage and unity could achieve.

When Caelum turned to the rest, the tension in his shoulders seemed to gather into something fierce. "I will not see this kingdom gripped by fear," he said. "Malakar used illusions to break our spirits, but that ends. With a final push and the guidance of the dreamweavers, we will be free of him."

Applause broke out across the hall—some hesitant, some loud. Soldiers banged gauntleted fists on their chests in salute, while guild members exchanged determined glances. The King and Queen shared a silent embrace before turning to address a steward, who hurried forward with parchment and fresh quills.

Slowly, conversation rose as smaller groups began to organize. A swirl of clusters formed: blacksmiths conferring over forging details, scribes preparing to record new orders, seamstresses whispering about urgent ward embroideries. Wooden benches scraped as individuals found seats to trade notes or gather supplies. Guards lined the walls, keeping watch for anything unexpected.

Elara's heartbeat thundered. She thought of how Malakar had once worn his polite smile while praising her illusions, determined to twist her gifts to his advantage. She refused to let him do it again.

Carmen tugged at Elara's sleeve. "We can start with my informants tonight," she said, her voice hushed. "If they've seen suspicious activity, we might pinpoint Malakar's route. Let me gather the details and pass them on to Lucian."

Elara nodded. "Be careful." She briefly touched Carmen's hand, a gesture that not long ago would have felt unthinkable, given their past rivalry. Now, the memory of illusions fueling Carmen's envy seemed distant. They had all grown beyond petty grudges.

Carmen squared her shoulders. "I intend to survive this," she said. "And to help you do the same."

At the same time, Lucian drifted closer. He clearly wanted to jump into action, though he spared a glance at Elara. "I'll get squads ready," he murmured. "If your dream incursion uncovers Malakar's location, we move swiftly. No illusions will blindside us this time."

She offered him a tentative smile, ignoring the quick flutter in her chest. "I appreciate it. Thank you, Lucian."

Finally, Caelum stepped away from the table, exhaling as he approached them. Concern etched faint lines across his brow, though a glimmer of steel remained in his eyes. "We can do this," he said firmly. "I will address the city wherever illusions flare. I will remind the people we stand with them."

They shared a quiet moment of renewed confidence, though Elara's heart still pounded with anticipation. She thought of the spool of shimmering thread tucked in her belt pouch, waiting for the next opportunity to harness dreamweaver power. And she thought of Malakar, presumably lurking somewhere, feeding on the fear that prickled in every corner of the kingdom.

From the dais, voices rose as the King and Queen officially dismissed the council, urging everyone to expedite the plan. Footsteps echoed in the cavernous hall. The tension in the air felt taut as a drawn bowstring. Elara turned to Carmen, bracing herself for the next step.

Carmen quietly pulled Elara aside. "My informants might bring word as early as midnight," she said, her voice trembling slightly with emotion. "If they do, I'll find you in the seamstress quarters or the library, wherever you need to prepare."

"And I'll coordinate with Lucian," Elara replied, "so he knows if we're moving out."

Around them, the grand hall began to clear, courtiers and guild members scattering to their assignments. Elara brushed shoulders with an overworked steward, then sidestepped a guard carrying a rack of extra swords. Caelum's parents lingered near a side corridor, exchanging low words with a squad of knights. Even in their exhaustion, both monarchs radiated renewed hope.

As Elara glanced toward Caelum, who was carefully making his way to rejoin his mother, she felt a pang of protectiveness. It was so easy to remember him frail and unresponsive in his bedchamber. Now he moved under his own power, determined to save the very people who had once considered him lost forever. She admired him more than ever.

In one final gathering of resolve, Elara, Carmen, Lucian, and Caelum, paused in an impromptu circle near a marble pillar. No one spoke. Their expressions said enough: Trust me. Rely on me.

"We go forward together," Caelum said, raising his voice just enough for them to hear.

Elara nodded. Carmen's composure remained steady. Lucian glanced around, then curved his lips into a tight, confident smile. "Then we'd better get started."

They split, each heading to their tasks. Elara tightened her hand around the spool of thread. She prayed her illusions could truly root out Malakar's final hold, that Carmen's repentant cunning would uncover the traitorous sorcerer's hiding place, and that Lucian's sword would keep them safe. Above all, she hoped Caelum's strength would endure. The entire kingdom rested on that fragile promise.

And as the council drew to a close, the King and Queen pressed a final vow upon everyone present: trust in Caelum's leadership. Though they had once deferred to Malakar's facade, they now embraced their awakened son wholeheartedly. Chairs scraped, voices erupted with fresh instructions, and the wide doors to the great hall were flung open to let the tense throng disperse.

Carmen lingered near Elara's elbow. "I can get the first leads on Malakar's last movements," she said, lowering her voice. "It might take me a few hours, but I'll return with whatever I find."

Lucian, overhearing, added, "Once I have that intel, I can divide the knights into maneuver squads. If Malakar's hiding in the outskirts, we'll flush him out. If he's lurking in the city, we'll isolate him."

Elara's heart felt like a drum in her throat. She clutched the spool at her waist. Despite bone-deep weariness, purpose flooded her veins. She glanced between Carmen, Lucian, and, across the hall, caught Caelum's resolute stare. Their gazes locked, and for a moment, time seemed to float—two dreamweavers, a swordsman, a once-cursed prince, and a kingdom's fate on the brink.

The King's herald rang out, announcing the council dismissed. The echoes ricocheted across the hall, and Elara swallowed hard. She felt the weight of the future pressing down on them all.

At last, the small group pushed forward. Carmen set off to find her informants. Lucian peeled away to summon his rebel knights. Elara and Caelum exchanged one more hopeful glance before turning to help quell any illusions that might arise in the next few hours. All around, the royalty, guilds, and grieving citizens alike placed their final hopes on this confrontation, trusting that by dawn, Malakar's hold on their nightmares would be broken forever.

CHAPTER

TWENTY-EIGHT

Night enveloped the city in a cloak of restless shadows. Rain hammered the rooftops, pouring in relentless sheets that turned every alleyway into a rushing gutter. Elara pulled the hood of her damp cloak tighter around her face and blinked water from her lashes. She kept a steady pace, matching Prince Caelum's measured steps, though her heart thumped with rising urgency. Citizens hurried past, clutching oilskin umbrellas or ducking beneath sagging awnings as thunder rolled overhead.

Flickers of whispered tension drifted with the rainfall. Rumors claimed Malakar himself was on the move, no longer satisfied with sending half-formed illusions. Elara's chest twisted at the thought of meeting him in person. She had witnessed the brutal power he wielded through nightmares, and the possibility that he would manifest in flesh and bone rattled every fiber of her being.

Beside her, Caelum inhaled shakily. The bitter chill and the lingering ache in his limbs tormented him, but he masked both behind grim composure. He wore a high-collared cloak of deep blue, its embroidered wards glinting under the torchlight that cut through the downpour. The palace had mobilized swiftly, dispatching loyal guards to every corner of the city, yet Elara felt no relief. Fear draped the streets like a tapestry of gloom, and every clap of thunder sounded like an omen of bloodshed.

Ahead, Lucian waited near a narrow archway. He stood with his arms folded across his breastplate, droplets clinging to the edges of his dark hair. At his side stood Carmen, her face angled downward. Lightning traced a ragged path across the sky and illuminated the determined set of her jaw. They glanced at Elara and Caelum with tense acknowledgment.

"You heard?" Lucian asked. His voice cut through the thunder, resolute yet edged with dread. "He shows himself in the main courtyard soon. People have been fleeing, though I saw some too terrified to move."

Elara nodded, breath catching in her throat. "Where is he exactly?"

"In the heart of the city," Carmen answered, lifting her gaze. "Word is that illusions swirl around him like a thundercloud. Windows are shuttering. Anyone brave enough to look claims he conjured shapes that twist into beasts whenever someone edges near."

Caelum exhaled, exhausted. "Then he is daring us to confront him openly. Either he wants the crowd's fear, or..." He fell silent and glanced at Elara. She knew what he meant. Malakar thrived on illusions that fed on raw terror.

If the kingdom's fear was a well, he was ready to drain every last drop.

"We should gather who we can," Lucian said. "I'm still uncertain how many illusions wander the outskirts, and the knights posted by the gates might not reach us in time."

Elara's heart pounded. She remembered sleepless nights forging protective illusions to block Malakar's nightmares. Now everything converged and they had no choice but to meet him face to face. She could still sense the faint echo of his vile presence from their last battle in the catacombs. If he had chosen tonight to appear, he believed his illusions would be unstoppable in the open square.

"All right," she murmured, "we can't leave him free to terrorize the people. Let's go."

The four of them stepped into the open. Rain pelted their cloaks in fierce gusts. The streets leading to the main courtyard formed a labyrinth of puddles and slick cobblestones. Shadowy doorways flickered with candlelight, and watchers peered nervously from behind half-closed shutters. Over the drumming rainfall, Elara heard distant murmurs of alarm. Her stomach knotted at the thought that the entire city teetered on the brink of chaos.

Their footsteps echoed as they neared Sunspire Plaza at the city's core. Lanterns swung precariously in the wind, their flames sputtering against the downpour. Bolts of violet-tinged lightning lanced across the clouds, illuminating clusters of worried citizens huddled under eaves or behind doorways. A hush fell whenever Elara and her companions passed, as if the crowd sensed a final standoff drew near.

She moved closer to Caelum and brushed his hand, silently offering reassurance. Despite the tension throbbing inside her, she found strength in his presence. Months ago, she had glimpsed him only in moonlit dream corridors, half believing he was nothing more than a fleeting vision. Now he was awake and determined to rid the kingdom of Malakar's twisted illusions, no matter the toll on his still-recovering body.

A shout pierced the night. Lucian froze, his eyes narrowing, then he pointed down a wide alley that opened onto the main courtyard. Ripples of shadow undulated in midair, casting monstrous silhouettes that flared whenever lightning struck. Elara's throat went dry. She felt a growing pulse of dark energy, so palpable it made the hair on her arms stand on end.

"Gods," Carmen whispered. "He is here in person, isn't he?"

Before anyone could answer, a jagged streak of silvery fire illuminated the courtyard. Malakar stood at the center. A swirling funnel of shadow seemed to cling to his shoulders, as though carved of living smoke. His cloak streamed in the wind, and an eerie reflection glimmered in his eyes, no longer the polished façade of a court adviser but a vessel of raw malice. He appeared taller, more ominous than any illusion from before. Bolts of crooked lightning webbed across the sky, drawn to the tempest of magic radiating from him.

Elara's pulse thundered as they stepped onto the

cobblestones of the plaza. The smooth stones were perilously slick underfoot, water pooling in shallow dips. The stench of fear hung in the air, carried on each sheet of rain. Townsfolk had scattered to the edges of the courtyard, peering ghost-like from behind pillars and doorways. A few small children pressed themselves against a stone wall, as if they yearned to vanish into the masonry. Their eyes shone with fraught alarm.

Malakar let out a laugh that echoed above the drumming rain. "You actually showed up," he said, voice smooth despite the roiling sky. "Willing lambs to the slaughter. Did you believe vanquishing my anchor runes would be enough? How quaint."

Lucian gripped his sword. Beside him, Carmen readied a shimmering whisper of illusion around her palms. Caelum stood taller, though Elara saw him swallow painfully and force himself to remain steady. She stepped forward, her spool of glimmering thread in hand, and her heart hammered so hard she feared it might burst. In all her nightmares of Malakar's scornful face, she had never imagined confronting him like this, in front of an entire city, with the sky boiling overhead.

Malakar's attention fell on Caelum. His lips curled in a sneer. "The prince stands upright at long last. Congratulations on your precious defiance, my liege. Have you even the strength to lift a sword?"

"Strength enough," Caelum rasped, though his cheeks were pale. "And I have the will of my people behind me."

Malakar's gaze slid over the huddled citizens, dismissing them with a flick of disgust. "They cower like mice, paranoid that each shadow may be a new illusion, and perhaps they should be. Fear is my greatest ally." His eyes turned on Elara. "And you, seamstress, always meddling in realms beyond your station. Did you intend to scold me for conjuring a little dread? Or perhaps you want one last demonstration of how illusions really bend reality."

"I've seen enough," Elara replied, keeping her voice as steady as she could. The spool of thread quivered in her hand. She thought of all the illusions she had banished, the nightmares she had painstakingly unstitched. Her dreamweaver magic still pulsed beneath her skin, waiting for her command. "You won't chain them again."

Malakar's laughter pealed, thunder rolling as if in answer. "You speak as if your trifling illusions could stand against me." Shifting his weight, he raised a hand. Shadows bled from his gestures, piling onto themselves like molten tar. The mass twisted into a towering shape with branching horns, ink dripping from its maw. Hisses and startled cries rose from the edges of the courtyard as the creature lurched forward, too tangible for anyone's comfort.

Carmen tensed. "Elara," she hissed, eyes on the monstrous silhouette. "That...that's bigger than anything we faced in the catacombs."

Elara swallowed hard. She felt Caelum's quiet presence at her side, and Lucian's intense focus behind her. She stepped closer to Malakar, demanding every shred of courage she possessed. Her spool of shimmering thread ignited with faint silver arcs, responding to the swirl of magic. "If you think your illusions can still terrorize us," she said, "you've already lost. We've learned how to fight back."

"Have you?" Malakar replied, pressing his hand against the torso of the horned illusion. Violet sparks spat across its surface, granting it a dreadful solidity. "Then show me."

He gestured, and the monstrous illusion charged forward, hooves thundering on soaked cobblestones. Rain sprayed in all directions. Lucian shouted for the small group to spread out as knights scrambled in from a nearby street to hold the perimeter. Caelum did not retreat. He angled himself in a guarded stance, though Elara's heart squeezed because she knew his strength was still precarious.

She flung a bolt of dream-infused energy, threads gleaming like filaments of moonlight that lashed at the creature's chest. The monster reeled but did not dissolve. Instead, it reared high, raking claws and spitting black droplets. Carmen unleashed her illusions in a radiant net over the monstrosity's flank, trying to peel away the shadows. The courtyard erupted in flashes of color and swirling darkness. Citizens cowered, some covering their heads, a few crying out as the illusions boiled toward them.

Lightning scorched the sky, its glare sketching the chaos below. Elara heard Caelum call her name over the roar of the storm. The horned beast lashed at him with a black tendril, but Lucian lunged between them, his sword cutting the living shadow. For a breathless second the illusions crackled with raw power, and Lucian staggered back, half blinded. Carmen shouted his name and raised an iridescent barrier in time for him to regain his balance.

"Elara, keep going!" Caelum said. He braced himself against the swirl of illusions and lifted his sword, his posture wavering yet determined. "We drive them back, show them we can banish it."

Pressing her lips together, Elara summoned the memories that fueled her magic. She remembered the lonely nights hunched over her spool, trembling with the knowledge that only her illusions could breach Malakar's curses. She recalled forging wards in the catacombs and felt life flare in Caelum when her illusions finally severed his chains. The recollections ignited a fierce power in her chest. She flicked her wrist, and her thread snapped into a bright lash of dreamfire. The horned beast howled, stumbling as the net Carmen held pinned it in place. Lucian hacked at the illusions, each slash biting deeper into the shadow's resolve.

Malakar's eyes narrowed. "You push me too far," he hissed, stepping back as the monstrous shape flickered, its edges unraveling beneath the combined assault. "Let's see how well you fare when the entire city quakes."

With a twist of his hand he hurled tendrils of darkness across the courtyard. Smaller illusions burst forth, warping into half-formed nightmares that swarmed the outer ring of stunned onlookers. Shock rippled through the watchers. Some tried to flee and slipped in the downpour, while others froze, unable to tear their eyes from the horrors blocking every path.

Elara's breath stuttered. Childlike shapes writhed among those illusions, pale faces twisted into silent shrieks. Each vision threatened to stoke the city's panic, and if terror took the crowd Malakar would only grow stronger. Her legs shook, yet Caelum's presence steadied her. His hand brushed her shoulder in unspoken encouragement.

She drew a long breath and turned fully to him. Illusions hissed and sparked in the rain, but for a moment she met his gaze. Pain and resolve mingled in his blue eyes. He stood ready to fight, trusting her to guide the dreamweaver magic that could break Malakar's lies. She gripped Caelum's hand, her fear hardening into defiance. She would not let Malakar reduce this kingdom to cowering shells.

Thunder rumbled overhead, a dire drumroll to what Elara suspected would be their hardest battle yet. The courtyard's torches sputtered in the wind, the storm unrelenting. The illusions tightened their circle, and the city braced for a nightmare given flesh and shadow. Through the dimness, Elara spotted Lucian rallying the knights along the courtyard's perimeter, barking orders for them to hold formation no matter what new horror emerged from Malakar's conjurations. Carmen hovered at Elara's left, illusions half formed in her cupped hands, eyes blazing.

Another arc of forked lightning illuminated Malakar's face. A triumphant, near manic expression distorted his features. He spread his arms, letting the swirling shadows intensify, and the monstrous illusions around him swelled, surging outward. Water surged at Elara's feet. It felt as though the elements themselves had turned to wrath.

Summoning her courage, Elara gripped Caelum's hand one last time, then signaled to Lucian to hold the line. The final battle between dream and waking nightmare was about to erupt.

CHAPTER

TWENTY-NINE

Lightning streaked the storm-wracked sky, sharp and blinding in its fury. Elara blinked hard to keep focus as thunder shook the city's main courtyard. Each crash reverberated through the ground beneath her boots. Rain pummeled her cloak, plastering it to her skin, but she refused to yield to discomfort. The entire world seemed to hover on a knifepoint, and every heartbeat hammered a reminder of what was at stake.

Searing light exposed the colossal illusions Malakar had conjured. They were monstrous, half-formed shapes lurching and twisting like living nightmares. Fanged heads thrust forward, snapping at the defenders who held a ragged line amid overturned carts and broken masonry. Elara watched in horror as a guard's protective ward flickered and failed. A spectral beast lunged, forcing an agonized scream from the man. She inhaled sharply and summoned calm despite the swirl of panic stifling the air.

"Hold formation!" Lucian bellowed. He slashed at a

327

rampaging shadow thing with a blade etched in warded script. Sparks arced where steel met illusion. More knights rallied around him, pressing forward even as the monstrous illusions threatened to devour their courage. Lightning illuminated Lucian's rain-streaked face, revealing a fierce determination that kept his squad from scattering. Phantom creatures screeched and flailed, oozing black vapor in every direction.

Carmen crouched behind a broken pillar and drew up a glowing thread of her own, illusions pulsing in her cupped hands. "Stay back!" she shouted at a pair of wide-eyed townsfolk clinging to each other. With deft motions, she conjured ephemeral chains that lashed two smaller nightmares and yanked the illusions apart with a crackle of dream light. Her illusions dissolved into shimmering motes that drifted upward, lost in the storm.

Elara's chest constricted when she glimpsed the one figure in the courtyard who did not flinch at the lightning, Malakar himself. He stood tall, robes dripping, and calmly orchestrated the chaos with a tilt of his chin and the unspoken mastery of illusions he had cultivated for so long. His gaze found hers, cold and knowing. A swirl of shadows coiled around him, giving him a regal, terrifying aura, as if he belonged to this storm more than any mortal soul. Dozens of illusions clawed the ground before him, each feeding on fear that thickened in the rain-drenched air.

At her side, Prince Caelum trembled in the downpour. Though his posture wavered, he refused to step back. A bruise across his cheekbone gleamed in the torchlight.

Every blow he and Lucian had traded against these horrors left its mark. The formidable illusions had battered Caelum's mind with haunting echoes of the coma he had recently escaped. Elara touched his elbow and sensed the hollow terror building in him. She recognized that look, remnants of the prison of nightmares he had once been forced to inhabit.

"Caelum," she said gently, trying to steady him. "Look at me." Rainwater ran down her face, mingling with sweat. Her heart twisted at the flicker of pain in his eyes.

"I...I see them everywhere," he whispered. Thunder cut across the end of his words, yet she heard him clearly. "They...they're the same illusions that chained me in those endless dreams."

Elara swallowed the knot in her throat. "You are free," she insisted. "He no longer holds your mind. We need you. Focus on me, on all of us who stand with you."

Caelum nodded. He tightened his grip on the hilt of his sword and refused to let the illusions reduce him to that broken state again. Drawing labored breaths, he took a defensive position.

Lightning revealed the king and queen perched on a nearby parapet, stricken by the devastation unfolding below. They flanked a handful of guards who struggled to keep them safe from stray illusions that sometimes spiked up the walls. Queen Meredith lifted a shaking hand to her mouth as another monstrous shape lunged at the defenders.

Elara steeled herself, recalling lines from Mistress Imelda's stolen notes. She had studied them in secrecy, learning how incantations might anchor her illusions when raw determination was not enough. Threads of fear, heartbreak, and fierce loyalty churned in her chest, letting her draw upon the dreamweaver powers that had started as flickers of magic at her needle's tip. Now those powers threatened to flood her entire being.

Malakar advanced by a single, measured step. More illusions spewed forward at his silent command: beasts with elongated limbs, eyes like shifting coals, teeth that dripped with an unsettling glow. One monstrous shape slammed into the ward line, sending knights stumbling. Another roared so loudly that dust rained from the stone ramparts overhead, and a wave of dread crashed through the courtyard.

Lucian's voice rang out again. "Shields up! Do not yield!" He tore through a manifested fang of darkness, shattering it into wisps. To hold their nerve under that onslaught took all his skill and fortitude. Another moment of hesitation, and the illusions would devour the entire front rank.

Elara clenched her fists around her spool of shimmering thread. She could not afford to falter. Turning her head slightly, she saw Carmen subduing two more illusions. The older seamstress offered Elara a look of urgency, beckoning her to do what only she could. Elara nodded. She steadied her breathing, cleared her thoughts, and spoke the incantation she had nurtured night after night:

"Threads of daylight, threads of night,
Unravel his grasp, restore our sight.

From dream's own heart, I summon might,
Banish illusions, reveal true light."

Her voice trembled at first. Then something in her center flared, bright and commanding. A swirl of pale fire lit her eyes from within, and the spool of thread in her hands radiated silver arcs. She almost felt Caelum's presence in her chest, sensing his compassion, his guilt over lost years, and his unwavering pledge to stand with the kingdom no matter the cost. She let that whirl of emotion fill her illusions with unstoppable force.

The ground quaked as her words vibrated through the courtyard. She recognized that Malakar's conjurations were anchored to multiple rift-nodes dotting the city, hidden under layers of malevolent design. Her dreamweaver senses picked up on their faint pulses, each one tethered to the illusions rampaging here. Malakar's greatest advantage was not only these monstrous shapes, but the entire network feeding them.

Elara spotted arcs of crackling blackness flickering at the corners of her vision. They pulsed in tandem with every hush of the wind and every wave of panic from the defenders. This network was the same twisted vein of magic that had once kept Caelum trapped in cursed sleep, but now it bared its fangs at the entire populace. She felt the anchor lines hooking into people's fear, turning their darkest dreads into tangible monsters.

"Stop!" she cried. Her voice reverberated with a thunderous echo that did not belong to her alone. Fragments of her dreamwoven illusions glowed in the air behind her, fluttering like ribbons of starlight. "Malakar, you will not cage us again!"

His mouth curved in a contemptuous smile. "You challenge the illusions I have cultivated for years?" His words came softly, yet they carried across the crashing storm as if he spoke straight into the minds of all present. "You are too late, seamstress. You cannot mend what I have already torn."

Elara exhaled, ignoring the droplets sliding down her forehead. "We will see about that," she hissed.

She sensed Caelum trembling at her flank, but when she shifted her gaze, she saw clarity in his eyes. He refused to wither before Malakar a second time. He raised his sword, jaw set tight. "We fight together," he said, and his voice was stronger than she expected.

Malakar flicked a hand and summoned a fresh wave of illusions. The monstrous shapes surged forward, throats rumbling with unearthly howls. Elara's heart hammered. She imagined the entire city trembling under illusions as relentless as these, and for a moment fear pricked her lungs. Then Caelum's steady posture called her back from the brink. She inhaled deeply and sank into the magic roiling within her.

Threads of pale luminescence coiled around her fingertips, shimmering in the storm. She let her heartbreak, her guilt over every moment she worried she was too weak, fuse with her deep love of the kingdom. She remembered the nights standing guard over Caelum's cursed body, the quiet devotion Lucian and Carmen had shown. She remembered the people who believed in her. All of it welled up, fueling the illusions she needed to craft.

"Focus on her illusions!" Carmen called out. She thwarted another snapping nightmare, the false vision unraveling in a blaze of sparks. "Create an opening!"

Elara did not need a second reminder. She poured the fullness of her dreamweaver might into the spool. A swirling tapestry formed in the air. Glowing threads twisted and wove themselves into a grand design. Hazy shapes became protective arcs of light, and each filament lashed the half-formed beasts Malakar had conjured. Where the beasts had gaping jaws only moments earlier, the spectral forms now shrank back, sizzling at the edges.

She felt malice radiate from Malakar. He extended both arms, and dark ribbons of magic flared from his fingertips. The illusions that answered him grew wilder, shapes blurring into sharp angles and spikes. Citizens screamed, and guards reeled under the punishing force. Some illusions battered the warded amulets the knights wore, testing for weak points.

Elara's spool glowed like a tiny star in her hand. Lightning danced above, and thunder clapped, punctuating her every heartbeat. She pressed forward and repeated the incantation:

"Threads of daylight, threads of night,
Unravel his grasp, restore our sight.
From dream's own heart, I summon might,
Banish illusions, reveal true light."

Her illusions flared so brilliantly that she felt the threads vibrate, scorching her palms with magical heat. The courtyard lit up like midday. She spotted Carmen, face streaked with rain and sweat, weaving ephemeral patterns that locked several feral illusions in place. Lucian, half masked by swirling shadows, roared a war cry and struck down another of Malakar's summoned horrors with a crackling slash. The black shape melted at his feet.

Caelum choked back a gasp, eyes widening as a specter lunged at him from behind. He pivoted just in time and parried with his blade. The sudden clash rattled him, but he did not fall. Elara's chest burned with pride. If Malakar wanted to see them cowering, his illusions had found the wrong court.

Finally, Elara unleashed the full wave of her conjured magic. She lifted her spool overhead and let her threads expand in a radiant spiral, lines of shimmering light swirling outward like an unfolding tapestry. In that moment, the illusions Malakar had flaunted lost cohesion. Limbs of shadow sagged, claws receded to dripping wisps, and horrific eyes went wide with surprise. Elara aimed her power at the hidden anchor lines she sensed beyond the courtyard, those rift-nodes distorting everything, and she visualized them dissolving beneath the weight of her dreamwoven onslaught.

Malakar hissed. His once-unbreakable illusions convulsed as if they faced raw sunlight after ages in darkness. "No!" he snarled. The cry echoed across the battered courtyard. The roiling storm overhead flickered, and lightning cut through the haze, revealing him fully. He looked diminished yet full of desperate fury, determined not to concede. A final monstrous wave erupted around him, thrashing wildly and reaching for any source of fear.

Elara inhaled. Every muscle felt on fire, but she refused to relent. Rain pounded her shoulders, and her hair clung to her cheek. She stepped into the midst of the swirling illusions, her eyes blazing with that pale, near-white brilliance. Directly behind her, Caelum braced himself as if ready to dash forward and shield her with his body. She felt his presence, heard his ragged breathing, and let that love anchor her. She spun a final lash of magic, using the spool as a focus point.

A tapestry of dreams burst forward in an unstoppable torrent. Every stitch shimmered with gold and violet. She poured her compassion into each strand, and pain and longing fueled the momentum, forging illusions immune to Malakar's hatred. The swirl of dream shapes crashed into his monstrous creations like a tidal wave.

An explosion of light flooded the courtyard so intensely that cracks of thunder seemed to vanish. For an instant nothing else existed. Knights toppled, covering their faces. High above, the king and queen watched, their voices caught in their throats. Caelum staggered, his sword dropping for half a breath as he blinked away tears. Carmen shielded her eyes with both arms, and Lucian froze mid-swing.

Then it happened: Malakar's illusions buckled under that raw might. One by one the savage spectral beasts disintegrated into drifting motes, powerless before the tapestry Elara had unleashed. She clenched her teeth and held the magic until the courtyard trembled beneath waves of bright, cleansing energy. The storm's thunder roared in agreement.

Jagged shapes collapsed where her magic landed, and Malakar's monstrosities turned to ash beneath an onslaught of vivid dreamweaver power that left the onlookers breathless and trembling.

THIRTY

Elara felt her heart hammer wildly as rivulets of dream-fire swirled around her hands and lashed into the center of Malakar's illusions. The tangled mass of prowling shadows convulsed, torn apart by her fierce surge of magic. She steadied her posture, boots gripping the rain-slick cobblestones, and focused on channeling her power with precision rather than desperation. She could almost taste the metallic tinge of fear in the air, an echo of the kingdom's terror that Malakar had feasted upon for far too long.

Sparks showered across the main courtyard, casting erratic flashes of light over the fearful faces of onlookers pressed against walls or peeking from shuttered windows. As the illusions around Malakar cracked, Elara saw a flicker of genuine alarm in his eyes. His once-impenetrable aura of confidence looked fractured, like a mirror smashed by a single lethal blow. Elara's dream-thrumming heart urged her onward: she had come too far to let him reinforce those nightmares again.

When her magic battered the final barrier around Malakar, Caelum stepped forward. He moved as though every breath pained him, yet he refused to let weakness command him. His shoulders trembled, but his sword remained steady, the deep blue folds of his royal cloak dripping with rain. A ragged hush fell around the courtyard when he lifted his voice. "Malakar," he said, voice hoarse but resolute, "by my right as prince of this kingdom, I name you a traitor and a murderer of hope. You tore my life from me. You twisted illusions to terrorize my people. You will have no more power here."

Clutching her spool of shimmering thread, Elara felt a surge of pride at Caelum's denouncement. While the courtyard had once been rife with illusions that made every step uncertain, her magic now rolled outward like a protective wave. Citizens stared as Malakar reeled, his smug smile contorting. The illusions that coiled around him melted away, as though the threads of Elara's dreamweaver powers snipped them at the root. Cries of relief and disbelief rose among guards, peasants, and guild members as the monstrous visions no longer towered overhead.

Malakar stumbled while struggling to keep his composure. "You dare speak to me of treachery?" He snarled. Rain splattered against his long coat, revealing a tremor in his posture. "You have no idea what it takes to rule these people, to harness their nightmares before they devour everything." Hatred burned in his gaze as he stared at Elara. "And you, foolish seamstress, think a spool of thread is enough to destroy all I have built?"

Elara's throat tightened, yet she refused to yield to fear. She steadied her shaking arms, and her magic surged from the tangle of emotions inside her, a swirl of heartbreak, devotion, and fierce resolve. This was the power that had disrupted Caelum's coma and had united guilds and knights for one desperate stand. "I do not destroy," she replied, lifting her spool with a trembling hand. "I mend what you have broken."

Something thrummed in the air as Malakar raised his hands. The stench of ozone followed, and darkness gathered in the courtyard. Forked lightning flickered across the sky, illuminating the maniacal glint in his eyes. He unleashed a final torrent of illusions, twisting them into a towering vortex of nightmares. Above the city square loomed clawed beasts, twisted faces, and shadows that melted and reformed like liquefied tar. The swirling storm cloud of illusions crackled with malevolence, hungry for the fear of those who watched from every corner.

Elara clenched her fists. The new illusions threatened to blot out every earlier victory. Her magic flared in answer, and she sensed movement to her left. Carmen, her dark hair slick from rain, stepped forward. She held a handful of shimmering thread tinted a pale blush, and her lips set in a determined line. For a moment, Elara and Carmen locked eyes. A silent understanding passed between them, no longer rivals, nor merely reluctant allies. They were two seamstresses forging illusions for the realm's survival.

Carmen raised her palms, and her spool unraveled in spirals. Glowing filaments linked her illusions to Elara's. Their strands merged in midair, shining with raw power that drove back the monstrous shapes swirling overhead. Each new creation Carmen summoned snapped at the nightmares' edges, fracturing the illusions before they could fully coalesce. The thunderous swirl above their heads began to shift, unsteady and no longer unstoppable.

Furious, Malakar cursed, his eyes wild as the illusions buckled. The courtyard shook with each tremor of his faltering storm. "I have shaped these illusions for years," he hissed. "I fed on the kingdom's fear. You cannot simply wash that away with your thread!"

Elara's breathing came in rapid gasps as she held the illusions at bay, but she found her voice. "Maybe fear sustained you," she said, "but it also unites the rest of us in courage. Look around you. We stand together." She gestured to the outskirts of the courtyard, where Lucian and the knights braced in a defensive line to guard any citizen who might be threatened by stray illusions. Some of the newly forged amulets glinted on the knights' chests, wards hammered lovingly by blacksmiths under Roderick's direction.

Malakar's illusions quivered again when Carmen poured more energy into the shimmering nets overhead. Elara sensed that Carmen was near her limit, but the older seamstress refused to back down. Sweat mingled with rain on Carmen's brow as she raised trembling arms to hold the illusions in place, preventing them from collapsing onto the crowd. The monstrous shapes overhead flickered with bright arcs, some half dissolved, others screeching as if they possessed voices of their own. The confrontation crackled, a standoff of illusions that robbed the air of breath.

Then Lucian shouted, "Forward!" The knights surged, steel flashing in the stormy light. They swarmed around Malakar and forced him to shift part of his focus to their physical onslaught. Elara heard the clash of metal and saw Malakar gesture frantically, illusions swirling in chaotic arcs to repel the attack, but his final conjurations weakened by the second.

Desperate, he sprang toward the swirling nightmares, hoping to lose himself in them. Elara watched his shifting silhouette flicker among the illusions, and dread spiked in her chest. Fear frothed in her veins. She could not let him vanish when they were so close to ending this nightmare forever. She raised her spool, letting the luminous thread unwind from her fingertips. A warm pulse of recognition swept through her, as though every ounce of her devotion, heartbreak, and longing converged in her chest.

She chanted an incantation under her breath, shaping the words from all the scraps of dreamweaver lore she had pored over. The spool glowed like embers at the heart of a fire. Bolts of shimmering light flashed from her outstretched hands and seared through the illusions. She had done this in nightmares, in catacombs, and in Caelum's bedchamber. Now she faced the origin of her fear in full daylight.

Malakar stumbled, illusions flickering around him in jagged shards.

Elara guided a final bolt of dream-fire into the collapsed center of his conjurations. She poured her entire will into unpicking every thread of his illusions from the inside. Needle-sharp arcs lanced outward. For an instant, she glimpsed the frantic desperation on Malakar's face as he realized the illusions he had relied upon were unraveling in a blink.

He let loose a raw scream, half fury, half despair. Then the illusions around him imploded, dissolving like black sand carried away on a tempest. Gasping, Malakar tumbled onto the slick cobblestones, his once-fine coat spattered with mud and torn from frantic spells. Rain plastered his hair to his scalp, revealing the gaunt angles of his face.

Elara's lips parted in one shaky breath. For a moment, the entire courtyard stilled, everyone frozen in disbelief, as though the heartbeat of the city paused. Lucian's knights closed in fast. She glimpsed metal shifting in torchlight as swords angled in a lethal arc. Malakar raised one trembling hand, eyes blazing with resentment and regret, but no illusions came to his rescue. His voice rasped out one final curse. Elara could not hear the words fully, but she felt the echo of venom in them.

The knights struck him down with swift, merciless efficiency. He jerked once, as though stunned by the mortal blow. The anger in Malakar's expression curdled into a terrible emptiness. A shudder wracked his body, and life fled from his eyes. Above them all, the last pockets of illusions sputtered into nothingness, their monstrous shapes flicking away like spent cinders.

Elara let out a trembling exhale and stopped the flow of her magic. Carmen dropped to one knee, arms still extended as though uncertain the threat had truly ended. The courtyard bristled with a shocked hush. Steam rose in patches around the knights, mixing with rain and the faint glimmer of spent illusions. The few watchers who had hidden behind archways now ventured out: merchants, guild artisans, and even frightened children creeping from doorways to see if the horror was truly over.

Slowly, Elara stepped away from where Malakar's lifeless form lay. Her legs felt weak, and each breath tasted of ash and adrenaline. She half expected some final shadowy beast to rise, hungry for vengeance, yet none came. The swirling nightmares had dissolved, leaving behind damp cobblestones and a battered city that had endured. The roil of thunder overhead began to ease, and the storm started to recede.

She felt a presence at her side. Caelum placed a hand on her arm. His touch steadied her heartbeat, reminding her that he was alive, free of the illusions that had once bound him. Though his voice quivered with exhaustion, he gazed into her eyes, relief shining there like the first sunbeam after a long winter. He turned to survey the courtyard, and the watchers parted in quiet awe. Few dared cheer yet, as if they waited for confirmation that Malakar truly lay dead.

Carmen rose and leaned on Lucian, who had hurried over to offer his shoulder. Her face showed shock and tear tracks, though the rain tried to hide them. She bowed her head toward Elara, a silent acknowledgment of what they had achieved. Gratitude welled in Elara's chest: gratitude that Carmen had chosen to stand against malevolence at a crucial moment, gratitude for Lucian's unwavering shield, and gratitude for Caelum's steadfast resolve. Through her exhaustion, she recognized that they had faced the nightmares at their fiercest. They had won.

As if in answer to the kingdom's relief, the clouds overhead shifted. A beam of pinkish-gold light broke across the sky. Breath caught in Elara's throat. Something in that gentle illumination made the gruesome scene at their feet feel smaller, like a memory already passing. The city exhaled in a wave of hushed release: children wept in startled calm, mothers gathered them close, and battered knights slowly lowered blood-smeared swords. The group that had dragged Malakar's body away stood uncertain, as though no one quite believed what had happened.

Elara did not know how much time passed while they stood in the courtyard, blinking at the fact that Malakar's illusions were gone. Carmen finally lifted her eyes to the brightening sky, and Lucian's hand settled on her back as if to confirm that they were both real and alive. Elara heard the faint shuffle of footsteps behind her. She turned and saw Roderick, the hard-edged blacksmith, remove his dented helm. His harsh features trembled with emotion. She had never seen him cry, but a suspicious sheen glimmered in his eyes.

Prince Caelum limped a step forward, pressing a hand to his chest. He tried to speak. His first attempts came out in a raw whisper. At last, he lifted his head and found a voice that carried through the quiet, though it wavered from strain. "The illusions are finished. Our nightmares have no master now."

Those words rippled across the onlookers, and a new hush descended, a hush of disbelief tinted with hope.

It was as though an entire realm could see color returning to the world.

Elara brushed damp hair from her forehead, still clutching her spool of thread in one trembling hand. She yearned to collapse, to find a quiet place where she could sob, scream, or laugh. Perhaps all three at once.

She felt Caelum's arm around her shoulders. He leaned against her for support, his body wracked with quiet tremors in the wake of the battle. Their gazes met, exhaustion and gratitude shared in equal measure. She inhaled shakily, the mingled scents of wet stone, discharged magic, and relief so profound it felt like a physical presence filling her lungs. The steady warmth in Caelum's eyes told her they had done enough. They had broken through illusions that had strangled the kingdom.

Carmen and Lucian joined them, forming a small circle. Carmen's expression was drawn, hair plastered to her cheeks, but her eyes shone with determination. Lucian stood protectively at her side, his breathing still harsh from the earlier combat. Together, they surveyed the scattered remnants of Malakar's final stand.

Guards fanned out and called to citizens that it was safe to return and that the dreaded illusions had collapsed. Several townsfolk stumbled forward in gratitude, though none dared cheer while Malakar's still form lay unmoving on the stones.

At last, the tension that had gripped the city for so long loosened, and the sky seemed to take a fresh breath with them. The distant clouds parted in wide arcs, and sunlight poured downward. It bathed the courtyard in a glow so startling that people covered their eyes for a few moments, unused to such brightness after the gloom.

Elara closed her eyes, the promise of long-denied daylight warming her face. She felt Caelum's hand tighten on hers. Nearby, Carmen let out a shaky sigh of release, and Lucian exhaled a silent prayer to the skies.

With Malakar's power broken and the dream realm's barrier shattered in a cleansing rush of Elara's dreamweaver threads, the sky cleared above, revealing a dawn so luminous it felt like a promise from the gods themselves.

THIRTY-ONE

The air in Mistress Imelda's small, herb-scented workroom, tucked away in a quiet wing of the recovering palace, was thick with the aroma of dried lavender, old parchment, and the faintest trace of lingering dream-thread magic. Days had passed since Malakar's defeat in the city courtyard, days filled with the slow, arduous task of mending a kingdom physically and spiritually scarred. Nightmares still flickered at the edges of the city for some, but they were fading, their power source severed. Prince Caelum, though still regaining his full strength, was a constant presence, his determination a beacon for the weary court.

Today, an unspoken summons had drawn Elara, Caelum, Lucian, and Carmen to Imelda's sanctuary. The old dreamweaver, her eyes missing nothing, had simply nodded when they arrived, a knowing calm about her as she gestured for them to sit on the worn cushions around her worktable. A pot of her familiar, pungent tea was already brewing.

Elara settled beside Caelum, his hand instinctively finding hers, a warm, reassuring pressure. Across from them, Lucian and Carmen sat a little straighter, a tentative understanding in the way their shoulders brushed. The ordeal had changed them all, forging new bonds and reforging old ones.

"There are questions that linger," Caelum began, his voice still bearing a slight rasp but gaining strength daily. He looked at Imelda. "Truths that Malakar buried, or that were never spoken. We hope you can shed some light, Mistress."

Imelda poured the steaming tea into chipped earthenware cups, her movements deliberate. "Ask, my Prince. Some threads are best unraveled in the quiet, after the storm has passed."

Elara spoke first, the question that had hummed beneath her magic for so long finally taking voice. "My grandmother," she said, her gaze finding Imelda's. "The spool of shimmering thread...it was hers. You hinted once that my ability might be a legacy. Was she...like me? A dreamweaver?"

Imelda's gaze softened with a blend of ancient sorrow and gentle pride. She set down the teapot. "She was, child. One of the strongest of her generation, though few knew it. Your grandmother, Lyra, possessed a rare and potent connection to the Veil. The shimmering spool was her heart-thread, an extension of her spirit, imbued with the very essence of her dreamweaving power."

Caelum's fingers tightened around Elara's. "Then Elara's gift…it is inherited?"

"Indeed," Imelda affirmed. "Dreamweaving often runs in bloodlines, though it can lie dormant for generations, only to awaken when the Veil is thin, or when a heart with true empathy is called upon. Your grandmother foresaw a time of great turmoil, a shadow that would fall upon the kingdom. She knew Malakar, you see. Long ago, before he twisted his knowledge into a hunger for power, they were both acolytes, studying the ancient arts, the delicate balance between worlds."

A collective gasp went through the small group. Carmen leaned forward, her usual composure replaced by avid curiosity. "She knew Malakar?"

Imelda nodded slowly. "Lyra recognized the ambition in him, the coldness that lurked beneath his intellect. She feared he would seek to control the dream realm, not protect it. Before she…passed from this world, she imbued that spool with her strongest protective enchantments and a binding of lineage. She hoped that if the time came, her gift would pass to one who would use it for healing, for mending." Her eyes rested on Elara with profound affection. "She left it for you, child, knowing that even if she could not guide you, the magic itself would."

Tears welled in Elara's eyes. A grandmother she barely remembered had, in effect, armed her for this battle. "But why didn't you tell me this sooner, Mistress Imelda? When I first came to you, so confused and frightened by the glowing thread?"

A shadow of pain crossed Imelda's face. "The truth of

your lineage, Elara, was a heavy burden and a dangerous one. Malakar was ever watchful. Had he known the full extent of your inherited power too early, he would have sought to control you, to corrupt your gift far more aggressively than he already attempted. Your grandmother's enchantments on the spool were designed to awaken your abilities gradually, in response to your own empathy and the kingdom's need. I sensed your burgeoning power, yes. I guided you with what lore I dared share. But revealing your direct lineage to Lyra, a known adversary of Malakar's earlier ambitions, would have painted a target on your back before you were ready to wield your own shield."

She paused, her gaze sweeping over them. "I have also been piecing together fragments of old lore, Lyra's hidden journals, which I only recently managed to decipher fully with the help of the symbols you and Lucian brought back from the restricted archives. Only then did I understand the full depth of the connection, the specific nature of the protection she wove for you, and the true reason Malakar was so obsessed with Caelum."

Caelum leaned forward, his eyes intense. "Malakar. Why me? Why put me through five years of cursed slumber? Was it merely to destabilize my father's reign?"

"It was far more than that, Your Highness," Imelda said gravely. "As I understand it now, from Lyra's writings and the texts you found, Malakar's ambition was to control the Veil itself, the very fabric that separates the waking world from the dream realm. He believed that whoever controlled the dreams of a kingdom controlled its destiny, its very soul."

Lucian shifted, his hand instinctively moving to the hilt of his sheathed sword. "And Caelum was the key?"

"Precisely," Imelda confirmed. She turned to Caelum. "Your Highness, you were born with an exceptionally strong natural resonance with the Veil, much like Elara's grandmother. Malakar knew this. He saw you not just as an heir but as a powerful, untapped conduit. By placing you in that cursed slumber, he wasn't merely removing a political obstacle. He was trying to use your spirit as an anchor, a living battery to draw power from the dream realm, so he could manipulate and eventually merge the worlds to his will, making him their ultimate master."

Carmen gasped. A faint memory of Malakar reflecting on his view of Caelum as a "conduit" and his plan to use Caelum as an "eternal anchor" for his "perfect dream" of a merged reality flashed through her mind. Imelda's words chillingly confirmed Malakar's own inner monologue. She shared this with the rest of the group.

"The reciprocal slumber the physicians named," Elara breathed as understanding dawned. "Every time Caelum's spirit tried to cross back, Malakar was siphoning that energy."

"And the dreambleed, the nightmares plaguing the kingdom," Imelda continued, "were both a byproduct of the Veil tearing under that strain and a tool for Malakar to sow fear, further strengthening his hold by weakening the collective spirit of the people."

Carmen shuddered. "He used my ambition, my jealousy of Elara, to get closer to her magic, didn't he? He wanted to understand her dreamweaving, perhaps to corrupt her as well or use her as another conduit."

Imelda nodded sadly. "Malakar was adept at exploiting any fissure in a person's heart, Carmen. Your latent sensitivity to the threads of illusion, however faint, likely made you an easier target for his manipulations. He sensed that you too possessed a sliver of the old magic, perhaps from a distant ancestor, enough for him to twist."

Carmen absorbed this, a flicker of understanding and a strange validation in her eyes. It was not an excuse for her actions, Elara knew, but it offered context for the intensity of Malakar's hold on her.

"So, the Serpent's Eye glyph...," Lucian began, "the one we found, the one he inverted on his seal..."

"Was a powerful symbol of severing and protection, yes," Imelda finished. "Malakar twisted it, turning a key into a lock, a ward into a siphon. Your discovery of the true glyph, Elara, in the Queen's tapestry, and your intuitive use of it in the anchor you stitched for Caelum began to unravel his deepest enchantments."

Elara touched the now-empty space where the emerald signet ring had rested against her skin, the one Queen Meredith had given her. That too had been a piece of the puzzle.

"And the talisman you gave me, Mistress?" Elara asked, her fingers touching the smooth stone at her collar. "It flared with heat during our final confrontation with Malakar's dream spirit."

"A gift from your grandmother, passed to me for safekeeping," Imelda said, a gentle smile touching her lips. "It was attuned to Lyra's bloodline, designed to awaken and amplify your own protective instincts when you faced true dream corruption. It also served as a beacon, a way for her spirit, and the benevolent dream spirits she allied with, to lend you strength from beyond the Veil when you needed it most."

A profound sense of connection to a grandmother she never truly knew washed over Elara. Her dreamweaving was not merely a skill. It was a birthright, a sacred trust. In her darkest hours she had not been entirely alone.

"There is one more thing I do not understand," Caelum said, his voice quiet but firm. He looked at Elara, then at Lucian. "The kiss in the dream realm. The one Malakar forced between you." He paused, the memory painful. "How did he gain such control over your actions within the Veil, and why?"

Elara's cheeks burned, and she felt Lucian shift uncomfortably beside Carmen.

Imelda sighed, her expression somber. "That was perhaps his most desperate, cruel gambit. By that point your combined efforts, yours, Elara's, Lucian's, and even Carmen's growing resistance, were unraveling his power. The dreamshield you wove around Caelum's waking mind was effective. Malakar, sensing his control over the prince waning, sought to strike at the emotional core of your alliances."

She looked at Elara and Lucian with sympathy. "He could not fully possess either of you, not with your own strengths and the wards in place. But he could manipulate the dream stuff around you, creating a powerful compulsion, an illusion so potent it could briefly override your will within that unstable space. His aim was twofold: to shatter Caelum's fragile trust in Elara by making him witness what appeared to be a betrayal, thus weakening his resolve to fight the curse, and to sow discord between Elara and Lucian, fracturing the bond of loyalty that was proving so threatening to his plans."

Lucian clenched his jaw, the memory of that unnatural compulsion still a bitter taste. Elara felt a wave of relief that Caelum now understood the truth of that violation.

"He underestimated us," Caelum said, his voice resonating with a newfound strength that surprised them all. He reached for Elara's hand again, his grip firm. "He underestimated the bonds forged not in ambition or fear, but in shared sacrifice and a commitment to what is right." His gaze moved to Lucian and Carmen, a silent acknowledgment of their hard-won unity.

Carmen, who had been listening intently, spoke hesitantly. "Mistress Imelda... you said I had a 'latent sensitivity' to illusions. Does that mean...?"

Imelda regarded her with a kind smile. "The old magics touch many bloodlines, Carmen, though often in whispers rather than shouts. Your ambition, your keen eye for patterns, even your earlier envy; these are all facets of a mind attuned to the subtle currents of influence, of how perception can be shaped. Malakar sensed it, twisted it. But that sensitivity, if guided by a mended heart, can also be a strength. You wove true illusions in the catacombs, not merely from borrowed skill, but from your own courage. There may yet be a dream-thread or two in your own ancestry, waiting to be patiently unspooled."

Carmen looked down at her hands, a thoughtful, almost wondrous expression on her face. Lucian reached over and gently took one of her hands, his thumb stroking her knuckles. Their shared smile was a quiet promise.

The small room was quiet for a long moment, the weight of Imelda's revelations settling over them. So many threads, so many lies, so many hidden intentions were now finally laid bare. Malakar's curse had been born of a desperate hunger for control over the very essence of their world, and Caelum, with his innate connection to that essence, had been the unwilling key. Elara's heritage, the silent gift of a grandmother she had never known, had become the counter-key.

"What of the Veil now?" Lucian asked, voicing the question that hung in the air. "Is it mended?"

Imelda shook her head. "Mending the Veil will take time, and the collective will of many. The dreambleed has lessened since Malakar's anchor was destroyed, but the scars on reality remain. Nightmares may still slip through, and the balance is fragile. It will require dreamweavers like Elara, and perhaps others who carry a sensitivity, like Carmen, to soothe the lingering echoes and reinforce the boundaries. The kingdom will need its prince, its knights, its guilds, and its weavers, all working in concert."

Elara looked at Caelum, her heart swelling with a love as vast and luminous as the dream realm itself. His journey back had been arduous, and the path ahead for the kingdom was still uncertain, but when she met the quiet strength in his eyes, she knew they would face it together. Her dreamweaving was more than a power. It was a promise to heal, to protect, and to love. With her prince by her side and their loyal friends around them, she finally understood the true design of her grandmother's legacy. The threads of the future were theirs to weave, bright and resilient against any lingering shadows.

Mistress Imelda smiled, and a deep, knowing look passed between her and Elara. The heaviest secrets had been aired, the most painful truths acknowledged. Now the work of true mending could begin.

EPILOGUE

Three months had unfurled like a bolt of the finest sun-bleached linen since the shadow of Malakar had been scoured from the kingdom of Celaria.

Once choked by fear and the insidious creep of nightmare illusions, prince Caelum's kingdom was slowly but surely mending. Autumn's gentle hand now painted the royal gardens in hues of amber, crimson, and gold, and the air, crisp and clean, carried the scent of woodsmoke and ripening apples rather than the acrid tang of dark magic.

Today the gardens and the grand courtyard beyond buzzed with a life that had been absent for too long. It was not an official holiday, but an impromptu celebration had bloomed, a day to mark the anniversary of the final battle in the catacombs, the severing of Malakar's spectral anchors, and the true end of his reign of terror. Laughter, a sound once precious and rare, now echoed from cobbled paths and beneath vibrant canopies.

Elara stood on a sun-warmed terrace with her hand

resting in Caelum's, his fingers interlaced with hers. The easy comfort between them testified to the quiet intimacy they had nurtured in the weeks following the kingdom's liberation. He was still the prince, of course, and his bearing regained its innate regality with each passing day as his strength returned, but to her he was also simply Caelum, the man whose mind she had touched in dreams, whose heart now beat in steady rhythm with her own. The subtle silvery scars on his wrists, remnants of the dream chains, were the only visible reminder of the abyss from which they had pulled him.

Her gaze drifted over the scene below. Mistress Imelda, her wise eyes crinkling at the corners, held court near the ancient willow tree. She had been appointed Royal Dreamweaver Advisor, a role created by a grateful king and queen to ensure the ancient arts were preserved and understood, never again to be twisted as Malakar had done. A circle of young apprentices, a few with the telltale shimmer of budding illusionists from the Mage's Guild and others with the nimble fingers of promising seamstresses from Elara's own Tapestry Guild, listened with rapt attention as Imelda spoke, perhaps about the delicate balance between the waking world and the Veil. Old Man Hemlock sat beside her, smiling at what she was saying but barely listening to a word. Elara smiled. The future of dreamweaving and the protection of the kingdom's spirit were in capable hands.

Near the newly restored fountain, its waters sparkling clear and untainted by dreambleed, Master Thomas, head of the Tapestry Guild, engaged in an animated discussion with Roderick, the blacksmith master. Between them, draped over a trestle table, lay a magnificent tapestry depicting a phoenix rising from stylized flames, its feathers woven with threads that shimmered with minute, protective runes, a collaborative masterpiece that symbolized Celaria's rebirth. The guilds, once fractured by suspicion and fear, were now working in concert, their combined crafts creating new forms of art and protection for the realm.

The king and queen moved through the assembled guests, their relief evident to all. The years of grief and anxiety had etched lines upon their faces, but today those lines were softened by genuine smiles. King John paused to clap a blacksmith on the shoulder, his laughter booming, while Queen Meredith accepted a posy of late-blooming roses from a shy village girl, her eyes bright with unshed tears of gratitude. They were no longer monarchs besieged but parents rejoicing in their son's full return and a kingdom slowly healing.

Elara's gaze found Lucian and Carmen. They stood near the sprawling rose bushes that she had once coaxed into peace with her illusions. Lucian, ever vigilant yet lighter in posture, leaned to whisper in Carmen's ear. Her laughter, rich and unburdened, danced on the breeze. Her hand rested easily in his, their fingers entwined. The ambitious, often sharp-edged seamstress who had been both Elara's rival and, in the end, a crucial ally had found her own peace. The shadows of Malakar's influence and the bitter tang of jealousy had finally receded, allowing genuine warmth and affection to bloom between her and the steadfast captain. Their happiness was a vibrant thread in the day's celebratory weave, a testament to the healing that extended beyond the royal family. Elara felt warmth spread through her chest. Their joy mirrored the kingdom's mending heart.

The sun dipped lower, painting the undersides of the clouds in strokes of fiery orange and soft lavender. A hush began to fall over the gardens as the assembled crowd, sensing a more formal moment approaching, turned their attention toward the central terrace. Caelum squeezed Elara's hand, his blue eyes meeting hers, full of a love that still made her breath catch.

"Are you ready, my dreamweaver?" he murmured, his voice for her alone.

A delightful shiver of nerves and anticipation danced through her. She thought of her journey, from an overlooked orphan in the Tapestry Guild's dusty corners, her only legacy a mysterious spool of shimmering thread, to this moment, standing beside her prince, her heart full. The path had been fraught with peril, exhaustion, and a confusion of feelings she was only now beginning to understand fully. Her connection to Lucian, forged in shared danger and mutual respect, had settled into a deep, cherished friendship, a bond of camaraderie she knew would endure. Carmen, too, had found her own way, her strength and talent finally channeled into creation rather than rivalry. And Caelum...Caelum was the anchor of her soul, the love that had called to her across realms, the steady beat against which her life now found its truest rhythm.

"As I'll ever be," she whispered back, a radiant smile blooming on her face.

Together they walked to the edge of the terrace, where the king and queen waited, their expressions beaming. King John stepped forward, his voice strong and clear, ringing out across the silent courtyard.

"My cherished people of Celaria," he began, his arms spread wide. "Three months ago, darkness threatened to consume us. Illusions born of malice and ambition sought to unravel the very fabric of our lives and imprison our spirits in fear. But we stood together, we fought, and with courage, sacrifice, and the extraordinary gifts of a few brave souls, we reclaimed our dawn."

A heartfelt cheer rose from the crowd, a wave of sound that seemed to sweep away the last vestiges of shadow from the palace stones.

The king continued, his voice thick with emotion. "Our beloved son, Prince Caelum, was returned to us from a cursed slumber that lasted five long years. His recovery, his presence here today, is a testament to the unbreakable spirit of Celaria." He turned, placing a hand on Caelum's shoulder, his pride evident. "And it is a testament to the unwavering dedication and profound power of one extraordinary woman."

He looked at Elara, his eyes filled with a gratitude that brought a fresh wave of tears to her own. "Lady Elara," he proclaimed, his voice resonating with royal authority and paternal affection, "you came to us a humble seamstress, but you proved to be the master weaver of our kingdom's hope. Your dream-threads mended what was broken, shielded us from despair, and guided our prince back to the light. For this, and for all you have done, Celaria is eternally in your debt."

He paused, then, with a joyous smile that encompassed both Caelum and Elara, announced, "And so, it is with the greatest happiness and pride that Queen Meredith and I declare the betrothal of our son, Prince Caelum, to Lady Elara of Celaria! May their union be a symbol of the new dawn that graces our land!"

This time, the cheer was deafening, a joyous roar that shook the very foundations of the palace. Elara felt Caelum's arm slide around her waist and pull her close as he leaned down to press a kiss to her lips, a kiss that tasted of sunlight, shared dreams, and a future brimming with promise. She laughed against his mouth, her heart overflowing, her spirit soaring. The weight of her past, the loneliness of her orphan years, and the exhaustion of the battles fought all seemed to lift, replaced by incandescent joy.

As the applause and well-wishes swirled around them, Elara caught Lucian's eye. He raised his goblet in a silent toast, a genuine smile crinkling the corners of his eyes. Beside him, Carmen beamed, her happiness for Elara unfeigned and true. Their support and their friendship formed another precious thread in this rewoven tapestry.

The celebration continued long into the evening, the gardens illuminated by thousands of tiny, softly glowing illusion lights that Elara and Imelda's apprentices had joyfully crafted, mimicking the fireflies of a summer night. Music drifted on the cool air, and the scent of roasted meats and spiced cider mingled with the fragrance of roses.

Later, when the revelry had softened to a contented murmur, Elara needed a moment of quiet. Caelum, understanding, pressed a kiss to her hair and let her slip away. She walked to the furthest edge of the royal gardens, where the meticulously tended flowerbeds gave way to the wilder growth bordering the ancient palace wall. The moon, a perfect silver disc, hung high in the inky sky and cast a serene glow over the sleeping city.

A cool night breeze rustled the leaves of the old oaks, carrying with it the faintest whisper of something...other. Elara frowned, her hand instinctively moving to the now familiar weight of the shimmering dream-thread spool still tucked at her waist, a habit, a comfort, a reminder. For an instant a flicker of movement in the deepest shadows beneath the wall caught her eye, then vanished as quickly as she blinked, a trick of moonlight on swaying branches, perhaps.

She shook her head, a small smile playing on her lips. The battles were over. Malakar was defeated; his dark magic unraveled. It was natural for lingering fears to surface, echoes of the terror they had all endured. The kingdom was safe, Caelum was by her side, and their future stretched before them, bright and full of love.

Yet...as she turned to walk back toward the warm glow of the celebration, toward the laughter of her friends and the embrace of her prince, Elara could not fully dismiss the faint, almost imperceptible hum that seemed to rise from beyond the borders of their hard-won peace. It was a dissonance, a thread out of place in the otherwise harmonious weave of the night, a fleeting sensation, nearly forgotten as soon as it was felt.

"Likely nothing," she told herself, only the wind.

But the dreamweaver within her, the part forever attuned to the subtle currents of the Veil, knew that the world was vast and magic, in all its forms, was a tapestry of infinite, ever-shifting threads, and some shadows, once awakened, might only be sleeping, waiting patiently for a new story to begin.

OTHER FLORID ROMANCE BOOKS

To be notified of new releases and special promotions from Florid Romance, please join our email list:

https://floridromance.lmbpn.com/about/sign-up-for-our-newsletter/

For a complete list of books published by Florid Romance please visit our website:

https://floridromance.lmbpn.com/

BOOKS BY RIVER TATUM

The Dating Diary
One is too Many BF's (Book 1)
Two Many Choices (Book 2)
Three is a Crowd (Book 3)
Four is a Disaster (Book 4)

<u>The Firebound Chronicles</u>
Forged in Flame (Book 1)
Bound by Flame and Illusion (Book 2)
Crowned in Flame and Oath (Book 3)

<u>Vows in Magic and Steel</u>
Duty Bound (Book 1)
Hearts in Conflict (Book 2)
Unbreakable Vows (Book 3)

<u>Sorcery and Secrets</u>
Sabotage (Book 1)

Suspicion (Book 2)
Seduction (Book 3)

Love on the MerChain Express
Route of Secrets (Book 1)
Merchant's Gambit (Book 2)
Without Illusions (Book 3)

The Dreamweaver's Pact
Whispering Dreams (Book 1)
Shattered Nightmares (Book 2)
Dawn Awakening (Book 3)

BOOKS BY MICHAEL ANDERLE

Sign up for the LMBPN email list to be notified of new releases and special deals!

https://lmbpn.com/email/

For a complete list of books by Michael Anderle, please visit:

www.lmbpn.com/ma-books/

CONNECT WITH MICHAEL ANDERLE

Connect with Michael Anderle

Website: http://lmbpn.com

Email List: https://michael.beehiiv.com/

https://www.facebook.com/LMBPNPublishing

https://twitter.com/MichaelAnderle

https://www.instagram.com/lmbpn_publishing/

https://www.bookbub.com/authors/michael-anderle